THE WEIGHT

A Legal Thriller

www.hubertcrouch.com

ISBN: 1548323969
ISBN 13: 978-154-8323967
Library of Congress Control Number: 2014920504
Serpentine Books, Nashville, TN

ACKNOWLEDGEMENTS

Thanks to my editors Char Vandermeer and Skip Hollandsworth, whose plot suggestions and editorial revisions were invaluable to the process, and to Courtney Bond for her keen eye and attention to detail. Thanks to Amy Nettle, Paula Lovell, Brooke Floyd, Shelly Waters, Nora Dobson, Donna Nicely, and Bev Toms for their constructive comments and insightful input. And thanks to my wife, Doris, whose candid criticism and enthusiastic encouragement kept me at it.

"Boy, you're gonna carry that weight
Carry that weight a long time"

—The Beatles *Abbey Road*

THE WEIGHT

A Legal Thriller

HUBERT CROUCH

PROLOGUE

She handed the taxi driver a hundred euro note and, in flawless French, told him, "Je ne devrais pås être long." *I shouldn't be long*. She opened the door and slid her long legs out of the cab and onto the cobblestone driveway. Standing, she looked out on the Mediterranean hundreds of feet below, and then she turned her gaze to the building looming in front of her—a former chateau, now transformed into a five-star hotel, with rooms starting at $1,000 a night. She began cautiously picking her path between the cobblestones in the black stiletto heels she had purchased just for this evening.

As she entered the lobby, she tilted the wide brim of her dramatic black hat down, casting a shadow over her face. She knew there would be surveillance cameras capturing her every move—and she wanted to reveal as little of herself as possible. Not that she had to worry. She was perfectly disguised. Her hat, trench coat, and slinky black dress underneath would never make it back to the States, nor would the high heels. Although she had never worn a wig before and actually liked the look—straight blond hair favorably highlighting her blue eyes—it too would be staying behind. Nothing she was wearing would ever be traceable to her—nothing.

She walked through the lobby attracting little attention and then exited through heavy antique doors. She hurried down a covered stone walkway, glancing at the numbers etched above each of the bungalows, looking for the one she had been given over the phone—113. After passing four of the detached cottages, she smiled, turned down a private sidewalk, and knocked on the arched wooden door.

Jamie Stein had been waiting nervously for Christine Connors. Although they had taken their business relationship to the bedroom on one previous occasion, his expectations for this visit ran low. He was reluctant to go back on their original deal and ask for more money, but there was no choice. To live the European high life to which he had become accustomed—with its expensive digs, high-priced hookers, and designer drugs—he needed the extra dough.

Besides, he knew she could afford it, with the millions she had made on the settlement he had thrown her way. He was entitled to a better deal, with better money. He had earned it.

Jamie opened the door wearing a white bathrobe with the hotel logo prominently displayed on the pocket, bright red Gucci slippers on his feet, and a broad smile on his face. As soon as he saw Christine, he couldn't help himself. He leaned forward to kiss her, but she slipped past his lips and into the suite.

As he closed the door behind them, she chided softly, "Not out there. Anybody could see us. Besides, there just might be time for that later."

Christine smiled coyly as she set her tote on the slender table on the side of the entryway. She took off her hat and coat, throwing them on the table as well. Jamie's eyes widened as he took in every inch of Christine's body.

"I don't know whether you look better as a redhead or a blonde," he said. "But I like the hell out of both." He moved toward her, put his arms around her waist, and pulled her close. "I've missed you, Christine. I can't tell you how many times I've dreamed about that night at the Ritz."

Christine wriggled out of his embrace and stepped down to the sunken living area, taking in the crackling blaze in the stone fireplace. Holding her hands toward the flames, she said, "Nice touch, Jamie. Sets the mood."

"I wanted everything to be perfect. How about some champagne?" Jamie gestured toward an oval-shaped coffee table in front of two wingback chairs that faced a floor-to-ceiling window framing the Mediterranean. An opened bottle of champagne sat nestled in an ice bucket, two flutes on one side and a tray of prosciutto, cheese, and pastries on the other.

Christine nodded approvingly as she took a chair, leaned over, and picked up a slice of cheese. After taking a bite, she said, "Mmm, this is delicious. What is it?"

"Something French and expensive." Jamie grinned at Christine as he filled the flutes with champagne. "Cheers," he said. "To the sexiest woman I know." They clinked glasses, and Jamie slid into the chair next to Christine's.

"And, believe me, I am so sorry about—"

Christine cut him off. "Look, let's not go over this again. I don't like it, but it is what it is." She paused and stared directly into Jamie's eyes. "Let's be clear about one thing—this is a one-time deal. No more sob stories, no more money. You understand that, don't you?"

"Absolutely. It's just that—"

"You've been getting money every month, just like we agreed. *Substantial* amounts of money, I might add. The problem is you're going through it like water. Jamie, don't kid yourself. I know about the high-end call girls, the drugs, the expensive hotels, the trips, not to mention the gambling debts you've piled up. I know all about what you've been up to over here. Don't think for a minute I haven't done my research. You can't go on like this."

Jamie took in a breath of air and slowly let it out. "I know, I know. It's been crazy. I've done a lot of stupid shit. But starting right now, that's all coming to an end."

Christine shook her head. "Please, I know it's not going to end. I'm not an idiot, Jamie. You've just got to bring it down a few notches. If you don't, you might as well start writing your own obit."

Jamie tried to contain his delight. Christine had been an easier sale than he'd expected. He did his best to sound rueful as he uttered, "You are right. I will be taking it down a notch from here on out."

Christine nodded. "What's done is done." Then, to Stein's surprise, her smile returned. She raised an eyebrow. "I guess I could leave now," she continued, and paused. "Unless you want to have a little fun. It would be a shame to fly all the way from Texas only to talk business."

Christine retrieved her faux leopard-skin tote bag, which, on this trip, doubled as a purse. She riffled through the contents and pulled out a small plastic vial.

"What have you got there?" Jamie asked.

"You'll see soon enough," Christine replied as she slid the champagne bucket and appetizer tray to the side, unscrewed the tiny cap, and carefully tapped out six lines of a white, powdery substance onto the tabletop. She fished two crisp $100 bills out of her bag and handed one to Jamie. "Voilà!"

Jamie cocked his head as a grin creased his lips. "Speaking of taking it down a notch, what's this little gift you've brought me?"

"Some of the most kick-ass coke you'll ever have. A little end-of-an-era celebration."

"Come on. I had no idea a nice girl—"

"Just goes to show how little you know about me. Shall we?"

Jamie replied, "Absolutely. Ladies first." He watched curiously as Christine rolled up her bill, leaned forward, and quickly inhaled three of the lines.

She threw her head back, closed her eyes, and gasped, "Damn! You're gonna love this shit. If you thought the sex we had in Dallas was good, just wait."

Jamie quickly rolled his bill and finished off the lines. His eyes narrowed as he leaned his head back on the chair and smiled.

Christine got up and headed to the bathroom. "Be right back. And while I'm gone, why don't you mosey on back to that big ol' bedroom and get under those sheets like a good boy."

Christine could feel herself getting groggy. She hurried into the bathroom, lowered the toilet lid, and sat down. She carefully took off her wig and pulled out the small syringe she had embedded in the lining. Tilting to one side, she pulled up her dress, stuck the needle into the muscle of her right buttock, leaned against the cool porcelain tank, and waited. After several minutes, she felt the naloxone begin to kick in. The powerful heroin antidote was taking effect. It wasn't long before she heard garbled yelling from the bedroom and knew she had to quiet Jamie down. She reinserted the syringe into the wig lining, hastily repositioned the wig on her head, and opened the bathroom door.

Jamie was on his back, robe open, genitals fully exposed. Christine winced at the sight. Oblivious to her distaste, he feebly smiled at her and mumbled something she couldn't understand, his eyes now narrow slits, his breathing heavily labored.

"Man, that coke knocked me upside the head," he whispered.

Christine smiled wickedly, leaned over, and whispered, "Oh, that wasn't cocaine, Jamie. That was the purest heroin money can buy—a little strong for you, I guess. And it's such a shame that I just brought enough antidote for one. How forgetful of me."

She paused to watch as a confused frown slowly formed on his face. He tried to reach for her arm, but his body was already shutting down.

"Well, I've got to be going," said Christine. "I wish I could say it's been fun." Before closing the bedroom door, she blew a kiss to a dying Jamie Stein and mockingly mouthed, "Sweet dreams."

Christine returned to the living area, rummaged through her bag, pulled out a scarf, and mentally retraced what she might have touched in Jamie's suite. She looked around the room, and her gaze stopped on the champagne flute in front of the chair where she had sat. She calmly scooped the flute into her bag. She grabbed the two rolled-up bills lying on the coffee table and tossed them in after the champagne flute. She wiped down the appetizer tray and moved it back into the center of the table. She inspected the chair carefully—it was completely upholstered, with no exposed hard surfaces that could harbor a fingerprint. Jamie had poured the champagne, so no need to wipe the bottle. She hadn't turned on any lights. She wiped the doorknobs on both sides of the bedroom and bathroom doors, as well as the toilet seat.

Satisfied, she threw on her trench coat and hat, once again concealing her face, and walked toward the door. She visually swept the living area one last time, making sure no clues had been left, and then scurried back toward the bedroom. She slipped inside, cautiously tiptoeing toward the bed. Standing to the side, she stared down at the blackmailing son of a bitch who had hit her up for money for the last time. His eyes were frozen open, vacuous, blankly staring into space. A trail of vomit trickled out of one side of his mouth and down his cheek, pooling on the satin pillowcase. She stood there for several minutes, watching for any movement, listening for any sound of life. Confident Jamie had breathed his last breath, she slipped back out of the bedroom and then hurried across the tiled floor to the door leading outside. With her scarf wrapped around her hand she opened the door and stepped out of the bungalow. After pulling the heavy wooden door shut, she uttered a sigh of relief and began to walk casually back toward the hotel reception area. Just after she walked through the arched entrance, a bellman, stacking large bags on a gold luggage cart, dropped a bag on the tile floor, startling everyone, including Christine. She looked up for only a second and then regained her composure, moving inconspicuously toward the door leading to the parking area, oblivious to the security camera positioned just to one side.

PART ONE

CHAPTER

1

In a corner office of the historic Flatiron Building in downtown Fort Worth, Jace Forman rose from the leather chair behind his desk. He began pacing around the hardwood floor of his office, stopped, and pivoted toward the speakerphone on his mahogany credenza. "Look, David, I've given you all the money I have. I've run out of line. You can either take it or we pick a jury on Monday."

There was silence.

"David, you still there?" Jace asked

"Yeah, I'm here," said David Raskin, one of the many plaintiff attorneys who over the years had tried his luck against Jace. A few months earlier, Raskin had filed suit on behalf of a down-on-her luck fashion designer who was claiming that Jace's client—Grace Summers, a Texas entrepreneur in women's accessories who had made her fortune designing and selling an insanely popular hair clip—had stolen some of her ideas. "Come on, Jace, I know you can scrounge up another twenty-five. That would make it a couple hundred even. I could sell that to my client. But anything less than that, I just don't . . ."

"I can't do it, David. There's no more water in the well. Not a drop."

Sitting on the other side of Jace's desk was Darrin McKenzie, his paralegal of over a decade. Jace winked at her. He knew that she knew he had another hundred thousand dollars' worth of authority from his client. If he could bring the case in under budget, his client would be ecstatic. There would be a celebration dinner at Bob's Chop House and maybe even a nice premium on the final bill. Grace was normally tight as a tick when it came to lawyer fees but, on occasion, would grudgingly agree to a little sweetener for a job well done. Jace could at least ask.

"All right, Jace, my client will do it if you can get me another ten. And that's my—"

"Listen to me, David. There's no more money. There's a lot of bad blood between our clients. I thought Grace was gonna come across the table when your client made that smartass remark during her deposition. Look, you and I both know you have no case. I'm only willing to settle because Grace doesn't want to waste her time on a frivolous lawsuit. We need to get this done—today. It'll knock us out of some fees, but worse things have happened."

"How quickly can you get me a check? The sooner the better."

Jace struggled to tamp down his jubilation. He wasn't staring down a weekend of fourteen-hour days of trial prep. The weekend was his. And best of all, he knew he'd sleep soundly on Sunday night without having to worry about picking a jury early the next morning.

Keeping his tone neutral to prevent David from sensing that the well wasn't all that dry, Jace replied, "I'll have to confirm, but normally they can cut a check within three business days—say, by Wednesday of next week?"

A sigh of disgust emanated from the speakerphone. "You really beat me up on this one," whined David. "My gut tells me I left some money on the table, but I can't chance being wrong. We need to get this wrapped up. Have a check delivered to my office first thing Wednesday morning. But you owe me one, Jace."

"Bullshit. Your client should be jumping for joy. My investigator had so much crap on her. She'd have been sweating like a pig once I got her on cross-examination."

"What are you talking about? What'd you have?"

"Can't give away trade secrets. Listen, I'll have Darrin draft a Rule 11 settlement agreement and get it over to you before lunch. If you could sign it and fax it back by 2:00 this afternoon, I'll start the process for getting you paid. Does that work?"

"Yeah, well, to be honest with you, I'd like to take off a little early myself. It looks pretty nice out today."

"Now you're talking. Hey, if I don't speak with you later today, have a good weekend."

"You too, Jace."

The line went dead, and Jace and Darrin gave each other a high five. The high five turned into a hug—and, as always, it wasn't just a friendly hug but one brimming with desire. No matter how many times they had tried to keep their distance, Jace and Darrin had a chemistry that had started the day Darrin walked into his office to apply for a job.

Jace gave her a look. Darrin, her hair blond and wavy, was wearing one of her black cashmere dresses that tastefully hugged her curves and fell just above the knee. As always, she looked much younger than her 38 years. "So," Jace said, "now that the weekend is free, you got any plans?"

"Actually, I promised my sister I'd visit her in Houston if the case settled." Sensing that Jace wanted to spend the weekend with her, Darrin found herself regretting her decision. But then again, she didn't want her feelings for him to consume her. She knew all too well that there was a private side to Jace that was, well, difficult for her to come to terms with. He always kept himself a little distant, always holding something in check. He had been that way since his wife's tragic death. The fact was that Darrin never could tell for sure just how he felt about her. There were some days when he acted as if she was the girl of his dreams. And then there were days when he seemed preoccupied, his mind somewhere else.

Quickly shifting her thoughts back to the case, she said, "I'll get to work on the Rule 11. It'll be in Mr. Raskin's hands within an hour."

Jace nodded. He too was back to business. "Thanks. And give Meg my best."

Right at that moment, Harriett, his secretary of many years, stuck her head in the door and, as Darrin was leaving, asked plaintively, "So am I going to be working all weekend?"

"Nope. Got it settled for $175,000. Would you get Grace on the line? She'll be pumped."

"Well, that's a relief! I'm getting too old for this," Harriett said, forcing a grin. "Oh, and I have a little surprise for you. Mr. Connors has been in the reception area for the last thirty minutes. He arrived right after you got on the conference call."

Jace stared at Harriett. "Cal Connors has been waiting a half hour to see me?" he asked. "I thought our meeting was later this afternoon."

"He dropped by early just in case you freed up. Should I bring him back?"

"Yeah, I guess so. We'll call Grace after I get finished."

"Will do."

Jace's mind began to race as he sat on the corner of his desk, waiting for Cal to walk through the door. Why in the world would his former adversary want to meet with him? They didn't currently have a case against each other and had only bumped into each other once or twice since the famous Stone case, which had attracted media attention from around the state. Cal had been representing the parents of a UT student who had sued a Fort Worth funeral home after they'd learned that their daughter's body had been dug up and stolen from the cemetery. The case had seemed all but lost until Jace began cross-examining the dead girl's father on the witness stand.

Why, Jace wondered, would Cal now want to talk with him? When Cal had called earlier that morning, saying he wanted to drop by, he had been anything but transparent. All he said was that he preferred to discuss things face-to-face.

Jace's thoughts were interrupted by a familiar baritone voice. "Jace, how in the hell have you been?"

Sliding off his desk, Jace turned to greet his guest. "I can't complain. Sorry about the wait. I was on a conference call with David Raskin trying to settle a case that's set on Monday." Jace offered his hand and Cal shook it firmly.

"Well, did you get it done?"

Jace nodded.

"I know David. He is an okay trial lawyer, but he'll nickel-and-dime you to death when you're negotiating a settlement with him. Seems to have a complex about not shaking every last cent out of you."

Jace laughed. "That's David all right."

With a keen eye, Cal glanced around the office and made a mental note of the stark contrast to his own. There were no signs of Jace's great success on display anywhere: none of the many awards he knew Jace had received over the years and no newspaper headlines featuring Jace's courtroom victories,only a modestly-framed law school diploma and Texas law license on the wall behind Jace's desk. "Like your digs here," Cal said. "I don't think I've seen 'em before. Best I remember, all the activity in the Stone case occurred over at my place."

"You're right about that. Hard to forget that Remington cowboy sculpture in your lobby. I bet it's worth more money than I made my first five years practicing law."

Cal chuckled. "Got to make an impression to make a living. Where do you want me to sit, Counselor?"

Jace motioned toward the circular conference table in the office corner, and the two took seats across from each other. Jace gave Cal the once-over. He was the same old Cal, dressed in a black suit with matching black Lucchese cowboy boots. His silver hair was swept straight back and his eyes were as blue as a mountain lake. Jace had to admit, Cal made a good impression. "Yeah," Cal said, pulling out an unlit cigar, "that grave robbery case you and I had was weird as hell. You ever had one any crazier than that?"

Jace thought for a moment before responding. "It ranks up there, that's for sure."

"And I thought I had you. Hell, I did have you. And then you pulled a Houdini on me with your cross of that son of a bitch I had for a client—lyin' bastard." Cal shook his head in disgust as the memory returned. "I gotta be honest. I don't know of another trial lawyer in town who could have figured that one out."

"Lucky, I guess."

"Lucky, hell! Luck never plays a part in anything. We have to scrape and claw to make things happen in this world. Those who aren't willing to do that don't make it, plain and simple—and then they blame their lackluster lives on not getting any breaks. That's a bunch of bullshit, and you and I both know it."

Jace changed course. "So, Cal, let's cut to the chase. Why did you want to meet with me?"

"We'll get to that but, before we do, I believe congratulations are in order." Cal leaned back in his chair, running both hands through his thick hair and then clasping them behind his head. "You know what I'm talking about. Crossing that line from civil defense attorney to Mr. Big-time Plaintiff Lawyer."

"I guess you're referring to the Brimstone Bible Church case?"

Cal leaned forward, his cold blue eyes zeroing in on Jace's smiling face. "Course to hell that's the case I'm talking about—those no-good sons of bitches protesting at the funeral of one of our fallen soldiers. Jace, I was pulling for you from the get-go. By the way, how did it feel to switch sides—representing real common folk rather than big ol' corporations? I bet you kinda liked it, now didn't you?"

"I have to admit, it was nice for a change."

"Well, that's why I'm here. I need a lawyer—a hard-charging son of a bitch just like you. I need someone who knows how to try a case, which most so-called trial lawyers don't know how to do anymore. All they are is a bunch of paper pushers. Like all those assholes over at your former shop—what was the name of that firm?"

Even though Jace was damn sure Cal knew the name of almost every attorney and law firm in town, he played along. "Hadley & Morgan."

"Yeah, that's it! I bet you were glad to get the hell outta there. Anyway, I had a case against one of those pompous pricks a year or so ago. I can't even remember his name. We got close to trial and he folded like a bad poker hand. I mean, tucked his tail like a scalded dog and ran for cover. Hell, I settled the case for three times what it was worth. You know the type of lawyers at that firm. They usually put an initial in front of their names and a third or fourth after, like they come from royalty or something."

"Come on, Cal, they're some—"

"Now don't get all diplomatic on me, Jace. You know just as well as I do we're a dying breed. There are very few real trial lawyers left. Damn shame. All this mediation and arbitration crap has taken all the fun out of things. You remember when we started out years ago? We tried cases by the seat of our pants week after week, and we loved every damn minute of it. You never knew what witnesses were going to say when they got up on that witness stand. You had to think fast, adjust, roll with the punches. Now we've got all of this damn discovery—documents and more documents, deposition after deposition. It costs a fortune to try a case these days. And if you get before a jury in two or three years, consider yourself lucky." Cal shook his head in disgust. "I know

I'm getting a little off track, but I can't help but get pissed about it. Now, let's get back to why I'm here. Like I said, I need you to represent me."

"For what? You haven't been sued for malpractice, have you?"

"I'll pretend you didn't say that. Of course I haven't been sued for malpractice. All my clients love me. Apparently, however, a certain publication does not." Reaching inside the leather satchel he had brought with him, Cal pulled out a copy of the latest issue of *Texas Matters,* the state's preeminent magazine, and slid it across the table.

Jace glanced at the cover. An unflattering caricature of Cal Connors, clad in his signature bolo tie and cowboy boots, was straddling a supine Lady Justice, her blindfold askew, one eye blackened, a frown pursing her lips. The words "TEXAS JUSTICE GONE WRONG" were stamped diagonally across the cartoon depiction in eye-catching red ink.

"You seen this crap?"

Jace picked up the magazine. Studying the cover, he couldn't help but grin. "Nope, can't say I have."

"This ain't a damn bit funny to me. That rag is no better than the *National Enquirer*—just one lie after another. They'll both publish anything to sell issues."

Sensing that Cal was really getting worked up, Jace opted not to respond.

"I want to sue that filthy rag and that little bitch who wrote the story," Cal continued, his voice growing more strained. "Leah Rosen. That's her name. When you and I get finished with them, hell, she'll never write another story and we'll own that damn magazine."

"What do you want to sue them for?"

"Lying, defamation, intentional infliction of emotional distress, business disparagement, whatever else you can think of. I want to throw the kitchen sink at 'em. Ask for a hundred million in damages—actual and punitive."

"Cal, don't you think you've got a First Amendment problem? For starters, you've got the burden of proving the story is false. Even if you get over that hurdle, they'll claim you're a public figure and you can't recover a penny unless you show they maliciously ran the article. It's a tough road, Cal."

"Proving the story is false? Are you kidding me? Course to hell it's false! I swear on my mother's grave that there's not an ounce of truth to that story. Read it and you'll see what I'm talking about. The idea that I rigged the system is pure bullshit. And come on now, Jace, I'm no public figure—I ain't the president or some rock star, for crying out loud. I'm just a country lawyer from Cowtown who's hit a few good licks, that's all. But even if I was a public figure, this story is a hatchet job with malice written all over it. They wanted to bring ol' Cal down, and if that ain't malice, there ain't a cow in Texas." Cal paused before continuing. "Jace, you keep saying I'd have to prove this and I'd have to prove that. Don't forget—we're in this together. You're my lawyer."

Making a halting motion with his right hand, Jace replied, "Not so fast, Cal. I haven't agreed to take this on. You know I'm not really a plaintiff lawyer. You can count on one hand the cases where I've represented the plaintiff. That's not what I do day in and day out."

"Jace, please. It don't make a rat's ass which side you're playing for as long as you know what to do when you step up to the plate. And you've been knocking it out of the park since you got your law license. I'd love to see you go after that snotty-nosed Leah Rosen on the witness stand. You'd have her so confused she wouldn't know whether she was afoot or horseback. You know I'm right."

Rummaging through his satchel again, he pulled out a check, which he pushed across the table to Jace. "That should seal the deal."

Jace glanced down. It was a $150,000 retainer payable to the Forman Firm. He closed his eyes and slowly rubbed his brow before responding, "Can't do it, Cal."

"What do you mean you can't do it?" Cal's frown morphed into a grin. "I get it. You're bargaining with me. You want more money, you sly dog. What if I double it?"

"It's not the money, Cal. I just don't feel I can take the case. I'd like to, but—"

"Are you crazy? This case is a lay-down. Hell, I'll pay you a half million up front. I'll even give you twenty percent of any judgment you recover as a bonus. You could retire off what you'll make on this case."

Jace squirmed in his chair. He was beginning to have trouble turning down that kind of money without sleeping on it, but an inner voice kept telling him to let it go.

"I'm sorry, I just can't represent you, Cal. There are a number of reasons. First, like I said, I'm not a plaintiff lawyer. Second, I've spent years building a law practice representing defendants. You even sued one of them. My clients wouldn't like it if I represented a high-profile trial lawyer who makes his living suing corporations. Taking your case might cause some of them to have second thoughts about using me, and I just can't afford to take that risk."

Jace paused briefly before continuing, wondering whether he should mention his final point, and then forged on. "And I have to level with you, Cal. I know the reporter you want to sue. I met her at a hearing in the Stone case, and she interviewed me several months later for this article."

Cal, appalled, responded, "She did what?"

"Now hold your horses, Cal. All she did was call me to find out what I thought about you when she was working on the story."

"So what'd you tell her?"

"I told her that you were a hard-nosed, competent trial attorney who'd tried a lot of cases."

Visibly calmer, Cal replied, "I appreciate that, Jace. Back atcha." He thought for a moment and continued, "Okay, I get it now. You're worried you might have some kind of conflict because you talked with her. I don't see it, but if it would make you feel any better, I'd waive the conflict in a heartbeat. I'll sign whatever release you want. That take care of your concern?"

"No, Cal, it isn't just that. Like I told you, there are a number of reasons." Jace slid the check back across the table.

Ignoring the gesture, Cal fixed his eyes on Jace. Suddenly the calm demeanor was gone. "I'll be a son of a bitch. You think you're too good for me. That's what it is, ain't it? You think you've got some friggin' halo over your head and I'm some kind of heathen, a lowlife you don't want to do business with—don't want to get your hands dirty."

Cal rose from the table, picking up the check and dropping it in his satchel. "Well, I'll tell you what you can do. You can kiss my ass. I'll find someone to represent me who can run rings around you."

"I hope you do, Cal."

Before leaving the office, Cal stopped and turned toward Jace. "And you can keep the magazine. That Rosen lady must not have thought much of what you had to say. She didn't even quote you."

CHAPTER 2

Cal burst into his daughter's office. Profanities spewed out of his mouth as he stormed angrily from one side of the room to the other, his eyes burning a hole in the thick carpet. Christine Connors sat behind her desk and watched silently. She had witnessed her dad throw many a tantrum, and she knew it was best to let him vent.

After several minutes, he collapsed in the chair across from her desk and sighed.

Christine got up and made her way to the chair next to his. "You ready to talk about it?" she said, grinning. "And I said 'talk,' not 'scream.'"

Cal reached over and put his hand on top of his daughter's. "You have a knack for being able to calm your ol' dad down. Thank the Lord for little things."

"So what happened? The only thing I could decipher between obscenities was that Jace Forman somehow pissed you off."

Nodding his agreement, Cal said, "And that's putting it mildly. I told you I was going to meet with him this morning, didn't I?"

Christine shook her head no.

"Well, I thought I told you, but maybe I didn't get around to it. Anyhow, I met with him about suing *Texas Matters* and that reporter—"

Knowing where this was going, Christine finished the sentence. "Leah Rosen. I thought I had talked you out of that. Dad, it's not a good idea."

"Yeah, you and I talked about it, but you didn't convince me."

"So Forman turned you down? I'm glad he did! Maybe you'll rethink the wisdom of stirring the pot. Like I said before, that's not a good idea. Better to let a sleeping dog lie."

"That dog ain't sleeping, young lady. You know that U.S. Attorney Cowan is sniffing around, looking for evidence to bring criminal charges against me. And, don't kid yourself, it's not just me he's after. He's after you as well. All because of Rosen's article. We need to nip this in the bud. Go on the offensive. You know the old saying—the best defense is a good offense. In fact, that's how I built this place right here—by taking chances, rolling the dice, going for the jugular. And I don't intend to change my ways now."

Jumping in before her dad could come up with any more old chestnuts, Christine said, "Will you at least hear me out one more time? Remember, I've got as much at stake here as you do. And I had a little to do with building this firm to what it is today, wouldn't you say?"

Cal sighed. "All right, I didn't mean to take all the credit. You're one helluva trial lawyer, and you're right—I couldn't have been near as successful without you. So talk to me. Convince me that I'm fixin' to head down the wrong path."

As she presented her case, Christine rose and began walking around her uncluttered, spacious office, in much the same fashion as she had before countless juries. "So you sue *Texas Matters* and

Ms. Rosen for defamation, slander, whatever. Who do you think they'll retain to represent them?"

"I don't know, but I'll hire someone better."

"Maybe, maybe not. I can tell you they will spare no expense on the lawyer they hire. The hourly rate won't be a problem. This is a bet-the-company case, and they *will* hire a bet-the-company lawyer."

"So?" Cal queried.

"I'm just setting the stage. You can't count on *Texas Matters* hiring some lightweight paper pusher, a term I've heard you use more than once, who's afraid of the courtroom."

"Your point being?"

"This will be all-out war. You ready for that?"

"I've never been afraid of the courtroom."

"As an adversary you haven't, but it's a different story being a party. It's a lot more fun asking the questions than answering them, wouldn't you agree?"

Cal didn't reply, and Christine continued, her closing argument taking shape.

"What's the first thing you think their lawyer will do?"

Cal thought for a minute and offered, "Probably send out some interrogatories and a document request."

"Right. They'll ask for everything we have—emails between you and Crimm, bank records, client files, phone records, you name it."

"Our lawyer will file objections to all that stuff."

"Sure he will. And some of his objections will be sustained and some won't. A lot will depend on the judge we get, and we won't know who that'll be until the lawsuit is filed and assigned."

Cal nodded, and then asked, "But what right would they have to our bank records?"

"You're suing for damage to your reputation. They'll argue they're entitled to see if our law practice suffered financially. If our revenues went up after the article was published, no damages."

"Okay, I see your point. By the way, you covered your tracks in that deal you did with that insurance guy, didn't you?"

For a moment Christine paused, trying to frame exactly what she wanted to tell her father. "As covered as they can be. It would take a savvy investigator to connect the dots, but that's not to say it's impossible.But let's stay with your case for now. So after bombarding you with discovery requests, they'll take your deposition. You can bet they'll go for broke there. And chances are they will have already talked with your expert about what he knows. Maybe he breaks, maybe not."

"I can handle myself, and I'll make sure Crimm holds up." Cal tried to sound confident, but on the inside, he was concerned about his former expert. The last year or so hadn't been good to him. He'd been down some rocky roads, which had left him shattered and broken and dangerously unpredictable.

"You sure about that?" Christine probed.

"I've known Crimm for years. If anyone pays him an unexpected visit, he won't say a damn thing without talking to me—nothing. I'm sure of that."

"Maybe, maybe not. You just never know."

"You about through?" Cal asked impatiently.

"You going to invoke your Fifth Amendment right at your deposition when you get questioned about Crimm's reports?" Christine asked, pausing to let the gravity of her question sink in. "You can rest assured that the U.S. attorney will get a copy of the transcript and go over it with a fine-tooth comb, looking for any inconsistency, anything he can charge you with."

"I'm going to tell it like it is," Cal responded defiantly. "I didn't do a damn thing wrong. Crimm gave his opinions, and those juries bought off on 'em, hook, line, and sinker. That's our system, plain and simple."

"You may be right, but I'm gonna stick with my opinion. Suing is a bad idea."

"So what would you do? Cowan is snooping around. We do know that."

"Let him snoop. The feds snoop around all the time and come up empty. Case in point, all those Wall Street bankers stole billions, brought the world's financial system to the brink, and not one of those crooks went to jail. Does that tell you anything?" Christine asked rhetorically.

"Yeah, it does. They hired high-priced, aggressive lawyers, smart as hell, and they just didn't sit around with their fingers up their you-know-whats, I can tell you that. They went on the offensive and it paid off. That's what I want to do here—hit 'em before they hit me."

"How, exactly, does suing *Texas Matters* help you with the feds?" Christine queried.

"The only reason Cowan and his FBI henchmen are coming after me is because of that article—he said as much. If I hire a mean-ass lawyer to take Rosen and her story apart, then Cowan will lose interest in a heartbeat."

Christine nodded. "That's a gamble I wouldn't take but, I admit, you may be right."

"Okay then," Cal said, and he suddenly switched gears. "So let's talk about your settlement with Stein. We still paying that bastard?"

Christine thought again for a minute before responding. "Dad, trust me, the less you know about that the better. This is my deal. I negotiated the settlement, and I had all the meetings with Stein. You wouldn't even know him if he walked through that door."

Cal nodded. "That's right. What's your point?"

"There's no way for Cowan, or anyone else for that matter, to tie you to that deal. Let's keep it that way."

"I follow you. Makes sense."

Christine continued. "Likewise, I had no dealings with Crimm. I didn't try any of those cases. They were all your babies, and I—"

Cal interrupted, finishing her sentence for her. "Would like to keep it that way."

"Exactly. I haven't decided yet, but I think it might be a good move for me to stay completely out of your lawsuit. And it might be best if I hire my own lawyer in case the feds start looking my way. After all, the charges that they might bring aren't related at all, the only connection being we're in the same law firm."

Cal gave Christine an admiring glance. "I agree with you, but we can still talk, keep each other up to speed on what's going on. Just leave no footprints, right?"

"That's what I have in mind. So now that Jace Forman is out of the picture, who you going to hire to represent you, Dad?"

"I've got several people in mind. I'll give you a heads-up before I pull the trigger." Cal walked over to his daughter and hugged her close. "You and me, we make one helluva team. Nobody's going to bring us down—nobody."

CHAPTER 3

An eerie silence fell over the Travis County courtroom in Austin as Judge Maureen Vasquez solemnly ascended to her seat behind a massive mahogany structure known in legal jargon as the "bench." She nodded at counsel seated at the tables below before turning toward the jury. "Mr. Foreperson, has the jury reached a verdict?"

A lanky middle-aged man with thinning black hair and a scraggly day-old beard rose. "We have, Your Honor. We find the defendant," an awkward pause as the man nervously cleared his throat, "not guilty."

Mayhem followed. There were gasps of shock, shouts of disapproval, choruses of "I told you so," and refrains of "I can't believe it!" Judge Vasquez brought down her gavel, restoring some semblance of order. Over the crowd's simmering murmur, she hastily thanked the jurors for their service before adjourning court and disappearing behind the door to her chambers.

The trial had taken a full week, generating daily coverage in the Austin press. Michael Randazzo had been arrested in Los Angeles and extradited to Austin to stand trial for the molestation, assault, and harassment of one of their own, a reporter for *Texas Matters*. It was big news. All three local television channels had recapped each day's testimony on the six o'clock and ten o'clock editions of the nightly news. The *Austin Sentinel* had a reporter cover every day of the trial. Courthouse junkies had arrived each day before the doors opened, jockeying for the best seats in the gallery and, during lunch recess at a nearby greasy spoon, gleefully expressing opinions on who should win.

Now the verdict was in, and Randazzo was about to walk out of the courtroom a free man.

Private investigator Jackie McLaughlin, standing in the back of the courtroom, couldn't believe it. She had been responsible for the indictment and extradition of Randazzo. What he had done to her poor client in a lakeside cabin in the Hill Country just outside Austin still haunted her. She grimaced at the mental horror show returning to focus in her mind and shuddered during the slow-motion replay. She had tracked him down to his lair in L.A. and, with the cooperation of the LAPD, brought him back to Austin for trial. And now the son of a bitch was walking the charges, a free and very dangerous man.

Dressed conservatively in a blue suit, white shirt, and striped tie, Randazzo dismissed Jackie with a sneer as he marched through the courthouse doors and onto the massive limestone steps, his high-rolling trial lawyer, Marty McCracken, glued to his side. The newspaper and television reporters, along with a few curious onlookers, gathered around McCracken's client, straining to get a look at the man who had beaten the odds.

Never short on words and always camera-ready, McCracken addressed the crowd in a booming, artificially inflected voice characteristic of lawyers who have higher opinions of themselves than anyone else does.

"Ladies and gentlemen, my client and I want to thank Judge Vasquez for a case well tried, and even more importantly, we'd like to thank those hardworking, honorable twelve men and women who dispensed true justice, something my client has been denied for way too long."

McCracken grabbed his client's hand and hoisted it up in the air in Rocky-esque fashion, grinning with satisfaction as camera bulbs flashed in their direction. "It's been a long week, and my client and I are both physically and mentally exhausted. If you'll excuse us."

The rakish lawyer and Randazzo, both with wolfish smirks on their faces, snaked their way through the crowded steps toward a waiting black limo. Dressed in wrinkled khakis and a button-down dress shirt, Abe Levine, executive editor for *Texas Matters,* blocked their path and shouted accusingly, "Mr. Randazzo, you were paid a lot of money to come here, to assault and torture Ms. Rosen, all to scare her off a story about one of your clients. Who was that client? Who paid you, you no-good bastard?" McCracken pushed Abe aside, and the two men ducked into the limo. Through squinting eyes, Abe watched as the limo turned and disappeared from sight.

Abe had been in the gallery when the verdict came in. Leah was waiting at the office, avoiding the courthouse and the circus she knew would follow, regardless of the verdict. Now he headed back to *Texas Matters,* went straight to her office, and sat down on the other side of her desk, his forlorn expression signaling trouble.

Leah was the first to speak. "I'm afraid to ask. It's bad news, isn't it?"

Knowing there was no good way to break the news, Abe said quietly, "I'm afraid so, Leah. The jury let him go."

Leah's eyes began to water, and tears rolled down her cheeks. As if willing herself away, she stared straight ahead at the wall and then softly uttered, "I don't know what to do. I know it was Randazzo, I just know it. And I'm sure Connors was behind all of it. He wanted to scare me off the story I was writing about him. The jury must not have believed a word I said."

Abe got up from his chair and made his way around the desk. Leaning down, he gently put his arm around Leah's shoulders and said, "The jury believed everything you said, I promise. You just couldn't swear for sure it was Randazzo who did those things to you. You were blindfolded, Leah. He planned things out so there was no way you could identify him. All the circumstantial evidence—the tattoo, the voice recognition testimony, Randazzo's past history—just wasn't enough for the jurors. I bet every one of them thought he was guilty, but they didn't believe the prosecutors proved it beyond a reasonable doubt. And that's the standard, whether we like it or not."

Leah looked up at Abe. "What should I do now? I can't pretend like it never happened."

Abe returned to his seat. "First, I think you should call Jackie McLaughlin. She was in the courtroom when the verdict came in. She wanted a conviction as much as we did. Get her thoughts. I know you don't want to hear this, but she's one of the best investigators—"

"I don't know if I can ever forget how she let me down. How do I know she won't again?"

"Jackie found Randazzo, didn't she? It was through her hard work that he was extradited to Texas and tried. She did everything she could to put that bastard behind bars. Trust me, Jackie feels terrible about what happened that night, but it wasn't her fault."

"Maybe you're right. I'll think about it."

"Good. Now, you've still got that Glock, don't you?"

Leah nodded toward her purse. "Never leave home without it."

"Why don't you stay at my house for a few days, until the shock of all this wears off a little? I can only imagine what you're going through right now."

"Thanks for the offer, but I can't impose on you every time I . . ."

Smiling kindly, Abe replied, "It's no imposition, I promise."

"The door to my condo is dead-bolted, and the security guys are great. One of them walks me to my door when I get home from work, and he does a quick walk-through before leaving. I feel as safe there as anywhere."

"Glad to hear it. So how about work? Do you need to take some time off?"

"I'd be climbing the walls. No need for that."

Abe stood up. "You'll let me know if anything changes?"

Leah nodded, trying hard to fight back tears.

Abe opened the door and, looking over his shoulder, added, "And you call me if you need anything—day or night. Promise?"

"Promise."

After Abe closed the door, Leah picked up her iPhone and ordered Siri to call Jackie McLaughlin.

CHAPTER 4

Jace threw on jeans, a polo shirt, and sandals and rushed into the kitchen. Pulling out a Pyrex dish, he made a generous pour of Caesar salad dressing into the dish, added a few drops of Worcestershire sauce and a dash of soy sauce, and tossed in a sprinkling of garlic salt before stirring his concoction with a fork. Then he dropped in two eight-ounce filets, cut to order by his favorite butcher. He flipped the steaks in the dish to make sure both sides were amply coated by the marinade, covered the dish with plastic wrap, and placed it in the fridge. He took a sip of scotch and glanced at his watch. Jackie would be there in less than thirty minutes. He would have to hurry if he wanted to have everything ready when she arrived.

Jace bolted out the side door onto a brick patio, which was furnished with a comfortable couch and swivel chairs, a built-in Weber grill, and a fireplace. After strategically placing several logs on the grate in the fireplace, he lit the kindling he had placed underneath. Seconds later, the fire began to crackle.

Rushing back inside the house, he headed for the den, opened the cabinet door to the right of the big-screen television, and began thumbing through the impressive collection of vinyl he had amassed over the years, stopping when he got to Rickie Lee Jones' debut album. Sliding the record out of the sleeve, he carefully placed it on his state-of-the-art turntable. After activating the turntable and speakers, he lowered the stylus to the first track, retrieved his scotch from the kitchen, and then stretched out on the leather chair and matching ottoman.

Five minutes later the doorbell rang.

Jackie was dressed in skinny jeans, a black halter top, and tan open-toed leather heels, her dark brown hair flowing over her shoulders, her matching eyes working their magic. As he stood in the doorway, Jace found himself uncharacteristically speechless.

"Well," Jackie said, a smile sliding across her face. "May I come in?"

"Of course. Sorry. You look so damn good I was distracted."

Following Jace into the kitchen, Jackie looked around and commented, "You have excellent taste, Counselor." She brushed the marble-topped island with the fingertips of one hand. "Very chic," she added. Her eyes darted to the gas range accented by a colorful backsplash depicting a wine bottle with several clumps of purple grapes strewn in front. "And nothing like cooking with gas. It makes a huge difference."

"Wish I could take the credit. I had the place redone six months ago from top to bottom. Cost me a fortune but I decided that if I was going to stay in this house, I needed to get rid of some memories.So, what can I get you to drink?"

Jackie grinned. "Hmm—choices, choices. What are you having?"

Jace held up his glass. "I started with scotch but I'm thinking about switching to wine. We're having tenderloin for dinner."

"Yum. You got any Pinot?"

"Need you ask?" Jace pulled a bottle from the wine rack next to the fridge and cradled it for Jackie to take a look. "This work for you?"

"I love Oregon Pinots. Let's do it." Jackie wandered out of the kitchen and into the den. Over her shoulder, she commented, "Great tunes! Who is that?"

"Rickie Lee Jones."

"I haven't heard any of her stuff, but I like it—kinda jazzy."

Removing the cork from the bottle, Jace poured two glasses of wine and followed Jackie into the den. He handed one to Jackie, who swished the contents around and then held the glass up to her nose. "Smells delicious." She took a sip. "And is delicious." Her eyes toyed with Jace's.

"Glad you like it." Jace gestured toward the side door. "Why don't we head out to the patio?" Seconds later, they were seated next to each other in front of a roaring fire, Jackie's bare feet propped up on the raised stone hearth. Her toenails, painted a bright blue, wiggled in front of the flames, occasionally brushing against Jace's leg.

"About time you made good on your promise to have me up for a weekend," she said with another smile, cocking her head playfully. "I was beginning to wonder whether you were just leading me on."

"Well, then," Jace said, lifting his glass, "we should make a toast to my case settling at the last minute."

They clinked glasses. "Were you surprised it settled?" asked Jackie.

"Not really. My opposing counsel doesn't like to try cases, but he held out for as long as he could, hoping to get my client's last dollar."

"And did he?"

"He left a little on the table." Jace grinned, and added, "The case wasn't as exciting as the ones you and I have worked on together, but it turned out just fine."

"I bet your client was happy."

"Very happy. And right after I called her with the news, I called you. I'm glad you didn't have any plans." Jace leaned over, gently squeezed Jackie's thigh, and brushed his lips against her cheek. The music stopped, and Jace, irritated at having to stop the flow, got up and headed inside. As he flipped the record over, he lamented, "That's the only problem with vinyl. Another glass of wine?"

"That would be great."

Jace returned with the bottle of wine. He poured another glass for Jackie and one for himself, and placed the bottle on a side table next to his chair. Before sitting, he threw another log on the fire and then turned toward Jackie. "Speaking of one of our old cases, guess who dropped by to see me this morning?"

"No idea."

"Cal Connors." Jace eased back into his chair and braced himself for the onslaught he knew was coming.

"What did that asshole want?"

"To hire me."

Leaning closer to Jace, Jackie laughed. "You've got to be kidding. What in the world for?"

"He wants to sue Leah Rosen and *Texas Matters* for defamation. They ran this article—"

"Cal Connors is nothing but a scumbag. He doesn't know the difference between right and wrong."

"You don't know that," Jace retorted.

Moving to the hearth across from Jace, her back to the roaring fire, her face betraying the frustration gripping her, she countered, "I do know that. He hired some sleazy PI to scare Leah off her story, but it didn't work."

"You don't know that either. Look, I heard the news on the way home from work. An Austin jury found Randazzo not guilty this morning."

"Jace, I didn't tell you when you called, but I was in the courtroom when the verdict came in. I was so shaken up that I didn't want to talk about it over the phone. I just couldn't believe it. The son of a bitch got away with it. But it happens all the damn time. The prosecution just got out-lawyered. It's as simple as that. Marty McCracken represented Randazzo. I'm sure you know who he is."

Jace nodded. "Well, if you can afford the best, why not get the best?"

"That's what's wrong with the system. The rich can pay for some hotshot lawyer and walk, while some poor kid from the projects does time for having a few grams of cocaine. That isn't right, and you know it." Jackie paused and stared straight into Jace's eyes. "You didn't take the case, did you?"

"If I said yes you wouldn't leave, now would you?"

"Don't screw with me, Jace. I really, really don't like that guy. And now he wants to sue Leah." Jackie pursed her lips. "Unbelievable."

"Okay, okay. I didn't take the case. I turned him down, along with the hefty retainer he offered me."

"Good for you."

"I don't know about that. Everyone is entitled to a good lawyer. I followed my gut and made the decision without anything to back it up. And now I'm the one who is leaving a lot of money on the table."

"You'll be glad you did, I promise. And just for your information, Leah Rosen called me after the verdict."

"And?"

"She's scared to death now that Randazzo is on the loose. She thinks he'll come back after her, and she wants to hire me again to protect her."

"I assume you agreed."

"Of course. I feel really guilty about what's already happened to her. It was on my watch when she got attacked. I'm sure she blames me. Who wouldn't? She needed me and I let her down."

"Don't beat yourself up, Jackie. You're the best private investigator I've ever met. I'm sure you did everything you could."

"I thought I had, but obviously it wasn't good enough."

Sensing he was on thin ice, Jace calmly stated, "But we still don't know for sure that Randazzo was the sick son of a bitch who molested Leah. And, even assuming he did, we don't know why."

"Oh, I do. I know it was him, no doubt in my mind. Connors hired him to scare Leah off the story she was writing about him. That's what Randazzo does for a living. Celebs out in Hollywood have been hiring him for years in divorce cases to threaten the hell out of their soon-to-be exes so they'll take less money. He also went after a reporter for the *LA Courier.* And she sued him."

There was an awkward pause.

"So did she win?"

"No, but that doesn't mean he didn't do it. He's slick, Jace. And so is Connors. You were smart not to take his case, and I'm proud of you for not stooping to his level."

Calming herself, Jackie returned to the chair next to Jace, swiveled it around, and gently nestled her feet in his lap. "I'm tired of talking shop. Let's change the subject. How's Matt doing?"

Smiling wistfully at his son's name, Jace responded, "Going through SEAL training. I don't get to talk to him that much, but he seems to love what he's doing. I still can't figure out why he signed up without even discussing it with me. I'm sure he hasn't gotten over his mother's death and blames me for it."

"Time will—"

"Oh, yes, I know the old adage. But it's been several years now, and not much has changed. If anything, our relationship has gotten worse. I wish Matt were still at the University of Texas, doing what young men his age do. You know, partying, enjoying life, chasing good-looking girls. There'll be plenty of time for the serious stuff later."

"And I guess there's nothing you can do now to fix it."

Jace turned toward Jackie and murmured as if talking to himself, "Believe me, I've looked at it from every angle. Unfortunately, once you enlist, you're hooked. No loopholes that I could find. Being young and using poor judgment just doesn't qualify."

"Come on, Jace. Give Matt the benefit of the doubt. Didn't he tell you the reason he signed up was to give back, do something for his country?"

"Yeah, that's what he said, and there may have been a little bit of that going on, but the main reason was to get back at me. I know him pretty well, and that's my take. I've spent enough sleepless nights tossing and turning, worrying about what could happen to him on a midnight raid in some godforsaken country halfway around the world. I hate to say it, but I may be just as pissed at him as he is at me right now."

Jace threw down the rest of his wine and began to massage Jackie's feet.

"Mmm," Jackie sighed, closing her eyes. Then she shifted them back to the hearth. "That feels so good, but I'm afraid we won't get around to cooking dinner if you don't stop."

"You're such a beautiful tease," Jace said.

"Hey, I'm a woman with big appetites. You ready to grill those steaks? You've sure bragged a lot about your forte in that department. Let's see if you can back up all that big talk. I'll get everything else ready."

Jackie got up and walked toward the kitchen, her bare feet gliding across the floor. Jace followed, taking in her tan shoulders, slender waist, and shapely hips.

Maybe dinner will have to wait, he thought to himself as he edged up from behind and slid his hands around her bare midriff.

CHAPTER 5

"So that's what your week looks like," said Darrin, glancing up from the detailed notes she had prepared for her meeting with her boss. "Bottom line, I think you are in good shape. That settlement you negotiated on Friday was a lifesaver. A two-week trial would have involved a lot of juggling on my part." Gathering her files, Darrin rolled her chair back from the table. "I guess that's it."

"Aren't you forgetting something?" Jace asked with a grin.

Darrin thought for a second. "I don't think so."

"Don't you want to know about my meeting with Cal Connors? You took off to catch your flight to Houston before I finished meeting with him."

"I totally forgot about that! What happened?"

"He wanted to hire me."

"Hire you? As co-counsel in one of his cases?"

"No. To sue Leah Rosen and *Texas Matters* over that article she wrote about him."

"Really! I read the article. It's pretty scathing. Basically, she called him a criminal."

"I agree. He left a copy and I read it after he blew out of here. I could tell from the cover it wasn't going to be very flattering, but holy shit, it was even rougher than I expected. I can understand why he was so pissed."

Jace chuckled as he retrieved the magazine from a stack of papers and handed it to Darrin. As she eyed the caricature of Cal, Jace continued, "And now the U.S. attorney over in Dallas is sniffing around to see if there is any truth to the article."

Darrin nodded. "So let me guess. Cal wants to go on the offensive and hire you to rip the reporter and the story apart, which will hopefully cause the U.S. attorney to drop the investigation."

"Exactly."

"So did you take the case?"

"Nope, turned it down, which, I might add, was damn hard to do. He offered me a $150,000 retainer. Then he upped it to a half mil."

"That's a lot of money."

"I'll probably regret—"

"No, you made the right decision. I saw the way Connors operated in that funeral home case, and I didn't get a warm and fuzzy feeling. He'll do whatever it takes to win, whether he has to step over the line or not. And that article is pretty detailed and well documented. I think Ms. Rosen is on to something."

Jace sighed. "Yeah, I just had a bad feeling about working with him."

"I bet he was mad as hell when you turned him down. People like that don't like no for an answer."

"You got that right. He had some choice words for me, but *c'est la vie*." Jace cleared his throat, hoping Darrin didn't catch his nervousness. "So how was your weekend in Houston? How are your sister and her husband doing?"

"Better, much better. They're going to marriage counseling, actually having a date here and there, taking baby steps."

"That's good. And the girls?"

"They were with their dad for the weekend. But I know they just want their parents back together." Darrin paused before asking, "And your weekend?"

Questioning the wisdom of bringing up the topic, he stumbled through an answer. "Fine, fine. Just stayed around the house and relaxed. I was whipped after last week."

Darrin wasn't biting. "I thought you would have celebrated, blown off some steam."

"That's coming up Wednesday night. Grace is treating me to dinner. She was thrilled with the settlement. Speaking of, you want to join us?"

"I think I'll take a rain check. Grace likes having all of your attention."

"Oh, come on. There's nothing between—"

"No, no! I know that. But you know how she is—she loves holding court."

Jace laughed. "I guess you're right."

Darrin rose from the table, files cradled in her arms. "Well, back to the grind."

Jace opened the door for her and watched as she walked down the hall, wondering what was going through her mind.

Turning into her office, Darrin dumped the files she was carrying into the chair across from her desk and kicked the door closed. After rummaging through her purse for her cellphone, she called her sister, who answered right before the call went to voice mail.

Out of breath, Megan gasped, "Darrin, hi! I was upstairs, straightening up. So how was your flight back?"

"Didn't you get my text?"

"Yeah. Thanks for letting me know you got in safely.I should have responded, but it was late by the time things settled down around here. I figured I would call you this morning but you beat me to it."

"Hey, I just wanted to tell you how much I enjoyed the weekend. It was so much fun! And I know it was a big imposition, considering all you are going through with Mark and the girls."

Megan scoffed. "Are you kidding? It was a welcome and much-needed distraction. I also think it was good for the girls to spend the weekend with their dad. They were on cloud nine when he brought them home last night. This was a big step in the healing process."

"That's so good to hear! Sorry I didn't get to spend time with them, but I'll make it a point next visit."

"So did you have a good time at the brunch yesterday? I noticed you and Dr. Pass seemed to be enjoying each other's company."

"He was fun to talk with and, I gotta say, damn good-looking."

"Do I sense a little chemistry going on, Sis?"

"Way too early to tell, but I did enjoy meeting him—not as conceited as some of the docs I've met."

"You know he lost his wife several years back."

"I was wondering but didn't want to pry. Did you know her?"

"Not well. I saw her at a few parties over the years but never had much opportunity to talk with her. You know how those things are—trying to eat, drink, and talk at the same time. You and Levi didn't seem to do much mingling. I don't know who cornered who, but y'all spent most of the brunch over in your own little world like long-lost friends. Did you meet anyone else?"

"A few people, but no one stands out, and you know I'm not much on small talk. And neither is Levi. He seemed serious at first, but after we talked for a while, he let his guard down. And he's got this wry sense of humor. Some of the things he said cracked me up."

"By the way, he probably didn't brag about it, but he's head of cardiology at St. Joseph's. He's one of the most respected doctors in Houston. I think Mark told me several years ago that Levi had been elected president of the Texas Medical Association, but I can't be sure about that."

"Impressive."

"Not to change the subject, but how's Jace?"

"That's a good question. I don't really know. We met this morning to go over his schedule for the week, and I asked him what he did this weekend."

"And?"

"He said he stayed around the house, but he wasn't too convincing. I'm not sure I believe him."

"Do you think he saw that investigator? What's her name?"

"Jackie McLaughlin. I don't know whether he did or not, but I didn't get a good feeling about things."

"Can I give you some advice, Sis? Jace doesn't know what he wants right now. He's been stringing you along for a while, and you need to make him commit, one way or the other. You know how men are—they'll straddle the fence as long as you let them."

"So what do you think I should do? Quit my job and move to Houston?" Darrin joked.

Megan answered earnestly, "That's exactly what I think you should do. Give him a taste of what life would be like without you. If he loves you, it will be a loud wake-up call and he will come crawling, begging you to come back. If not, then you'll know where you stand."

"It's not that easy, Megan. Jace's practice depends on me more than he likes to believe. I know things wouldn't run very smoothly around the firm if I left."

"It would be good for Jace to sweat a little. Like I said, learn what life would be like personally and professionally without you."

"I'd have to find a new job, a place to live . . ."

"As good as you are at what you do, I bet you would have more offers than you knew what to do with. You could live with me and the girls while you tested the waters. I promise you, it wouldn't be as hard as you think. And I bet Dr. Pass would come knocking when word got around."

"I don't know, Megan. I'll think about it."

"It's a big decision, I know that, but I really believe moving to Houston is the right thing."

"I hear you. Well, I've got to get back to work."

"And I'm late for my yoga class. Love ya, Sis."

"Love you too."

Darrin stared out the window. She hadn't wanted to fall in love with Jace Forman. Somehow love had just crept up on her. Nothing overnight, nothing immediate, just gradual and sure. The late evenings getting ready for trial, the lingering looks, the subtle gestures—all had slowly morphed into something she couldn't, and didn't want to, let go of. And their weekend in New Orleans after their last trial victory had been surreal—a romantic dinner at Bayona, after-dinner drinks at the Carousel Bar in the Hotel Monteleone, and then a night of passionate lovemaking she had hoped would last forever. The next day had been spent wandering down Royal Street, occasionally ducking into art galleries, antiques stores, and those cluttered shops unique to the Big Easy, arm in arm, sneaking a quick kiss now and again, and then relaxing on a bench as the sun slowly set over the Mississippi. They had grabbed an early dinner at Killer PoBoys on Conti Street before catching a cab to the Blue Nile, on Frenchmen, where they listened to jazz and sipped cognac, which sparked a second night of lovemaking, more careless and confident than the first. The next morning they savored Bloody Marys and bananas Foster pain perdu at the Ruby Slipper before heading to the airport.

The following Monday, however, Jace had been all business, acting as if their magical weekend together had never even happened. There seemed to be some invisible shield in place, separating her and Jace, a shield she had tried to penetrate with little success. For weeks she had hoped for things to improve, which they did, to a degree. But the fire that had burned for two days and nights in New Orleans now merely simmered, a shadow of a flame now and then, and she could only wonder, as she had so many times, why. Why couldn't Jace take the next step? Why couldn't he love her for longer than a weekend? Was there something wrong with him—or with her?

CHAPTER 6

The elevator stopped at the eleventh floor. The door opened to a spacious, modern reception area—tiled floor, white leather furniture, teak wood with abstract art on the wall. Two young women with expensive haircuts and sleek, stylish dresses sat behind a massive L-shaped block made of opaque glass and white marble. Behind them stood a stone wall with the eye-catching imprint "Law Offices of Sharlene Knox."

"Howdy, ladies," said Cal, winking at the prettier of the two as he signed his name to the guest register. After he finished, the young woman escorted him down the hall, stopping at a corner office where, with a graceful sweep of the arm accented by a suggestive smile, she motioned him inside. Sharlene Knox was waiting behind a glass desk. After a brief exchange of pleasantries, she got up and walked over to a mahogany cabinet anchored to one of the walls of her office. She opened the doors and picked up a marker from the tray below a whiteboard.

Turning to her new client, she smiled. "Ready for a little brainstorming?"

There was something about Sharlene that drew Cal in, but he couldn't put his finger on exactly what it was. She wasn't beautiful, certainly not in the way his first two wives had been. They had literally turned heads—long, flowing hair, blue eyes, and plenty up top. Sharlene was just the opposite. Her amber hair was cut fashionably short, bangs swept across her forehead. She wore a sleeveless blue dress, simple pearl studs, and a matching double strand of pearls around her slender neck. Her figure was graceful and well proportioned, nothing overdone or artificial, with legs so perfect and defined they could be mistaken for those of a twentysomething.

"Cal, you sure you're ready to get started? You seem a little distracted." Sharlene smiled, business mode momentarily muted, her brown eyes searching for clues.

Flustered, Cal muttered unconvincingly, "Oh, I was just thinking about this case I'm handling. Sorry."

"Okay, I want to start by saying I know that lawyers can be difficult clients. I have represented my share, and they think they know everything. As I told you over the phone, I've agreed to take your case on one condition. I call all the shots. You and I will discuss trial strategy, but at the end of the day, I'll make the calls. You're just too close to this. You still on board with that?"

Cal nodded his agreement.

"Just making sure there aren't any misunderstandings before we get started. I know this case is important to you. And believe it or not, it's just as important to me. I'm in this with you—all in. But we don't need two cooks in the kitchen."

"I'll try to stay out of your way, but I may forget from time to time. I'm sure you'll let me know if I step out of line." Cal shot her an aw-shucks grin that he used from time to time and then eased back in his chair, his eyes glued to his new lawyer.

He knew he had picked right this time. Screw Jace Forman. Sharlene could run circles around him. She had graduated salutatorian from St. Agnes, a prestigious prep school in Austin. UT-Austin was next, and then law school at Yale, after which she had worked for a law firm in New York that specialized in entertainment law, representing Hollywood actors, recording artists, professional athletes, and renowned authors. Although she quickly established herself in New York, making critical connections and getting more hands-on experience than she'd expected, the concrete jungle got to her after a couple of years, and she decided to move back to Texas and open an office in the Oak Lawn area of Dallas. It wasn't long until her New York connections paid off. A Dallas Cowboy football player charged with domestic assault was referred to her by her old firm for representation. Though the charges repulsed her, she eagerly took the case. She had a reputation to build and, more importantly, needed the dues. Twenty years later, she was now regarded as one of Dallas's premier trial lawyers. From the ground up she had built a highly lucrative boutique trial practice with four seasoned lawyers, two paralegals, and three investigators working for her. Home was the penthouse of the Warwick, an exclusive condominium development on Turtle Creek, with the skyline of downtown Dallas as the backdrop. Life had been good to Sharlene, very good indeed.

"Cal, let's talk about the elements of your case. First, we've got to prove the story Ms. Rosen wrote about you wasn't true."

As she spoke, Sharlene wrote "LIES" in bold letters on the board. "Okay, you've read the article. What about it wasn't true?"

"The whole damn thing. The whole damn article was one big lie."

"We've got to do better than that. We're going to have to spell them out, one by one." Under LIES, Sharlene slashed the number 1 on the board. "So, what's the most glaring falsehood you can recall?" After a lengthy pause, she added, "I've got the article on my desk if you need to refer to it."

"I remember it well enough. It starts off with this pharmaceutical case I tried down in the Valley. I tagged the company for selling a drug designed to beat depression but it did the exact opposite. This so-called wonder drug screwed up one man's brain so bad that he shot his family, execution style. It was a righteous case, Sharlene. Those crooks from up east deserved to get hit. And this reporter—hell, she ain't even dry behind the ears—her first allegation was that I got my expert, Dr. Howell Crimm, to file false reports with the court about the drug's side effects. There's not a lick of truth to that. Dr. Crimm is credentialed out the wazoo, more awards than you can shake a stick at. He formed those opinions on his own without any interference or suggestions from me, and the jury obviously believed him. Rosen then goes on to criticize jury verdicts I've gotten against other companies throughout the nation without an ounce of support for anything she says. Hell, those big-ass companies I sued had the best lawyers money could buy, some of 'em billing at one thousand dollars an hour or more. They just got whupped, that's all—just sour grapes. I'm sure the bastards got to that reporter and put her up to this."

Sharlene wrote "EXPERT REPORTS FALSE" next to her number 1 and then, in parentheses, "Howell Crimm's testimony, Howell Crimm's credentials, opposing counsel's right to contest, jury's right to believe."

Turning to Cal, she said, "I like it. Anything else I can add to that one?"

"Ain't that enough?"

"Okay, let's go to the next one."

"That I forum-shopped, looking for the most favorable trial court. Well, I don't guess that's a lie. I do it in most, if not all, of my cases. Hell, all good plaintiff lawyers do. It would be malpractice not to, in my opinion. And filing my lawsuit in South Texas was the smart call. But Rosen implies that picking where you sue is somehow illegal, and that's just plain bullshit."

"I agree with you." Sharlene penned the number 2 on the board, scribbled "FORUM-SHOPPING" next to it and then, in parentheses, wrote "legal."

Cal stared at the board. "Can we go back to number one? Let's say Howell gets cold feet about testifying. Would we have to have him?" Cal was priming the pump. He wanted to make sure Sharlene had a backup plan in case Howell tucked tail and ran.

"That'd be my preference, but a jury just might be convinced by reading his reports, reviewing his résumé, learning that opposing counsel had every opportunity to present expert reports, and did. They could definitely be swayed by our argument that the juries in those cases believed Dr. Crimm rather than opposing counsel's hired guns. Any reason you think he might not want to testify?"

Cal sighed. "Well, to be honest, the last time I used him he was going through this nasty divorce, and I mean nasty. He was cheating on his wife, hitting the craps tables in Vegas, and drinking way too much—and all of that put his life in a real tailspin. I hate to say this, Howell being a longtime friend of mine, but in a matter of months he went from being one of the best in the business to a worthless drunk. Shit, I tried my best to help him, even guaranteed his lease when he moved to Santa Fe, but it didn't do any good. He was too far gone."

"Such a shame. Sorry to hear that, but it happens. So you're saying we might not even want him to testify? Hmm." Sharlene leaned against the wall as she thought, the marker lodged between her fingers like a cigarette, her mind going back in time. "I had this witness once. When we started his deposition at nine in the morning, he did great, I mean great. And then he came back after lunch and caved—he'd hit the sauce over the noon hour. I had no idea he was a closet drunk or I wouldn't have let him out of my sight."

Relieved, Cal saw an opening and added, "That's what I'm afraid of with Howell. You just don't know what he might do. He's a loose cannon."

"Well, we don't have to decide that today. What else you got?"

"Rosen mentions that Howell's reports are similar in all of my cases, him saying exactly what I needed him to say, but that don't prove a damn thing."

"I agree, but let's jot it down anyway." Sharlene added number 3 to the board and wrote beside it "SAME TESTIMONY."

"And Rosen made a big deal of the fact that the jury awards I received were all in the millions."

Shaking her head, Sharlene said, "I saw that. Again, so what? That just means you're a good lawyer—a great lawyer. It's not even worth writing on the board."

"What's next?" Cal asked.

"Let's go back to number one a moment. In her article, Rosen mentions some research assistants that Dr. Crimm used in forming his opinions. You remember that?"

"Yeah, I remember that."

"You wouldn't know their names, would you?"

"Nah, but I bet Howell would. I'll call him."

"That would be great. Let me know what he says." Sharlene looked at her watch. "Cal, this has been helpful. I'll have a draft of the petition to you later today, and we'll get it filed as soon as you give me the go-ahead."

"Sooner the better."

Sharlene extended her hand. "Cal, it's been a pleasure."

Cal shot her a grin. "Take no prisoners, Sharlene."

"Don't worry. I never do."

CHAPTER 7

The lawsuit was served on Leah mid-morning the following Monday. In disbelief she paced back and forth in her office as she read the allegations against her. According to the document shaking in her hand, she had been negligent, grossly negligent, malicious, incompetent, and wanton, and she had intentionally caused millions of dollars in damage to the reputation of one Calvin Connors.

She staggered over to Abe's office, closed the door, and gasped, "Have you seen this?" She held the petition up and shook it in his direction.

"Afraid so." Abe rose from behind his desk and approached Leah. "It's just a bunch of garbage. Nothing to any of that crap, I promise."

"So how did you learn about it?"

"*Texas Matters* was served on Friday. I didn't tell you. There was no point in ruining your weekend."

"It wasn't much of a weekend anyway, and yes, it would have been a lot worse if I had known about this." She held up the petition again for emphasis and continued, "We're going to fight it, aren't we?"

"You bet we are, and we're gonna win. This is nothing more than a bullying tactic—typical of Connors and people like him."

Collapsing in the chair across from Abe's desk, Leah said, "I can't afford a lawyer."

"Not a problem. The magazine will pay all of your defense costs."

"Well, that's good. Who's going to represent us?"

Hesitating, Abe responded, "*Texas Matters* has retained the Ralston firm. They handle all of our legal matters. But Steve and I felt you should have your own lawyer."

Steve Blumenthal was *Texas Matter's* publisher. Alarmed, Leah cried, "You don't think I did anything wrong, do you?"

"Not at all. It's typical in cases where there are multiple defendants for each defendant to be represented by separate counsel to make sure there are no conflicts and that everyone's interests are protected."

"Aren't we all in the same boat here? I mean, I wrote the story, you and Steve approved it, and the magazine published it."

"Right on all points. Like I said, this is just a precaution."

"Confusing, but I sorta get it." Leah continued. "Who will represent me?"

"We wanted you to make that decision."

"Abe, I have met some lawyers down at the courthouse while covering the beat, but I don't know whether they'd be right for this type of case. What do you think? Do you know any good lawyers?"

Abe smiled. "Isn't that an oxymoron?"

"Come on, Abe. This is serious."

"I know a lot of lawyers, but they're mainly 'deal' guys who've never been inside a courtroom and have no desire to go in one."

"Well, that doesn't help much."

"Look, I'll call the Ralston firm and see if they can recommend someone."

Standing, Leah sighed. "Thanks, Abe. Not a great way to start the week."

"Look on the bright side. It can only get better from here."

"I hope you're right."

After she got back to her office, Leah called Jackie's cell.

"Leah, how are you?"

"Not great. Just got served with a lawsuit. Cal Connors is suing me and *Texas Matters* over that story I wrote."

Jackie feigned surprise. "I guess I should have seen this coming. He is such a dirtbag. Who's representing him?"

Thumbing to the last page, Leah replied, "Let's see. Here it is. Sharlene Knox, Law Offices of Sharlene Knox, the Grinder Building, 2020 Oak Lawn Avenue, Dallas. You know her?"

"Name doesn't ring a bell. Let me Google her." There was a brief silence as Leah listened to Jackie punching on her computer keyboard. "Okay, here she is. Graduated from UT and then Yale Law. Looks like her client list is a who's who of celebrities—professional football players, country music folks, politicians. Pretty impressive."

"I wonder why Connors hired her?"

"On her website, she lists defamation as one of her specialties."

"That's just great!" said Leah, worried once more. "Connors hired the best in the business."

"Who is going to represent you and the magazine?"

"I just got out of a meeting with my boss. He told me I needed to have my own lawyer."

"Sounds like they want to make sure you get the best representation possible. It'll cost *Texas Matters* a lot more since they will have to pay two law firms instead of one, but it's a smart move."

Feeling better with the strategy, Leah asked, "So who would you hire if you were in my shoes?"

Jackie didn't hesitate. "Jace Forman," she said.

"I know him. I've seen him in court before and interviewed him for the article. Seemed like a good guy."

"He is a good guy, and he's a great lawyer. I've worked with him, and I can tell you he knows what he's doing."

"I wonder if he's ever handled a case like this one."

"I can't answer that. Why don't you call him and ask?"

"I will. Thanks for the reference. Any update from your contact at the LAPD about Randazzo?"

"I haven't heard anything else, but I'll give her a call and let you know if I learn anything."

"Thanks, Jackie. Hey, I know you're doing everything you can to protect me, and I appreciate it."

"Leah, this is not just a routine case to me. It has become really personal. When I heard the verdict, I can't tell you how pissed I was. But that's water under the bridge. I promise you that sick son of a bitch will never lay a finger on you again."

"I hope you're right."

Ending the call, Jackie dialed the cell number for Officer Flannigan in the LAPD's main office. "This is Jackie McLaughlin in Austin. Just following up on our man Randazzo."

"Hey, I meant to call you earlier but I've been underwater. I've got news. Randazzo may have changed his appearance."

"Plastic surgery?"

"We tailed him to a surgery center, one used by the celebs. He made two visits before we lost him. We've kept an eye on his residence, and he hasn't made it back there. Jackie, I'm starting to worry that he's taken off."

"Damn. Any idea where?"

"We don't have any leads. I'll let you know if anything comes up on our radar."

"I appreciate your help."

After Flannigan disconnected, Jackie glanced at her watch. It was 6:30 in Austin. She wondered if Randazzo was headed their way or if he was already there. She considered calling Leah but decided against it. She needed a plan first. Leah would pepper her with questions, and she wanted to have all the answers so she could give Leah as much peace of mind as possible when they talked. She called her former partner with the Austin PD, Officer Jorge Gomez, who had worked side by side with her on her last investigation of Randazzo.

"Jorge, I hate to bother you but—"

"Hey, Jackie. Good to hear from you. What's going on?"

"Randazzo's headed this way. At least I think he is."

"How do you know?"

"Just got off the phone with Flannigan out in L.A. She's had one of her officers trailing Randazzo since he got back to L.A.—long story short, he's probably had a face job and hasn't been seen since. I have a bad feeling he may surface here in Austin. Only this time, we might not recognize him."

"Shit."

"Shit is right."

"Do we have any idea what he looks like?"

"Not a clue. But, of course, we do know what he used to look like, including his height, build, skin tone, and, if he didn't have it removed, his neck tattoo."

"I'll circulate his previous mug shots to all the beat cops and let them know his appearance may have changed. It's a long shot, but we may get lucky."

"Thanks, Jorge."

"Glad to help."

Jackie's thoughts rewound again to that horrible night. A hulking figure, clad totally in black, methodically and without emotion ordered Leah to take off one piece of clothing after another until she was standing before him shaking, totally nude. An image of dark eyes, staring at a helpless Leah through the eyehole slits of an ink-black stocking mask, flashed through Jackie's mind. Shuddering, she considered heading to the kitchen for a shot or two of whiskey in hopes of dulling the image. She rejected the idea. A cloudy mind was the last thing she needed.

CHAPTER 8

Darrin had spent the last several days obsessing about Jace and whether or not she should leave the firm and move to Houston. She kept coming back to the same place: she could handle having her professional life in upheaval, and she could handle her personal life falling apart, but she didn't think she could handle both at the same time. It was just too much.

She was tired and worn out from it all when she got to work that morning. She decided to take an early lunch and bought a takeout salad from a sandwich shop around the corner. Heading to her office with her lunch, she overheard Jace on the phone. "Jackie! Great to hear from you!" Then the door to Jace's office closed.

The afternoon crawled by, and Darrin couldn't focus on work. The call from Jackie had pushed her over the edge. A decision had to be made. Later that day, she walked into Jace's office and stood in front of his desk.

"Darrin, I haven't seen you all day. Sit down and stay awhile, as the saying goes." Jace smiled. It wasn't returned.

Still standing, Darrin said firmly, "Jace, I've done a lot of thinking, and I've decided it's best if I leave the firm."

"What in the world are you talking about?"

"I'm leaving, Jace. I've been thinking about this for quite a while, and I'm sure it's the right thing for me."

Jace just stared at her in silence. He drew a hand down across his face. Finally, he replied, "Darrin, to say this is a big surprise would be an understatement. Why didn't you talk to me? I had no idea." Jace rose from his chair, but Darrin waved him back down.

"It's too late for that. I've made up my mind."

"What brought all of this on?"

"Come on, don't play Mr. Innocent, Jace. I'm not a fool."

"I didn't say you were. I just think we should talk this through like adults rather than play some guessing game."

"Okay, let's talk. You've been acting cool and distant ever since New Orleans. I don't know what I did or said, but things haven't been the same since."

"I don't know what—"

Cutting him off, Darrin felt her voice intensifying. "Sure you do. You know exactly what I'm talking about. And how about that weekend after you settled the Moore case? I assume you were with Jackie."

"Let me—"

"Don't make things any worse than they already are, Jace. Anyway, I'm giving you my notice. I'll stay until the end of the month. Don't worry, I'll make sure no deadlines are missed and that you're not left hanging on anything. I'll work directly with Kirk and, if you have any questions or need anything while I'm here or after I'm gone, you can talk with him. That will make it easier on both of us."

Jace rose from his chair, his body literally trembling. "This is such a shock, Darrin. You can't leave. I won't let you. I don't know what I've done, but you've got to give us some time to—

Shaking her head emphatically, Darrin cut him off. "No, I don't. It's been hard enough—coming in, looking forward to seeing you every day and then you blowing me off, acting like there is nothing between us, like New Orleans never happened. I'm not going to put myself through this anymore. I can't."

"Darrin, I'm sorry. I just need—"

Her voice quivering, Darrin said, "I'm moving to Houston, Jace."

"Your sister put you up to this, didn't she?"

"Don't put this on Megan. This was all my decision."

"Do you have a job yet?"

"No, but I assume you'll be getting calls once I start interviewing. I hope you'll give me a good reference. I think I've earned it."

"Darrin, you've got to rethink this. You're making a huge mistake."

Fighting back tears, Darrin turned toward the door. "No, Jace, you did."

After Darrin left, Jace made his way back to the credenza, opened a cabinet door, and pulled out a bottle of Glenlivet 12. He didn't often drink at work—he couldn't even remember the last time—but he was definitely about to make an exception. He poured the glass half full and emptied it, squinting his eyes as a slow burn made its way down his throat and into his gut. He poured another, swishing it around, looking for answers in the gold liquid, before throwing it back. The hoped-for dullness didn't come. He considered pouring another but rejected the idea. What good would getting drunk do?

The questions began to bombard him. Should he walk down to Darrin's office and try again to talk her out of it? Maybe he could get her to postpone her move, which would give him more time to come up with something, maybe work some magic. Jace shook his head. Her body language had told him she was emotionally devastated and just couldn't take any more. He eyed the scotch bottle again. Another wouldn't hurt—he could handle it. He poured a third and down it went. His mind took a turn.

So, he asked himself, what was so wrong with his taking a step back after New Orleans? No question the weekend had been special, but on the flight back things had gotten a little too heavy, and he had begun to feel trapped. Darrin told him she loved him, and the word "married" reared its frightful head. No, she hadn't put any time constraints on him, but it was clear where she wanted the relationship to go, and he got the sense she wasn't going to wait much longer. But he wasn't even close to ready. His marriage to Camille had been rocky for years before her accident, and he was anxious about taking that step again—at least anytime soon. Darrin was coming from a different place, and he could understand her desire to tie the knot. She too had been married once, but it was years ago and only for a short time. And there had been no kids in her marriage. It was a totally different picture for her than for him.

Jace's thoughts turned to Jackie—he clearly wasn't ready for a serious commitment with Darrin. He had tried to buy some time, but Darrin had called his bluff.

C'est la vie or *c'est la guerre*. Jace threw on his sport jacket, and headed down the hall. Walking past Darrin's office, he glanced in—she was gone. Maybe her leaving was for the best. He wouldn't try and talk her out of it. He would let things take their course and try not to peer too far down the road.

Heading to his car, he felt the alcohol kicking in. Fortunately, he was sober enough to know he couldn't drive and instead pulled out his phone and tapped on his Uber app. A few minutes later he was on his couch with a glass of pinot in one hand and a slice of cold pizza in the other. It was going to be a long night and an even longer tomorrow.

CHAPTER 9

Dressed in a tight-fitting pencil skirt, black sleeveless top, and matching heels, her auburn hair flowing down her back and her ears adorned with aquamarine studs that highlighted her blue eyes, Christine Connors stood in the reception area of Travers & Chalmers, thumbing through a lawyer magazine as she waited.

"You must be Ms. Connors? I'm Reed Travers."

A broad-shouldered man of medium height, dressed casually in a sport jacket and slacks, walked forward and offered his hand. He looked to be in his early forties. Christine immediately noticed his brown eyes, with crow's-feet at the corners, and crooked nose, as if it had been broken on numerous occasions and never properly set. Reed was not attractive in a Hollywood sense: he was certainly no Paul Newman or Leonardo DiCaprio. If anything, he was more of a De Niro or Stallone. There wasn't a single feature that stood out, that held any attraction for her. It was the total package: the rugged looks, the confident air, the smile—oh yes, the smile, a smile that lit up his entire face, that warmed her, that made her want to join in. Christine was impressed. Reed was dead attractive in an unconventional way—an attraction that didn't come across from the photo on his website but was intoxicating in the flesh.

Taking his outstretched hand, she replied, "Christine, please."

"Christine it is. Come on back to my office." Leading the way down the hall, he motioned her inside his office and toward a seating area where two upholstered chairs faced each other on either side of a rectangular aged-oak coffee table.

"Something to drink? Coffee, tea?" Reed asked.

"I'm fine. I had several cups of coffee before I left home." She glanced at Reed, noting for the first time a faint scar under his right eye.

Pouring a cup of coffee for himself, Reed took the chair next to Christine. "I don't think we've ever met before. Of course, I've read all about you and your father."

"You're not going to hold that against me, are you?" said Christine in a joking tone.

"Oh, don't be modest. Most of it has been favorable," Reed flashed a grin at Christine.

"You haven't read the most recent article then, the one in *Texas Matters*." Sitting up in her chair slightly, Christine pulled her skirt down to just above the knee. Reed couldn't help but notice her tan, well-defined legs.

"I haven't," Reed said, "but I did see the cover while I was waiting in the checkout line at the grocery. I'd be lying if I didn't tell you I laughed out loud at that caricature of your dad riding Lady Justice."

"Well, I'm glad *someone* found some humor in it, because we didn't. In fact, it's part of the reason I'm here."

"Before we get to that, how did you hear about me anyway?"

"We don't do criminal work, just like you don't handle civil cases, but I do keep up with what's going on in the Fort Worth legal community. You've made the news more times than I can count, and the recent acquittal you won for that woman who shot her husband four times in the back—come on, Reed. Self-defense? You've got to be kidding me!"

Reed didn't budge an inch. "She had been abused by that no-good son of a bitch for years," he replied. "As the saying goes, he had it coming."

"No need to convince me. It obviously worked on the jury. But before I hire you, I'd like to know a little bit more about you."

Reed sighed and then shot her another one of those boyish grins. "So where do you want me to start?"

"I have all morning."

"Okay, then, I'll give you the lengthy David Copperfield version. I was born in Texas City. You know where that is?"

"Near Galveston. Was your dad in the oil business?"

"If working in a refinery counts, you could say that. My mother taught sixth grade. I was born and raised Catholic, though I haven't gone to church in years. I went to public school in Texas City through high school, played football, and lucked into a scholarship at Trinity, in San Antonio. Too much detail?"

"You're doing just fine." Christine had momentarily forgotten why she was there. She was enjoying being with Reed and hearing all about him. She could almost convince herself that it was a little like a first date. "What did you play?"

"Linebacker."

"And after Trinity, SMU Law? I think I remember that from your website."

"Yep. My grades were pretty good but not good enough to get into UT. I wanted to stay in-state, and SMU was my second choice."

"So how did you end up practicing criminal law in Fort Worth?"

"I never really warmed up to Dallas—a little snooty for me—so I applied to the Tarrant County District Attorney's office. I had spent some weekends during law school in Fort Worth, and I loved the laid-back feel of the town. Plus, I wanted to try cases in the worst kind of way and felt being with the DA's office would give me that opportunity. And I wasn't disappointed. I was picking juries right after I passed the bar exam."

Christine could feel the approving smile on her lips. "Nice. So when did you go into private practice?"

"I was with the DA's office for a little over five years. During that time I went up against this local defense lawyer named Joe Chalmers—a helluva lawyer, kicked my butt more times than I'd like to admit. He called me one day out of the blue and asked me to come to work for him. I didn't hesitate—gave my two-week notice and ended up on the other side of the docket learning from the best in the business. Did you know Joe?"

"No, but I bet Dad did."

"Wouldn't surprise me at all. Anyway, I tried several cases with him, learning some of his tricks and getting used to the defense side, and then he cut me free. He was there as a sounding board but I was trying cases solo."

"I noticed his name is in the firm. Is he still practicing?"

"Nope, he came in my office one day several years back and told me he was moving to Belize. He was burned-out on the practice and wanted a Jimmy Buffett kind of lifestyle."

"I bet that was a shocker."

"Not really. I had seen it coming. His personal life was a mess, he had gone through several wives, he had been hitting the bottle pretty heavy for years, and his health wasn't good. So he decided to do something about it. Told me he just wanted to leave it all behind and get a clean start."

"And I guess you left his name in the firm as a kind of tribute?"

"Yeah. I put my name first, though." Reed smiled before concluding, "And I guess that's about it. Did I pass the audition?"

"With flying colors."

Their eyes met and fixed on each other for an instant before Christine looked away.

"So, you ready to tell me why you're here?" Reed asked.

"I've never been a client before. I hate to admit it, but I'm kind of nervous. I don't know exactly where to start."

"Well, you quizzed me about my background. Why don't you start by telling me a little about yourself?"

"Let's see. I grew up here in Fort Worth, went to Baylor undergraduate, and then Harvard Law. Got offers from a lot of firms all over the place, like New York, San Francisco, Denver, but decided to come back to Fort Worth to practice with my dad."

"You and your dad close?"

"Very."

"And your mother?"

"Dad's good at a lot of things, but marriage isn't one of them. He and my mother divorced when I was pretty young, but it was about as friendly a divorce as you can have—no trial or custody battle. Dad knew he was at fault and gave my mom a very generous settlement. They agreed on joint custody and that was that. I was an only child, and the way my parents handled things meant a lot to me."

"How is it working with your dad?"

"Honestly," said Christine, surprising herself, "it was difficult at first. It was his firm. He loved his nickname, the Lone Wolf, which pretty much says it all. It was an adjustment for both of us, shall we say."

"But you made it?"

"We did. And I've never looked back. The firm's been very successful, and I've enjoyed practicing with him. He still likes to try cases by himself, but it's pretty special being able to walk into his office and chat whenever I want."

"I bet. You and your dad have a specialty area?"

"We used to concentrate on personal injury, but tort reform took a bite out of that, so recently we've been taking on some patent cases, business torts, that type of thing."

"Okay. Now let's focus on why you're here today."

Clearing her throat, Christine braced herself. "You know the U.S. attorney over in Dallas?"

"Cowan? Yeah, I know who he is. I haven't tried a case against him yet. He's pretty new. I think he received his interim appointment about a year ago. He was an assistant DA down in Austin."

"That sounds right. Anyway, his office subpoenaed some of our firm's records several months back."

"Dealing with what?"

"Some silica cases I settled."

"Why would he want those records?"

Hedging, Christine responded, "Your guess is as good as mine. The settlement was for a lot of money, but that's not unusual for our firm."

"So how did you respond to the subpoena?"

"We didn't have anything responsive to his request, and I filed a pleading saying just that. Once a case is settled, it's our firm's practice to destroy all the files. What's the use in keeping them around?"

"Nothing illegal about that," Reed offered. "Did you hear anything back from Cowan after you filed your response?"

"Not a peep, which began to worry me. You know, it felt like the calm before the storm. That's why I decided to hire you. It made sense to me to do it sooner rather than later. I've never been charged with anything more than a speeding ticket in my entire life and don't know the first thing about criminal law. I need you to keep me from doing something stupid."

"Good thinking."

"One other thing. You remember I mentioned that *Texas Matters* article as being part of the problem?"

Reed nodded.

"Well, it was a hatchet job on Dad. The magazine accused him of rigging jury verdicts throughout the country by using tainted expert testimony. After the article came out, Cowan called Dad in and asked him some questions."

"Are you mentioned in the article?"

"In passing, but the reporter who wrote the story didn't say anything derogatory about me."

"You mentioned earlier that your dad liked to try cases alone. Did you work with him on any of the cases that were the subject of the article?"

"No, I didn't. In fact, some of those cases were tried years ago, before I even joined the firm."

"Don't read anything into this, but I have to ask. Do you have any knowledge your dad did anything wrong in obtaining those verdicts?"

"None whatsoever."

"Okay then, let's put that aside. Going back to the silica settlement, anything you can think of, anything, that might have the slightest appearance of illegality, impropriety, anything of that nature?"

Her stare staying with Reed, Christine responded smoothly, not a hint of equivocation in her voice, "No, nothing comes to mind." Picking her purse up off the floor, she fished out a check for $25,000 payable to Travers & Chalmers and handed it to Reed. She noticed he wasn't wearing a wedding band.

"Christine, that's not necessary at this point. Let's see what happens with Cowan."

"No, I want it to be official. Now that I've given you a retainer you're my lawyer, and everything we discussed here today, or may discuss in the future, is privileged." Christine lamented, "I wish we were meeting under better circumstances."

Reed grinned. "There's always tomorrow. Shall I show you out?"

But Christine had already risen and was walking toward the door, making sure her heels gave Reed the best of her calves. Peeking over her shoulder, she said, "No need. I know where I'm going."

CHAPTER 10

The alarm on Jace's phone buzzed and vibrated, prompting him to fumble blindly across the top of his bedside table. He punched the clock icon and the dot next to "6:45," and the annoying buzzing stopped. Sitting up, he perched on the side of the bed, head bowed and throbbing. In the days since Darrin had told him she was leaving, he had been hitting the bottle too hard. *I've got to cut down on my drinking*, he thought to himself as he stood up.

He had learned that a greasy breakfast was one of the more effective antidotes for a nasty hangover, so he threw on a robe and ambled into the bathroom and on into the kitchen. Bachelorhood had taught him to be a passable short-order cook. After sliding two pieces of wheat bread into the toaster, he laid out a couple of slabs of bacon on a microwavable tray, and then dropped a pat of butter in the skillet. Minutes later, he was reading the digital version of the *New York Times* while enjoying eggs over easy, bacon, toast, and a cup of steaming coffee.

After finishing, he checked the calendar on his phone. Shit! He was booked on a 10:00 out of Love to Austin. He had a meeting with Leah scheduled for 2:00 that afternoon. He glanced at the time. It was almost 8:00. He could probably make the flight, but it would be close. He called Harriett and asked her to cancel his reservation. He had decided to drive.

After showering and dressing, he slid into his Range Rover and drove in the direction of Cleburne. He opted not to take I-35 to Austin—too much truck traffic, intermittent road construction, and drab scenery. Instead, he would take state roads through Hico and Lampasas and then on to Austin. He loved small-town Texas, and maybe the trip would give him a chance to think.

He got to Hico in a little over an hour and decided to make a pit stop, grabbing a cup of coffee at a local favorite, the Koffee Kup. Driving into town, he grinned as he read the town motto: "Where Everybody Is Somebody." He pulled into the restaurant parking lot and went inside. The place was hopping with the breakfast crowd, the rumor mill in full swing.

After hitting the restroom, he ordered a cup of black coffee from the tired-looking waitress behind the counter. A gray-bearded fellow sporting a cowboy hat commented on the weather. Jace agreed, finished his coffee, and then slid off his stool and walked over to pay the bespectacled, blue-haired lady at the register. Leaving a tip that was twice as much as his coffee had cost, Jace stopped to gaze longingly at the homemade pies prominently displayed at one end of the counter. He walked out the door, and a couple of minutes later he was driving down Highway 67 toward Lampasas.

The scenery was not pretty but ruggedly pleasant, scrub oak and mesquite dotting the landscape. As Jace drove, taking in the open vistas on either side of the highway, he winced as he relived the verbal beating he had taken from Darrin. The exchange kept sneaking up on him, as if it had just happened yesterday. Was it justified? Did he deserve it? Yes to both. Subconsciously, he had probably known it was coming. There was no way to keep doing what he was doing without things coming undone, which they had—and in a big way.

But Darrin had been right: he hadn't treated her the way she deserved since their weekend trip to New Orleans. Still, Jace wasn't ready to settle down, and he knew he shouldn't force things. These were two immutable truths, there was no right or wrong, no way to work out these differences as things stood. Leaving was the only choice Darrin had. They both needed some space, time to figure things out.

He punched the voice command icon on his steering wheel and had Siri call Jackie.

"Hey, Jackie," said Jace in response to her voice mail greeting, "this is Jace. I'm headed your way. If you're not busy tonight, let's get together for dinner. Let me know. Look forward to seeing you."

Disconnecting, Jace returned his attention to the harsh Texas landscape.

Several hours later, Jace and Leah were seated at a conference room table at the *Texas Matters* offices in downtown Austin.

"So, Ms. Rosen," Jace began before being interrupted by Leah.

"Leah, please."

"Okay, Leah. I'd first like to thank you for calling me on this case. I know we spoke when you were writing the piece on Mr. Connors. But the circumstances are a little different today. Do you have any questions for me or about my practice that you'd like to ask?"

"You come highly recommended. A mutual friend of ours, Jackie McLaughlin, gave me your name. She said y'all had worked together on several cases and that you were the best."

"She's a great investigator. I'll have to thank her for the referral."

Continuing, Leah said, "And, actually, I saw you in action once. When I was doing research for the article, I attended a hearing where you were on the opposite side of Mr. Connors. You had his client on the witness stand. It was quite a show!"

"I believe you introduced yourself to me at that hearing. Things turned out pretty well at the end, but it was a rocky road until then."

"Isn't that the way all cases are?" Leah asked.

"Some more than others. Did you talk with Connors at the hearing?" Jace asked.

"Briefly. On his way out of the courtroom, I told him I was writing a piece on him for the magazine and asked if he would like to see a draft before it went to press—you know, for comment."

"And how did he respond?"

"Well, I can't recall exactly what he said, but I can tell you he wasn't pleased," Leah laughed.

"Cal wasn't a happy camper after that hearing," Jace agreed. "So, I understand you graduated from the University of Texas here in Austin and were hired right out of college by *Texas Matters*. Is that correct?"

"That's right. Majored in journalism. Had always been a fan of the magazine and was thrilled when I landed the job."

"Who is your direct supervisor?"

"My boss is Abe Levine. He's an executive editor. Abe reports to Steve Blumenthal, who's the big cheese. By the way, they both want to meet you before you leave today. You'll like them—they're great guys, and wonderful to work for."

"I look forward to it. You mentioned earlier that it's your practice to give an advance copy of an article to the subject for comment. Any other practices you follow?"

"I make sure I have reliable sources for each factual statement I make in an article. Then I run it by our fact-checking department and I also run a draft of the article past Abe, of course, to get his input. In this instance, I gave a copy to Steve as well."

"By the way, thanks for faxing me a copy of the petition. I bet it threw you for a loop when you got served."

"Are you kidding me? I couldn't believe it. Accusing me of slandering Calvin Connors. *Pleeeaase*. And after all that man has done to me!"

"I followed the Randazzo trial. I understand you've been through quite a lot lately."

"I *know* Cal Connors hired him to scare me off the very story he's suing me for! It's crazy. Is there any way we can use that against him in this case?"

"As it stands now, no. But once we get into the discovery phase of the case, we'll take another look at it. And I plan on getting the transcript from the Randazzo trial. By the way, have you talked with anyone about this lawsuit?"

"Ran down to Abe's office and cried on his shoulder right after getting served. Then we both met with Steve."

"Anyone else?"

"Not about this case, but I did get a call from the U.S. attorney's office inquiring about my article."

"I'm not surprised. Your story did point to some laws being broken. Do you remember who called you?"

Leah flipped some pages on her notepad until she came to the page she was looking for. "Here it is. His name is Reginald Cowan. Do you want his contact information?"

"No, I have it. What did Mr. Cowan want?"

"He asked me about the article, if I fact-checked it, who my sources were. And then he asked me if I knew anything about some high-dollar settlement the Connors firm had been involved with."

"Okay. Let's back up a minute. Walk me through how you came to work on this story, who your sources were, and the steps you took to make sure you got it right. I want to know everything. We'll get back to Mr. Cowan in a minute."

Good journalist that she was, Leah displayed remarkable attention to detail. Methodically, she took him through her reporting. Abe, she said, had assigned her to cover a case Connors was trying against Big Pharma in the Valley. She had sat through the trial and had been surprised that Connors won a huge verdict in the case. Her "bigger story" sense triggered, she began to research Connors's other successful verdicts and noticed a pattern: Connors had used the same expert in all his pharmaceutical cases, Dr. Howell Crimm.

Leah recounted how she had tracked down Crimm's research assistants and uncovered evidence that he had distorted their research on the drugs in question. After an initial reluctance from Abe and Steve to print the story, her persistence in getting verified sources paid off, and Steve finally gave her his go-ahead, congratulating her on a job well done.

"So that's it," she said. "The story behind the story."

"Leah, I know you're not going to like this, but I need to know the names of your sources."

"Jace, I can't give you those. I didn't give them to Cowan either. I promised them confidentiality."

"I figured as much. Look, everything we've talked about today is covered by the attorney-client privilege. Anything you tell me going forward is protected as well, including the identities of your sources. And, obviously, I can't disclose any of the information you give me, including your expert's names, without your consent."

"Can't do it, Jace. I keep my promises. I made it clear I would tell no one."

"I understand, but since you made that promise, you've been sued in a multimillion-dollar defamation case. Their testimony might make the difference between winning and losing."

"Well, I might reconsider down the road, but of course I would still need to get their approval."

"Fair enough. Now, getting back to your call with Mr. Cowan. You mentioned he said something about a settlement of some sort?"

"Yes. He asked me if I had any knowledge or information about a silica settlement the Connors firm had with a company called . . ."

Leah looked down at her notes from the call with Cowan. "Here it is. Empire Risk, out of Connecticut."

"And do you?"

"No. Do you think it's important? It was like Cowan was talking Greek to me. I don't even know what silica is."

"I'll check it out and let you know. What do you know about defamation law? Connors' lawyer has thrown in a lot of claims, but defamation is at the heart of all of them."

"I know just enough about it to be dangerous. First, I know that truth is always a defense. I learned that in one of my journalism classes at UT, and it's common knowledge around here."

"If we can prove every word of your article is true, Cal goes home with nothing," Jace added.

"Every word is true, I'm sure of it. But what if we can't prove it? Is there any other way out?" Leah queried.

"Absolutely. Connors still has to prove you were negligent in order to recover a dime."

"I saw that term used time and again in the petition. What does it mean?"

"Negligence is the failure to use reasonable care in the performance of a duty."

Leah furrowed her brow.

"Stated another way, if you do everything a reasonable journalist would do in researching and writing an article, you cannot be found negligent in a court of law." Jace eyed Leah to see if the concept was sinking in, and then added, "Even if some of the statements in the article turn out to be untrue."

"Got it," Leah replied, and then continued, "Like checking sources, giving the subject an opportunity to weigh in, what we talked about earlier."

"Exactly. There's another wrinkle in the law that makes things a little more complicated and, fortunately for us, more challenging for Connors."

Leah leaned forward. "What's that?"

"If we can prove Connors is what the law terms a 'public figure,' then his standard of proof goes way up. To be clear, famous people are considered public figures under defamation law—current and past presidents, senators, politicians in general, movie stars, professional athletes, or someone like Khloé Kardashian. People who have put themselves in the limelight."

"I understand, but it doesn't seem to me that Connors falls in that category. What am I missing here?"

"He may be a 'limited purpose public figure,' which I know complicates the picture even further."

"You've convinced me not to go to law school," Leah laughed. "It's a little confusing, but keep going. I'll try to stay with you."

"Connors has handled a lot of high-profile cases over the years, and he's given plenty of interviews to newspapers and local television stations, bragging about the results he obtained for his clients. So—for the limited purpose of those lawsuits, some of which you wrote about in your article—he would arguably be a public figure. Stated another way, he knowingly thrust himself in the public view for the limited purpose of touting his legal skills in those cases."

"Okay. So where does that get us?"

"He would have to prove malice rather than just negligence. Basically, he would have to prove you knowingly published an untruthful story with the intent of damaging his reputation."

"That's a big hurdle to get over and totally not true in this case."

Jace nodded. "Very big."

"In the petition, he's suing me for millions in actual damages and millions in punitives. Where did he get those numbers?" Leah asked.

"First of all, actual damages would include financial damage to his law practice, like a drop in revenue after the article ran. Punitive damages, on the other hand, are not designed to compensate the victim but rather to punish the defendant. Does any of that make sense?"

"It's a lot to take in."

"I know. We'll have plenty of other opportunities to discuss defamation law. I just wanted to give you an overview." Jace paused and then said, "Leah, there's one other thing I want you to know before we go any further."

"What's that?" Leah responded, a concerned look on her face.

"Connors came to see me and asked me to represent him."

"On what?"

"He wanted me to file the case we've been discussing."

"He wanted you to sue me?"

Jace nodded.

"That son of a bitch. Well, I assume you wouldn't be here if you had taken him up on his offer."

"You're right. I turned him down."

"May I ask why?"

"There were a lot of reasons, but there's no need to get into those now."

"Jace, I don't know what to say, except thank you. I'm glad you're representing me and not him. So where do we go from here?"

"I'll get to work on filing an answer on your behalf in the case. In the meantime, do you have any other questions?"

"Not that I can think of. I'm sure a million will come to me once you walk out the door. Don't forget, Abe and Steve want to meet you before you get away. Abe is just down the hall and Steve one floor up. I promise—no lengthy meetings. You can just stick your head in their offices, say hello, and that'll be it."

"Lead the way."

After meeting Abe and Steve, Jace said goodbye to Leah and headed to the parking garage. Checking his cell on the way, he played the voice mail Jackie had left while he was meeting with Leah.

"Jace, thrilled, just thrilled you are in town! What a nice surprise! Hey, I'm on my way to Central Market right now, and I'm going to cook you a dinner you'll never forget. When you get this, call me, and I'll give you directions to my place. And, Jace, I hope you brought an overnight bag."

He pressed "call back" and smiled as his gaze landed on the leather tote in the passenger seat next to him.

CHAPTER 11

FBI agent Stan Tipps arrived at the Albuquerque Airport at 1:15 mountain time. After picking up his rental car, he hopped on I-25 toward Santa Fe. Assuming no wrecks or road construction, he figured he would arrive at his destination in a little over an hour.

He spent a few minutes returning phone calls, and then he settled back in the driver's seat, his mind churning, weighing the pros and cons of different approaches to the interview he was about to conduct.

He had done his homework on Dr. Howell Crimm and knew all about him—where he had grown up, his former wives' names, the number of children he had, where he had obtained his multiple degrees, the places he had lived, and, most importantly, the expert opinions he had given in cases throughout the country. There was only one problem: he couldn't force him to say a damn thing. Crimm could just sit there like a wooden Indian, and Tipps would be helpless to do anything about it. After all, this was not an interrogation session. Crimm hadn't been formally charged with a crime, and he could simply refuse to answer any questions. He could ask for a lawyer, or he could even order Tipps out of his house. Those were all possibilities.

Tipps had decided not to call Crimm ahead of time. He wanted to stage a surprise attack. There would be no time to call lawyers, postpone the get-together, or concoct a plan. Maybe, just maybe, Crimm would panic and spill the beans. It was a long shot, but stranger things had happened. Tipps would do his best to act politely and be deferential toward Crimm, hoping this would make him feel important. He'd be easy on him, blow some smoke up his ass, and, when the moment was right, go in for the kill. Tipps felt confident he had come up with a good strategy. In the next hour or so, he would find out whether it would pay off.

Stopping the rental car in front of an attractive adobe hacienda set back from the road and up on a hill, Tipps checked the number on the mailbox against the information in his files. He had the right house. It was classic Santa Fe architecture, with a flat roof, multiple wood columns, iron-paned windows, and a soothing color palette.

The early afternoon sun felt nice as he stepped out of the car, adjusted his coat and tie, and walked up the stone pathway toward the house. He stopped in front of a wooden door, antiqued in teal blue, and knocked firmly. There was no response. Worried that Crimm might not be home and that he'd made the journey for nothing, Tipps knocked again. He was relieved to hear the faint sound of footsteps approaching.

A voice from the other side of the door called out, "Who is it?"

"Dr. Crimm, my name is Stan Tipps. I am an agent with the FBI. I need to ask you a few questions."

Leaving the chain lock on, Crimm cracked the door open to get a better look. "I need to see some identification."

Taking out his wallet, Tipps offered his identification and badge to Crimm, who pulled it close to the small opening for a closer look.

Reluctantly, Crimm unlatched the chain and opened the door a little wider. "What's this about anyway?"

Tipps was ready with his story. "One of your former research assistants has applied for a job with the agency, and we're doing a background check."

The door opened to a short, bald man sporting a goatee and mustache and clad in a loose-fitting Hawaiian shirt, worn blue jeans, and Indian sandals straight out of the sixties. He handed the badge and identification card back to Tipps and said, "I apologize for putting you through the wringer, but I don't like to take any chances. Come on in." Crimm turned and made his way down a hall. "Let's talk in the study."

Tipps followed Crimm into a rectangular room, flagstone tile covering the floor, the ceiling planked with what appeared to be cedar logs running in the opposite direction. A fireplace, cluttered with ashes, filled a corner and a floor-to-ceiling bookcase the adjacent wall.

Crimm motioned for Tipps to take a seat before offering, "I've had a lot of research assistants over the years, so it's unlikely I'll remember this person you're investigating."

Tipps smiled. "I understand. And it's not an investigation, just a routine background check."

"Pardon me, bad choice of words. So what's his name?"

Tipps took a chance. "It's a she. Her name is Elizabeth Chen."

Crimm leaned back in his chair, pressing the back of his head against clasped hands. He shook his head and replied, "Sorry, but that name doesn't ring a bell. I've had a slew of female assistants—more in recent years, as you'd expect—but I don't remember anyone by that name. What type of job is she applying for with the FBI?"

Wanting to solidify his bona fides, Tipps replied with authority, "There are five entry-level programs for acceptance to the agency. One of them is in foreign languages. Elizabeth was born in China and is fluent in Chinese."

Crimm nodded. "I see. That skill would probably come in handy these days."

"That's why we are very interested in her."

"Sorry I can't help. It's too bad you made the trip for nothing." Crimm began to rise from his chair.

"Hold on, let's talk for a minute. Maybe something will come to you."

Crimm sat back down but didn't respond, and Tipps continued. "What kind of medicine do you practice?"

"I haven't had a clinical practice for a number of years. But I have taught, done research, consulting, that type of thing."

"Sounds like you've had an interesting career."

Crimm laughed. "I hope it's not over quite yet."

"You do any forensic consulting? Occasionally we need someone outside the department to testify in a criminal case."

"That's outside my area of expertise. I have testified as an expert in civil cases, though."

"Yeah, what type of cases?"

Feeling more at ease, Crimm began to open up. "Mostly medical malpractice. But lately I've been consulting on pharmaceutical cases."

"I guess you testify for the companies?" Tipps knew he didn't.

"Not as a rule. In my research I've found that many times their R&D departments cut corners in the approval process."

"Is that right? Concerning, isn't it?"

"Very," Crimm shook his head disgustedly.

"And where do you testify?"

"All over."

"Really. Ever worked with an attorney by the name of Cal Connors? We're looking into some allegations a reporter made about him."

Crimm's expression soured. He gave Tipps a lingering look. "You didn't come here to talk about Elizabeth Chen, now did you?"

Deciding it was time to cut bait, Tipps came clean. "No, Dr. Crimm, I didn't. I came here to talk with you about your work with Mr. Connors. Let me start by saying you are not under any type of investigation whatsoever. An article about Mr. Connors ran in a magazine, and we don't know whether there is any truth to the allegations the reporter made. But the U.S. attorney feels an obligation to look into them. You can understand that, can't you?"

Crimm frowned. "I suppose so. But why did you give me all that bullshit?"

"I didn't want to, but you seemed so suspicious. No need to spook you any more than I already had."

"So what do you want to know?" Beads of perspiration started to dot Crimm's forehead. He knew he should end the interview, but curiosity had taken hold. For now, he decided, he would play along and see just what this Agent Tipps had.

"How long have you known Mr. Connors?" Tipps asked.

"It's been years, I can't tell you exactly how long."

"Over ten?"

"I would say so."

"Over twenty?"

"Probably, but I can't be sure."

"Do you recall how many cases you have worked on for Mr. Connors?"

Crimm paused for a moment, pretending to search his memory. "Hard to say. It's been in the double digits—ten to twenty, but that's just a guess."

Tipps continued. “Do you have any files here that might jog your memory?”

Crimm replied quickly—perhaps, thought Tipps, a little too quickly. “No, I’ve gotten rid of all those files. No sense in keeping them around. They just take up space.”

Tipps nodded courteously, convinced his subject was lying.

Figuring he had played this game long enough, Crimm glanced at his watch. “I hate to do this, but I’ve got an appointment on the square with my accountant in ten minutes, and I need to get ready. Now, if you’ll excuse me . . .”

Tipps grinned apologetically as he handed Crimm a card. “Sorry to barge in on you like this. If you run across any of your files or think of anything that might be helpful, I’d sure appreciate your giving me a call.” Tipps knew he wouldn’t.

Crimm took the card but didn’t respond and then closed the door firmly. Tipps could hear the dead bolt turn as he walked down the stone steps toward his car.

Cracking the curtains, Crimm watched as Tipps backed slowly out of the driveway onto the blacktop, switched direction, and then drove out of sight.

Scouring his memory, Crimm quickly replayed their conversation. He assured himself that there had been no occasion, not even a minute or two, when he had left his uninvited visitor alone. No, they had been together from the moment Tipps crossed the threshold until he walked out. There had been no opportunity for Tipps to plant any recording device. Crimm was almost sure of it. He rushed back to the study and dropped to his knees, inspecting with squinty eyes the undersides of the arms and cushion of the chair where Tipps had sat. Nothing. He struggled to his feet, 100 percent sure the FBI agent had not planted any type of electronic eavesdropping device anywhere in the house.

He was too nervous to sit, so he punched in a familiar number and hit the speakerphone button. Seconds later, Cal Connors' boisterous voice filled the room. "Howell, how in the world are you, my friend?"

"I've been better—a lot better."

"What's going on?"

"An FBI agent just left here." Glancing at the card between his fingers, Crimm added, "Special Agent Stan Tipps."

With limited success, Cal tried to disguise his concern. "What in the world did he want?"

"After telling a bald-faced lie to get in the door, he started questioning me about the cases you and I worked on together."

"What did you tell him?"

"Nothing. I told him absolutely nothing other than that I had worked with you for years."

"Good, good," said Cal, pacing around his opulent office.

"Are you under some kind of investigation?" Crimm asked.

Cal decided to play it straight with his longtime expert. "I don't know what they're calling it internally, but the U.S. attorney over in Dallas set up a meeting with me several weeks ago. He drilled me about some allegations made by a rookie reporter at a local rag." Stopping suddenly, Cal whispered into the phone, "No chance we're being recorded, is there?"

"Nope, I checked out everything once Tipps left. All clean on this end."

"Good. Well, like I was saying, he wanted to know about the verdicts I got in those cases we worked on together against Big Pharma."

"Yeah, so what specifically did he ask you?"

"He asked me about the allegations made in the article. I'll bottom-line it for you: this sleazy reporter claimed that me and you got together and came up with a fraudulent scheme to trick juries throughout the country into giving us a shitload of money. You supplied false expert reports, and I sold them to the folks in the box."

Silence on the other end of the line.

"Howell, you still there?"

"Of course, I'm still here. But after what you just told me, I'd like to be in the Caribbean somewhere. This scares the shit out of me. I'm sure this is not the last I'll hear from Tipps. He asked me if I still had any of my files."

"And?"

"I told him no, that I'd thrown them all away."

"Good answer."

"You know that's not true."

"So?"

"Cal, you think I need to hire a lawyer?"

"Hell, yes, I think you need to hire a lawyer."

"Won't that make me look guilty?"

"Had you rather look guilty or play the fool? Anyone being investigated for criminal conduct is an idiot if he doesn't hire a lawyer, it's that simple. Hell, I've hired my own lawyer to handle this crap."

"Why didn't you call me, give me a heads-up? Tipps's visit caught me totally by surprise."

"Sorry about that. I was going to, but I didn't think the feds would move so quickly. You know how incompetent those bastards usually are."

"Well, Tipps didn't seem incompetent at all, but like I said, I didn't give him anything. You got any recommendations for a lawyer?"

There was a pause before Cal responded, "As a matter of fact, I do. You remember that Mendez case we tried out there?"

"Of course I remember. I remember all the cases we worked on together. We were ginning money."

"I hired a Santa Fe lawyer to sit next to me at counsel table—you know, a Mexican to work the Hispanics on the jury."

"I vaguely remember. What was his name?"

"Medina."

"Oh, yeah, I remember him."

"He's a good guy and a capable lawyer," Cal added, and then thought but didn't say, *and someone I can control.* "I'll give him a call and have him get in touch with you."

"What's his last name again?"

"Medina. Donato Medina."

Crimm wrote it down. "Cal, I'm scared shitless about this."

"Look, your defense is solid as a rock. You gave your honest expert opinion in all of the cases and the juries believed you. That's what our judicial system is all about. And don't forget, it's not like those lying companies didn't have counsel. They hired the best lawyers they could find."

"That's all true with one major qualification—in practically every case, I disregarded the conclusions my research assistants gave me."

"So what if your professional opinions diverged from those of your inferiors? Nothing criminal about that, now is there?"

"You make it sound so cut-and-dried."

"It is, Howell. Trust me on this one. If it makes you feel any better, I haven't heard a peep out of the U.S. attorney since we met."

"That's because his folks are busy scaring the shit out of people like me, going for the smaller fish first."

A slight tension rose in Cal's voice. "You're going to stay with me on this, aren't you, Howell? You're not thinking about breaking rank, are you?"

"No, I'd never do that to you. Although I'm not excited about it, I'm in for the long haul."

"Good," Cal replied before adding, "and watch for Donato's call. I'm going to give him a ring right after we hang up."

"I will, Cal. And in the future, it would be helpful if you'd keep me in the loop. I don't like surprises. Also, send me a link to that article. I want to know what I'm dealing with here."

"You got it, Howell."

The line went dead as Crimm continued to pace back and forth in his study, wondering if he was playing the fool to put his trust in one Calvin Connors.

* * *

Slamming his fist down against the top of his desk, Cal uttered a series of expletives. His secretary stuck her head in and, with a concerned look on her face, asked if everything was all right. Cal waved her off dismissively, and she disappeared behind the door.

The questions bounced inside Cal's head like pinballs. No doubt, there was panic in Howell's voice. Was there a chance he would flip? Cal winced, thinking about Howell's personal problems: his failed marriage and estranged children, his massive gambling debts and his drinking issue. It wasn't just an issue—hell, Howell was a raging alcoholic. No doubt about it, Cal's partner-in-crime was about as unstable a son of a bitch as you could find. He had to take control of the situation, and quick.

Cal looked up Donato Medina's number and immediately called him. When Donato got on the phone, Cal said, without caring, "Donato Medina, it's been a while. How in the world have you been?"

"I can't complain, Cal. How about yourself?"

"Life is good, life is good, *mi amigo*."

"I hope you have another case for me. We sure hit a home run on that last one."

Cal swallowed his first thought, which was, *What's with the "we"? I did everything. You made several million by just sitting next to me at counsel table and "looking Mexican" to that Santa Fe jury.*

Finding his slickest voice, Cal said, "I've got my feelers out. I'll let you know if something firms up." Cal lied convincingly and then cleared his throat before continuing. "But I'm calling for a different reason. I need your help, Donato."

"Shoot, Boss. You know you can count on me."

"You remember Dr. Crimm, the expert we used in the Mendez case?"

"Yeah, I think I remember that dude—kinda funny-looking, thick glasses, short. Is that the guy?"

"Yep, that's Howell. He lives in your neck of the woods and got an unexpected visitor today. An FBI agent dropped by to visit him."

"Shit. What about?"

Cal filled him in on the article and Cowan's investigation.

"So how can I help?"

Cal carefully contemplated his reply. "Howell has had a rough go of it the last few years. He went through a nasty divorce, his kids disowned him, he started hitting the bottle pretty heavy, and you know where that leads."

"Oh, man, I'm sorry for him."

"And he's piled up several million in gambling debts."

"Damn. Doesn't sound like things could get much worse for the poor bastard."

"Yeah, that's what's worrying me. He's a very desperate man."

"What can I do?" Donato asked.

"Howell called me after the FBI agent left. He was beside himself. I calmed him down a little, told him he had nothing to worry about, that things were going to turn out fine. I didn't want to spook him, but I didn't have a choice. I told him he should hire a lawyer. Donato, I told him to hire you."

"What did he say?"

"He said he would."

"So you want me to represent this dude?" Donato asked.

"That's the idea. I told him you would call him today."

"Glad to. Should I tell him to plead the Fifth?"

"Not exactly. Can I be honest here? I think Howell is a ticking time bomb that could bring us all down—and that includes you, Donato."

"Say again? How am I involved?"

"You were my co-counsel in that Mendez trial, and that's one of the cases the U.S. attorney in Dallas is investigating."

"*¡Jodido!*"

"You got it. Howell turns and we all go down. You and I need to make sure that doesn't happen."

"I'm not sure I understand . . ."

"Well, let me be a little clearer then, *mi amigo*. We—that includes both of us—can't take a chance on Howell talking. Like I said, he has a shitload of gambling debts, and you know how the mob feels about not getting paid."

"Boss, I would do anything for you, but—"

Cutting him off, Cal said, "Look, Donato, I made you a fortune. You live in that big house because of me—and only because of me. I don't ask twice for a favor. This is the one and only time I will."

"I have never . . ." Donato sputtered as his voice trailed off.

"You don't have to do anything personally. I'm sure you have low-life clients that owe you or would be glad to earn a quick buck. I don't care how you do it. Just get it done and make sure there's no trace back to you or me. Understand?" Cal wasn't asking any longer, he was telling.

Resigned, Donato asked, "How quickly?"

"Soon. Before this agent comes snooping around again."

"I'll see what—"

"There's no 'seeing' to it. Just get it done!" Cal abruptly ended the call, tossed his cell on the desk, and then coursed his fingers through his silver mane. He wouldn't tell Christine. As they had discussed, this was his problem and his problem alone. He had to fix it and he would, no matter what he had to do.

CHAPTER 12

Before exiting the parking lot, Jace directed Siri to call the U.S. attorney for the Northern District of Texas. Two options popped up, and he tapped the one for Dallas. After a few rings, an efficient-sounding woman answered, "How may I direct your call?"

"This is Jace Forman. I'm a Fort Worth attorney, and I'd like to speak with Mr. Cowan."

"Just one moment, please."

Seconds later, Cowan was on the line. "Jace, it's been a while. What's going on?"

Easing his Range Rover out of the garage and into traffic, Jace winced as his thoughts took him back to Cowan's days as a prosecutor in the Austin district attorney's office. Cowan had tried to implicate his son, Matt, in a possible homicide and had likely had a hand in Jackie's dismissal from the Austin PD. He hated the son of a bitch but needed his help on Leah's case.

"I'm in Austin and just left the offices of *Texas Matters*. I've been hired to represent Leah Rosen in a defamation case brought by Cal Connors."

"He sued her?"

"Yep, and the magazine as well," Jace answered.

"Doesn't surprise me. I've known Connors a long time. He always, *always* goes on the offensive."

"I understand from my client that the two of you have talked."

"Yes, we have. I read Ms. Rosen's article, and based upon what she reported, I called Cal in for a sit-down."

"And?"

"Of course he denied everything. Used some choice words to describe your client. I then called Ms. Rosen."

"How did that go?" Jace asked.

"She was very professional. Walked me through the basis for her allegations. She wouldn't give up her sources, though. I assume, after your meeting today, you know who they are?"

"No, she wouldn't tell me either. She takes her confidentiality vow very seriously. As she should."

"I've run into this issue with reporters before. They can be pretty obstinate, but a balance has to be struck. If giving up a source can lead to a criminal conviction, the scales have to tip in favor of justice."

Jace didn't respond.

Cowan continued. "So, Jace, what do you have in mind?"

"Well, our clients' interests are aligned when it comes to Connors. You want to put him in jail, I want to get his case against Leah thrown out of court, and Leah wants both."

"So you want to pool our efforts, share information?" Cowan asked.

"I think that makes a lot of sense, don't you?"

Cowan thought for a moment. "I don't see any downside. Let me talk to my team, and I'll get back to you."

"Sounds good. And there's one other thing. Leah mentioned another investigation you might be conducting against Connors, something having to do with a large settlement?"

Jace fished, doubting Cowan would take the bait. Federal prosecutors almost never reveal the details of cases they are investigating. But to his surprise, Cowan came around.

"Yeah, we got a call from the Hartford U.S. attorney's office. An insurance company there by the name of Empire Risk filed a criminal complaint against one of its claims adjusters. The complaint alleges the adjuster made a multimillion-dollar settlement with Connors' law firm that was not on the up-and-up."

"Can you give me the names of your contacts at the insurance company?" Jace asked.

"As long as you agree to tell me everything you find out in the matter."

"Agreed."

There was a brief pause while Cowan sifted through some files on his desk before finding the one he wanted. "Okay, there are two contact people listed: Andrew James, Empire's general counsel, and Weldon Trapp, their outside lawyer."

Pulling into a strip mall, Jace quickly grabbed a pen and his notepad. "Could you repeat that?"

Cowan repeated the information as Jace jotted it down.

"And the name of the adjuster?"

"Jamie Stein."

"I assume your office has talked with Mr. Stein?" Jace asked.

"I wish we could. Stein's dead."

"The Hartford PD investigating?"

"Now, as I understand it, when Empire and its lawyers began to turn up the heat, Stein hightailed it to the South of France. Several months later, he turned up dead in a resort near Nice. The cause of death was ruled an accidental drug overdose. It seems Stein liked to run with a fast crowd. He had an insatiable appetite for recreational drugs and high-priced hookers."

"And I assume your office is looking into it?"

"We are, but France is a little bit out of our jurisdiction. I'm not optimistic our investigation will turn up much of anything."

"Well, I appreciate your sharing this information with me."

"Not a problem. Jace, I may need your help in getting Ms. Rosen to turn over her sources. That could break this investigation wide open."

"I hear you. I'll do what I can," Jace offered.

"I'll get back in touch about teaming up."

* * *

Minutes later, Jace grabbed his overnight bag from the car and hustled toward the arched front door of a small limestone Tudor-style house with French-blue shutters.

Before he could knock, Jackie opened the door. She was dressed in a seamless white cami and beige tie-dye lounge pants, a drawstring cinched at the waist, her tan midriff tauntingly visible.

Draping her arms around Jace's neck, Jackie rose to her tiptoes and gave him a long kiss. "I've missed you," she whispered.

"I've missed you too. A lot."

Taking his hand, she led him into a cozy den. "Okay, get on the other side of this coffee table. I want to move it against that wall over there," she said, nodding in the direction she wanted it.

"*Okaaay*. Uh, why?"

"You'll see, Mr. Impatient."

Not satisfied with the result, Jackie ordered, "And the rug. It goes against the same wall. Help me roll it up."

"Come on, Jackie. What are you up to?"

"You ask too many questions, Counselor. Just do what I say, please."

"Okay, okay."

After the rug had been rolled up and leaned against the wall, Jackie picked up a remote and, seconds later, Ben Harper's voice came through the stereo speakers mounted on the bookcase. He was singing an acoustic version of Marvin Gaye's classic "Sexual Healing." Loosening Jace's tie, she threw it on the couch and put her arms around his neck once again, swaying slowly to the music. Jace's hands slipped under the back of Jackie's top and found her soft skin. Thirty minutes later, their clothes were strewed all over the floor and their bodies wrapped together on the couch.

Resting her head on Jace's bare chest, she whispered, "So did you like my little surprise?"

Stroking her bare back, Jace replied, "Do you have to ask?"

"I was so happy when I got your message today, I can't tell you."

"I was hoping you wouldn't have plans."

"Wouldn't have mattered. I'd have canceled them."

After slipping into her panties and top, she walked into the kitchen while telling Jace, "I picked up a rack of lamb, wild rice, and a French baguette. Lamb's in the oven. How about a scotch or a glass of wine?"

"I'll drink whatever you're drinking."

Jace shimmied on his pants, pulled on his T-shirt, and joined Jackie in the kitchen. There was a cheese tray on the table and two glasses of red wine. Jackie looked into the oven to check on the lamb. Satisfied, she closed the oven door and sat with Jace at the table.

"I think I may know, but tell me why you're in Austin today." Jackie smiled.

"Because you gave my name to Leah Rosen and she hired me as her lawyer in that case Connors wanted me to file. I drove down this morning to meet with her."

"Smart girl. Glad she took my advice." Jackie nibbled on a slice of cheese and then chased it with a sip of wine. "How did your meeting go?"

"Good. Leah is going to make an excellent witness. She seems very smart and, just as important, honest as the day is long. I believe her."

"You should," Jackie agreed.

"Poor girl, she's been through hell and back."

"That bastard Connors, he ought to be behind bars."

"Well, with a lot of hard work and a little luck, maybe that's where he'll end up."

Jace recapped the information he had gathered, saving the Stein investigation for last. "The whole thing smells fishy to me. Stein settles a bunch of dog-ass cases for a shitload of money and months later ends up dead of an overdose in some high-rent hotel in the South of France. I'm just not buying into the accidental overdose finding and need you to dig deeper. I want to know whether that multimillion-dollar settlement was dirty and whether Connors had anything to do with Stein's death."

Scrounging in his pant pocket for the note he had made while talking with Cowan, he pulled it out and handed it to Jackie. "That's the contact information for Empire Risk's general counsel and their outside lawyer. You might start by giving both of them a call. Maybe they'll share some of the findings from their internal investigation and let you look at Stein's files on the cases he settled with Connors."

Filling their wineglasses, Jackie smiled. "Hey, I'd love a trip to the French Riviera. Think that's in the cards?"

"Clear it with me before you book your flight. I might want to join you," said Jace, returning the smile. "I'm scrambling at the office right now. Darrin turned in her notice and is moving to Houston."

"Wow! That's a surprise." Jackie tried to sound concerned but was truly gleeful.

"It was a total surprise. She has been with me for years, and it will be difficult to replace her." Jace didn't add, *in so many ways,* but thought it.

"I'll be happy to help in any way I can. Just let me know."

"Thanks, Jackie, I may take you up on that offer."

"One question. What's this insurance case have to do with your defense of Leah in the defamation suit? I mean, it's interesting stuff but—"

"If we are able to show Connors' firm was mixed up in another fraud, the jury will likely believe this wasn't the first time but rather part of a bigger picture, a pattern of illegal conduct."

Jackie nodded. "I see."

"Even more importantly, if we can tie Connors to Stein's death, he goes to jail and the defamation case goes away."

Jackie smiled. "I like it."

"Oh, one other thing. I talked to Cowan today, after I called you."

"What did that prick have to say?" Jackie asked.

"I know. I don't like him any more than you do."

"He cost me my job, Jace. Although that turned out good for me, I'll never forget it. And what he tried to do to Matt!"

"I know. I have to bite my lip whenever I talk with him. But he's got the resources of the federal government behind him. He can subpoena records, do things you and I can't. He could help us bring Connors down, and he seems willing to work with us."

"I get it, but I don't have to like it."

"I asked him if he wanted to mount a common defense against Connors."

"What did he say?"

"He seemed to like the idea. He's going to check with his team and get back to me."

"So I might have to work with him."

"Your contact with Cowan would be very limited, I promise. You'd more likely be talking with the FBI agent who has been assigned to the case. I don't know who that is yet, but I'll find out from Cowan when he calls me back."

"Okay, I'm on board." Jackie got up to open the oven and check on the lamb. "Dinner's ready."

"I'm starved. What's for dessert?"

Jackie coyly replied, "You'll find out soon enough."

CHAPTER 13

Glancing anxiously over his shoulder, Michael Randazzo turned the key and pushed open the front door. Satisfied no one had followed him, he stepped inside, closed the door, and turned the dead bolt, which he had installed several days before. Stepping lightly, he watched for loose planks as he navigated his way across the wooden floor and through the room. It was eerily empty: no furniture, no pictures, no rugs, no signs of life. But he didn't give a shit. He wouldn't be there long—just long enough.

He had liked the Mexican woman who'd rented him the dump. She didn't speak any English, and that was just fine by him. He asked her how much for three months, which she conveniently understood, and then paid her in cash—$1,200. She didn't ask him his name, why he was there, what he did for a living—nothing. She just took the money and left. He would never see her again. Exactly the way he planned it.

Walking to a door in the hallway, he opened it and peered down the stairs and into the utter darkness below. It was pitch-black, a dank chamber below ground with no windows, no vents, no openings of any kind to let the world in. He flipped the switch to his right and stepped down into the man-made cave.

Constructed out of cinder block, the room mirrored the footprint of the house, with more than enough space for his purposes. He had purchased a cot from Walmart in East Austin, which he'd pushed against the wall in a corner. There was no need for sheets. It was just a place where he could grab a few hours of shut-eye when he wasn't getting things ready.

He had found a rickety aluminum table and chair upstairs and brought them down. A state-of-the art Wi-Fi modem and a brand-new laptop were on the table. He had discarded his old computer, which had been returned to him after the trial. Those bastards had searched and searched it, looking for something incriminating, and hadn't found a damn thing. And now they never would: he had taken the computer apart piece by piece, discarding the remnants in dumpsters when he had returned to L.A. He had purchased and activated his new laptop under a nerdy fake name: Alvin Jernigan. Once he finished his work, it would be dismembered and discarded as well. There would be no evidence of anything. It would be as if nothing had happened. She would just disappear into thin air, like magic. Poof.

Randazzo reached up to feel his new nose—one that was much smaller and more defined. He had considered himself handsome before, but he liked the change and thought it made him look more aristocratic. Letting his fingers run over his lips, he could tell that the bottom one was narrower and not as puffy. It was unbelievable what a difference that made. The doc had worked wonders.

But Randazzo was a careful man—a very careful man who left nothing to chance. He had wanted a complete makeover, and getting new hair was a major part of his new look. He knew many male celebrities in L.A. were bald as a baby's butt and, by necessity, had purchased the finest hairpieces money could buy. And he wanted one that looked real, just like theirs did, and he had known where to find it. He didn't think he looked as good with gray hair as he had with his natural hair, dark and thick, which for years he gelled and swept back. But it was one more change. No one who knew the real Michael Randazzo would recognize him now. The transformation to Alvin Jernigan was complete.

The basement was hot. Stripping down to his T-shirt and shorts, Randazzo opened his laptop. Taking a deep breath, he typed in a familiar search phrase and then clicked on the video that appeared on screen. A woman clad only in a black bustier writhed wildly against leather restraints secured to four bedposts. She was gagged and blindfolded, her legs spread wide. A man dressed in a black robe, a hood over his head, entered the frame and walked slowly toward the woman. The clip had no audio, but the man's lips moved, causing the woman's body to convulse even more wildly. As the man removed an object from the pocket of his robe, Randazzo, his breath labored, impulsively reached for his shorts.

PART TWO

CHAPTER 14

After taking the last bite of her bagel, Jackie poured another cup of coffee and made her way to her study. These days her work clothes consisted of T-shirts, jeans, and sandals. She smiled, remembering her former life when she was with the Austin PD: the uniform, the hours, the hierarchy, the reviews, the rigid protocol. It was quite the contrast to her work life now: no dress code, no hours, no boss, no commute—the list went on. Of course, no steady paycheck had been hard to get used to, but she was paying the bills. And her freedom, of course, was priceless.

Clutching her coffee mug in one hand, Jackie retrieved her laptop from the built-in desk in the corner of her study and settled into a comfy leather chair.

Popping open her laptop, she Googled "Jamie Stein." She scrolled through the search results and, finding nothing of interest, went to the next page, and the one after that. On the fourth page, she came across a reference to an article in the *Hartford Courier*. Clicking on the link, she read:

> "Jamie Stein, a former employee of Empire Risk Insurance Company, has been charged with embezzlement. Andrew James, general counsel for the company, reports that Stein was employed by Empire Risk for three years as a claims specialist before mysteriously disappearing. According to James, Stein entered into a multimillion-dollar settlement with a Texas law firm on behalf of the company without following proper protocol and is alleged to have received an illegal kickback. Stein is currently believed to be somewhere in France."

Jackie printed the article and continued her search, landing on a story that had appeared in an English publication reporting news in the South of France, the *Riviera Times*:

> "Èze, France. Jamie Stein, a United States citizen, was found dead in his seaside suite at the Chateau La Femme **d'Été** in this medieval village, just miles outside of Nice. Inspector Laurent Rousseau, who was in charge of the investigation, reported that the cause of death was an accidental drug overdose and that there was no indication of foul play. Stein was thirty-five years old and had recently been the target of a bribery investigation in the United States."

Again, Jackie hit the print icon and continued scrolling through several more pages before concluding her online research. She walked over to her desk and slid the printed articles into a manila file labeled "Stein Investigation." Before closing the folder, she dialed a number she had jotted down under the heading "Contacts." A woman answered, and Jackie asked to be transferred to Andrew James.

There was a lengthy pause before the receptionist returned to ask Jackie why she was calling.

"I'm calling in relation to the Jamie Stein investigation."

Within seconds, a voice inflected by an overdone aristocratic accent came on the line.

"This is Andrew James. How can I help you, Ms. McLaughlin?"

"I appreciate your taking my call, Mr. James."

James replied, "I understand this is about the Jamie Stein matter?"

"Yes. I'm an investigator for Fort Worth attorney Jace Forman. He's hired me on a case he's handling against Cal Connors. I believe you know Mr. Connors?"

"Clarification. I know of Mr. Connors. I've never personally met the man. Please continue, Ms. McLaughlin."

"Mr. Forman knows the U.S. attorney in Dallas, Reginald Cowan. I understand you have spoken with him?"

"Yes, several times. He is heading up the Jamie Stein investigation in Texas."

"Mr. Stein settled a number of silica cases with Connors. You believe the settlement was dirty and that Stein received a kickback for doing the deal. Is my information correct, Mr. James?"

"Mr. Stein certainly did not follow company protocol. So what is the purpose of your call?" James asked.

"I believe we can help each other by sharing information. Mr. Forman is defending a case brought by Mr. Connors, and he would like to be able to establish a course of illicit conduct by Mr. Connors. Are you interested?"

"Please continue."

"I assume someone has been through all of Stein's files?"

"With a fine-tooth comb," James said. "There were no smoking guns. However, it doesn't take a smart man to know that this settlement was a scam. Those cases had been sitting around collecting dust for years, and then all of a sudden, Stein goes around defense counsel and straight to Connors' office and pays a lot more money in settlement than the cases were worth. He wouldn't have done that unless he was getting something in return. Something substantial, we believe."

"How about a paper trail? Have you been able to trace any money coming back to him?" Jackie asked.

"No, but we do know he bought a brand-new Ferrari, which he damn sure couldn't afford on the salary we were paying him."

"At least he had good taste. Where's the car today?"

"No idea. I confronted him about it before he fled the country and he simply shrugged it off, saying he had rented it for a weekend from someone in Brooklyn who was trying to subsidize his car payments. Of course he couldn't come up with a receipt or a name for the person he rented it from. Just days later, he evidently left for France, which has an inexplicable reluctance to send known criminals back to the U.S. for trial."

"And then Stein turns up dead."

"Correct."

"Have you spoken with the French investigator?"

"Yes, a Mr. Laurent Rousseau. He spoke very little English and seemed eager to get off the line."

"Seen any of the police investigation files?" Jackie asked.

"No. Rousseau did manage to tell me there was nothing indicating foul play—an apparent heroin overdose."

"I assume you've been through all of Stein's emails?"

"Every last one of them. Interestingly, there are no emails between Stein and the Connors firm. Our IT department spent hours trying to determine if there had been any emails deleted from the hard drive and came up empty. All the settlement discussions must have been in person or from another account."

"That's a shame," Jackie said. "I know you probably don't want me going through Stein's company files, but would you mind if I talked with the person who did?"

"Weldon Trapp, our outside counsel, is conducting the investigation. Feel free to call him." James paused briefly before continuing. "I should clarify a previous answer I gave you. There is a bit of a paper trail. There were settlement documents signed and orders of dismissal entered in the cases."

"Signed by Connors and Stein?" Jackie asked.

"No, by Christine Connors. Mr. Connors' name doesn't appear in any of the files. Only hers."

"Now, that's interesting."

"Excuse me, Ms. McLaughlin, but I have a conference call in two minutes."

"I understand. If you turn up anything else in your investigation, please let me know."

"I assume you'll do the same."

"Of course."

Hanging up the phone, Jackie began jotting down a few notes on a memo pad. She hadn't known about the Ferrari, clearly an important piece to the puzzle. James was right. A claims adjuster couldn't afford a car like that, and it had to be more than a coincidence that he had made the purchase right after the settlement was funded. Couple that with his disappearance to France after James confronted him, and the settlement began to reek.

And how about the actual settlement documents? Jackie had erroneously assumed they had been signed by Cal. *Well,* Jackie thought, *the apple doesn't often fall far from the tree.* She needed to find out more about Christine and the circumstances surrounding Stein's death.

Glancing at her Apple watch—it was 10:43 Texas time—she asked Siri the time in France, and 5:43 appeared on the watch face. It was probably too late to reach Inspector Rousseau, but Jackie decided to give it a try anyway. She dialed the international number, and, surprisingly, she caught him.

Their conversation was a struggle. Jackie spoke slowly, keeping her explanation as simple as possible, but still had to repeat almost every word, and Inspector Rousseau the same. Since Jackie had no knowledge of French, they spoke in broken English, in phrases, working hard to get through to each other. Jackie had to suppress a chuckle now and then as Rousseau's accent conjured up an image of the mustachioed Peter Sellers' infamous Inspector Clouseau, bumbling through a crime scene, asking all the wrong questions and reaching all the wrong conclusions with an amusing appearance of unshakable confidence.

Jackie explained her interest in the Stein investigation, and Rousseau feigned understanding. In truth, she was pretty sure he had no idea what her role was but didn't want to appear stupid by saying so. In stop-and-start fashion, he took Jackie through the investigation as best he could, with her interrupting from time to time with a question.

There was a pause, and then Rousseau asked if he could be of any further help. Now Jackie got to the real purpose for her call: her desire to see his files. She was especially interested in the hotel video and crime scene photos. Already, in her mind, Stein's death was no accident.

"Inspector Rousseau, I would like a copy of your files."

"Mademoiselle, uh, uh, the in-ves-tee-gay-shawn is complete, *oui?*" Rousseau responded slowly, weighing every word.

Jackie clarified, "No, no, I know your investigation was very good, very complete, but I would like copies, for my own file, you know."

"But, Mademoiselle, for what reee-son? Excuse *moi,* but you are not po-leese."

Finally Jackie had to accept the fact that Inspector Rousseau was not going to release his files without the proper authority to do so. She thanked him for his time, hung up, and then promptly called Jace. She suspected Cowan had already received all of Rousseau's investigative files and materials, and she wanted Jace to get them for her.

CHAPTER 15

Rolling over in bed, Howell Crimm squinted at the neon digits of the clock on the bedside table. It was 3:36 in the morning. After struggling to sit up, he swung his legs over the side of the bed and instinctively reached for the bottle of George Dickel next to the clock, poured himself a generous double, threw it back, and then poured himself another. As he sat there, staring blankly into space, he thought about getting up. No, he decided, he would give the Tennessee whiskey a chance to kick in. He slipped one foot and then the other back under the sheets, hoping sleep would come. It didn't. The thoughts kept coming at him, gnawing at him, refusing to be pushed away.

Tipps's visit had definitely unnerved him. What a shitty way to start the day—some bastard you don't even know knocking on your door, acting like he's your friend when you know damn good and well he isn't, and then slowly circling in and trying to get a kill. But Howell had sensed a rat, and Tipps left empty-handed, with no scalps under his belt, nothing to show for his surprise attack.

Unfortunately, the story wouldn't end there. Howell knew Tipps would be back, and he had to be ready.

The call to Cal had been calming at first but, upon reflection, confusing. Cal had been Cal, with answers for everything, Mr. Cool, seemingly in control. But Howell wondered whether, underneath the polished veneer, there was real concern. Cal was just a little too self-assured, a little too dismissive of the gravity of the situation. Going to the slammer certainly wasn't anything to shrug off. This was serious shit, and Cal knew it—he just didn't want to give anything away, send any signals that might cause panic in his partner in crime.

Then came the call from Donato Medina, which had been a mixed bag. Howell hardly knew the guy, and yet Donato had acted like some trusted confidante who had been there for him through one crisis after another. Donato told him, over and over again, that there was nothing to worry about, nothing at all, that things were going to turn out fine.

How in the hell did Donato know that? And what kind of lawyer was he, anyway? Howell remembered him only vaguely from the Mendez trial, but Donato had hardly uttered a word. Cal did all the talking, put on all the witnesses, made the opening statement and delivered the close. Donato just sat there like a Charlie McCarthy dummy, nodding whenever Cal gave him the cue. Was this the kind of lawyer Howell could trust to represent him in an investigation that would determine whether he spent the rest of his life in jail? But what choice did he have? None at the moment, so he decided to play out the line and, if things turned south, recalibrate.

Donato's advice was simple. All Howell had to do was pack up his case files and bring them, along with his computers and cellphone, to Donato's office the next morning at 9:00. They would meet for however long it took. Donato had cleared his calendar for the whole day. Together, they would put together a game plan.

If Tipps came calling again, Donato would be a phone call away. There would be no ambush. There would be no interrogation in a windowless room with a video camera overhead. There would be no documents produced for inspection. They would yield no ground. They would be ready.

Howell wondered if Donato had fed him a line of bullshit. Only time would answer that question. Meanwhile, he had to live in the present and make the best decisions he could with the facts at hand. Donato had assured him that everything they discussed would be covered by attorney-client privilege, and he had also mentioned that Cal had taken care of his fee. So why not pull together what Donato had requested and show up at 9:00? No harm in meeting.

Giving up on sleep, Howell wobbled into the bathroom, turned on the light, and scowled at the man in the mirror. Wincing at the bloodshot eyes, he wondered what had happened to the earnest young doctor he used to be. What had gone so wrong? There were diplomas from the finest schools, countless academic and professional awards, an endowed chair at a prominent medical school, and, most of all, a devoted family standing behind him. It had all been his.

And then he'd met Cal Connors.

They'd been introduced at a seminar in Las Vegas where Howell was a featured speaker. This seemingly random introduction to a silver-haired, smooth-talking Texan wearing a bolo tie and custom boots had changed his life forever—not immediately but gradually, like a slow-working poison.

After the seminar, Cal had called him. He had this case he wanted Howell to review. As Cal told it, the facts were pretty cut-and-dried. His client had asbestos-related lung cancer, and Cal just needed a reputable doc, one with unassailable credentials, to swear to the obvious. And money was no problem, Cal pointed out. The expert fee would be $2,500 an hour. Howell agreed to think about it and call Cal back with his answer.

It didn't take him long. An endowed chair at medical school looked good on paper, but it hadn't made Howell a wealthy man. In fact, money in the Crimm household had been tight for years. With two kids in college and a wife who enjoyed the finer things, Howell had found himself scrambling from month to month just to make ends meet. He had been ready for an easy way out, a way to have the kind of life he had always dreamed of, the kind of life he deserved. He had hoped that his chance encounter with the lawyer from Texas might just be an answered prayer. He would take Cal up on his offer. He remembered feeling that his luck was about to change. He just knew it.

But the case wasn't so cut-and-dried after all. Yes, Cal's client suffered from lung cancer, and yes, he had worked around asbestos for a couple of weeks one summer, helping his dad change out brake pads back in the eighties. But he was also a longtime smoker—two packs a day for thirty years.

Howell called Cal to voice his concerns, and, in trial lawyer fashion, Cal schmoozed him: "Come on, Doc. Just read the literature. I'm sure you can find some article out there that will support an asbestos diagnosis. Be resourceful. You're one smart son of a bitch. Hell, you've got more degrees than Einstein. And I'm sure you can understand that it just wouldn't be right for me to pay you if you came to the wrong conclusion."

His ego sufficiently stoked, Howell did find an article that, if stretched a bit here and there, could be read to bolster an opinion that the plaintiff's cancer was asbestos related. And that was the opinion Howell gave. He expected a vigorous cross from the opposing lawyer, which mercifully never came. The case later settled for millions, and Howell received $100,000—$25,000 for the hours of work he had actually put in on the case and a premium of $75,000 Cal graciously paid as a "merit bonus" when the settlement train pulled into the station. A lucrative, long-lived partnership was born.

With his newly found income source, Howell bought a ten-thousand-square-foot house, surprised his wife with a five-carat diamond ring, and paid off all the loans he had taken out to put his kids through expensive private schools. Life couldn't have been better. In addition to being the faculty chair at a prestigious medical school, he was now a highly paid consultant on big-ticket litigation. Howell Crimm had it all.

And the cases kept on coming, three or four a year. But the opinions Howell was asked to render became increasingly difficult to support. There were no scientific articles to stretch, no sources to quote out of context, no treatises from some random researcher in a foreign country. So Howell decided to support his testimony with his own "in-house" research; through the university, he had several research assistants assigned to him. He would suggest potential outcomes to the eager assistants and then use their work to justify his scholarly opinions. Initially this arrangement worked well. Generally speaking, their findings were consistent with his initial "hypotheses," but over time even that began to change. Their analyses would come back at odds with the positions Cal wanted to take in court. Cal suggested an out. He told Howell to reference his assistants' research in his reports and then discard any problematic data.

Howell had been raking in several million a year under his arrangement with Cal, and he had ratcheted up his lifestyle to match. Unbeknownst to his wife, he began stealing away to Las Vegas for weekend betting binges disguised as paid speaking engagements. He liked the high-roller lifestyle—the big bets, the free-flowing liquor, the unrestrained sex with beautiful escorts—but it didn't like him. The debts began to pile up, and Howell morphed from a man of fortune to a man in trouble. He had no choice but to do what Cal suggested. The opinions, flawed as they might be, kept on coming. And so did the big bucks.

And then Howell hit a wall. His wife became suspicious of his out-of-town forays and hired a PI to follow him on one of his "speaking engagements." She wanted rid of him, and she wanted the millions she suspected he had stashed away somewhere. She got her first wish but not her second. She divorced her husband several months later, ending up with the house, all the contents, and her Mercedes SUV, but there was no secret stash, only a few thousand in a checking account and a shitload of gambling debt. After their acrimonious divorce proceedings hit the local and campus newspapers, Howell soon lost his tenured faculty position and, with nothing more than a suitcase full of clothes and his Cadillac, moved to Santa Fe. There he rented a house, one too expensive for him, but made possible by his old friend and partner Cal Connors, who guaranteed the lease.

Howell shook away the reveries of his past and made his way into his office, where he scoured the file drawers for every folder having anything to do with Cal or his law firm. With few exceptions, the folders were virtually the same—retention letters from Cal, background information on the plaintiff, medical records, maybe a deposition or two, interrogatory answers, data analyses from his research assistants, and, most important, expert reports sworn to by Howell Crimm, M.D. By the fourth cup of coffee, he had finished boxing up the files. He took a long, hot shower to try to clear his muddled mind and calm his frazzled nerves, shaved, and threw on a rumpled sport jacket in need of cleaning and a pair of worn khakis. He glanced in the full-length mirror on the inside of his closet door and frowned at what he saw. But what the hell difference did it make? He wasn't meeting with a hot Las Vegas escort. He was going to see some ambulance-chasing lawyer who spoke tortured English and probably didn't know shit from Shinola. He would soon find out.

Loading up the boxes into the trunk and placing his worn leather briefcase containing his laptop in the backseat of the car, he patted his pocket to make sure he had his cellphone. Then, after fishing out his car keys, he slid behind the steering wheel, inserted the ignition key, and gave it a turn. For a moment, nothing happened. Then came a loud blast, and the light blue Cadillac became a blazing inferno. By the time emergency crews arrived, there was little left of the files, the briefcase, the laptop, the phone—or Howell Crimm.

CHAPTER 16

Cal's secretary buzzed him on the intercom. "Sharlene Knox is on line one for you."

Putting down the newspaper he was reading, Cal answered, "Sharlene, always good to hear from you."

"Good morning, Cal. Did you receive the fax I sent over? Ms. Rosen filed her answer to our lawsuit this morning. You know this guy who's representing her?"

Cal cupped his hand over the receiver and yelled at his secretary to bring him the fax. "Hold on a second, Sharlene. I'm getting it right now." His secretary brought in the fax, closing the door as she left. Glancing at the signature block on the last page, Cal grimaced and uttered through clenched teeth, "Yeah, I know the son of a bitch. I had a case against him several years back."

"And?"

"Decent," Cal forced the reply, reflecting back on Jace's refusal to represent him.

"What kind of case?" Sharlene asked in a businesslike manner.

"One of the craziest damn cases I've ever had. I represented these folks whose daughter was a student down in Austin, at UT. She died from an apparent overdose and was buried over in Fort Worth. Two days later her body was found on the altar of a church on the outskirts of the city."

"I think I may have read about—"

"You probably did. It was all over the news. Her parents came to me with the case. They were shook up as hell and wanted to sue someone, so I came up with this idea that we could sue the cemetery. We had no idea who dug up the body and the cemetery had money, so—"

"And your argument was they should have had security patrolling the cemetery grounds," Sharlene interrupted.

"That was our position."

"So did you win?"

"We settled, for a substantial sum."

"And your clients were happy, I assume?" Sharlene asked.

"Well, Forman asked for a prove-up hearing, and that's when the wheels came off."

"At a prove-up? What happened?"

"Let's just say my clients hadn't been on the up-and-up with me and leave it at that."

Sensing she had hit a nerve, Sharlene didn't dig any deeper. "I've been there," she said. "It's not a good feeling."

"No, it isn't. But back to your question, I've got to give it to him—ol' Forman did a good job. I thought I had him, and I did." Cal took a deep breath before adding, "But my clients didn't square with me. I got caught with my breeches down at that hearing. I will say this. You can't underestimate Forman. He comes to play."

"That's not one of my weaknesses. I do my homework on opposing counsel. I find out everything I can about them, look for their strengths and weaknesses, but I never assume they're not going to work as hard or prepare as well as I do. Can you tell me any more about Forman?"

"He's got a solid reputation here in Fort Worth. The local judges love the guy. And he has an impressive record with Fort Worth juries as well. I wouldn't call him flamboyant. Come to think of it, he's pretty low-key—you know, the aw-shucks type who tries to catch you with your guard down. He started out with Hadley & Morgan and then opened his own shop."

"I did an internet search on him this morning. Is there anything else you know about him that I can't find online?"

"Not that I can think of. I'll let you know if anything comes to mind. So what's the plan?" Cal asked.

"Have you been in touch with Dr. Crimm? I'd like to get him in and see how he might hold up as a witness."

"I've tried to reach him several times since you and I met. I'm afraid he might have gone on a bender," Cal smoothly lied. "I'll keep after it, though, and let you know. By the way, you ever get over to Fort Worth?"

"Very rarely."

"Well, I know you Dallas folks think we are a bunch of rednecks over here, but you might like our laid-back style more than you think."

Shalene took the hint. "Maybe so. I'll let you know if I'm headed your way."

"Please do. You won't regret it, I promise."

Cal hung up the receiver and smiled. He thought about Sharlene, not the lawyer but the woman. Cal had always had a wandering eye. A pretty girl hardly ever escaped his notice. But Sharlene was not a pretty girl. She was an attractive woman, a successful woman who had made her own way in the world, who had taken men on and beaten them at their own game. He didn't know for a fact, but he guessed she had been divorced several times. It would take a special type of man to handle Sharlene Knox—someone like him, someone who had worked hard for everything, someone who played for keeps, someone who wasn't afraid to take a chance. She had probably been unlucky at love, just like he had. Maybe that was why she was ignoring his overtures. But he wouldn't give up easily. That just wasn't his way. He'd continue to dangle the bait and hope for a strike.

CHAPTER 17

Randazzo watched from a side window as boxes were placed on the covered front porch just outside the door. Once the UPS truck lurched forward and disappeared down a hill, he quickly dragged the heavy boxes inside, closed the door, and turned the dead bolt. He decided to move all the packages to the basement before opening any of them. There were no curtains on the living room windows, and he didn't want to take a chance on a passerby casting a curious eye on his activities—better to be safe than sorry, an adage he had learned to live by.

Randazzo was a strong man. While in L.A., he had regularly worked out at a gym close to his apartment—he boxed, lifted, and even ran the bleachers at the local high school football field. He was in his early forties but ripped like a twenty-something. Before his stint in the can, he weighed just shy of 200 pounds and could bench a little over 300. He had lost some muscle in jail but had done his best to stay in shape, doing several hundred push-ups a day and an equal number of sit-ups. Jail food sucked, but he forced it down. Although he hadn't been to the gym since beating the rap at trial, he figured he could still bench at least 250. Once he got through with what he had to take care of, he would be back in L.A. and back to his old routine. He would be stronger than ever.

Randazzo picked up the largest box first and carried it through the kitchen, then down the stairs to the basement. He repeated the exercise until all the boxes had been moved. After placing the last one on the concrete floor, he jogged back up the stairs and closed the metal door to the basement. He heard a click as the auto-lock was triggered. He punched in the code he had programmed and then heard the lock disengage. He smiled—everything was working perfectly. He had bought the metal door and keypad lock the day after moving in. They had been easier to install than he'd expected. Now an escape from the windowless dungeon was impossible: only Randazzo knew the combination, and he intended to keep it that way.

He went back down the stairs and pulled out a box cutter from his jean pocket. He slit through the taped seam and peered inside the first of the boxes. The contents were packed tight and wrapped in plastic, making it difficult to tell what it was. Carefully, he turned the box on end and tugged the cardboard toward his body. It was the bed frame. He tore open the plastic and checked the parts against the instructions—everything was there. In less than thirty minutes, the frame was assembled.

The next box contained a padded top for the bed made of leather-covered foam. Randazzo rolled it out on the frame and laid down on top. Not bad—it wouldn't be great for sleeping, but that's not what he had in mind. There were holes in the supports of the frame so the bed could be adjusted to different heights and positions. He tried several of them, tilting the bed at different angles. Getting down on his knees for a closer inspection, he saw that the bed frame had been customized so that wrist and ankle restraints could be easily attached. They had thought of everything.

The next box weighed a little less than the first. He knew what was in it and couldn't wait to open it. This time he slit the sides of the box and peeled open the cardboard. Inside were several metal pieces, which Randazzo removed separately. First was the metal platform, where her bare feet would be. Holding it toward the light, he inspected it carefully. It had a grooved opening in the center. He placed it to the side and picked up an adjustable metal pole with grooves on one end. He lined up the grooves with the opening and then screwed it in—perfect. He stood and then adjusted the pole to different heights. Next came the attachments to keep her ankles spread and her hands behind her back. Randazzo noted that the ankle bar was about twice as long. He nodded—there was good reason for that. And finally there was an L-shaped metal structure, which fit onto the adjustable metal pole. It could be moved up and down and then tightened into place once he had it at the desired height.

The next box contained a suspension ring with the parts needed to hang it from the ceiling and adjust it mechanically. This would take a while to install. He made sure all the parts had been shipped and then pushed it aside.

There were two more boxes, both smaller and lighter than the others. He cut into the first package—careful not to damage any of the contents—and pulled out a variety of whips, crops, and ticklers; a pair of leather fur-lined ankle restraints and a matching pair of restraints for her wrists; and an adjustable gag, which he looked over carefully before trying it on. He just couldn't resist. But would he want to muffle her screams? There was no doubt the dungeon was soundproof. He might enjoy hearing her scream in addition to watching her writhe in agony. After all, it was payback time, and he planned on dragging out the punishment for as long as possible, until his captive could take it no more. Last there was the leather blindfold. Again, he might not use it—looking deep into her eyes and seeing the terror in them could be the ultimate turn-on.

His victim's attire for the evening was in the final package: a front-zipping black leather bustier for easy access, black thigh-high stockings with garters, and stiletto heels. He laid them on the adjustable bed, carefully positioning them in the approximate places they would be on his victim that night—a night soon to come, one he had dreamed about constantly in that cramped, filthy jail cell. His breathing became labored, and beads of sweat popped out on his forehead, as an image began to take shape in his twisted mind.

Randazzo hustled over to the cheap boom box he had purchased the day before. What would their special night be without music? Sliding the Stones' *Sticky Fingers* into the player, he selected the sixth track—the first cut off side B on the vinyl edition—and "Bitch" blasted into the room. As Keith's primal guitar began to bounce off the cinder-block walls, Randazzo started moving to the beat, swaying slowly at first and then jerking convulsively back and forth in time, his voice starting low, getting louder, and then at fever pitch, screaming along with Mick, "kicking the stall all night."

CHAPTER 18

"So what do we have, Stan?" Reginald Cowan III rose from behind his massive desk and sidled up onto one of its corners. He sported a three-piece suit, bow tie, and suspenders, which had become his trademark attire since getting the interim appointment as U.S. attorney. He had decided he needed to look the part, stand out, appear important. When he entered a room, he wanted everyone present to take notice. He was royalty now.

"Where do you want me to start?" Agent Tipps asked, stroking his neatly trimmed goatee, his head shaved smooth as a cue ball. "With the judicial scam or the insurance fraud?"

"Let's start with the scam. I know you paid Crimm a visit and now the son of a bitch is dead. Where does that leave us?"

"Well, I was hoping to get him to turn, and I think I might have been able to with a little time."

"You think he called Connors after you left?" The way Cowan spoke, it was more of a statement than a question.

"I have no doubt he called Connors. We can get Crimm's phone records to verify, but we'll need a court order."

"You think Connors had anything to do with Crimm's death?" Cowan asked.

"It's awfully suspicious. But I can't prove anything—at least, not right now."

"What about the Santa Fe PD? What do they say?"

"They've conducted a half-assed investigation—about what you would expect. The preliminary conclusion is that this was a mob hit." Tipps scoffed.

"Mob hit?" snapped Cowan. "Hell, the mob doesn't use car bombs anymore. They haven't for years."

"That's what I told their lead investigator, but he just wants to take the easy path, close the case as quickly as he can."

"What evidence supports his theory that the mob cared anything about Crimm?"

"Big gambling debts. Owed a lot of money to several Vegas casinos and some in New Mexico as well."

"How much are we talking about?"

"Millions."

"That's a big chunk of change. To be honest, you can't rule out a mob hit with those numbers out there."

"I know, but I'm not buying. I brought in the ATF. They gave the evidence a second look."

"And?"

"The car bomb was very amateurish. It's a miracle the damn thing even went off. Which would be very uncharacteristic of the mob."

"Anything else?" Cowan asked as he slid off the desk and ambled over to the window.

"The ATF examined all the fragments from the wreckage to see if they could get any fingerprints. No dice. But they were able to get some DNA. They're running it now to see if they can find matches to anyone other than the deceased."

"Good. Let me know as soon as you hear something."

"I will. A few other things you should know. The Santa Fe PD searched Crimm's house. Standard shit. But no laptop, no cellphone, and it looks like he cleaned out some files. There were file cabinets in his office that were open and empty."

"You think he had those with him in the car?"

"That would be my guess. The ATF is still searching the debris, but it's slow going. The fire burned for a while after the explosion, and then the fire trucks drenched everything. Hard to tell what was in that car."

"You really think Connors would stoop to murder? I don't like the son of a bitch, and no doubt he'd do anything to win in the courtroom, but to hire a hit man to kill his old friend? I don't know about that."

"If we're right and all those jury verdicts were obtained through fraud, Connors' world is getting ready to come down around him—his money, his airplane, his vacation homes, all gone in a flash. And from what I've learned about Crimm, he was one screwed-up son of a bitch. He stayed drunk all the time and ran up huge gambling debts. That's why I thought I could get him to flip. He would have cracked in time and ratted out ol' Cal. And Cal knew it."

"You may be right, but we need hard evidence," said Cowan. "I would love nothing more than to hang a murder one charge around Connors' neck. I want to see him carry that weight, spend the rest of his fucking life in jail."

"If there is a way to get there, we will."

"You mentioned Crimm's phone records. What are we doing on that?"

"Yeah, the Santa Fe PD agreed to get a warrant from one of the local judges. We should have the records in a day or two."

"Good. Just keep me posted. Assuming we can't prove your murder-for-hire theory, what do we have?"

"Same shit we had before. Similar affidavits, big judgments—not much unless you can get that reporter's informants to testify."

"I mentioned that to Forman. I'll circle back with him and let you know." Sighing, Cowan collapsed in his chair and propped his tasseled loafers on the desk. "Okay, let's turn to the insurance fraud case—the kickback scheme. Where are we there?"

"We've got a similar problem. A key witness is dead."

Cowan smirked. "Seems like we're running into a familiar pattern here."

"Sure does." Tipps ran a hand over his smooth head like it was some crystal ball with all the answers.

"You talked with the French police?"

"Yeah, and there's not much there. But I do have the wheels in motion to get a copy of their files, like you asked. You know the way they are. They don't like working with us any more than we like working with them."

"I hear you. What else?"

"Andrew James over at Empire Risk calls me on a daily basis. He's bugging the shit out of me about this investigation."

"You can't blame him for that. They lost a lot of money, and he's taking the fall for it."

"Yeah, I know. Don't guess you can blame him for being pissed."

"Have you had any luck tracing any of the settlement money from Connors to Stein?" Cowan asked.

"We've got people in Hartford now, two or three forensic accountants, trying to piece it all together."

"Nothing yet?"

"Not yet."

"So what do we have at this point, Stan?"

"All circumstantial. A bunch of shitty cases that had been sitting around for years are settled for a ton of money by an adjuster who, right afterwards, is seen in New York in a brand-new Ferrari. When asked about it, he makes up a bunch of crap and then high-tails it to France, where he ends up dead. Looks fishy as hell, but at this point we can't prove anything."

"I just wonder if Connors might have had something to do with Stein's death."

"I've wondered the same thing, but I don't think we should be wasting the government's money flying off to France, going down rabbit trails."

"You've got a point. For now let's see what the bean counters come up with. And thanks, Stan, for your hard work."

"Wish I had more progress to report, but I'll stay on it."

Cowan leaned back in his chair, cupped his hands behind his head, and wondered aloud, "Do you think we should consider having a sit-down with Connors' daughter? She's in the same firm with him, and her signature is on all the settlement docs. I doubt she'll give us anything, but it might be worth a try. I know it would be a waste of time trying to get anything out of her old man."

"She lawyered up yet?"

"Don't know, but if we gave her a call, we'd sure find out in a hurry."

Tipps thought for a moment. "I don't see any downside."

"Neither do I."

As Tipps walked toward the door, Cowan buzzed his secretary and asked her to get Christine Connors on the line.

CHAPTER 19

"This is one of my favorite Houston restaurants. I've been coming here for years," said Dr. Levi Pass, before extending his thanks to Charles, the maître d', who had seated them across from each other at one of the most intimate tables in the restaurant.

Glancing around at the exposed-brick walls and the hardwood floors, Darrin took in the romantic fire flickering in a fireplace catty-corner from their table, bathing the room in a warm glow.

"Nice choice, Levi. I like this place."

"It was named after the architect who designed the building, John Staub. I assume you haven't been here before?" Levi asked.

"No, I don't know Houston at all. Whenever I visited Megan and Mark, we usually ate in or went to a neighborhood Mexican restaurant. They have two young daughters . . ."

"I understand. My sons were young once. By the way, I think you know that Megan, Mark, and I have been friends for years.

He's an excellent surgeon. We have referred patients to each other when the circumstances called for it. I was sorry to hear about their separation."

"It's been tough, but they seem to be working things out. Mark hasn't moved back in yet, but they're seeing each other and actually getting along better than they have in years."

"That's wonderful to hear."

The waiter appeared, took their drink orders, and disappeared.

"I was glad to hear about your move to Houston. Megan called to tell me, and she seemed excited as well. Have you found a place to live yet?"

"I have. I just signed a lease a couple of days ago on a townhouse in Montrose."

"Great area, within a stone's throw of downtown. When I first started my medical practice, it wasn't a place you wanted to be after dark, but it's gone through a renaissance."

Their drinks arrived, a dirty martini for Levi and a Pink Lady for Darrin.

"If you need any help getting settled or finding your way around, let me know. I've lived here for years."

The waiter returned to take their orders. Levi recommended the crawfish enchiladas, the gumbo, and the Gulf Fish Pontchartrain, and the waiter seconded. Happy for the recommendations, Darrin nodded, the waiter took the cue, and they were left alone once again.

"So have you found a job yet?"

"I have. I'll be working downtown at Bass & Culbertson. Do you know the firm?"

"I know it well. An old-line firm that's been around forever. I believe a toast is in order. Welcome to Houston."

They clinked glasses and each took a sip, the fire's flicker highlighting their faces.

"As I recall, you worked for a law firm in Fort Worth for a number of years," Levi said.

"Yes, a small litigation boutique firm."

"Bass & Culbertson will be quite a change, I assume."

"A welcome change." Darrin forced a smile.

"I find lawyers interesting," Levi said with a chuckle. "They have egos almost as big as doctors."

"I don't know about doctors, but I certainly agree with you on lawyers, and trial lawyers especially."

Their appetizers were served, and the conversation continued.

"Who will you be working with over at Bass?"

"Frank Powell. He's chair of the antitrust section. Seems like a nice man."

"Don't know him, but it's a big firm. They must have several hundred lawyers."

"In the Houston office alone! I think they have ten offices in the U.S., and three or four international offices. Don't ask me where."

There was a slight pause in the conversation, and Levi shifted in his chair. "Darrin, you may not believe this, but you're the first date I've had since I lost my wife."

"How long ago, Levi?"

"Two years and two months, almost to the day. And it's been a difficult journey. Darrin, I have to tell you, though, I've really been looking forward to this evening. Ever since we talked at the brunch, you've been on my mind."

"I'm flattered." Darrin smiled, allowing herself to enjoy the compliment. "To tell you the truth, I've been looking forward to seeing you again as well."

It was true. Darrin couldn't get Jace off her mind, and she thought going out with Levi might help. And, although she couldn't imagine having the same feelings for Levi as she had for Jace, she was moved by his openness and sincerity.

Taking the last bite of her appetizer, she placed her fork to the side of the plate. "That was delicious but filling. I don't know if I can handle gumbo and an entrée!"

"I think I got a little carried away." Levi motioned to the waiter and canceled the gumbo. Their appetizer dishes were removed, and another round of drinks appeared.

As the night progressed, they made light conversation about the legal and medical professions and what they did on a daily basis, leaving their personal lives at bay for the present. Their dinner plates were removed, and the waiter tried to tempt them with a dessert menu.

"Darrin, we have to split the bananas Foster. It's the house specialty and known throughout the country."

Normally Darrin would have begged off—too many calories—but she was having a nice evening out with someone other than Jace and opted for dessert and an after-dinner drink.

On the ride to Megan's house, their conversation continued. There was no intimacy to it, Levi concerned about pushing too far too fast and Darrin not interested in delving any deeper.

Pulling into the driveway, Levi cut the ignition and walked Darrin to the house.

When they reached the front porch, Darrin softly said, "Thank you for a wonderful evening."

"The first of many, I hope," Levi replied and kissed her gently on the cheek.

Darrin went straight to her bedroom and began undressing for bed. As she leaned over to turn off the light, she glanced at her phone, which she had left on the bedside table to charge. Jace had called three times without leaving a message. And just like that, all the old feelings came flooding back. She debated calling him. What if it was something important? What if he had changed his mind and wanted to move forward in their relationship instead of back?

She chided herself for even giving it a second thought. Things were over with Jace. She was on the road to a new life.

She turned 18the switch, and slid under the covers. After a brief fight with her feelings, she let the tears come.

CHAPTER 20

After meeting with Jackie and learning that Randazzo could be somewhere in Austin, Leah realized she just couldn't concentrate on her work any longer. She decided to take Abe up on his offer. She needed some time off to try to regroup. She was constantly looking over her shoulder, as if Randazzo might suddenly appear out of nowhere. An eerie paranoia had set in. She was never without her Glock—in her purse whenever she went out, on her bedside table at night.

She still saw Chip Holt several times a week whenever she went to his rifle range to practice her shooting. He was so, so good-looking, a Greek god with sun-bleached hair, blue eyes, tan skin—and, oh, was he ever ripped! Unfortunately, he wasn't the right match for her; the two simply had very little in common. He wasn't much of a reader, and she wasn't much for the great outdoors. She liked to curl up with a good book and a glass of wine. He liked to go two-stepping at the Broken Spoke and throw down shots of whiskey. He had little ambition and was comfortable just to hang out and let the winds of fate take him wherever. Leah, in contrast, was driven, eager to find her passion and make it to the top. They were cordial with each other, still friends, but there was no chemistry between them, something they had been disappointed to discover over time.

It was an effort, but Leah forced herself out of bed. She threw on her robe and shuffled barefoot into the kitchen. After fixing a cup of coffee and sliding onto a bar stool, she propped up her iPad on the counter and began reading the *New York Times*: ISIS cutting off the heads of Christians on a beach somewhere; Democrats and Republicans accusing one another of everything but incest; a car bomb killing thirty men, women, and children in Baghdad; the Israelis and Palestinians blaming one another for the recent flare-ups in the region. The depressing headlines weren't helping her mood. She closed out of the news and started working the crossword. It was Monday, and the puzzle should have been easy for her. But it wasn't; her mind was such a mess. She decided to try again later and closed her tablet, troubling questions consuming her thoughts. Robotically, she sipped her coffee and stared into space.

She had never imagined Randazzo would get off. There was not a doubt in her mind that he was the one who had done those terrible things to her, no doubt at all. What was wrong with that jury? And now he could very well be back in Austin, except this time as a free man, walking the streets, watching her come and go, tailing her at every turn. She just knew he was there, she could feel it. Randazzo was back, and who knew what he might have in mind for her this time.

She shivered, got up, and zapped a bowl of oatmeal in the microwave. As she took a bite, she spotted a large brown envelope on the tiled entryway to her condo. She was about to pick it up when she noticed there wasn't anything written on the front—strange.

Picking up her cellphone, she called down to the doorman in her building.

"Yes, Ms. Rosen. How may I help you?"

"I was just wondering if management, or anyone there at the office, slipped an envelope under my door last night or this morning."

"Let me check." There was a pause as the doorman riffled through an activity log. "We haven't had any tenant deliveries yesterday or today. Were you expecting something, Ms. Rosen?"

"No, no I wasn't. Thanks," she mumbled before disconnecting. Her stare returned to the brown envelope. She considered her options and decided to call Jackie.

Jackie answered on the first ring and was at Leah's condo in less than fifteen minutes. Leah cracked the door, and Jackie inched her way sideways through the opening, careful not to disturb the envelope.

"Leah, you were smart to call me. There's no telling what's in there."

"So what should we do?"

Jackie leaned over and examined the envelope. "Looks like it's sealed—no chance of spilling any of the contents. And it's way too flat to contain an explosive device. I'm just going to bag it and take it down to police headquarters."

Jackie pulled on a pair of latex gloves, carefully picked up the envelope, and then placed it in a transparent plastic bag. When it was securely sealed, she sighed in relief and said, "I'll get this over to Officer Gomez and ask him to have the lab take a look at it as soon as possible. We might know something this afternoon, tomorrow at the latest. I'll come back here after I drop it off."

The wait, though relatively short, seemed like forever. An hour after returning to Leah's, Jackie's cell sounded. It was Gomez. The good news: there was no toxic substance in the envelope. The bad news: there was a DVD and a note. Gomez refused to describe the contents of either over the phone. They needed to get down to the station immediately. Leah, he said, was in danger.

Randazzo was definitely in Austin.

* * *

Ushering Jackie and Leah into a conference room at the Austin PD, Gomez wasted no time. "There were no fingerprints on the envelope, DVD, or note. Whoever put that envelope in Leah's condo was wearing gloves. Although we'll check the condo for prints tomorrow, I'm ninety-nine percent sure we won't find any."

Jackie interjected, "Back when we were pretty sure it was Randazzo that broke into Leah's condo, I had a camera installed above the door leading to the hallway. I thought about getting a copy of the video from the past twenty-four hours but held off until we knew what was in the envelope. I was hoping this might be a false alarm. I'll go and pull it so we can take a look."

"Let me know what you find out, Jackie. Okay, now comes the hard part. I have put the DVD that was in the envelope in that player over there." Gomez nodded in the direction of a crude metal table on rollers, with a monitor on top and a DVD player underneath. "All you need to do is press play." Gomez sighed and shook his head. "You're not going to like what's on there, but you need to know." He left the room.

Jackie turned to Leah. "Are you prepared for this?"

"No, but what choice do I have? Not knowing would drive me crazy."

Jackie walked over to the monitor and rolled it closer to the conference table. She positioned it at one end, looked at Leah, who nodded, and then hit the play button.

A blindfolded Leah stood totally nude in a shower, a stream of water beating on her naked body. A deep voice instructed her to play with herself.

Leah screamed, "Enough, Jackie, stop it! Just stop it . . ." Her voice trailed off, tears streaming down her face.

Jackie paused the video and wrapped her arms around Leah, pulling her close. "It's going to be all right. I promise."

"I just don't know how much more of this I can take!" Leah screamed. She broke away from Jackie's hold and began pounding furiously on the table as Jackie watched helplessly. After several seconds, the pounding stopped, and a seemingly broken Leah Rosen stared at Jackie, her eyes pleading for answers.

"We're gonna get him. He's going to make a mistake. They always do. He'll get careless, and when he does, we'll get him," Jackie said, her voice strong and sure.

There was a knock on the door. It was Gomez.

"Y'all okay in there?"

Jackie answered through the door, "Leah's pretty upset, but come on in."

Gomez walked in. "I'm sorry you had to see that, Leah."

No words came. Leah nodded uncertainly as tears continued down her cheeks. In a quivering voice, she asked, "What did the note say?"

Hesitating, Gomez reluctantly handed Leah a note in a sealed evidence bag. The words, scrawled in red marker and clearly visible through the plastic, screamed, "I AM DONE WATCHING!!!!"

Gomez took a seat at the conference table. "I think we all know who is behind this, or at least we are pretty sure we know."

All three looked at one another but said nothing. Gomez continued. "We may not be able to prove it yet, but we have to assume Randazzo is here in Austin. So we need to take every precaution." Gomez slid what looked like a Dr. Scholl's shoe insert across the table in Leah's direction. "I want you to slip this in one of your shoes."

With a puzzled look, Leah responded, "What is it?"

"It's a tracking device and will let us trace your whereabouts 24/7."

Leah went pale. "You think he might try to kidnap me?"

"I have no idea what the sick bastard is up to, but it's important for us to know where you are at all times, just in case."

"Do what he says," Jackie advised Leah, and added, "It can't hurt, and it might save your life."

Gomez slid an identical insert in Jackie's direction. "I want you to wear one as well."

Jackie smirked. "Come on, Jorge. Now you're going a little overboard."

Gomez didn't back off. "I'm serious, Jackie. I don't want to look back and second-guess myself for not doing this or that. Wear it. If not for yourself, wear it for me. It'll make me feel better."

Jackie stared at the insert for a second and then put it in her bag. "I'll think about it, but no promises."

Gomez nodded and turned to Leah. "You still carrying your Glock?"

"Everywhere I go."

"Getting security at your complex to walk you up to your condo?"

Leah nodded, and added, "And locking the dead bolt after they leave."

"Good." Gomez stood up and cautioned, "If either one of you notices anything suspicious, anything out of the ordinary, call me. I mean it. Both of you have my cell number."

They nodded, and Gomez left the room.

"You want me to spend the night at your place tonight?" Jackie asked.

Leah nodded. "It would make me feel a lot better considering what I've just been through."

As they walked out of the police station and down the steps, a nondescript man with gray hair and a small nose watched intently and then took a long drag off a cigarette, inhaling deeply. A wolfish sneer creased his lips.

It wouldn't be long now, not long at all.

CHAPTER 21

Christine Connors and her attorney, Reed Travers, were escorted down a long hallway in the Fort Worth office of the U.S. attorney for the Northern District of Texas. They didn't speak as they walked. At the end of the hallway, they were motioned into a conference room. Interim U.S. attorney Reginald Cowan III and FBI agent Stan Tipps were seated on one side of a long conference table. They rose when Christine and Reed entered the room. After an awkward exchange of forced pleasantries, Christine and Reed sat next to each other across from their hosts.

Cowan stood and draped his suit jacket over the back of his chair, exposing in dramatic fashion his red suspenders and polka-dot bow tie. He began to roll up his shirtsleeves slowly and methodically, signaling he was fully in charge and it was time for business.

"Ms. Connors, would you mind if I called you Christine? I hate being so formal." Cowan sat back down, awaiting Christine's reply.

"Yes, I would." Christine glared through him, overtly broadcasting her contempt for the man across the table.

Cowan cleared his throat. "All right then." He adjusted his bow tie before continuing. "As you know, we are here on a very serious matter." His eyes darted back and forth between Christine and her lawyer. Neither replied.

"A very serious matter indeed. We are in the midst of a troubling investigation into certain activities of your law firm, Ms. Connors," said Cowan, enunciating her name in a passive-aggressive manner.

His opening salvo was met with silence.

"We have strong evidence, very strong evidence, that your law firm was involved in a far-reaching scheme to obtain, through perjury and other means, fraudulent jury awards." Cowan took a deep breath before adding, "Jury awards in the millions and millions of dollars."

Still, no response.

Cowan rose and sauntered cockily toward the end of the conference room. He opened the doors to a cabinet mounted in the middle of the wall. There was a dry-erase whiteboard behind the doors upon which he began to write as he spoke.

"I'm sure you would like for me to detail the evidence we have uncovered so far, which I am more than glad to do." After he finished writing, he turned to face his audience and read what he had written on the board. "Howell Crimm. False affidavits. Suborned perjury. Multimillion-dollar jury awards."

Christine doodled on the front of a legal pad, her eyes focused on her drawings and away from Cowan. Reed listened courteously, his expression giving away nothing, the legal pad in front of him blank.

"So, you might ask, how are we going to prove these affidavits are false?" Cowan paused as he surveyed his audience.

Christine rolled her eyes. She hadn't asked a damn thing. Her doodling continued.

"In every single case, every single one, no matter what pharmaceutical product was involved, and there were many different ones treating a variety of diseases, the language of the affidavits was almost identical, the conclusions the same."

Reed spoke. "I hate to interrupt, but that doesn't prove anything. As you know, I do civil and criminal work, and I have seen form affidavits used in both. That's not unusual."

Cowan politely scolded his newfound pupil. "Not taken alone, but we have more—much more."

Reed shrugged as if to say, *then show me something and quit wasting my time.*

"Dr. Howell Crimm used research assistants to help him with the backup data for these reports," Cowan continued, his thumbs pulling his suspenders forward.

Christine stopped doodling and rested her chin on a palm, her lips partially covered, eyes staring straight ahead and away from Cowan.

Cowan continued. "There's nothing unusual about that unless their data were disregarded intentionally to reach the desired conclusion." He then paused, allowing for the inference to sink in.

Reed spoke. "Again, I hate to interrupt your flow, but you're not telling us anything that wasn't in the article. Obviously we take issue with virtually every word written by Ms. Rosen. In fact, my client's father has sued the tabloid for defamation. If you have some concrete evidence to give us today, we are glad to stay and listen. Otherwise, we both have active dockets and would prefer to spend our time on paying cases as opposed to listening to a regurgitation of the unsubstantiated allegations of a neophyte reporter trying to make a name for herself."

"What if I told you we had the names of those research assistants?" Cowan offered.

"Then I would ask you to turn them over. Do you and will you?" Reed replied instinctively and without hesitation.

"I am not prepared to do that quite yet."

"I bet you're not." A disgusted smirk from Reed followed.

"Another piece of troubling evidence for your client. Howell Crimm is dead."

"And I'm sure Mr. Connors is very upset about that. I understand they had a long professional relationship," Reed said.

"I should tell you that Dr. Crimm's death is being actively investigated by this office." Cowan nodded at Agent Tipps. He weighed the idea of saying that Cal Connors was a person of interest in Crimm's death, but he thought better of it.

Reed pushed his chair back. "I think we're ready to leave." He looked at his client, who nodded her agreement.

Cowan ignored the comment and pushed on. "In all candor, I want to fill you in on another investigation we are conducting. It also involves the Connors & Connors law firm but more directly pertains to your client."

Reed considered leaving but stayed in his chair. He had come to get a preliminary showing of what Cowan had, so why leave before his adversary had shown all his cards?

Cowan walked back to the board and wrote: "Multimillion-dollar settlement, Jamie Stein, kickback, Stein dead."

"Let's talk about what is uncontroverted first. Your client," Cowan nodded in the direction of Christine, "entered into a settlement with Empire Risk Insurance Company, settling a number of silica cases. The settlement amount was negotiated, and I use that term very loosely, between Jamie Stein, then a claims adjuster for Empire Risk and now a dead man, and Ms. Connors. We have obtained copies of all the settlement documents, and every single one is signed by Ms. Connors."

Christine's chin was now cradled in her palms, her elbows on the table and her gaze still away from her accuser.

"These cases had sat around for years, gathering dust. They were worthless and should never have been filed. I provided ten of the files, randomly selected, to a local defense firm here for evaluation. They reviewed the materials and gave me a written legal opinion that the claims were meritless and had no value."

There was no visible reaction from Christine. Reed made a note and asked, "Could you tell me the lawyer's name who gave you that opinion? I might know him or her."

"Nice try, Reed. I will consider doing so, depending on whether we make some progress today. Ms. Connors, are you following all of this?"

Reed responded before she could reply. "She's here to listen, not to be interrogated."

"Fine. I just wanted to make sure I wasn't making things too complicated. To continue, we believe Stein would never have settled these cases unless there was something in it for him. He went around the defense lawyers Empire Risk had retained to represent the silica companies, which is highly, highly unusual, and we are confident he received a substantial kickback for making the deal. We also have a team of forensic accountants working around the clock to prove it."

"So what you're telling me is you have no hard evidence to back up these fantastical assertions you are making against my client?" Reed retorted.

"We're getting there, shall I say."

Reed turned to Christine. "You ready?"

"Just one last thing before you go. I have some video surveillance I would like for you to see."

Cowan took his time. He knew this was his big moment. He slowly pulled down a projector screen and walked back to his laptop. In seconds, the screen lit up as a figure clad in a black trench coat and hat made her way across what appeared to be a hotel lobby, then returned, the lower facial features faintly visible.

"I had my tech folks splice together the disks we received from the French police. Jamie Stein was found dead the day after this surveillance video was taken. Does anything look familiar about the star of this little film?" Cowan asked, his voice tinged with sarcasm.

Christine stood and headed toward the conference room door. "I don't have to put up with this crap."

After she exited, Reed turned to Cowan. "I guess you have your answer."

As Reed rose to leave, Cowan replied, "Yes, I think I do."

* * *

Cowan waited several seconds after the door closed before asking, "So what did you think?"

Tipps stroked his goatee and then answered, "She was damn hard to read."

"She is one cold bitch, I can tell you that."

Tipps changed course. "I thought you were going to bring up a plea deal."

"The timing wasn't right. I want to let all of this sink in. They are probably headed back to Travers' office right now to sort through what I threw at them today. He put on a good front, but I'm pretty damn sure he was hearing a lot of this for the first time."

"Ain't that the way it always is? Clients rarely tell their lawyers everything. So you just gonna wait and see if Reed calls you?" Tipps asked.

"That's my plan. And, Stan, let's go balls to the wall on this one. My instincts tell me father and daughter are both guilty as hell. Let's put 'em both away."

Nodding his agreement, Tipps left the conference room. Cowan played the video one more time, pausing near the end, at the frame where the subject's facial features were briefly revealed. Was there a resemblance to Christine Connors? He was no expert in this area, but there seemed to be. And from what he could tell of Ms.

Connors, she certainly appeared capable of murder. The question remained: would she risk it?

They had no hard evidence that she was anywhere near Jamie Stein when he died. And even more problematic was the finding of the French investigator that Stein's death had been an accidental overdose. There were some big hurdles to get over, but Tipps was the best agent he had ever worked with. If there was something out there, Tipps would find it.

* * *

The car ride back to Reed's offices was cloaked in silence. Christine looked straight ahead, as if in a coma. Reed considered turning on the radio to ease the tension but rejected the thought. This was serious shit, and he needed to let his client think without distraction.

Once they were both seated at the small conference table in his office, Christine wasted no time. "Reed, I don't believe in beating around the bush. If you don't mind, I would like to address every damn allegation that no-good son of a bitch made against me, and then you can ask me whatever questions you want."

Without waiting for a response, she continued, "Let's talk about this alleged kickback scheme with Stein. First of all, I wouldn't have filed all those cases if I didn't think they had merit. Why would I waste my time? I have more cases than I can handle as it is. That's just a crock of shit. I don't know what lawyer Cowan hired to look at those claims, but I think it was pretty damn telling that when you asked for a name he wouldn't give it to you."

Reed nodded. His client was on a roll—no need to break the flow.

"And of course I met with Stein. You don't make multimillion-dollar deals in this business without meeting face-to-face with the other side. That's the way I have always negotiated. I want to check out the opposition's body language. When someone tells me there is no more money, I want to look him right in the eye to make sure he's not screwing with me. That's what good plaintiff lawyers do, don't you agree?"

Another nod coupled with a supportive smile. Boy, was she persuasive! Her demeanor, her emotional delivery, her common sense and logic—he certainly wouldn't relish having her on the other side of a case.

"Sure my name is on the docs. Duh! And if I felt like I was committing some crime, why in the world would I sign all of them? Geez!" Christine poured herself a glass of ice water from the pitcher Reed's secretary brought in, took a hurried sip, and then continued. "Oh, and the reason Stein went around the lawyers—are you ready for this? He told me they had plucked him like a chicken, charged him so much in fees that he had no choice but to settle and stop the hemorrhaging."

"That doesn't surprise me," Reed replied, affording his client a chance to catch her breath. "Hell, with the hourly rates those big firms are charging these days, it sometimes makes more sense to settle."

"And this kickback claim—you've got to be kidding me! Did you hear Cowan offer one shred of evidence supporting that ridiculous allegation?" Christine asked rhetorically. "Did you hear what he really said?" She deepened her voice to mock Cowan's, "*We're working on it.*" She changed back to her normal tone and added, "And they won't find a damn thing. You know why? Because there isn't anything. There was no kickback, period."

"I believe you."

"Oh, and the video surveillance." Christine leaned her face tantalizingly close to Reed's. "Do I look anything like the person in the video? Wait, that's an unfair question. Hell, there was no way to tell who was in that video. It could have been a man dressed up like a woman, for all we know."

"I agree. I couldn't tell much from it, and that's probably the way whoever was in the video wanted it."

"I can tell you one thing about Stein from the two meetings I had with him. Boy, did he like to party! The police determined he died of an accidental overdose. Maybe he was doing drugs with some high-priced call girl and got a little carried away with whatever he was taking. Then she freaked out and hauled ass after he died on her. That's certainly more logical than what Cowan dreamed up about me."

"You've convinced me. So what about the allegations involving your dad?"

"You know his nickname is the Lone Wolf, don't you?" Christine asked.

"I had heard that."

"And for good reason. He likes to fly solo and try cases by himself. In the years we have practiced together, I can't recall one case we actually tried together. I take that back. He did come with me to watch on the first couple of cases I handled on my own and critiqued me afterwards. But we never actually tried a case together—never." Christine took another sip of water before resuming. "The reason I tell you that is to explain why there was no reason for me to work with Dr. Crimm. I met him once or twice in the office, but that was it. I had no involvement in the cases where he gave expert testimony—zippo."

"Do you think any of what Cowan said about your dad is true?"

"Knowing Dad like I do, I don't believe a word of it. Just like you said, that Rosen woman was trying to make a name for herself and slandered Dad in the process."

"What about Crimm's death?"

"Dad mentioned it to me. He was pretty shaken up by it, told me he had been trying to straighten Dr. Crimm out for months."

"What was the problem?"

"He was an alcoholic and a gambler."

"That'll do it."

"No doubt about that. In any event, that's all I know."

"All of this is very helpful."

"So what's next? Do you think Cowan will charge me? And what was the purpose of that little dog and pony show today?" Christine asked in rapid-fire succession.

"Cowan was trying to scare you. He wants your dad's head on a platter and hopes to make a deal with you to help him get it."

"Well, he can forget that."

"I know, I know. As far as charging you, that's anybody's guess. I just don't know at this point."

"They won't just come up to my office and cuff me, will they?" Christine asked, with her first hint of concern.

"Probably not. In a situation like this, where someone has hired a lawyer, Cowan would probably call me and ask if you would turn yourself in voluntarily."

"Well, that's good to know. Whew, I feel like I've been run over by a train. Guess I'll go home and make myself a strong drink."

Reed laughed. "I have a better idea. I'll buy you dinner. Mi Cocina is just a stone's throw from the office. I bet a frozen margarita would taste pretty good about now."

Christine cocked her head. "Do you think that's a good idea, you being my lawyer and all?"

"I can't think of a better one."

* * *

The next morning, Christine was hiding out in her office. She had gotten to work an hour later than usual and had slipped by her dad's open door while he was on the phone, gazing out the window, his boots resting on the credenza.

Her hand clutched a cup of black coffee. This was her fifth cup of the morning—one too many margaritas the previous night. She had taken some Advil before falling into bed, but that hadn't done the trick. Her head felt as if a game of ice hockey were being played inside, with plenty of violent forechecking going on.

She smiled despite the lingering effects of a bad hangover—it had been well worth it. There had been no talk of her current dilemma, just a wonderful evening with someone she found dead attractive and enjoyed being around. The good news was he wasn't married and never had been. She had thought about asking him up when he dropped her off after dinner, but she opted not to. She decided she wanted to take this slow and easy and not let impulse drive the wagon. This could turn into something that just might last, and she intended to do everything in her power to make that happen.

Her trance was shattered when her office door was abruptly opened. Her dad was standing there in the doorway, a knowing grin on his face: "Long night?" Cal plopped down in the chair across from her.

"You might say that." Christine was not in a talkative mood.

"Hell, I been on pins and needles. I knew you were meeting with that worthless bastard Cowan yesterday, and I wanted to hear how it went. I called you several times late in the day—even texted you, which is a real effort for me—but I didn't hear back."

"Sorry, Dad. I cut my phone off when I went into the meeting and forgot to turn it back on."

"Well, how was it?"

"Pretty much what I expected. Cowan strutted around like a show pony, throwing out one accusation after another, trying to act important and scare the crap out of me."

"And did he?"

"Well, it isn't any fun sitting there while someone rails on you, but I was as prepared for it as anyone can be, I guess." Christine drained her coffee and poured another cup from the carafe on the credenza behind her.

"Cowan have any surprises?"

"He thinks you had Crimm killed. Does that count?"

"I didn't know the son of a bitch would stoop that low. He knows better. I may not be perfect, but I wouldn't kill anybody. I'm not that damn stupid. He's grasping at straws."

"Well, he had an FBI agent there. I didn't pay attention to his name—"

Cal interrupted. "Tipps?"

"That was it. How did you know?"

"That was the guy who paid Crimm a visit before he died."

"Well, he's Cowan's go-to investigator, evidently."

"What'd you think of him?"

"He didn't say a word. It was the Reginald Cowan show."

"Figures. He loves to hear the dulcet tones of his own voice. Hell, if bullshit were music, he'd be Sousa's band." Cal laughed disgustedly.

"Oh, and Cowan implied he knew the names of the research assistants Crimm used."

Cal perked up. "Did he tell you who they were?"

"No. Reed asked but Cowan held back, saying he might later."

"He doesn't have shit. That was just a bluff."

"I agree."

"Anything else I should know?"

"Not that I can remember. He pretty much tracked the accusations Rosen made in the *Texas Matters* article. The only things he added were that he knew the names of her sources, Crimm's research assistants, and believed you put a hit out on your old friend."

"Did the meeting end after that?" Cal asked.

"Oh no. He fired some shots in my direction about the silica settlement."

"Like what?"

"Like the cases were dogs, that the settlement was a sham, that Stein got a kickback, same song, different verse." Christine didn't mention the video and Cowan's inference that she might have killed Stein. No need to worry her dad with that. Besides, she had told him that she would handle that prong of the investigation.

"So how do you like your lawyer?"

"Very much. He stood up to Cowan—put him in his place several times. I have a lot of confidence in Reed."

"And I sense there may be a little more to it than that. Am I right?"

Christine grinned. "Dad, I've got work to do."

"Be careful about mixing business with pleasure."

"You don't need to worry."

Cal rose from his chair, went around behind the desk, gave his daughter a peck on the forehead, and then left.

Christine smiled. She loved her dad. Even if they were never in the courtroom together, they were a team. They always had each other's back and this would be no exception. They would get out of this—someway, somehow.

CHAPTER 22

Jace bustled into the *Texas Matters* conference room, briefcase in hand. "Sorry to keep the two of you waiting, but my flight was late." He took a seat and pulled two folders out of his leather satchel, sliding one across the conference table to Leah and one to Jackie.

"Connors answered the discovery we served on him. I made a copy of his responses for each of you. Just so everybody's in the loop, I also sent copies to Cowan and Aaron Heidrick. Heidrick's the lawyer with the Ralston firm who's representing *Texas Matters*."

Leah and Jackie opened their folders and began to peruse the contents. Leah was the first to speak. "Wow, there is a lot of material here. What is all of this?"

"Let me walk you through it. First, we served interrogatories on Connors. Basically, they're questions for him to answer under oath. For example, the first question asks him to name all of the persons who participated in answering the questions, and his answer was 'Cal Connors.'"

Leah nodded. "Oh, I see."

"In almost every instance, Connors lodged an objection to the question we asked and stated the grounds for his objection. Sometimes he answered the question subject to the objection and other times he didn't." Jace thumbed through his file materials and then said, "Take a look at interrogatory number fifteen. I asked him to list all of the clients he had represented over the last thirty-six months. He objected on the basis that the information was privileged and the question was overly broad, and refused to answer."

"Why did you ask him for that information?"

"Two reasons—one, I knew it would hit a nerve and I wanted to get under his skin, and two, I thought we had an argument to get it. After all, he's claiming millions of dollars in damages, and I wanted to test that."

"How will the objection be resolved?"

"We'll have a hearing before the judge at some point, and he'll rule on all of the objections Connors made. Judges usually split the baby in rulings of this nature and give each side something."

Leah shook her head as she flipped through an eight-inch stack of documents.

Jace smiled. "Don't worry—we're not going to go through all of this page by page. That's why I had Kirk prepare a summary. It's the three-page memorandum at the back of the folder."

Leah and Jackie shuffled through their files and pulled out the summary.

"Take a moment to read it."

They did, and then looked up after finishing. Leah shook her head. "He is such a liar. He wouldn't know the truth if it hit him in the face. I can't believe he denied knowing Randazzo. He hired the sick son of a bitch."

Turning toward Jackie, she asked, "Have you told Jace what happened?"

"We've traded calls, but no, I haven't had the opportunity to tell him."

Leah's gaze returned to Jace. "He's back. Randazzo is back in Austin. He left an envelope under the door of my condo. It . . ."

Leah's voice trailed off as she looked to Jackie for help.

Jackie brought Jace up to speed.

"I'm so sorry, Leah. Did Gomez have any recommendations?"

"Yeah, he wants me to wear a tracking device. And Jackie too, for that matter."

"Sounds like a good idea."

"I'm wearing it now," Leah offered. "It was a little uncomfortable at first, but I've gotten used to it."

Jace turned to Jackie. "And you?"

"I haven't decided yet. Seems like overkill for me to wear one."

"I'd rethink that if I were you," Jace argued.

"We'll see," Jackie cursorily responded, and then pivoted to another topic. "So let's get back to the discovery responses. The recap seems to say that we didn't get anything helpful. Is that right?"

"Pretty much. Connors denied knowing Randazzo, denied knowing the identities of Crimm's research assistants, denied he had suggested any of the conclusions contained in Crimm's reports. Basically, he denied everything."

"That wasn't unexpected, was it?"

"No, not really. He did produce some documents—emails between him and Crimm."

Leah began flipping through her folder.

Jace noticed and offered, "If you're looking for the emails, they're at tab D. I would encourage you both to read them at some point. Kirk and I have carefully reviewed every single one of them. There were fifty-two, but in our opinion, only three had any relevance to this case."

"And?" Jackie asked.

"I made separate copies of those. They're at tab F."

As Leah read the first of the three emails, a subtle smile took shape. "Can you believe it? He actually wrote 'The end justifies the means.' That just kills him. It proves everything we've been saying. Come on, this case is over. Connors is admitting Crimm lied to win all of those cases."

"No doubt that's good stuff, but take a look at the next two."

Leah read the first out loud. "Howell, if you don't feel comfortable giving an opinion in this case, then don't. I wouldn't want you to do anything you consider the least bit unethical. Just give me a call after you have made a decision."

Leah scoffed. "It's apparent what he's doing. He's covering his tracks plain and simple, creating a false paper trail. Anyone can see that."

"That could be, but his lawyer will blow that email up, stack it on an easel positioned strategically in front of the jury box, and let those twelve folks read it over and over again as she is putting on her case. It certainly takes some of the sting out of the previous one."

Leah ignored Jace's comment, flipped to the last email, and read, "Howell, I've learned through the years that there is very little black and white in this world. The world is full of grays. You may have one opinion and another expert an entirely different opinion. That doesn't mean one of you is right and the other is wrong. You just see things differently. There is nothing unethical or illegal about that. Think about what I've said and let me know how you come out."

After finishing, her eyes darted back and forth between Jace and Jackie. "It's clear to me. He's asking him to lie. Crimm got cold feet about giving the opinion Connors wanted and Connors was trying to shame him into doing so."

Jace shrugged. "That's one way to look at it, but I'm sure Connors' lawyer will put a different spin on it."

Jerking back from the table, Leah jumped to her feet and began pacing around the room. "So are you saying we've lost, Jace? Have you given up on this case?" She leaned across the table in Jace's direction and spewed, "I thought you were a fighter. That's what Jackie told me before I hired you. Now I'm not so sure—"

Jackie calmly interceded. "Leah, it's Jace's job to see the case from both sides, the strengths and the weaknesses."

Still not satisfied, Leah continued her tirade. "I get that, but I haven't heard him mention one thing that's in our favor. Is there anything, Jace?"

"If we go to trial now, with what we have, it's going to be tough for us to win this case."

Leah was boiling. "So what are you saying? What happened to what you told me during our first meeting? You said Connors would have an uphill battle because his burden of proof was going to be so high. You said he would have to prove I intentionally set out to destroy him. You said it would be even tougher for him if we could show he was a public figure. Were you just feeding me a bunch of bullshit to get me to hire you?"

"Leah, I understand you are upset. Everything I told you in our meeting was true, and I'm not backing off any of it. But with regard to those emails, they are ambiguous. And as I said, once Connors' lawyer mucks up the water, they'll be a wash at best. Crimm's dead, so we can't depose him, break him, or find out what was going on between him and Connors. The fact that there were big jury awards doesn't prove a damn thing. There are big jury verdicts in this country every single day. So what? Picking where to file his cases amounts to nothing but just smart lawyering. The bottom line is this: the key to successfully defending this case is what those research assistants told Crimm—the ones whose names you won't give me. If they get up on that witness stand and testify they told Crimm there was nothing wrong with those drugs, it'll blow the case wide open. Couple their testimony with the emails, the big jury verdicts, and Crimm's murder, and then you've got something. They're the thread that ties everything together."

Leah sat back down. "But I promised them."

Jackie spoke up. "At a time when you and your magazine weren't being sued for a gazillion dollars."

"She's right, Leah. Things have changed since you made that promise."

Leah looked at Jace. "I need to think about this. And like I've said repeatedly, I would have to talk with both of them before I disclosed anything."

"Of course. They might be more understanding than you think. After all, they know what went on in those cases—that Crimm ignored their findings so that he and Connors could get rich. They're not fools."

"When do you need an answer?"

Jace grinned sheepishly. "Yesterday."

"I want to talk with Abe and sleep on it. I'll call you in the morning."

"That works."

"Is that it for today?" Leah asked.

"One other thing. You know that Jackie has been working on an insurance fraud claim involving Connors' law firm?"

"I don't understand why that has anything to do with the case he filed against us," Leah said, a puzzled look on her face.

"It establishes a course of conduct. If Connors defrauded an insurance company out of millions, then it makes sense he would do the same with Texas juries."

"I get it. Will the judge let that evidence in?"

"Maybe, maybe not. Depends on whether he finds that the probative value of the evidence outweighs the prejudicial effect it will have on the jury."

"What in the world does that mean?"

"Whatever the judge wants it to mean. If he wants to let the evidence in, he will. If not, he won't. The law gives him plenty of latitude to do what he thinks is fair under the circumstances."

"Well, at least we've got a shot."

Jace nodded and then said, "Anyway, Jackie and I are going to review what she's learned about that claim. You want to sit in?"

"I'd like to, but I've got a lot to sort out. If you don't need me . . ."

Jace shook his head no. "But we would like to use this conference room, if that's okay."

"No problem. I'm going to meet with Abe right now. I'll let him know you will be here for several more hours." Gathering herself, Leah continued, "And, Jace, sorry about the outburst. This has been a rough time for me, and I had to take it out on someone."

"Apology unnecessary. Just know that we are doing everything we can to win this case—everything."

Leah reached her hand across the table, and Jace took it. "I know you are." She then excused herself and left the conference room.

After the door closed, Jace and Jackie stared at each other for several seconds before Jackie said, "That last episode was what pushed her over the edge. She didn't mean any of—"

"I know. I just let her vent. It was probably good for her."

"You should have seen her down at the station when we played that DVD. She literally lost it."

"And who wouldn't? Unfortunately, things aren't going to get any better—for a while, anyway. In the meantime, we've got to do our best to help her get through this."

"Well, I think I'm making some progress on the Stein matter."

"Did Cowan get the French investigation file over to you? He promised me he would."

"He did, and I've been through everything in it more times than I can count."

Jackie replayed her review of the photos taken of Stein's hotel suite, the toxicology reports, and the fingerprint analysis. She saved the video surveillance disks for later.

"So what conclusions did you draw from the file?"

"That Stein definitely died from a heroin overdose."

"Is that it?"

"The rest is conjecture at this point. Could have been a night of fun with a prostitute that got out of control. The hooker panics when Stein overdoses, wipes down the place for prints, takes the champagne glass she used, and then hauls ass."

"Why wouldn't she call the police?"

Jackie smirks. "Come on, Jace. Do you have to ask that? She's a call girl doing illegal drugs with a john who ends up dead. If she calls the cops, she gets charged with prostitution, possession, maybe even dealing, and possibly gets slapped with a murder charge. I don't think so. She gets the hell out of there—hopefully without a trace."

"Good point. It's definitely a possibility. How about murder?"

"Can't rule it out. Maybe the hooker is hired to kill Stein and make it look like an accidental overdose. There was no trail, though—pretty professional."

"And Connors might have hired her?"

"We don't have any evidence of that, but again, it's a possibility." Jackie opened up her laptop. "There was some video surveillance from the hotel cameras."

Jace rolled his chair closer to Jackie's and focused on the screen as she played the video, pointing out pertinent details. When they got to the frame where the bottom half of the woman's face was briefly revealed, Jackie paused the disk.

"Okay, if you look closely, you can make out the nose, the lips, and the chin."

Jace leaned closer to the screen, squinting as if that would give him a better look. "I can, but that doesn't tell me a lot."

"It doesn't tell me a lot either, but I know an expert who might be able to crack the code. He has this software that allows him to match subjects by their facial features. It's called facial recognition software, or something like that."

"And?"

"Assuming I get him photos—preferably video showing movement—of the person I think might be in that surveillance video, he can do a comparison of their size, the way they walk, and, most importantly, their facial features."

"And how certain can he be of a match?"

"Depends on how much he has to work with. The more video and the better the quality, the higher the probability his conclusion will be accurate."

"Does he have the surveillance video yet?" Jace asked.

"Not yet. I have talked with him about it. He wants me to bring him photos and videos of the suspect at the same time."

"And who might that be?"

"Christine Connors."

"Oh, come on, Jackie. You don't think she would fly all the way to France and murder someone, do you?"

"Stranger things have happened."

"I think there is a greater likelihood Connors hired a call girl to do it. Those high-rent folks don't like to get their hands dirty."

"They don't, but they will if their future is riding on it. Pretty damn risky to hire a stranger to do your dirty work for you—no way to know how that person will hold up if things go south. And Christine was the one who signed the settlement documents, every single one of them."

"I suppose it's worth a shot."

"I'll make a trip to Fort Worth and do a little filming."

"Be sure and pack an overnight bag." Jace grinned impishly.

"If you're lucky. On a serious note—"

Jace interrupted. "Come on. I am being serious."

Jackie playfully squeezed his hand. "I'm not through talking shop yet." Flashing a "maybe later" grin, she continued. "Cowan getting me that French investigator's file was a big help. I understand he has the FBI working with him on this. I plan on giving the lead agent a call, maybe suggest angles for him to pursue and, you know, make him think they were his ideas. He'd have the resources and power of the federal government to get them done."

"I think that's a good plan." Jace glanced at his watch—5:35. "I sure don't feel like driving in rush hour across town to the airport."

"You don't have to. Your rental car in the parking garage?"

"It is."

"Let's head that way. You can drive me to my car and then follow me home, catch the first flight out in the morning."

"I like the way you think."

"I thought you might. Lead the way, Counselor."

CHAPTER 23

He paid too much for the van: $1,200 in $100 bills. Maybe it was worth $500, and that was a stretch. The front windshield was cracked, the seat on the driver's side badly ripped, the tires bald. But none of that mattered. He wouldn't need the van for long. His job would be finished in a matter of days.

He turned the ignition key. The engine coughed once and then died. Randazzo glared at the salesman standing in the parking lot, who shrugged, a "what me worry" expression on his face. On the second try, the engine struggled but finally came to life. The salesman smiled in relief as Randazzo shifted into gear and merged slowly onto a pockmarked street that took him past a mixture of run-down shacks, seedy-looking bars, and a strip mall housing a carnicería and a panadería with some loan shark operation dubbed Dinero Rápido wedged in between.

Randazzo took the ramp to I-35 North. He glanced at the speedometer and then the rearview mirror, staying well within the speed limit. The temporary license plate and inspection sticker were both current. He had made sure of that before buying the van. There would be no reason for the cops to stop him. He would obey all laws—traffic laws, at least.

After he entered the city limits of Round Rock, he noticed he was low on gas. He cursed the asshole that had sold him this junk heap for leaving the tank nearly empty. Spotting a full-service truck stop on the side of the freeway, he exited and pulled up next to one of the pumps, went inside, and gave the attendant a fifty for gas. On the way out, he spotted some baseball caps on a swivel rack emblazoned with the interlocking red-and-white *R*s of the local minor league baseball team. Grabbing one, he returned to the cashier to pay for it. He wanted to look like a local, and there was no better way than wearing a hat no one would want but some snuff-dipping redneck from Round Rock.

After filling the tank, Randazzo eased back onto the freeway and drove toward his first destination, EZFind Discount Warehouse. The parking lot was practically empty. He parked the van in a remote section and, after cutting the engine, looked to either side and into the rearview mirror. There were no cars in the area and no sign of activity. Stepping out of the van, he pulled the bill of his new cap down. He didn't overdo it, just enough to obscure his features.

Once inside the store, he dislodged a cart from the rack and pushed it slowly toward the tool department. After searching the wall rack, he placed two handsaws and an industrial power saw in the cart and strolled toward the checkout area. A talkative teenager with bad acne ran the three items through the scanner while making teeny-tiny talk that went unreturned except for the occasional nod. After paying in cash, Randazzo walked out the sliding doors toward the van, stopping to stuff the sales receipt in a trash can just outside.

Randazzo was no chemist—far from it. He had almost flunked science in high school. But he did know how to use the Internet, and he had done his research: he needed hydrochloric acid. His research had told him that this was an extremely corrosive substance—more corrosive than sulfuric acid, lye, or bleach. It could dissolve bone, teeth, hair, fingernails, and every tissue and organ found in the human body. And it was easily attainable at any EZFind. But he couldn't buy it at the same location where he had just purchased the saws. That might arouse suspicion. After putting the saws in the back of the van, Randazzo drove out of the massive parking lot and toward the freeway.

The EZFind in Temple was only twenty minutes away. He knew where to find the hydrochloric acid. He had checked while at the previous location. There were only a few stragglers left in the store; closing time was in a little less than an hour. He walked inconspicuously toward the aisle he wanted, placed the merchandise in his cart, and breezed through the checkout lane. A short time later, the acid containers were on the metal floor in the back of his van, and he was on the way to his last destination, the EZFind store in Belton. There, he bought duct tape, black automotive paint, and several plastic drums. After loading the drums, duct tape, and cans of paint, he headed south on I-35 toward Austin. He would spend the rest of the night in the rat-infested garage of his rental house painting the van ebony black. His preparations would then be complete.

CHAPTER 24

"Darrin, you sure are working late," said a middle-aged man in a custom-tailored gray suit. His thick dark hair was stylishly streaked with gray and professionally coiffed. With a proprietary air, the man walked behind Darrin's desk and stood uncomfortably close to her, peering over her shoulder at the file that lay open on her desk.

"Oh, you're finishing up the discovery responses in the Miramar Petroleum case. But they're not due for a week."

Nervously, Darrin closed the file. "I know, I know—but that's just me. I'm always worried I'll miss a deadline." She turned and looked awkwardly up at her new boss, her eyes radiating discomfort.

Taking the hint, Frank Powell sat down in the chair in front of her desk. "So, how are things going so far? You getting settled in?"

"I can't complain. Everyone here has been so nice and helpful," Darrin said, forcing a smile.

"That's good to hear—probably a bit of a transition from your old firm." Before Darrin could respond, Powell continued, "By the way, I don't know if I told you, but I had a really good visit with Jace during the interview process—seemed like a nice guy, and boy, did he have great things to say about you."

Darrin smiled and politely nodded but offered nothing.

Powell looked at his watch. "I didn't realize it was so late. Why, it's almost seven. You interested in getting a bite to eat? They serve a mean steak over at Vic & Anthony's."

"That's so nice of you, but I have plans," Darrin lied.

"Well, maybe some other time." Powell rose from the chair and, before walking out of her office, turned and commented, "We sure are lucky to have you. See you tomorrow."

"Night, Mr. Powell."

"It's Frank, remember." He shot Darrin a suggestive grin as he disappeared down the hall.

Closing her office door, Darrin pressed Megan's number. "You won't believe what just happened. The nerve . . ."

"Uh, could you back up a bit? How about 'Hello, Megan, how are you'"?

"Sorry, but I'm a little upset, and that's putting it mildly. My boss just asked me to have dinner with him at some place called Vic & Anthony's. Can you believe that?"

"Well, at least he has good taste in food. Mark and I have eaten there a number of times, and their steaks are delicious."

"Megan, that's not the point! The guy is married and has three kids. One of the secretaries even told me he was a deacon in the church. Everyone around here thinks he hung the moon, and I think he's hitting on me!"

Megan snickered. "Doesn't surprise me one bit. Those are the kind you really have to keep an eye on. The ones that have that holier-than-thou air about them—you just can't trust 'em."

"The way he looked at me, peering over my shoulder—I could even feel his breath on my neck," Darrin shuddered. "It really gave me the creeps. What am I going to do the next time he comes in? And I have no doubt there will be a next time."

"Simple. You're going to do the same thing you did tonight—politely say no."

"I get the feeling he might not like hearing that over and over. I can tell he has an ego bigger than Texas."

"So what's he going to do? Attack you in the office? He may be a lech, but he ain't stupid. Otherwise he wouldn't be a partner in one of the best firms in Houston. After a while, he'll give up trying. You also might avoid working late at the office. If you have to get something out, work on it at home. Less chance Romeo will get frisky if there are people around."

"Good point. So, enough about me. How are you and Mark doing?"

"Really good. I don't think counseling will be necessary much longer. We have talked and talked, I've cried, he's cried—nothing more to put out on the table."

"Have you set a date for him to move back home?"

"We are thinking two or three more weeks. We just don't want to rush it."

"Megan, that's such great news. Have you told the girls yet?"

"No, we decided it's better to hold off until we get closer to the move-in date. Don't want to get their hopes up if there is a chance things might take a bad turn."

"That's probably best."

"Hey, you still liking your new digs?"

"I'm getting settled in slowly but surely. Haven't met any of my neighbors yet, but I'm in no rush. Just taking things one day at a time."

"And how's Dr. Pass?" Megan asked nonchalantly.

"Fine, as far as I know."

"Come on, Sis. You're holding out on me."

"Not really. There's not much to tell. We've been out to dinner a few times. Levi is a very nice man, but he's a little too needy for me. Honestly, I don't think he has gotten over losing his wife. We have pleasant-enough conversations, but that's about all there is to it."

"That's too bad. I thought you two might be a match. I know some other—"

Darrin stopped her with a laugh. "Look, I'm fine. Honestly, I would just like a little 'me' time to figure things out."

"You haven't gotten over him yet, have you?"

"Come on, Megan. It's been a little over a month since I moved to Houston. Jace was a part of my life for years. I wish I could just snap my fingers and forget about him, but things don't work that way. You know that."

"I understand. Look, I'll quit bugging you about it, but if you feel up to it, I know plenty of—"

"You've made that clear, and when I'm ready, I'll let you know." Darrin sighed and switched topics. "So you think I'm overreacting to what just happened?"

"Absolutely. Guys pull that kind of crap all the time. It's part of their DNA. If your boss comes on to you again, which he very well might, just come up with another excuse. Like I said earlier, he'll get the message after two or three polite turn-downs."

"You're probably right. Well, it's past time to get out of here, and I need a glass of wine."

"Know the feeling. Now don't be a stranger, Sis."

"I won't. Night, Megan." Darrin picked her purse up off the floor, dropped her phone inside, and walked out of the office. As she headed toward the elevator, she glanced over her shoulder. She hoped Megan was right about Frank Powell, but that queasy feeling inside hinted otherwise.

CHAPTER 25

It was the tail end of rush hour, and traffic was snarled on I-35. What had he been thinking? He should have stayed at Jackie's another thirty minutes; he would have missed most of this. He reached for the coffee mug and took a sip. He was still a little hungover, but not too bad; the bacon and eggs Jackie fixed had been a lifesaver.

The tractor-trailer in front of him came to a complete stop. Jace eyed the other lanes—no better. He then glanced at his watch. His plane was scheduled to leave in a little over an hour. He reached for the cell in his jacket pocket and ordered Siri to call Leah Rosen's cell. She answered on the second ring.

"Jace, I was just about to call you."

"I'm in traffic on I-35—what a mess. It's like a damn parking lot out here. No way I'm going to make my flight."

"I thought you were going back yesterday."

"That was the plan, but some things came up."

"Anything I should be worried about?"

"Oh, no. It had nothing to do with your case."

"That's good to hear. Okay, I know why you're calling. I promised you a decision and I've made one." Leah paused, stoking the suspense.

"And?"

"Well, I talked with Abe, and I don't think I have a choice." Leah hesitated before saying, "I'm going to give you the names of my sources."

"That's what I wanted to hear. Like I told you yesterday, their testimony could very well make the difference."

"That's what Abe said too. I just had to think things through. But there are some conditions."

"Now, wait a minute, Leah—" The traffic began to creep along, causing Jace to shift the cell to his left hand and take the wheel with his right.

"Hear me out. I want to be involved every step of the way. My contacts don't know you, so we have to handle this carefully."

"Understood. So who are they and where are they?"

Leah ignored the question. "Do you have to go back to Fort Worth today?"

"I don't think I have anything urgent. I can call my office after we get off the line to make sure. What are you thinking?"

"Well, neither of my sources lives in Austin."

"That's what I figured."

"I want to tell one of them in person. His name is Dr. Sanjay Patel. He works at Vanderbilt Medical Center, in Nashville. I thought we might pay him a visit today. I could introduce you, let you explain all the legal mumbo jumbo, make him feel more comfortable working with us."

"I like it. Do you know if he is available today?"

"I'm going to call him after we hang up to make sure."

"There are several flights from Austin to Nashville, so that shouldn't be a problem. If he can meet, it would be great if you could make us reservations. Normally I would call and ask Harriett to do it, but with this traffic . . ."

"I got it covered. Not a problem."

"Who's your other source?"

"Dr. Seth Coleman. He's in Topeka. I haven't talked directly with him. All of my contact has been through his lawyer, a guy named Berry Spitz."

"Is he in Topeka as well?"

"Yeah, you want his cell number?"

"If you don't mind, go ahead and text it to me. Let's talk about how we handle Mr. Spitz when we meet at the airport.

"That sounds good. I'll call you back in a few."

"Perfect."

Jace slid the cell back in his pocket and smiled: Game on.

* * *

Leah confirmed Dr. Patel was in but didn't speak with him directly. She left a message on his voice mail, advising that it was urgent they talk. She then booked the 12:20 Southwest flight that arrived in Nashville at 3:40 and texted the flight number and departure time to Jace. After hurriedly throwing the bare essentials into an overnight bag just in case the meeting ran late, she scheduled a ride to the airport through Uber. As she waited in the lobby of her condominium complex, her cell rang. It was Patel. Yes, he could meet that afternoon, but why? Was there a problem? He wasn't in any trouble, was he? After reassuring him, Leah sidestepped any further interrogation and told him she would bring him up to speed once they got there. Patel was even more curious. What did she mean by "they"?

"Oh, yeah, I've been sued, and I'm bringing my lawyer with me. See you this afternoon," Leah quickly said. Spotting her ride, she stuffed her cell in her purse, grabbed her tote in one hand and briefcase in the other, and sprinted toward the car waiting at the curb.

Jace got to the airport a little after 10:30 and, after returning the rental car, breezed through security and got to the gate an hour early—plenty of time for a rib platter and a Shiner Bock at the Salt Lick BBQ. After placing his order, he asked Siri to search the Internet for "Berry Spitz lawyer Topeka." Several websites came up, and Jace tapped on the one that read thespitzfirm.com.

Spitz was the founding partner of an eight-man litigation boutique firm similar to the one Jace had started—a definite plus. Jace had learned over the years that people bonded with those who shared similar backgrounds and experiences. In jury selection, he always looked for folks who could relate to him, scouring the juror information sheets and tailoring his questions in voir dire to find that common connection. When he did, it usually paid off big-time.

Spitz had attended undergrad and law school at the University of Kansas in Lawrence. No overlap there. Jace had been to a UT football game in Lawrence years ago, but that was the only visit to KU he could remember.

Spitz worked the defense side of the docket. He was a member of the Defense Research Institute, commonly referred to as DRI—another plus. Jace was a member as well. Maybe their paths had crossed at one of the DRI conventions, although that was unlikely.

Jace scanned Spitz's practice specialties. There was no mention of media law. That was no big deal. Few lawyers specialized in that area. Jace didn't have it listed on his website, and here he was defending Leah in a libel case with millions at stake.

Jace put down his phone, picked up a rib, and, in time-honored primal fashion, pulled the flavorful meat off the bone with his teeth and chased it with a sip of ice-cold Shiner. In less than fifteen minutes, the plate was nothing but a pile of bones, the mug drained dry. He put his iPhone in his pocket, grabbed his briefcase and tote, and made his way toward the gate. Leah was waiting.

"We board in ten minutes. I was getting a little worried," Leah chided.

"I should have texted you. I stopped off to get a little barbecue. How long have you been waiting?"

"Not that long—twenty minutes or so. Have you talked with Mr. Spitz?"

"No, but I looked him up on the Internet."

"What'd you think?"

"Hard to tell a whole lot from a website, but he looked okay to me. I was glad to see he wasn't some ambulance chaser."

"That's a relief. Like I said, I haven't spoken with Dr. Coleman. Mr. Spitz has been the go-between on everything. He drafted the statement Dr. Coleman gave that supported my story."

"Do you happen to have a copy with you?" Jace asked.

"As a matter of fact," Leah rummaged through her briefcase and handed Jace a three-page document, "I do."

After reading through it, Jace whistled through his teeth. "He really puts it to Crimm. Doesn't call him a fraud but damn near. He should be a great witness for us at trial, assuming he holds up under cross."

"Are you going to call Spitz now?"

"I think I'll wait until after we meet with Patel. I want to see what he says before I talk with Spitz. It would really be nice if their stories lined up. I assume you have a copy of the statement from Patel as well."

"Of course." Leah pulled another document from her briefcase and handed it to Jace.

Jace nodded as he read through the affidavit and then said, "Patel and Coleman's stories are remarkably similar, the only real difference being the medications."

"That's what it seemed like to me."

"And I assume they didn't compare notes before signing their statements?"

"Not that I'm aware of."

A voice came over the loudspeaker, asking group A to get ready to board. A herd of people rose from their seats and took their places in line.

"The flight is sold out, so we probably won't get to sit together," Leah lamented.

"When we stop over, I'll switch seats. That will give us some time to talk before we get to Nashville."

"Good idea."

The gate agent called for group C, and Jace and Leah boarded, both ending up in cramped middle seats toward the rear of the cabin. The plane took off as scheduled and landed in Houston forty-five minutes later. After the Houston passengers deplaned, Jace and Leah huddled in two seats next to each other and settled in for the flight to Nashville.

As the 737 rumbled down the tarmac, Jace turned to Leah and said, "Let's talk about Dr. Patel."

Leah recapped her history with Patel. She explained how she had discovered the identities of a few of Crimm's research assistants through Midwestern Medical School, where Crimm had been employed at one time. She had tried to obtain Patel's contact information but struck out. Fortunately, Midwestern agreed to forward her email to Patel so he could respond if he chose to. Patel had contacted her after the Samson verdict but was initially reluctant to get involved. Understandably, he was concerned for his wife and baby. Leah explained how her persistence paid off and Patel eventually acquiesced if she promised not to disclose his identity.

"I feel for Dr. Patel. He is so torn about all of this, really worried about his family and his career." Leah took a sip from the Diet Coke the attendant had put on the tray in front of her.

"And you can't blame him for that. He's just getting started in his practice and now might be a witness against his former boss, who was blown up by a car bomb. That's pretty damn scary. So what time, and where, are we meeting?" Jace asked.

"I told him we'd call him when our plane landed. He said his office is only thirty to forty minutes from the airport, depending on traffic. When we get there, I'll introduce you and then explain why we've come to see him. I was planning on putting it on a personal level—let him know my neck is on the line, that Connors is suing me for millions. Drive home that the stakes have gone up since he and I last talked."

"I like that," Jace replied, shaking peanuts into his hand.

"You can answer any of the legal questions he might have."

"Leah, you know I'll have to tell him that we might subpoena him if he refuses to cooperate."

"Let's hope it doesn't come to that."

The attendants advised everyone to drink up, and began collecting trash and making sure everyone's tray table was in the upright and locked position. The plane touched down in Nashville shortly afterward, and they were at Patel's modest office an hour later.

* * *

"Dr. Patel, I'm so sorry I couldn't give you more notice, but things have been moving pretty quickly. And I can't thank you enough for meeting with us." Leah rushed the words out anxiously and then turned toward Jace. "I told you over the phone I had a lawyer. This is Jace Forman."

A small, thin man with dark skin and even darker eyes rose and leaned across the desk to shake Jace's hand. He was wearing a white lab coat and black tie, his name embroidered above one pocket. His ebony hair was neatly parted to one side, his oval-shaped wire-rimmed glasses drawn tight against his face and resting on a prominent nose.

"Please sit." Patel motioned toward two wooden chairs in front of his desk. He sighed and said, "Well, Ms. Rosen, I have to say I have not been looking forward to this visit. I was hoping my involvement in this matter had ended."

"I can certainly understand that. There are a lot of things I would rather be doing right now as well. If you don't mind, I'd like to fill you in on what's been going on."

"Please."

Leah brought Patel up to speed on the defamation lawsuit and the criminal investigation being conducted by Cowan.

"Well, a lot has happened," said Patel, shaking his head. "So, what do you need from me?"

Leah turned to Jace, who took the cue. "Well, there's no way to sugarcoat this. You're a critical witness in the defamation case Connors has filed, and also in the criminal investigation the U.S. attorney is conducting."

"I was afraid you would say that."

"Without your testimony, Connors just might win his case against Leah and *Texas Matters*. Remember, he is asking for millions in damages. A judgment of that size would bankrupt Leah and would likely end her career in journalism. It could also put a good publication out of business."

"I see."

Jace added, "Not to mention the fact that the criminal investigation would fall apart and Connors would get off scot-free."

Patel removed his glasses and rubbed his eyes.

"To keep that from happening, we need your testimony. Will you help us?"

"I don't know. This is more than I bargained for. Yes, I want to help, but I'm concerned about my family, my career, everything. I am sure you can understand that."

Leah stepped in. "Of course we can. There's a lot at stake here for everyone. I took a big chance when I wrote that story about Connors, but I don't regret it, not one bit. Something had to be done. We all know the guy's a crook. We just can't let him continue to do what he's been doing for who knows how long."

Patel nodded in agreement. "Okay, why don't you walk me through what would happen if I agree to help."

Jace sensed progress and responded, "First, I need to get some personal information from you. Please keep in mind that I'm not trying to pry. I'm just doing my job."

"I understand."

Jace asked Patel about his personal background, making sure there were no skeletons that could be used by Sharlene Knox for impeachment. There were none. Satisfied, Jace then moved to the work Patel had done for Crimm at Midwestern Medical School.

"Tell me how you came to work as Crimm's research assistant?"

"The position was advertised on the medical school website. I felt I met the qualifications and applied for the job. I had recently married and needed the money."

Jace nodded. "What did the job entail?"

"Helping Dr. Crimm on any number of research projects."

"What type of projects?"

"At the time, he was writing a paper on epilepsy, and I worked on that."

"So you weren't just doing research that related to lawsuits Crimm was working on?"

"Oh, no. There was much more to it than that."

"All right. I want to talk about the work you did on the drug known as Fosorax."

Patel shifted in his chair, leaned forward toward Jace, and asked, "Where would you like for me to start? I assume you've read the affidavit I supplied to Ms. Rosen."

"I have read your affidavit." Jace took the document out of his satchel and rested it on his lap. "One thing it didn't cover was the drug approval process. Can you help us understand that?"

"Certainly. Let's assume my company has developed a new drug we believe treats anxiety more effectively than medications currently on the market. The first thing I would do would be to file an Investigational New Drug application, or IND, with the Federal Drug Administration."

"What's in the application?"

"The results of any animal studies, manufacturing data on the proposed drug, and a detailed protocol on how clinical trials on humans would be conducted. Basically, the FDA wants to make sure all i's are dotted and t's crossed before human testing begins. After the application is filed, there is a thirty-day holding period to give the FDA an opportunity to review the application. If they find things in order, then the company gets the go-ahead. If not, it's back to the drawing board."

Jace looked up from his legal pad where he had been jotting down notes. "I know the application is filed with the FDA. Is there a specific—"

Patel interrupted. "The Center for Drug Evaluation and Research, or CDER, as it's commonly referred to."

Jace grinned. "The government loves acronyms, doesn't it? POTUS—that's the one that gets me. Anyway, what's the next step in the process?"

"If CDER finds the application in order, the clinical trials are conducted following the protocol outlined in the application. After they are completed, the results are submitted."

"And the drug is either approved or denied?"

"Correct."

"Now, going back to Fosorax, what did Crimm ask you to look at?"

"Everything—the application, the animal studies, the clinical trial results, you name it. He told me to see if I could find anything irregular in the approval process. He said he didn't care what it was. I thought that was odd, but I was getting paid a nice hourly wage and figured he had good reason for making a request like that."

"Did you know he had been retained by Connors as an expert in a case involving Fosorax?" Jace asked.

"Not at the time. I learned that much later."

"Okay, so what did you find?"

"Nothing out of the ordinary. The application was in order. The clinical trials appeared to have been conducted properly. Some of the subjects reported feeling more anxious, some even reported having suicidal thoughts—but it was a very, very small percentage of those participating in the trial. Plus, those anxious or suicidal feelings could have been explained by other causative factors. And the manufacturer could have warned of these possible side effects. You see that all the time."

"So you reported your findings to Crimm?"

"I did. My practice has always been to put my findings in writing so there can be no question regarding the conclusions I have drawn. And that's what I did here."

"Which are contained in the email you sent Crimm that is an exhibit to your affidavit?"

"Precisely."

"Did you receive any response from Crimm?"

"Nothing. He didn't ask me about my findings. He acted like I hadn't even worked on this. It was all very strange."

"You didn't ask him?"

"I didn't feel like it was my place. After all, he was my boss and I certainly didn't want to get fired."

"When did you find out Crimm had been hired by Connors as an expert in the Fosorax case?"

"When I received the forwarded email message from Ms. Rosen. I didn't respond at first, but I did call her after I read about the big verdict Connors had gotten in the *New York Times* and saw that Dr. Crimm had testified. I was shocked. I couldn't understand how that could have happened. That was when I decided to get in touch with Leah—excuse me, Ms. Rosen."

"Please, Leah's fine."

Patel nodded and said, "Now that you know the full story, tell me what you want from me."

"First, I want to be able to use your affidavit in the defamation case Connors has filed against Leah. I'll try to keep your identity shielded from the other side, but I think the likelihood of that happening is low. I also would like for you to consider testifying if that becomes necessary—by deposition or in trial, or both for that matter."

Patel didn't respond, his stare staying with Jace.

Jace continued. "Turning to the criminal investigation, I know the U.S. attorney wants to talk with you. I haven't given him your name yet, but I'd like to. If you don't agree to cooperate, he's going to file a motion with the court, and the judge will likely order Leah to give up her sources, which obviously includes you. If he has to go to all that trouble, he's not going to be too happy, and that's not a good thing."

"I understand, and I sense the urgency of this. I will call you with my answer tomorrow before noon. I thank you both for coming." Patel looked at his watch, and said, "I'm sorry, but I've got to go. My wife is expecting me home and I don't want to give her any cause for concern. Mr. Forman, do you have a business card?"

Jace pulled one from a satchel pocket and handed it over.

"Now, if you'll excuse me." Patel shook hands with Jace and Leah. "We will talk soon."

As Leah and Jace walked toward their rental car, Leah asked, "So what do you think?"

"He's with us. I could tell. I'll call Spitz once we get to the airport. Unless his client crawfishes, we can count on his testimony as well. This was not a good day for Cal Connors. That son of a bitch is going down."

CHAPTER 26

"Hot damn!" Reginald Cowan exclaimed, slamming the phone down in its cradle. "Now we're talking."

Buzzing his secretary, he ordered her to call Agent Tipps and get him over immediately. Tipps was seated in front of Cowan's desk in less than thirty minutes.

"I understand you have some good news?" Tipps probed.

"Not good news—great news!" Cowan sprang out of his chair and started prancing around the office. "No, this is a game changer, Stan—a fucking game changer."

"I'm about to die over here. Fill me in, Boss."

"Forman called this morning. He gave me the names of Rosen's sources for the story and faxed me their affidavits."

"That's great news. You got copies for me?"

Cowan handed the affidavits to his go-to investigator and continued to celebrate as Tipps read through them.

"These witnesses, Patel and Coleman, will be dynamite. They have no reason to lie and their affidavits are pretty damn clear that Crimm totally disregarded their findings—basically made up all that shit he put in his expert reports. Hell, he knew what he was telling those juries was nothing but a crock of shit, and so did that no-good bastard Connors."

Tipps finished reading through the affidavits and slipped them into his briefcase. "Sure seems that way. Are the docs willing to testify?"

"That's what Forman told me. Obviously they don't want to, but they will if we need them."

"So what's the next step?" Tipps asked.

"I want to turn up the heat some more on the old man's daughter. If we could flip her, it would be light's out. We just need a little more leverage with her, that's my bet."

"I don't know, Boss. She seemed like a pretty tough cookie to me."

"I've seen a lot of tough cookies crumble when the walls start closing in—lots of them." Cowan walked back behind the desk and collapsed into his oversized leather throne. "Forman is working with a PI. I know her—she used to be with the Austin PD while I was a prosecutor down there."

"Yeah?" Tipps rubbed the back of his shaved head, which he tilted to one side as if he knew what was coming and didn't like it.

"Forman suggested that we pool our investigative efforts, and I agreed."

"You want me to work with the PI they've hired?"

"That's right."

Tipps frowned as he asked, "What's her name, anyway?"

"Jackie McLaughlin. Stan, I know you like doing things on your own, but I can tell you McLaughlin was one of the most respected officers in the Austin PD."

Skeptical, Tipps countered, "So why isn't she still there?"

"I don't know the details, but my recollection is she wanted to be her own boss," Cowan lied.

He knew, of course, that he was the reason Jackie had left the department. He thought back to when he was the assistant DA in Austin and how he had filed a report with Jackie's supervisor, recommending she be fired because of the help she had given Jace Forman in investigating the mysterious death of a UT student. That's what Cal had wanted him to do, and he'd had no choice. After all, Cal had gotten him his job at the DA's office in the first place. Oh, but how the tables had turned!

Tipps shook his head and said, "Well, I'll give it a shot."

"I think you'll be pleasantly surprised. Like I said, she's damn good. Besides, Forman showed some good faith by giving up Rosen's sources, and this is my way of reciprocating."

"Did you and Forman discuss what Ms. McLaughlin has turned up?"

"We didn't discuss that in any detail. Besides, I was too focused on getting Rosen's sources. Forman did mention some things, but they went in one ear and out the other. I think it would be better if you got it directly from her anyway."

"You have her contact info?"

Cowan gave it to him, and then said, "After you talk with her, let me know what you think."

"I will." Tipps rose and made his way to the door. Before leaving, he turned and said, "And don't worry. I'll give this arrangement a chance. I'm just pretty set in my way of doing things."

"Aren't we all? See you, Stan."

The door closed, and Cowan propped his loafers up on the desk. An image of the Lone Wolf in an orange jumpsuit popped into his mind, bringing a satisfied grin to his face.

* * *

Thirty miles west, as Cowan and Tipps concluded their meeting, Jackie McLaughlin exited I-35 toward the offices of Connors & Connors. A borrowed Sony high-resolution camcorder lay on the passenger seat.

She pulled up in front of one of the gaudiest office buildings she had ever seen. It was a four-story glass box built in the late eighties that screamed "Connors & Connors" on the side in platinum letters. On one side of the firm's name was a large symbol of the state of Texas and, on the other, a replica of the scales of justice.

There was a visitors' parking lot to one side of the building. She turned in and stopped, surveying the lot for the clearest view of the building's entrance. As she did, she noticed there were several reserved spaces closest to the building entrance. "Christine Connors" was painted at the top of one of them. It was empty.

Jackie cursed her luck. Maybe Christine was out of town. If so, she had driven all the way from Austin for nothing. She glanced at the time on the dash—12:35. Maybe Christine was at lunch with a client, maybe she was meeting someone for a midday tryst, or maybe she had run a quick errand and would be back shortly. Jackie had no choice but to hunker down for a while. She would wait until she was damn sure that Christine wasn't going to show up. It was that important.

Pulling into a space in a corner of the lot across the street, she killed the engine and removed the camcorder from its case. Adjusting the lens, she took several practice shots and played them back. She was good to go.

She didn't have to wait long. Thirty minutes later, a jet-black Mercedes E-Class Cabriolet pulled into the space. Jackie rolled down her window, positioned the camcorder on the driver's side door, and pressed record.

The convertible top was up when Jackie started filming. There was no way to get a good view of the driver's face, the tinted side window blurring the image. Then the door swung open, and a high heel made its way to the asphalt, followed by another. An attractive woman of medium height dressed in a conservative blue jacket and matching skirt emerged from the car and closed the door before quickly looking around and walking toward the office entrance. The camcorder captured it all—every movement, every feature—the eyes, the mouth, the nose, the legs, the gait. It was all there to be enlarged, slo-mo'd, and massaged in any number of ways. Jackie's expert had been thorough in his instructions. She had everything she needed—she was sure of it.

Jackie returned the video camera to the seat next to her and turned the ignition key. Her intuition told her there was going to be a match. She had no doubt that the woman she had just filmed was the same woman who had been at the hotel the night Jamie Stein was murdered.

* * *

Jackie had just gotten back on I-35 when her cell sounded. She glanced at the screen—unknown caller—but decided to take it anyway. The voice on the other end was deep and unfamiliar.

"Ms. McLaughlin, this is Agent Tipps with the FBI. Is this a good time?"

"Yes, of course."

"I'm working with Reginald Cowan—the U.S. attorney over in Dallas—on an investigation involving a Fort Worth attorney, Cal Connors. I believe you are familiar with Mr. Connors?"

"Yes, yes, I am. In fact, Jace Forman, the lawyer I'm working for, called me earlier today and told me I might be hearing from you."

"I thought he might have. Looks like we may be helping each other out on this investigation."

"That's what Mr. Forman said."

"He and my boss talked this morning. I understand your client's sources are going to cooperate with the investigation. Their testimony is pretty damn strong. I read their affidavits this morning."

"I've been traveling and haven't had a chance to see them, but that's what I've been told as well."

"Anywhere exciting?"

"Actually, I'm just outside of Fort Worth."

"Really? My meeting with Mr. Cowan put me a little behind this morning and I haven't eaten yet. You have any interest in joining me for a little barbecue?"

"Sounds great. Where do you want to meet?"

"Angelo's—some of the best you'll ever have, I can promise you that. Meet you there in thirty minutes?"

"Deal. How will I know you?"

"Shaved head with a goatee. Just think Jesse Ventura with facial hair."

Jackie laughed. "Got it. See you shortly."

Twenty minutes later, she pulled up to the side of a barnlike structure a few miles west of downtown Fort Worth. Hurrying into the restaurant, she spotted Agent Tipps sipping beer from a mug the size of a fishbowl. He stood as she approached. They shook hands and she took the seat across the table from his.

"Well, I do see the resemblance to the former governor of Minnesota," said Jackie, smiling.

"I don't know how to take that."

"Take it as a compliment." Jackie looked around. "Angelo must be a hunting enthusiast. I've never seen so many stuffed animal heads in my life."

"I would say that's a pretty good guess. Hey, you ready to eat, or do you want to talk first?"

"Actually, I'm starving. And that beer you're drinking looks tempting. Shall we?" Jackie pushed her chair back and made her way toward the short queue of people waiting to place their orders, and Tipps followed. As they waited in line, they traded small talk.

Back at their table, Jackie took a bite of brisket followed by a sip of the coldest draft beer she had ever tasted, and then got down to business. "Any idea why I was in Fort Worth today?"

"Not a clue."

"I was videoing Christine Connors." Jackie tried the potato salad and then took another sip of beer. "You're right about this place—fabulous food."

"Yeah, it's pretty special. So, care to explain your film shoot?"

"You've seen the video surveillance from that hotel where Stein was murdered?" Jackie cleared her throat sarcastically, and added, "Oh, excuse me, died of an accidental overdose."

"I've watched it a number of times. Pretty damn poor quality, and I couldn't tell much about the person going into Stein's room. Looked like a woman—you know, the high heels and all—but who knows?"

"I thought that too when I first watched it, but now I know it was a woman."

"You've confirmed that?"

"Hang with me for a minute. You saw the part of the video when she was walking through the hotel lobby after she had been with Stein, right?"

"Yeah, I remember seeing that."

"She looked up, just for a millisecond, but long enough for the camera to capture most of her facial features—the nose, mouth, chin, and neck."

"That I don't remember."

"It was easy to miss. I didn't catch it until the seventh or eighth time I watched it." Jackie exaggerated to make Tipps feel better. "So back to your original question about why I filmed Christine today. You ever worked with a facial recognition expert?"

"Can't say that I have."

"On a few cases I did, back when I was with the Austin PD."

"I didn't know that type of evidence was admissible," said Tipps. "I've heard judges are tossing it. Remember those forensic dentists using bite mark comparisons to tie defendants to the crime? Sounded good at the time but turns out it wasn't very scientific at all. A lot of those convictions are getting thrown out."

"I admit that facial recognition science is cutting-edge, but so was DNA evidence not so long ago. Now defense lawyers are routinely using it to try and free clients who they contend were wrongly convicted. Whether judges will let facial recognition experts testify to their opinions depends on a lot of factors."

"So your guy is going to compare the features of Christine Connors with those of the subject captured at the hotel where Stein was staying?"

"Precisely."

"Interesting. If he finds a match, that will definitely give us some additional leverage. When will you have the results back?"

"Couple of days."

"You'll let me know what he finds?"

"Of course. We're a team now, right?"

"I guess you could call us that." Tipps felt himself warming to his new partner.

"Now I need something from you. If I'm right, and she did kill Stein, she would have flown to France before the murder and back to the States afterwards. If you could get the manifests from flights going from DFW to Paris and back, we might get lucky."

"I like it. I'll see what I can find out. Any other thoughts?"

"Follow the money. If we could trace payments from the Connors firm to bank accounts controlled by Stein—"

Tipps cut her off. "We would need Connors's bank records to prove that, and we don't have enough hard evidence to get any judge to give us a warrant to get those."

"Good point. But if we can put Christine in Stein's room the night of his death, that might be enough."

"It just might."

"Okay, I've got to get a move on. Don't want to get caught in that rush-hour traffic."

"I don't blame you. Hey, I gotta be honest. I was a little skeptical about working with you on this, but . . ."

"Don't blame you a bit. I like to go it alone most of the time. Others usually just get in the way." Jackie offered her hand, which Tipps grasped firmly. "I'll call you when I get Giff's report. If you find out anything on the flight manifests—"

"You'll be the first to know."

CHAPTER 27

Cal stared blankly at the stack of mail his secretary had placed in the inbox on his desk. He had neglected going through it for several days—rarely did anything important come by mail anymore. E-filings, e-transcripts, email—they had replaced the paper filings and correspondence of yesteryear. He laughed to himself as he recalled his first years of practice, when lawyers engaged in legal sparring through lengthy epistles arguing about this and that, when clients were apprised of the progress of their cases through multipage status reports, and when depositions came in booklet form searchable only by keen-eyed paralegals.

And the idea of a thorough and detailed exchange of information before trial—well, that was a joke back then. It was trial by ambush; maybe a few depositions were taken, but that was about it. You tried cases by the seat of your pants, and whether you won or lost depended on how you were able to handle that surprise witness or that unanticipated revelation from the witness stand or that "smoking gun" document conveniently produced on the eve of trial—or all of the above.

Cal rolled his chair back and sauntered over to the "memory wall," as he endearingly called it, where framed photographs in all shapes and sizes were displayed in haphazard fashion. His gaze traveled from one to the other and sometimes back again: a tuxedoed Cal with his arm draped around Bill Clinton, Cal eating at Hut's with former Texas governor Ann Richards, Cal shaking hands with President Obama, Cal and Christine at a fundraising event with abortion rights activist Wendy Davis, Cal backstage with Willie Nelson, Christine and Cal relaxing at their island retreat off the Mexican coast. As his eyes darted from one photograph to another, he grinned. It had been a good ride so far, a damn good ride. One he had enjoyed every minute of and was proud to call his own.

Cal's mood abruptly soured as a mental image of Reginald Cowan III came into sharp focus, interrupting his stroll down memory lane.

Shaking his head in disgust, he ambled back to his desk, muttering to himself, "That backstabbing son of bitch ain't gonna tear down what I've spent my whole life building—no damn way."

Before he could sit down, his cell vibrated in his jeans pocket. He remained standing as he put the phone to his ear.

"Cal, this is Donato. You got a minute?"

"Always." Cal closed his office door and then eased into his chair.

Donato asked, "We don't have company, do we?"

"I check every morning for bugs. We're clean. What's going on?"

"I wanted to give you a heads-up on the investigation."

"I'm listening."

"Preliminary conclusion is a mob hit."

"That's what we were hoping."

"Yeah, my buddy at the department tells me Crimm was drowning in gambling debts. And not just in Vegas, but here in Santa

Fe, in Albuquerque, all over the place. I don't know how long he thought he could get away with that shit."

"Well, he didn't, now, did he?" asked Cal, playing along with the charade. "You think they're close to wrapping up the investigation?"

"He thinks it'll take several more months. Can't look like a rush to judgment."

"What about Crimm's family?"

"The police interviewed them over the phone, but they said they were too busy to come in person—kinda sad. I guess he really pissed off his ex, and his kids as well. Looks like they pretty much disowned the poor bastard."

"That's a damn shame, it really is. You feel good about your source?"

"Better than good. We've been friends since we were kids. When I asked him about the investigation, he didn't ask why I wanted to know. He gets it. Sometimes the less you know, the better."

"You know the police chief as well, right?"

"Yep. I'm not as tight with him as I am with Manolo, but Garcia and I get along just fine."

"Did your friend say whether the feds were snooping around?"

"That's the bad part. That FBI agent, Tipps—he's been asking a lot of questions. He even brought in the ATF to go through the wreckage."

"That ain't good."

"No, it isn't. The local police don't have any choice but to cooperate. They don't like it, though."

"You need to stay on top of this. What are you going to say if Tipps pays you a visit?"

"I'm going to tell him the truth. Crimm called me after Tipps came to see him. He told me he had never been interrogated before and was scared shitless. He said he called me because I worked with him on a case and I was the only lawyer he knew in Santa

Fe. We scheduled a meeting for the next morning and he never showed—end of story."

"What if he asks you the name of the case?"

"I could say I don't remember, I handle a lot of cases. Or I could give him the name, but that would tie me to you."

"Let's go with the first option. He'd have a helluva time making the link. He might be able to find out from the court records that you and I had a case together, but we can't do anything about that. You'll let me know if he contacts you?"

"Absolutely."

Clearing his throat, Cal asked, "You're on a disposable, right?"

"Did you have to ask?"

"Hey, thanks for the call, Donato."

"No problem. I'll be in touch."

The phone call ended. Cal swiveled around toward the credenza, opened a drawer, pulled out a cigar, and, after performing his usual ritual of licking both ends, slid it into his mouth. As he rolled the cigar from side to side, he propped his boots up on the desk and stared up at the ceiling. He felt a little better after talking with Donato, but he still had concerns. How well would Donato hold up if Agent Tipps came knocking?

Cal chewed on his cigar and sighed. No need to worry about Donato now, he said to himself. There was nothing more he could do but wait and see.

CHAPTER 28

Jackie's meeting with Gifford Duncan, the facial recognition expert, had lasted all morning. He had painstakingly walked her through each step of his analysis of the hotel surveillance video, and his conclusions had been a mixed bag.

She drove home after the meeting, fixed a sandwich, and then settled in behind the desk of her home office. From her briefcase, she fished out Giff's report and the notes she had taken during the meeting. Between bites of a turkey on wheat, she carefully reviewed both.

During their meeting, Giff had detailed the methodology used in arriving at his conclusions, sprinkling in various caveats, qualifications, and questions. He had prefaced his remarks by reminding her he had a reputation to protect. He would not testify to any opinion he did not firmly hold and that had not been scientifically tested. He followed with an explanation of the science of facial recognition.

Her notes read:

- *faceprints are like fingerprints—they are unique*
- *every face has defining characteristics, like the width of the nose and eyes, jaw and cheekbone structure*
- *facial recognition software takes these features, and others, and converts them to a numerical code*
- *comparison of this code or faceprint can lead to matches in databases or photos/videos taken of individuals*
- *comparison of 3-D images can be more accurate than comparison of flat 2-D images*
- *accuracy of the comparison depends on many factors, such as lighting, angle, expression*
- *facial recognition on still frontal frames can be 99% accurate*
- *accuracy percentage can decrease as a result of bad lighting, makeup, facial tilt up or down*
- *facial recognition testimony has been admitted and excluded in courts across the country*
- *need to prove up hotel surveillance tape—affidavit from hotel management?*
- *Giff made a copy of the disk and did not manipulate or alter the one we gave him*
- *did enlarge, enhance, adjust the color of the images on the copy compared height, size, gait, and other non-facial traits of the subject in the surveillance video with the digital video of Christine Connors*

Jackie put her notes aside and began to read the conclusion of Giff's report. It was 33 pages long, including exhibits. The first part recited his credentials and referenced his curriculum vitae, which was attached as Exhibit 1. Next came a detailed description of the science of facial recognition, followed by the methodology he had used in reaching his opinions, every statement supported by scientific references.

Finally, there was Giff's conclusion:

> *"In my expert opinion, it is more likely than not that the subject in the hotel video described above and contained in Exhibit 4 hereto is the same as the subject contained in the video taken of Christine Connors described above and contained in Exhibit 16. My opinion is based on the factors listed in my report above, including comparison of the noses, lips, cheekbones, and jaws of both subjects using facial recognition software, as well as a comparison of their heights, weights, gaits, and other non-facial features."*

Jackie flipped through the exhibits, including still frames taken from the video footage at the hotel, as well as the footage she shot of Christine Connors. Some of the frames had been enlarged, some had dots and measurements on them, and some were close-up shots of individual features.

She laid the report on her desk and rubbed her eyes, Giff's caveats coming back to her: this was a very close call, and he'd put the chances at just over fifty-fifty that there was a match. If the eyes had been captured he could have been much more certain in his conclusion, but all he could offer was to do his best on cross. To be honest, he had serious questions about whether his conclusions should even be admitted in court as evidence.

Jackie had promised to contact Tipps after she got Giff's report. She nestled in the chair in the corner, kicked off her flats, and gave him a call. She got voice mail and left him a short message. He returned the call fifteen minutes later.

"I saw you called. Sorry I couldn't take it. I was in a meeting. What's up?"

"I met with Gifford Duncan this morning, my facial recognition guy."

"I hope you have good news for me?"

"Well, it's not bad news," Jackie replied timidly.

"What did he say?"

"He believes the woman in the hotel surveillance video is likely Christine Connors."

"That's fantastic—"

"Don't get too excited. Because we don't have the subject's eyes on the surveillance video, his opinion doesn't carry a high probability."

"How high?"

"The best he can say is it is more probable than not that it is Christine in the hotel surveillance video."

"Shit, that may not be enough to get it into evidence at trial."

"I know. If I were the judge, I don't know if I'd let it in."

"Would you email me a copy of the report?"

"I'll send it over right after we get off the phone."

Tipps thought for a moment, and then asked, "You don't mind if I use his findings in our discussions with Christine Connors, do you?"

"What discussions?"

"Cowan wants to make a deal."

"Has he offered her anything yet?"

"Not yet, but we've met with her. She stonewalled—didn't say a word until she walked out of the meeting and basically muttered over her shoulder that . . ."

Jackie finished his sentence. "You were full of it."

"Rhymes with."

Jackie laughed and then asked, "So what do you think of her lawyer?"

"Reed Travers? He's one of the best. I actually like him, and that's rare for me. You can probably guess what I think of most criminal defense lawyers."

"Yeah, I'm the same way." Jackie paused, and then added, "I'll have to get authorization from Jace, but maybe you can use the report as leverage. You don't have to give it to them. Just say you've got an expert who can put her in Stein's suite the day he died."

"That's what I was thinking."

"You find out anything from the airline records?"

"Christine didn't fly to Paris before the murder but . . ." Tipps let the suspense build for a moment before saying, "I looked at a map and noticed Milan is much closer to Èze than Paris."

"So you checked the flight manifests from DFW to Milan?"

"Yep, and she was on one of the flights two days before Stein was killed."

"Great work, Stan! Did she fly back from Milan afterwards?"

"Nope—she was smarter than that. Her return flight was out of Paris. It's one more piece of the puzzle. Hey, I'm sorry, but I've gotta run. I have a conference call in a few minutes. When you headed this way?"

"Don't have anything planned."

"Well, if you do, you've got my number."

Jackie clicked off and wondered if Tipps was going to keep sharing information if she didn't acknowledge his interest in her. She knew he was hitting on her. All the signs had been there when they had first met in person at Angelo's—the lingering looks, the overexuberant laughs at her jokes. She shrugged it off and called Jace to fill him in on the latest.

CHAPTER 29

He wanted everything on videotape—every movement, every look, every shudder, every squirm, every scream—muffled or not, he hadn't decided which. He wanted her eyes, her lips, her nipples—he was sure they would be hard that night, hard the entire time, he knew this from experience—her legs, her feet, and, of course, her pussy captured from every angle. Should he shave it, like some of the porn stars did, so every detail could be seen, every penetration intimately documented? Or should he film some of their activities that night with her au naturel and then shave it later? He would let primal instincts dictate—no need to script things too carefully. After all, spontaneity could be a very good thing.

In his line of work, he had learned how to use a camera. It was a requirement of the trade. Catching the cheating husband pumping his wife's best friend, his law partner's daughter, or getting a blowjob from some male intern had resulted in some high-dollar divorce settlements for his female clients over the years. But those clips had been taken on the fly with a handheld and were usually jumpy and of non-Hollywood quality. This would be different.

He was looking for perfection this time. Although he had never used a tripod before, it was easy to set up. Satisfied, he screwed the Canon Vixia into place, and then he practiced maneuvering the camera up and down with the elevation crank and moving it from side to side with the pan handle, eyeing the images in the camera window as he did so. It was time for the dress rehearsal.

The voluptuous silicone mannequin lay on the iron bed frame, blue eyes wide open, staring contently at the drab concrete ceiling above. Leather restraints bound her wrists and ankles. She looked eerily real, her lips puckered as if she were about to say something.

Randazzo, barefooted and wearing a wife beater and jeans, walked silently over to his date for the evening, whispered something in her ear, and kissed her gently on the lips before lifting up her head and tying a black blindfold over her eyes.

He returned to the camera, adjusted its height one last time, and began filming. After shooting from several different angles, Randazzo rewound and watched. Not satisfied, he repeated the exercise—better, much better. He returned to the mannequin, which he affectionately called Liz.

Randazzo unhooked the restraints, lifted Liz off the bed, and moved her to a metal chair. It was time to get her dressed for the evening, and he felt quite sure a black leather bustier would be perfect for the occasion. He hurried to a bench where he had methodically laid out all of what he—and she—would need for the evening. Bustier in hand, he returned to his date and guided her arms between the spaghetti straps, carefully positioning her breasts so that the desired amount of cleavage showed, and then zipped her in. Randazzo's gaze veered toward the triangular steel structure he had assembled hours—or was it days ago? Time had become elusive and, quite frankly, meaningless. His mind had literally become one-track, with a singular, all-consuming goal.

Randazzo squatted down to Liz's level and lifted her arms around his neck, placing his around her waist. He stood, holding her tightly, and waltzed around the dank basement in perfect time to a tune he hummed loudly and off-key before coming to a halt in front of the Tower of Pleasure. Since Liz couldn't stand on her own, he decided to attach the neck collar first; it would keep her firmly in place while he slipped her wrists and ankles into the restraints. His plan worked without a hitch. He stepped away to admire his date, blindfolded and helpless, a hard-to-read expression on her face. He returned and adjusted the metal pole in the middle of the Tower base so that it was inches below Liz's pussy, then he placed an electronic massager on top of the pole and turned it on. A pang of pleasure surged through his groin as the massager began to buzz, his thoughts fixating on what it would be like when make-believe became reality. Randazzo darted over to the camera, made some adjustments, and began filming.

The handcuffs dangled from a remote-controlled pulley Randazzo had attached to the ceiling. After freeing her neck, arms, and wrists from the Tower restraints, he slow-danced her over, her feet grazing the top of his. With the remote, Randazzo lowered the pulley and slipped the cuffs over Liz's wrists, securing them in place, stepped back, and raised the pulley until the tips of Liz's toes brushed back and forth across the concrete floor. He retreated to the camera, took some practice footage, and then unhitched Liz and laid her carefully back on the bed.

After removing the camera from the tripod, Randazzo collapsed in the metal chair and scooted up to the table. With a cable, he connected his camera to the laptop. As he watched the screen fill with images of Liz, he felt himself grow hard. He reached for his zipper but tamped down the urge. The night would be here soon enough—a night with no moon. And then the real fun would begin.

CHAPTER 30

Dressed in a navy blue suit, white blouse, and black heels, Christine Connors followed her lawyer's lead into the windowless conference room and took a seat at the table. Reed slid into the chair next to her and pulled out a legal pad from his leather briefcase, which he placed on the table. Neither spoke—there could be a hidden camera in the room, for all they knew. Reed monotonously twirled a pen between his fingers while Christine toyed with a ring she had purchased several years back.

Five minutes later, their hosts appeared: Reginald Cowan III, wearing his signature red suspenders and bow tie, and Agent Stan Tipps, clad in a sport jacket and button-down dress shirt, open at the neck. Reed rose and shook hands with both men. Christine remained seated, nodding in their direction as they greeted her but saying nothing.

Cowan sat across the table from Christine. She thought about moving to the other side of her lawyer but decided against it. She didn't want to give Cowan the satisfaction of knowing he had gotten to her.

Tipps stood for a moment, looking around the room, and then slowly made his way to the end of the table and took a chair. Then Cowan draped his suit jacket over the back of the chair and rolled up his sleeves, just like he had the last time she and Reed had been there. Christine sensed this routine had been used on countless occasions. She shook her head and muttered something under her breath.

No one took notice, and Cowan began.

"First, I want to thank both of you for coming. I know everyone has busy schedules, but I thought it important that we meet."

His eyes darted back and forth between his guests before he continued. "What I wanted to meet about is—well, honestly, I wanted to be up front with both of you and share some information I thought might be of interest. Information that pertains to our investigation."

Cowan pulled two manila folders from the briefcase next to his chair and slid one across the table toward Christine and one toward Reed. Reed opened the folder and began to scan the contents. Christine glanced down at the folder and then looked up, her expression one of disinterest.

Cowan caught her eyes and challenged, "I wouldn't be so dismissive, Ms. Connors." He flashed her a just-wait-and-see smile before continuing. "Under the first tab of the folder in front of you you will find copies of plane manifests. Do you see those?"

Reed busied himself reading the first documents in his packet. Christine called Cowan's bluff and left her folder undisturbed.

"You will note that, for privacy purposes, we have blocked out the names of all passengers except for," Cowan paused and nodded in the direction of Christine, "Ms. Connors."

Reed interrupted the flow. "What does my client going to Milan have to do with anything?"

"A great deal, I'm afraid. You see, the Malpensa airport in Milan is only a four-hour drive from Èze. And you will recall, Reed, that's where Mr. Stein was staying when he . . ." Cowan allowed his sentence to die, his stare staying with Christine.

Changing tactics, Christine met Cowan's stare, her blue eyes steely and unforgiving, admitting no guilt, granting no ground.

Reed asked, "And the plane manifest from the Paris flight?"

"Glad you brought that up. It shows Ms. Connors flew back from Paris rather than Milan, a very clever move that would have thrown off most detectives but not Agent Tipps."

Reed scoffed. "All this shows me is that my client went on a shopping spree abroad, plain and simple. It's no secret that Milan and Paris are the gold standard when it comes to fashion."

"You'll have to save that for the jury, Reed, and I am pretty damn confident they won't be buying. You see, juries don't like coincidences, and it just so happens that your client flew to Milan days before Stein's murder"—Cowan mockingly cleared his throat—"oh, excuse me, his untimely demise, and then returned to the States just days later via Paris. That's a big pill for a jury to swallow, don't you think?" Cowan hesitated for effect and then continued. "But there's more. I like to save the best for last. Please turn to the tab in your packet labeled 'Expert Report.' Do you see that?"

It was Barnum & Bailey time and Cowan was the ringmaster.

"A facial recognition expert compared video surveillance footage taken at the hotel in Èze where Mr. Stein met such an ignominious end with footage taken of Ms. Connors getting out of her Mercedes and walking to the office building owned by her and her daddy just days ago."

Christine sensed a slow burn in her stomach and noticed her fingers shaking ever so slightly, but shaking nevertheless. She lowered her hands under the table and, as inconspicuously as she could, took a deep breath. Cowan glanced up from his folder, and their eyes met once again and remained locked in a mental duel much like that of two arm wrestlers desperately vying for advantage. Reed's voice broke the deadlock.

"So my client was in Italy within days of Mr. Stein's death as a result of an accidental drug overdose. As you will recall, that was the conclusion reached by the French authorities and one you will have to rebut if you continue to pursue this preposterous theory. And this, this expert—"

Cowan interrupted, "Will testify that the woman who was in Stein's bungalow the day he died was none other than your client."

Banging his hand against the table angrily, Reed responded, "That's ridiculous. I've seen the hotel video, and there's no way any expert could draw that conclusion and justify it scientifically—no way. I'll keep it out. No judge will allow that kind of voodoo in the courtroom."

"I beg to differ. Facial recognition is highly scientific. It has been widely discussed and vouched for in numerous well-regarded journals. The link is made by visual observation in conjunction with a detailed analysis of characteristics performed by a software program—the same software used, I might add, to identify one of the Boston Marathon bombers. You remember that case, don't you?"

Reed didn't respond. Christine shifted in her chair, pretending to adjust her skirt. She thought about leaving but nixed the idea, instead electing to go on the offensive. "Mr. Cowan, your absurd assertions and easily debunked evidence—and I use the word 'evidence' very loosely—don't merit a response."

Pushing his chair back from the table, Reed interrupted his client. "We are through here. Christine?"

"No, I want to finish. I repeat, they don't merit a response, Mr. Cowan. But I do have one question. Why do you keep asking to meet with us? If you have a case, then file it. That's the way I practice law. Otherwise, you go your way and I'll go mine."

"What I'd like is your cooperation, Ms. Connors."

"Excuse me?" Christine glared at the enemy.

"There is no doubt in my mind that you know all about the scheme your father and Dr. Crimm carried out for years to the tune of millions in fraudulent jury awards. I want you to testify to what you know."

"You want me to rat out my dad. Is that what you're saying?"

Cowan nodded.

"It'll be a cold day in hell when I turn on someone who has been everything to me. Even if I knew something, I wouldn't tell you." Christine turned to Reed. "Now I'm ready to go."

Reed and Christine rose and stormed out of the conference room. Christine's manila folder lay on the table, Reed's parked in the briefcase at his side.

* * *

Moments later, in Reed's office, Christine was pacing from one side of the room to the other.

"Reed, I hope I didn't give anything away in there. I gotta admit, Cowan scared the shit out of me. Like I said when we first met, I've never been a client before, so I'm not used to being on the receiving end, and I'll tell you, it doesn't feel very good."

"I hear you, but trust me, you kept your cool just fine. I really liked the way you took over at the end. You seemed totally in control, like nothing he said had shaken you in the least."

"It was all an act. I mean, my stomach was literally—I kid you not—in knots at the end of the meeting. I had to do something to take my mind off how nervous I was." Christine sighed and asked, "So what do you think? He threw out some pretty strong stuff in there."

"Let's talk about the flight manifests first." Reed retrieved the folder from his briefcase but, before opening it, added, "By the way, I noticed you left yours on the conference table, never even opened it the whole time we were there—very ballsy."

"Glad you enjoyed the show, which is all it was. Curiosity was killing me. I wanted to know what that son of a bitch had on me in the worst kind of way."

Reed smiled and said, "Okay, here we go. According to this document," he held it up, "looks like you flew from DFW to Milan via Miami leaving DFW on American Flight 1596 at 9:05 a.m. and arriving in Milan at 9:15 the next morning. That was two days before Mr. Stein was found dead at the hotel in Èze. Any reason—"

"Could I see that?"

Reed handed her the document, which she closely inspected and then replied, "No, that seems right. I can't remember the exact date I left, but I don't have any reason to doubt what this shows."

Christine read through the document once more before handing it back to Reed.

"What was the purpose for the trip?"

"Just like you said. I had been burning the candle at both ends and needed a break. No better way for me to let off some steam than to go on a shopping spree in Europe. Look, this isn't the first time I've hopped on a plane and flown to Milan or Paris or London or Madrid. I bet I've been on European shopping jaunts four or five times in the last ten years or so, and I like going by myself. Having someone tag along just complicates things. I do what I want, when I want."

"I get it. If you have any evidence of purchases you made while in Milan, where you stayed, any documentation that establishes when you were there and what you were doing, that would be great."

"I'm sure I do. I remember buying some gorgeous shoes. Maybe I'll wear them for you sometime." Christine grinned suggestively and then added, "And, if I'm not mistaken, a suede outfit that almost broke the bank. It was knockout. I simply couldn't help myself."

"How long did you stay in Milan?" Reed asked.

Christine thought for a minute and then answered, "Two or three nights. I can't remember exactly. I was pretty jet-lagged when I first got there, and slept most of that day. I went shopping the next day, and then headed to Paris."

"Why Paris?"

"Why not? First of all, it's my favorite city in the world—so beautiful. I love the architecture, the museums, riding up and down the Seine on the Batobus, strolling through Notre Dame, going to Montmartre, you name it. Paris is just the best. And the shopping and food are over-the-top great. As a matter of fact, I don't think I've ever gone to Europe without including Paris in my itinerary. That would be nothing short of blasphemy!"

Reed was momentarily mesmerized, his eyes on Christine's, his thoughts on strolling down the Champs-Élysées with her arm locked in his.

Forcing the image out of his mind, he said, "I know what you mean. I have only been there once but I loved it. Can't wait to go back." He flashed her a look that made his intimation clear before continuing. "Did you keep any receipts?"

"I am sure I can get my hotel receipts. I think I put them on Amex. I took the train from Milan and might have that receipt as well. I'll just have to check. I don't think I will have any problem at all giving you what you need to show that I was in both Milan and Paris, shopping, sightseeing, and, in the case of Paris, eating."

"One thing I don't enjoy is eating alone."

"Doesn't bother me at all. I love to people-watch, and you can get plenty of that over a long meal at an expensive Parisian restaurant."

"Well, I feel pretty confident we can make a convincing argument that you were in Europe for reasons unrelated to Stein. The fact that he died while you were on the Continent doesn't prove anything."

Christine nodded, and then asked, "What about this expert Cowan was talking about?"

Reed turned back to the folder and thumbed to the appropriate tab. "We only have excerpts from the report. We don't know who authored it. The name has been redacted. Cleverly, Cowan left in portions of his, or her, professional résumé."

"And?"

"Graduated from MIT with honors. Looks like he has done a considerable amount of testifying, although Cowan has redacted the case names. The subject matter of his testimony is detailed, and some of it deals with perp identification through facial recognition."

"Does that mean the court admitted his testimony in those cases?" Christine asked.

"I can't tell from this. You take a look." Reed handed the folder to Christine, who studied it for several minutes and then gave it back.

"Neither can I. So what's our plan?"

"If Cowan files charges against you, I'll file a Daubert motion to exclude it."

"I have had a few of those motions filed against my experts in some cases."

"So you know the drill?"

"Yep, the methodology the expert uses can't be junk science. I think that's the term the Daubert opinion uses. It's got to be accepted in the scientific community. There are other hoops the proponent of the evidence has to jump through, but that's the gist of it, as I recall."

"You got it. I've never had a prosecutor try to use an expert like this one. I'll do some research, but my instinct tells me we have a reasonably good chance of keeping the testimony out."

Christine stared into space for several minutes before asking, "Don't read anything into this, but what do you think Cowan would be willing to do? You know, if I cooperated?" She was uncomfortable asking the question but she needed to know.

"Are you thinking—"

"No, no, no—don't get the wrong impression, but it's always good to know where the other side is coming from, whether you're seriously considering trying to do a deal or not. At least that's the way I operate with my civil docket."

Reed bit his lower lip while he thought about the question and then offered, "My guess is he'd probably drop the murder charge if you pled to commercial bribery and paid some restitution. Like I said, that's just a guess."

"And when he talks about cooperation, what do you think he means?"

"He'll want to pin down what you're going to testify to before he even considers making a deal—the stronger your testimony, the better the deal."

"I know you've got good arguments to make on my behalf, but let's face it, a trial is a crapshoot. There's no way to know what twelve people are going to do. And although Cowan is full of it, the jury might go with him."

"There's always that chance, but—"

"And if that happened, I could spend the rest of my life in prison. I've got to consider all my options here. Let me ask you this. Any deal I might make wouldn't be contingent upon the jury finding my dad guilty, would it?"

"I've never heard of that."

"Any chance of immunity? If I could walk, keep my law license—"

"You'd consider testifying?"

"I didn't say that. I just want to know how the system works."

"I doubt Cowan would give you immunity, but it depends on how strong your testimony is and how bad he wants to see your dad behind bars."

"I bet you think I'm a real bitch, don't you—asking questions like that?"

Reed considered the question before replying, "Not at all. This is serious stuff. We've got to look at all the possibilities."

"I could really use a drink right now."

Reed walked over to the built-in bar in the corner of his office, opened a cabinet door, and held up a bottle of Jack Daniel's. "A little Tennessee sipping whiskey sound good?"

Christine kicked off her heels, took off her suit jacket, and tiptoed over to Reed. She put her arms around his neck and kissed him—at first gently and then feverishly, as if she couldn't get enough. Before he could pour the first drink, she led him back to the couch and pushed him down. As he watched, she began undressing slowly, in striptease fashion, unbuttoning her blouse and sliding it gracefully off each shoulder, unzipping her skirt and swaying gently in time as it dropped to her ankles, reaching behind for the bra clasp and gracefully unhooking it—holding the bra in place for a tempting second and then letting it go, her eyes never leaving Reed's. She ringed the top of her see-through lace panties with slender fingers and moved closer to the couch. Reed reached for her hand and gently pulled her toward him. As he leaned up to kiss her, she placed a finger over his lips and then whispered, "Not just yet. I want that drink first."

CHAPTER 31

Tipps glanced out the plane window. The pilot had just announced they would be landing in Albuquerque shortly and should be at the gate on time.

The ATF had finished its examination of the bombed-out Cadillac where Dr. Howell Crimm had met his fate. DNA had been found on fragments from the car hood and the door on the driver's side. Some of the DNA samples taken from the wreckage matched that of Crimm; two of the samples did not.

After running the DNA through a database, investigators had found a match to one Jaime Garza, a Santa Fe resident with multiple brushes with the law, ranging from lifting a hoodie at a local Walmart to hotwiring a Nissan truck and slamming it into a telephone pole during a high-speed chase by local police. He had spent time in jail—two years for the latter offense—but, in most instances, pled guilty in exchange for short prison sentences or probation, depending on the gravity of the offense. With only one exception, his counsel of record had been Donato Medina, Esquire.

Before making the trip to Santa Fe, Tipps thought about calling the local police and having them pay Garza a visit but rejected the idea. His instincts told him he couldn't trust them. He had talked with the officer in charge of the investigation on several occasions and had gotten the distinct impression he wasn't the least bit interested in seeing the real culprit behind bars. Comments like "Hell, the bastard owed the mob a ton," "This has all the markings of a mob hit," "From what I can tell, the guy was a drunk and a gambling addict," and "Hell, his family didn't even come to his funeral" all spoke volumes to Tipps. No, he needed to interview Garza personally to have any chance of getting at the truth.

As Tipps started up his rental car, he asked Siri for directions to the address he had pulled up for Garza. Thirty minutes later, he was in front of a run-down apartment complex in a seedy part of town. He walked up to what appeared to be the complex entrance, and he noticed a door to one side with a sign above it with metal letters that spelled "Man g r's O fi e." He knocked on the door, worrying that the peeling and rotting wood would disintegrate under his fingers.

Almost immediately a short Hispanic woman cracked it open and said in a heavy accent, "I hep you?"

Tipps introduced himself, making it a point to speak slowly, and flashed her some identification. The door opened, and he was ushered inside. There was a folding metal chair in front of a metal desk, but Tipps elected to stand, as did the woman, who said her name was Gladys Sanchez. He got right to the point.

"I am looking for one of your residents—Jaime Garza. Do you know him?"

Señora Sanchez nodded. "I know him, but he not here any longer."

"Do you know where he is?"

There was a shake of the head accompanied by "No, I not know."

"How long ago did he leave?"

"I not know—*una semana*, a week? Somethin' li' that."

"Could I see his apartment?"

"I sorry, Señor. I already rent it."

Sighing, Tipps looked around the room. He didn't have a search warrant and probably wouldn't turn up anything anyway. He thanked the manager and walked briskly back to his car. Hopefully, his meeting with Donato Medina would go better. Tipps didn't like dry runs.

Medina's office was in a nearby strip mall. As Tipps walked through the front door, he was greeted by an attractive, thirty-something Latina seated behind a desk.

She asked, "Sir, how can I help you?"

"I'm looking for Mr. Medina. Is he here?"

"Do you have an appointment?" She smiled and worked him with her brown eyes.

He thought to himself that the woman could have been a model but kept his business face on and replied, "I'm Agent Tipps with the FBI, and I need to talk with him."

He showed her his badge, causing her eyes to widen. She rose from the desk and said, "I'll be right back."

She opened the door at the back of the reception area and disappeared. Several minutes later, a short, rotund man with thinning black hair slicked over from one side of his head to the other followed the receptionist out of the office and walked confidently toward Tipps.

Donato Medina thrust out his hand. "Agent Tipps, it's a pleasure to meet you."

"Likewise. Do you mind if we talk in your office?"

"Not at all. Come on back." Medina headed back the way he had come, and Tipps followed. After Medina was seated behind his desk and Tipps in the chair in front, Medina asked, "So how can I help you?"

"Jaime Garza. I believe you know him."

"I do. I have represented him on a number of criminal matters. He's not in trouble with the FBI, is he?"

"He could be. I assume you know about the murder of Dr. Howell Crimm?"

"I do. It was all over the local news. I knew Dr. Crimm. Such a tragedy! I was scheduled to meet with him the morning he died." Medina decided to go on the offensive and show he was a concerned citizen who wanted to help in any way he could. "We worked together on a case years ago."

"Do you remember the name of the case?"

Leaning back in his chair, Medina stared at the ceiling, massaging his forehead as if that might jog his memory. After several seconds, he looked at Tipps and shook his head. "I just can't think of it—sorry. I am sure you can understand. I've handled a lot of cases over the years."

"So what were you and Crimm going to meet about?"

"He called me and said that someone with your agency had paid him a visit. It scared him half to death. He wanted to meet with me and get my advice on what he should do."

Tipps thought about fessing up to the fact that he was the one who had dropped in on Crimm but decided against it.

"I assume he told you what the FBI agent had asked him about?"

"Actually, he didn't, but that's not unusual. A lot of my clients don't like to discuss their sensitive matters over the phone."

"Do you remember anything else you discussed over the phone?"

"Let's see. I did tell him to bring anything with him that might relate to what he and the agent discussed. He said he would, and then we hung up. That's all I can remember. The call didn't take very long."

"What was the name of the case you worked on together?"

Medina thought for a moment and replied, "I honestly can't remember."

"So he didn't show for the appointment?"

"That's right. Our meeting was scheduled for nine or ten the next morning. And he never made it."

"Why didn't you call the police?"

"If I called the police every time one of my clients, or potential clients, didn't show for a meeting, they would be ready to shoot me—sorry, bad choice of words." Medina smiled. "No, really, no-shows in my line of work happen all the time."

"Do you remember how you learned about Crimm's death?"

Medina shook his head. "Not really. Could have been someone told me, or I might have heard it on the local news. I have no idea."

"So why didn't you alert the police then?"

"And tell them what? That Crimm had missed a meeting with me that morning? I had no idea what he wanted to talk with me about. I hadn't seen him in years. I didn't think a call from me would be of any help at all or I would have."

"Going back to Jaime Garza—I assume you kept files on all of the cases where you represented him?"

"I did at the time but probably threw them away. That's my practice once I plead a client. What's the sense in keeping the files?"

"When was the last time you spoke with Mr. Garza?"

"The last time I represented him—probably over a year ago, at least. And you say he is in trouble? Do you mind telling me what for?"

"We think he may have had something to do with Crimm's murder."

"And what makes you think that?"

"His DNA was found on some of the car fragments."

Medina shook his head. "Jaime had a hard time staying out of trouble, but they were petty crimes. Except for the time when he stole that car or truck, I can't remember which. Before going to jail, he swore to me he'd never do anything like that again. Said it wasn't worth it. I mean, he wasn't a bad kid. I just can't imagine Jaime being involved in a murder. Blowing up someone in his car? No way."

"I assume you don't know where Garza is?"

"Like I said, I haven't talked with him in over a year. I have no idea."

"If he contacts you, you'll let me know."

"Of course," Medina responded without hesitation.

Tipps rose from his chair and Medina did the same. The two men shook hands, and Tipps gave him a business card.

Medina followed Tipps to the front door and watched him get into his rental car and pull out of the mall parking lot. He returned to his office, retrieved a disposable cell phone from his desk drawer, and dialed a number from memory.

CHAPTER 32

"Do you think he was lying?" Cowan asked as he gazed out the third-story window of his office on Commerce Street in downtown Dallas. "Did you get any sense at all?"

"Lying like a rug, no doubt about it. He was just too smooth. Acted like he wanted to help in any way he could. Overplayed the part."

"Any idea where Garza might be?" Cowan asked, his back still to Tipps, eyes fixed on the street below.

"No way to find that son of a bitch. He's probably somewhere south of the border. You know how that goes."

Sighing, Cowan wheeled around and ambled back to his throne. "So we're pretty damn sure we know what happened, but we don't have any hard evidence to prove it. Would that be a fair statement?"

Tipps nodded. "I'd agree with that. We have a strong circumstantial case, but that's all it is—no DNA proof linking Connors or his daughter to the murders, no fingerprints, no money trail, nothing that juries have come to expect these days after watching all those true-crime shows on TV."

"No doubt about it. The bar is higher than it used to be to get a conviction. We need more. I don't suppose you think there is a chance the daughter will flip?"

"I couldn't tell. No way to predict what she'll do."

"We need to get a look inside that fucking law firm—see their accounting records, their emails, who they sent texts to, who they called. We need their laptops, their phones—everything."

"No way a judge is going to give us that, not based on what we have now. It would shut down their law firm."

"You're probably right. But we do have the affidavits of Crimm's assistants, and we could get one from Leah Rosen as well. With the circumstantial evidence we've got, along with those affidavits, we might just have enough."

"Didn't you agree not to do anything with those affidavits unless you got Forman and his client to go along?"

"I did, but I'm not going to let a technicality get in the way of putting Connors and his daughter behind bars. We'll give Forman a courtesy call, and if he and his client agree—great. If not, we'll go forward without them. Hell, let's call him right now."

Without waiting for Tipps to comment, Cowan swiveled around, buzzed his secretary, and asked her to make the call. Minutes later, Jace was on the line.

"Jace, I've got Agent Tipps in here with me. Mind if I put you on the speaker?"

Jace agreed, Cowan pressed a button on his speakerphone, and the three were in conference. Jace spoke first. "I've got a meeting out of the office in thirty minutes. We'll have to keep this brief."

"No worries. We'll be done in five, ten minutes at the most. I just wanted to bring you up to speed. Stan just got back from Santa Fe. We've learned that the guy who planted the bomb under

Crimm's car was a former client of a local lawyer out there—Donato Medina—who, interestingly, has ties to Connors."

"What kind of ties?"

"Tipps searched the court records in Santa Fe and found that Connors hired Medina as local counsel in a case they tried together years ago. And guess who their expert was? Dr. Howell Crimm. No doubt Connors brought Medina in as local counsel to sway the Hispanic jurors. And it worked—they got a several-million-dollar verdict."

"Fits the pattern."

"Absolutely does. I'm sure Medina was given a nice slice of that recovery, probably more than he had made in his entire career. Hell, he's a bit player—handles divorces, slip and falls, criminal cases, whatever it takes to pay the rent. And the prints our ATF guys lifted from the car wreckage match those of one of Medina's clients. We are pretty damn sure Connors called in a chit for referring that lucrative piece of work to Medina, told him he wanted Crimm dead."

"And you think Medina hired his former client to do the bombing?"

"Right. And that former client has, unfortunately, disappeared somewhere south of the border."

"So you're confident that Connors is not only a liar and a crook but a murderer as well?"

"You got it. But all we have so far is circumstantial stuff. We can't pin the tail on the donkey. Not yet, anyway."

"Jackie tells me the investigation into the insurance fraud is progressing nicely."

"It is. By the way, Stan has nothing but good things to say about Ms. McLaughlin. I told him he'd like her, that she was one of the best on the force back when I was a prosecutor down in Austin."

It was all Jace could do not to respond. He so desperately wanted to call Cowan out for the skunk he really was. But his contempt for Cowan and those like him needed to remain under cover. He stifled a response and let his former nemesis continue.

"Stan and Ms. McLaughlin have come up with some good stuff. But it's all circumstantial, which brings me to the purpose of my call."

There was a pause, and then Jace asked, "And?"

"I want to get a warrant. I want their laptops, their financial records, their phones. We've got to connect the dots, show a kick-back payment to some sham corporation set up by Stein, find an incriminating email from Connors to Crimm, that type of thing."

"Don't you have enough to get a judge—"

"I don't think so. Hell, Jace, we'd be shutting down Connors' firm. A judge is going to want some pretty strong evidence before he'll even think about doing that."

"So you want to use the Patel and Coleman affidavits."

"Yep. We don't have a choice. And we need an affidavit from your client as well, swearing to what she wrote about Connors. Those could carry the day with the judge."

"I'll have to talk with all of them."

"That's why we're calling. This is urgent, Jace. Can you get back to us by this time tomorrow?"

"I'll do my best." Jace glanced at his watch.

"Thanks for your help," Cowan responded as he hit the button ending the call and turned his chair back toward Tipps.

"What if you don't hear from him by then?" Tipps asked.

"Like I said, we'll go forward with or without their approval. I just don't like ruffling feathers if I don't have to."

CHAPTER 33

Darrin waved to Levi Pass as he made his way down the sidewalk to his car. After closing the door to her condo, she walked barefoot into the kitchen and poured herself another glass of pinot grigio. Chris Isaak was crooning "Wicked Game" from the speakers in her den. She thought about turning off the stereo but opted to let him sing on, the guitar haunting, the lyrics conjuring up not-too-distant memories.

She was confused, so confused. Where was her relationship with Levi going, anyway? He was pushing way too hard, and she just wasn't feeling much of anything. Sure, she liked spending time with him, but she just couldn't get Jace out of her head. Thoughts of their late nights at the office together, their dinner dates, their surreal trip to New Orleans kept snaking their way into her mind. While she was trying to concentrate on a file at work, while she was trying to fall asleep at night, even while she and Levi were together, Jace always seemed to show up, no matter how hard she fought it. Damn it!

Darrin took a healthy sip—more like a chug—of wine, closed her eyes, and winced. She hadn't seen it coming, but if she were honest with herself, Levi's confession of his feelings toward her that night shouldn't have been much of a surprise. Her unconvincing and noncommittal response led to questions about the *real* reason she'd left Fort Worth. He was right. She wasn't being fair. While Levi was thinking about her, her thoughts were with another man. So Darrin had told him about Jace—not everything, but enough. Enough to cause Levi's mood to darken, his eyes to lose their luster, his voice to take on a somber tone.

Obscured if not lost—at least for the moment—were the feelings he had just professed for her. She could feel his hurt but had no soothing balm to offer. What she had told him was the unvarnished truth: she was not over Jace, not yet, anyway. Levi had pushed her, he had wanted to know, and now he did.

The night had ended soon afterward. Levi told her he needed time to think. Losing his wife had taken a heavy toll. Plunging headfirst into an uncertain relationship, where his feelings might go unrequited, could leave an emotional scar impossible to erase. Without hesitation, Darrin had voiced her understanding and given him a free pass out of the relationship if he wanted one.

She looked at her empty wineglass and wondered whether she should pour another. She had a big day coming up at work, but what the hell. After finishing off the bottle, she collapsed on the couch and changed the music selection with her iPad. She had listened to enough of Chris Isaak for one evening. Taj Mahal's signature harmonica filled the room, followed by a raspy, soulful voice singing "she caught the Katy." She sang along with "and left me a mule to ride," a smile creasing her lips. Tonight had needed to happen. It was time to step back, take a deep breath, and not force the hand. Patience was definitely a virtue, just not one of hers. She would override impulse this time and let things play out in their own time.

* * *

Leah turned over in bed and looked at the clock on her bedside table. It was 2:30 in the morning. She was still awake, very awake, her mind revved up like a V-8 engine hitting on all cylinders. What to do? She had already taken one Ambien. Should she risk another? She had downed several gin and tonics over the course of the evening. Was it two or three? She couldn't recall for sure. She remembered her doctor telling her it was not a good idea to mix Ambien with alcohol. But don't they all say that? They're just afraid of getting sued. There you go. Those damn plaintiff lawyers screwing things up for everybody: warnings for this, warnings for that. She always laughed when she saw those Big Pharma commercials on television. They had a list of possible side effects that ranged from headache to death. Really!

Leah looked at the clock again. Now it was 2:35. What was the sense in just lying there, staring at the ceiling, pretending sleep was on the way? No way that was going to happen. No, there was too much going on in her life, too much bad shit happening with no end in sight, no escape hatch within reach. When would it all end? No one could say—not Jace, not Jackie, not even her old gun-range-beau-turned-friend Chip Holt. Sure, they all tried to reassure her with empty clichés reinforced by empathetic hugs and consoling looks: hang in there, it's going to get better, it's just a matter of time, the darkest hour is just before the dawn—words that rang hollow and did little to ease the pain.

Leah sat up on the side of the bed, her feet dangling short of the floor. She glanced at her Kindle next to the clock and thought maybe she should read. Before going to bed, she had downloaded a book at the top of the *New York Times* Bestseller List. Written in moronic prose with a plot that was implausible and excruciatingly boring, this "thriller" had all the characteristics that, in theory, should have taken her to dreamland. But soaking in a warm bath and reading a dull book hadn't done the trick on this occasion. There was no point in repeating the drill.

Leah picked up her cellphone. Was there anyone she could call? Her parents had moved from Chicago to a retirement community just outside Phoenix several years back. It was two hours earlier there—almost 1:00 in the morning—but her mom might still be up, night owl that she was. Leah shuddered. What a terrible idea! What was she thinking? Her relationship with her parents had been a rocky road for as long as she could remember. She had moved in with her grandmother at age sixteen, for crying out loud! She had nothing in common with her parents, nothing. They were regular churchgoers, Leah an agnostic; they were staunch Republicans, Leah leaned left; they were anti-gay, anti-abortion, anti-everything except guns, which they cherished as one of the great freedoms in America, and Leah was at the other end of the political spectrum on each issue. No way she should call them. She had made her way without their help all these years, and there was no need to change course now.

What about Abe? She knew he had trouble sleeping; he had complained about it occasionally. Maybe he was still up. Maybe he was sitting on the side of the bed just like she was. There was no one—no one—who could calm her down like Abe could. His willingness to listen, his kind eyes and soothing voice—they had worked their magic on her from time to time. It didn't matter whether he offered real solutions to her problems. What mattered was that he was there for her, ready to listen to whatever was bothering her. He had given her his private cell number and told her to call him anytime, day or night. And he didn't make hollow offers. So she scrolled through her contacts and tapped on his number. Abe answered on the second ring.

"Leah, is everything all right?"

"Everything is fine, relatively speaking anyway. I just couldn't sleep."

"Welcome to the club. I gave up an hour or so ago, and came downstairs and fixed a sandwich. It doesn't help the waistline but sometimes helps me get back to sleep."

"I've tried everything and nothing's working. I'm sorry to be calling—"

"Hey, I'm glad you did. It's nice to have some company at three in the morning."

Leah felt better already, Abe's charms relaxing her.

"You know, it's funny. I get through the days pretty damn good. But when I'm lying in bed alone, it feels like the walls are closing in on me, all these bad thoughts circling around in my head. I feel like everyone else in the world is asleep but me."

Abe laughed. "I'm probably not."

"These last few months have really worn me down. Did I tell you I'm seeing a psychiatrist?"

"You did. I think it's a good idea. Sometimes it can get a little overwhelming to go it alone. Leah, it's not a sign of weakness but a sign of strength, being willing to own up to a need and looking for a way to meet it."

"I've never thought of it that way."

"I saw a psychiatrist after my wife left me. I was in such a bad place back then. He helped me see there was life afterwards, helped me find my way to the other side. What's that saying about hard times? If they don't kill you, they make you stronger. Always nice to have someone reinforcing the thought that you are going to make it, and that's what he did for me."

"I just wish this whole lawsuit thing were behind me, but it keeps dragging on. And there's always the possibility of a jury not going with us. Abe, have you ever been sued—personally?"

"Technically, yes, when I went through my divorce. But not like you're talking about."

"Well, I hope you never are. Add to that this criminal investigation the U.S. attorney up in Dallas has launched. Don't get me wrong. I'm glad he's going after Connors and his daughter, but I'm all tangled up in that as well. Today Jace called and said the U.S. attorney wants me to give an affidavit for a motion he's filing."

"What kind of motion?"

"He wants the judge to let him seize the computers, accounting records, cellphones, you name it, of Connors's law firm."

Abe whistled. "They're going for the jugular."

"Yep. And I was on the phone all day with Patel and Coleman's lawyer, getting them to go along with the plan. It was a frigging nightmare."

"Which explains why you can't sleep."

"That's part of it. But I've been having trouble sleeping since all of this happened. That's one of the reasons I decided to see a psychiatrist. Plus, I've been looking over my shoulder ever since the jury let Randazzo go. You should see me. I have this ritual I go through every time I enter my condo and every time I get ready for bed. I look under the furniture, in all the closets, and every time I take a shower I have a flashback to that video the son of a bitch took. Sorry, Abe. I know I'm babbling."

"No, it's good for you to talk it through. You've still got Jackie on this, right?"

"Yeah, but there's not much she can do. We don't know where he is or what he's up to."

"You sure you don't want to move in over here until all of this blows over?"

"I'm sure. I've got to get through this on my own. Like you said, if it don't kill me—"

"Yeah, yeah. I get it."

"Abe, I think I'm ready to give sleep another try. I feel a lot better than I did before I called."

"You sure?"

"I'm sure. I've been droning on and on about me. What's keeping you up?"

"Oh, I don't know—just the way I'm wired, I guess. Get some sleep now, but if you can't, you have my number."

"Night, Abe."

"Night, Leah." Abe kept the cell to his ear for several seconds before placing it on the table in front of him. Talking with Leah had been good therapy for him as well. Maybe the demons would stay at bay long enough for him to grab a few hours of shut-eye too.

CHAPTER 34

Cowan was reading through the final draft of his motion when his secretary interrupted him to tell him that Jace was on the line.

"Jace, I've been waiting for your call. Hope you've got good news for me."

"I do. Leah will sign an affidavit, and Patel and Coleman are on board. I told them you would file their affidavits under seal. I assume that won't be a problem?"

"Not at all. You know I can't guarantee they will stay that way. I'm sure, once the shit hits the fan, opposing counsel will be bombarding the judge with motions, including one to unseal the affidavits. And my guess is the judge will allow them to test all the evidence supporting our motion, including cross-examining anyone who has sworn to facts that implicate their clients."

"That would be my guess as well, but I assured Patel's and Coleman's lawyers that we would do our best to keep their identities confidential."

"Understood. Say, would you mind drafting the affidavit for Ms. Rosen to sign?"

"No problem. I'll take care of it. I'll get it to you later this afternoon."

Cowan cleared his throat before saying, "There is one other thing. I was thinking about this last night. Even with the affidavits, there is a chance the judge might deny our motion." Cowan paused.

"I'm listening."

"What if you noticed Connors up for a deposition in that defamation case he filed against your client?"

"I plan on taking his deposition down the road, but only after I get complete answers to the discovery I served. Hell, his lawyer objected to everything. I've got one of my associates drafting a motion to compel as we speak."

"I understand, and normally that's the way to proceed. But as you know, this is not a normal case. We've got parallel criminal and civil proceedings going on, the outcomes dependent on one another to some degree. Sure, I know the burdens of proof are different, but the issues are damn similar. With what Stan and Ms. McLaughlin turned up, you might be able to trip him up in a deposition, piss him off and make him lose his cool. Look, I know this may be a long shot, but it's at least worth a try."

"Are you thinking I should depose him before or after you file your motion?"

"I say before. Once the motion is filed, he'll have his guard up. Knox probably wouldn't even produce him for deposition. She'd find some lame-ass excuse to delay. I think we may have a window here to get some valuable admissions out of the old bastard, admissions we could use to buttress my motion so the judge will have little choice but to grant it."

"Aren't you chomping at the bit to get your motion filed?"

"I am, but I'm more anxious to see it granted. Let's face it, our ability to nail Connors and his daughter could be riding on whether I can look up their skirts, see what kind of dirty laundry the two of them are hiding."

"I'll have to talk with Leah. Once I notice his deposition, I'm sure Knox will notice hers."

"Of course. When can you talk with her? Obviously the sooner the better."

"I'll call her right after we get off the line."

"Good. I'll hold off on filing my motion until I hear back from you."

* * *

Leah paced nervously back and forth in the common area of her condo as she talked with Jace on her cell. "So do you think we should do this? Look, I know what Connors is like. I don't know his lawyer—Sharlene whatever—but if she is anything like him, the gloves are gonna come off once you ask for his deposition."

"I can't argue with that," Jace said. "They'll go on the offensive, no doubt. That's his style, and hers too, from what I've heard."

"But you still haven't answered my question. Should we go down this road?"

"If I were you, I would—for a variety of reasons. Number one, you're going to have to give your deposition at some point. It's not something you can avoid. Two, you and I have gone over that article word by word on more occasions than I can count, and there is nothing in it that presents a problem. You painstakingly documented everything you wrote, and Coleman's and Patel's affidavits are a testament to that. Third, we get to take the first shot. I'll depose Connors before they depose you. If things go as Cowan and I hope, Connors might flip a switch and your deposition would get postponed and, in a best-case scenario, never taken. And last—"

"Hold on, I don't get that." Plopping down on the couch, Leah ran her free hand through her hair. "What do you mean my deposition might get postponed?"

"Well, if Connors gets flustered, his lawyer might stop the deposition, in which event we wouldn't get to you."

"I get it. Sorry I cut you off. What was the last reason?"

"We know Connors has a short fuse and a massive ego. I'm going to work on both and, if things come together right, we just might get the break we're looking for." Jace paused and then added, "Which might give Cowan what he needs to convince the judge to grant his motion."

"In a worst-case scenario, what should I expect?"

"Connors doesn't flinch during his deposition, I finish with him, and then you're up."

"What will they try to get from me?"

"Anything they can, anything that might embarrass you. I'm sure they have an investigator turning over rocks right now."

"Can they do that? I mean, what does that have to do with the case?"

"They want to find ways to impugn your credibility, make you into a bad person and hope that influences the jury's decision."

"But you'll object, won't you?"

"Depositions are different from trials. Judges frown on objections. The standard is whether the questioning is reasonably calculated to lead to discoverable evidence, a pretty loose standard."

Leah reflected back on some past indiscretions of her youth and could feel her face flush. She took a deep breath and then said, "I've made my decision. Go for it."

"Okay, I'll call Knox and get back to you with some dates."

"Thanks, Jace. The sooner the better."

CHAPTER 35

It was déjà vu: walking down this hall in this building toward this conference room. The case had been different, of course—a young student's body stolen from the grave and the cemetery sued for not doing more to prevent something so sinister from happening—but the central figures were the same.

They had tangled in the courtroom before, the headline-grabbing Cal Connors and the no-frills Jace Forman. They were stark contrasts in style, both finding their own way of connecting with those twelve people behind the rail.

Jace shuddered as they approached the conference room, remembering how scared his client in that grave-robbery case had been walking down this same corridor several years back—a country boy trying to make it in the city, finding himself a long way from the hills of Tennessee and getting ready to enter the lion's den. Jace hadn't been able to find the right words to calm him, making him easy prey for the Lone Wolf.

As Jace walked through the entryway to the conference room, he smiled faintly as he glanced up at the inscription in bold gold letters: "The Boneyard." Some people never change, Jace thought: once an asshole, always an asshole. But this time the circumstances were different. Jace was asking the questions. The tables had turned, at least for the time being.

Leah followed Jace into the conference room. The court reporter and videographer were already there. The court reporter was pecking on the keyboard of her steno machine, and the videographer was adjusting the angle of his camera.

After exchanging introductions, Jace took a seat on one side of the conference table, Leah sliding into the chair next to him. Sharlene Knox and her client made their grand entrance minutes later.

"Mr. Forman, although we haven't met, I feel like I know you."

Jace took her hand politely and replied perfunctorily, "My pleasure, Ms. Knox."

In a blustery tone, Cal exclaimed, "Damn, it's good to see you again, Jace. The last time you were here in the Boneyard was when I deposed . . ." Cal snapped his fingers, like that might make him remember, and asked, "What was his last name?"

"Masterson."

"Oh, yeah. Lonnie Masterson. Damn shame what happened to that poor boy." Cal shook his head and made his way around to Jace's side of the table.

Jace rose, bracing himself for what he knew was coming. With one hand, Cal grabbed Jace's hand and with the other squeezed his shoulder, pulled slightly away, and gave Jace the once-over. "I wish to hell we weren't always on the other side of the docket from each other. We'd make one helluva team." Cal winked and then released his grip. Pointedly ignoring Leah, he ambled around the end of the table and planted himself next to his lawyer.

"So, you ready to get this show on the road?" Cal flashed a give-me-your-best-shot look in Jace's direction and leaned back in his chair.

After the court reporter administered the oath and the videographer made a few final adjustments to the camera, the jousting commenced. Jace had decided to dispense with the preliminary admonitions and background questions. He wanted to draw blood early, before Cal had a chance to settle in.

"Mr. Connors, you know Donato Medina, don't you?"

"I do. Fine lawyer."

"You actually retained Mr. Medina to work with you on a case in Santa Fe, didn't you?"

"Let's see. Yeah, I think I did."

"Do you recall the name of that case?"

Cal thought for a moment before answering, "I'm sorry, but I can't recall it. Wait, maybe it was the . . ." Cal paused, shook his head, and then said, "No, that wasn't it. Sorry, but it just won't come to me."

Jace took a second to admire Cal's acting ability before prompting, "Could it have been the Rodriguez case? Does that jog your memory?"

Cal tapped the tips of his fingers on the tabletop and replied, "No, I can't say that it does. But I've handled a lot of cases over the years, and my memory ain't what it used to be."

Jace opened the manila folder next to his yellow legal pad and pulled out a two-page document. He handed it to the court reporter and asked her to mark it as Exhibit 1 to the deposition. She placed an exhibit sticker on the front page and handed it back to Jace, who glanced at it before sliding it across the table to the witness.

"Does Exhibit 1 refresh your recollection?"

Cal picked up the document and began to read, with his lawyer leaning in to do the same. After several minutes, Cal asked, "Would you repeat your question, Counselor?" He obviously was playing for time while he considered his response.

Jace asked the court reporter to read back the question, which she did.

Before Cal could respond, Sharlene interjected condescendingly, “I’m sorry, but what in the world does a case that was filed over seven years ago in Santa Fe, New Mexico, have to do with the case we’re here on today? Help me out here, Mr. Forman.”

“If you want to instruct the witness not to answer, fine. We can get the judge on the line and he can rule whether your instruction was proper. Otherwise, I don’t need you weighing in on any of my questions. I’m not taking your deposition, Ms. Knox.”

Sharlene was about to respond when Cal’s memory returned. “I remember now. Donato and I worked on that case together.”

“And you hired him to help, not the other way around.”

“That’s the way I remember it.”

“It was a chemical exposure case. You were alleging Mr. Rodriguez had contracted liver cancer as a result of a pesticide manufactured by the defendant. Would you agree with those statements?”

Cal’s lips formed a tight line as he nodded.

“As you know, Mr. Connors, the court reporter can’t take down a nonverbal answer. Would you answer out loud, please?”

“Yes.”

“And would it be a correct statement that you hired an expert to prove causation—that is, to prove that the pesticide caused your client’s liver cancer?”

“Yes.”

“Do you recall the name of the expert?”

“Let’s quit playing games here, Forman,” Cal sneered.

Jace feigned innocence and replied, “I need to get a clear record. What’s your answer, Mr. Connors?”

“I do. Dr. Howell Crimm.”

“And Dr. Crimm gave you the opinion you were looking for, isn’t that correct?”

"He objectively reviewed the facts, the medical records, everything else he deemed relevant, and came to a scientific conclusion."

"A conclusion that enabled you and Mr. Medina to get a three-million-dollar verdict, the largest ever rendered in Santa Fe County, isn't that so?"

Cal Connors, defender of the common man, instinctively retorted, "Mr. Rodriguez died a horrible death. He had a wife and seven children to support. The jury got it right."

"Mr. Connors, you asked the jury for three million and they gave you exactly what you asked for, isn't that true?"

"I don't recall the exact amount, but it was a sizable verdict."

"Now, do you know if Dr. Crimm was a medical school professor at the time?"

"That sounds right."

"Do you know whether he ever used medical students to help him with his scientific research on cases like the one I just mentioned?"

"I don't know."

"Assuming he did and then disregarded their research to come to a contradictory conclusion, that would concern you, wouldn't it?"

Cal chuckled and then answered, "Not in the least. Experts disagree all the time. Hell, look at global warming. Half the eggheads say it's real and the other half say it's not. It's anybody's guess who's right. No, that wouldn't surprise me one bit."

Jace decided not to push it. Cal had obviously been prepped in that area, as evidenced by the smirk his lawyer flashed at Jace.

"Dr. Crimm would be the only person who could tell us how he reached the opinions he did in the cases he worked on for you, would that be a fair statement?"

"He would certainly be a good source. I think he also outlined the methodologies he used in each case in the reports filed with the court."

"Fair enough. But you would agree that Dr. Crimm would be the most important resource to determine how he reached his opinions?"

"Possibly." Cal was becoming more confident, giving up less ground. The initial shock of Jace's line of questioning was beginning to ebb.

"But Dr. Crimm can't tell us because he was murdered, isn't that correct?"

"Damn shame. I miss the old coot." Cal grimaced, clearly hoping a tear or two might follow but none did.

"How did you learn of Dr. Crimm's death?"

"I honestly can't remember—could have heard about it on the news, read about it somewhere. I really don't remember."

"When did you last talk with him?"

"Oh, a long time ago. As you probably know, Mr. Forman, Howell had some problems."

"What kind of problems?"

"I hate to talk this way about a friend, but Howell was a raging alcoholic. The juice ruined his marriage, that along with the gambling. I had no choice but to stop sending him cases, which I did a year or so ago. I hated to do it, but I couldn't rely on him anymore."

"So if I looked at your phone records, you wouldn't expect me to find any calls to Dr. Crimm for a year or longer?"

Seeing where this was going and not wanting to get walled in, Cal answered, "First, you have no right to see any of my phone records. That being said, I can't say with any certainty what they might show. Maybe he called me after he'd been drinking one night, I don't know. What does it matter, anyhow?"

"Don't you think it might matter a great deal if you talked with him right before he was blown to pieces by a car bomb?"

Cal began to rise from his chair, only to have Sharlene gently pull him back down. "You are way out of line, Mr. Forman.

Go on to something else or I'm going to instruct my client not to answer. This is nothing more than a poorly disguised fishing expedition."

Ignoring the comment, Jace continued, "Do you know Jaime Garza?"

Cal furrowed his brow before replying, "Name doesn't ring a bell. Should it?"

"Did you know Mr. Garza was a repeat client of your friend Donato Medina?"

"No. Why should I?"

"Did you know that the FBI has linked Garza to the car bomb that killed Dr. Crimm?"

Sharlene interjected, "Don't answer that."

"You directed Medina to hire Garza to put a hit on Dr. Crimm so the FBI couldn't question him about all of those fraudulent reports he signed off on, isn't that true, Mr. Connors?"

"I don't have to listen to this shit." Cal pushed back from the table, and before bolting from the room, he leaned across the table, jabbing his finger in Jace's direction. "You're over your head, Forman. Way over your head."

Jace turned toward the empty chair and started to ask a follow-up question before Sharlene interrupted him. "Your theatrics are underwhelming, Mr. Forman."

"I was just getting warmed up." Jace thumbed through his legal pad. "I had another half-day of questions, at least. I guess you won't agree to bring the witness back in here and let me finish."

"No way. I'm filing a motion with the court. Your conduct today was some of the most unprofessional I've seen in all my years of practice. I'll have you and your client sanctioned." Sharlene stuffed her file into her briefcase and hustled out of the conference room, slamming the door behind her.

Jace exchanged grins with the court reporter and videographer and then leaned over and whispered to Leah, "Doesn't look like your deposition is going forward anytime soon."

* * *

Later, in Cal's office, Sharlene admonished, "What was that, Cal? You know better than walking out in the middle of a deposition. The judge won't like it."

Cal remained in front of the memory wall in his office, his back to his lawyer, and didn't reply.

Sharlene walked over to the conference table, and Cal followed. "What happened in there?" she asked.

"I don't know. I guess I snapped. I've never had anything like that happen before. But I've never been accused of killing someone either. The nerve of that son of a bitch! I'd like to knock the shit out of him."

Staring earnestly into Sharlene's eyes, he hoped she believed the crap he had just spewed out. He hadn't snapped. It had all been an act. Forman was on to something with his questioning and, if Cal hadn't thrown a monkey wrench in the works by storming out, would have taken him down a path Cal didn't want to go.

"What happened after I left?"

"I threatened Forman with a contempt motion for acting so unprofessionally. I figured it was better to go on the offensive than to run out with my tail between my legs."

"I'd like to see you do that someday." Sharlene ignored the remark, and Cal awkwardly cleared his throat before asking, "So what did Forman say?"

"As best I recall, nothing. He just smirked at me. So tell me about this Medina guy."

"Nothing much to tell. I needed local counsel for a trial I had in Santa Fe and he was my pick. He didn't have to do much—just enough so he didn't look like a token Mexican, which is all he was. We hit a good lick and he got his cut. That's about it."

"And you haven't talked with him since the trial?"

"Not that I recall."

"What about Jaime Garza?"

"Everything Forman said today was news to me. I've never heard of any Jaime Garza. That whole theory about me asking Medina to find a guy to put a hit on Crimm—shit, that's the most ridiculous thing I've ever heard. Hey, if it would make you feel better, give Donato a call. Just tell him you are representing me in a slander case against an upstart reporter, and he'll fill you in on whatever you want to know. You want his number?"

"No need. I'll find him if I need to."

"So what's the next step, Counselor? By the way, it's pretty damn weird being the client. You ought to try it sometime."

Sharlene grinned. "No thanks. I like being in charge. I guess I'll let this little escapade blow over, give it a couple of days and then call Forman to reschedule."

"I can't wait for you to get a shot at Rosen."

"Won't be able to do that until Forman finishes your deposition. That was our agreement, which he wisely confirmed in writing."

"When you thinking about rescheduling?"

"Let me talk to Forman first, and then I'll be in touch." Sharlene stood and, with briefcase in tow, walked gracefully toward the door, stopping at the threshold. "You're squaring with me, aren't you, Cal?"

"Now, why wouldn't I? You're my lawyer, aren't you?"

Sharlene sighed and shook her head as she pulled the door closed.

After Sharlene left, Cal waited for a few minutes and then walked down the hall to Christine's office. She was behind her desk, reading a document. After stepping inside, Cal closed the door and cleared his throat for attention.

Finally looking up from her document, Christine asked, "How did your deposition go?"

Somberly, Cal replied, "It wasn't the way I answered the questions that troubled me; it was the questions he asked, and the way he asked them. He knows too damn much. We need to circle the wagons."

* * *

Jace pulled out of the parking lot and into traffic. "So what'd you think?"

"Well, I've never been to a deposition before. I read a few while I was researching the Fosorax case Connors had down in the Valley, but it was a lot different being there in the flesh. I really wasn't prepared for that."

Jace turned toward Leah and smiled. "They can get pretty nasty at times. But you get used to it."

"I guess people can get used to just about anything if they do it long enough."

"I always wondered how brain surgeons could sleep before a day in the operating room, but I talked to one of my doctor friends and he explained they just grow accustomed to it—no big deal if you do it day in and day out."

"I guess that's right. What did you think of Ms. Knox?" Leah asked.

"About what I expected—tough, smart, not easily intimidated. You?"

"Same. She kinda scares me. I'm glad my deposition isn't going on right now, that's all I can say."

"You have nothing to worry about. You'll do fine. Speaking of, what are your thoughts on Cal's testimony?" Jace asked, turning his eyes away from the road and toward Leah.

"He was pretty smooth, but I could tell you got under his skin when you started poking around the relationship between Medina and Garza. I don't think he saw that coming."

"That's what I was hoping. I think that's why he put on that show at the end. He didn't like where the interrogation was headed and wanted a time-out. We're on the right track, no doubt about it."

CHAPTER 36

Magistrate judge Darden West slowly read through each page of the application for a search warrant as Cowan and Tipps watched intently, trying to read his expressions and body language. After getting to the end of the document, the magistrate, without looking up at the attorneys standing before him or uttering a word, flipped back to the start and began reading again. When he finished, he rested his half-glasses on the top of his head and rocked back in this chair.

"You realize what you are asking me to do, Mr. Cowan?"

"Yes, Your Honor but—"

"You are asking me to shut down the law office of one of the most . . ." he paused, searching for the right adjective, and then said, "well-known firms in this area and, for that matter, the state of Texas."

"I know that, Your Honor, but—"

"Mr. Cowan, sometimes one better serves his client by listening rather than talking, so I would ask you to hold your tongue until I finish. Am I making myself clear?"

Afraid to say anything, Cowan simply nodded.

"Now, you want federal agents to seize practically everything in their offices—computers, cellphones, accounting and other financial information, client files, am I right?"

Again, a nod from Cowan.

"Not only that, you want to seize the same property from the homes of Connors and his daughter." The magistrate glowered at Cowan and, without waiting for affirmation, continued. "And what support have you given me for your application? Three affidavits, which you want me to place under seal, a redacted expert report, and some travel manifests."

Cowan considered responding but thought better of it. Afraid to move a muscle, he felt like a schoolboy about to be disciplined by a hard-ass principal.

Then, suddenly, the magistrate's demeanor changed, a warm smile dressing his face.

"Had you worried for a minute, didn't I, boys?"

Sighing as the magistrate laughed boisterously in response, Cowan and Tipps allowed themselves a small celebration.

"Well, no more joking. Hey, I'm glad you're after that son of a bitch. I've been watching the shenanigans he's been pulling for years. I had a feeling things weren't on the up-and-up with the Lone Wolf—isn't that what he calls himself? I don't know his daughter, but I suspect she's not all that different from her dad. I'm going to sign your search warrant, place the affidavits under seal, and give you all the relief you asked for."

Magistrate West began to scribble on the documents in front of him, talking as he wrote. "I can't guarantee that I'll keep these affidavits under seal if the other side files a motion. They do have a right to confront their accusers."

He looked back through the documents to make sure he hadn't missed anything and then handed them back to Cowan.

"Happy hunting!"

* * *

At 8:00 the next morning there was pounding on Cal's door. Still in his bathrobe, a cup of coffee in hand, he opened it. An FBI agent identified himself and simultaneously handed Cal a copy of the warrant. While Cal was still reading, the agent and several of his cohorts rushed by and started going from room to room, pulling out desk drawers, looking in closets, searching under beds, and dumping clothes on the floor. Cal was suddenly in hot pursuit, screaming obscenities at the top of his lungs, threatening them with multimillion-dollar lawsuits. His insults and threats fell on deaf ears. They ignored him—they had heard it all before. They had a job to do.

As agents boxed up all the files in his office, unhooked his computer, took photographs and books off his desk, Cal pulled his cell from his robe pocket, but before he could call Sharlene, an agent grabbed it out of his hand and zipped it up in a plastic bag. Cal tried to speak, but nothing came out of his mouth.

An hour after they'd arrived, the agents had done their damage, their van now fully loaded and on its way back to headquarters.

Cal picked up his landline and called his daughter—voice mail. Shit! They'd probably raided her house and confiscated her cellphone as well. Quickly, he called the firm.

"Mr. Connors, I've been trying to reach you," his receptionist said in a rush of words. "You wouldn't believe it. There are FBI agents all over the place. They've taken everything. This place looks like a war zone. They've shut us down—there's no other way to describe it. How can they do that?"

Cal had no response. Without a word, he disconnected the call and placed another.

"Sharlene, we need to meet. Now!"

CHAPTER 37

Christine didn't take time to change clothes or put on makeup. Dressed in a T-shirt, jeans, and sandals, she waited anxiously for the elevator. Men in suits and women in skirts and heels waited next to her, occasionally throwing curious glances her way. The elevator arrived, and she stepped on first, ignoring her fellow passengers as the elevator began its ascent, her eyes fixed on the floor indicator above the door.

Getting off on the fourth floor, she hurried past the receptionist and down the hall to Reed's office. He was on the phone, smiled when he saw her, and gestured with his thumb and index finger that the call was about to end. As she waited, Christine marched back and forth in front of his desk, signaling for him to hang up. He got the message and signed off.

"You won't believe what happened this morning! It was terrible, just terrible!" She continued to pace, gesturing with her hands, her voice shrill, breaking at times.

"Calm down, calm down. What's going on?"

"I had just gotten out of bed. Ron, the security guy downstairs, called and warned that the FBI were on their way up with a warrant! Then I heard banging on my front door. I threw on what I'm wearing right now and hurried to the door, peppering the guy on the other side with questions, stalling for time and trying to figure out what I should do. The agent got pissed and threatened to kick the door in. When I opened the door, he shoved some identification in my face and thrust a warrant at me!" Christine shuddered. "What happened next was a nightmare. There were five or six agents, swarming around my condo like a SWAT team, going from room to room, zipping things up in bags, stuffing files and documents in boxes. It was utter chaos. Reed, they took my laptop, all the files in my home office, they even took my cellphone—that's why I didn't call you. It was . . ." She didn't finish the sentence but just shook her head.

"Okay, okay. Take a breath and try to calm down."

"Calm down? Are you kidding? Did you hear what I just said?"

"Please sit down. You're even making me nervous."

"I don't care whether I am or not. I am so shook up, I can't tell you. I have always been able to keep my cool, always—until this morning." Christine took a deep breath and then continued. "So I went to the office before I came here. It looked like—and I'm not exaggerating—a fucking tornado had hit. Empty file drawers all pulled out, furniture thrown all over the place, cords dangling from desktops, the staff hysterical, asking me questions like 'What happened? What about our jobs? What was the FBI looking for? We aren't going to jail, are we?'"

"Have you talked to your dad?"

"He's on his way to meet with his lawyer."

"Any idea what they were looking for? Do you have a copy of the warrant?"

Christine pulled a crumpled document from the back pocket of her jeans and handed it to her lawyer. "I read it, but nothing stuck. I couldn't concentrate on what I was reading with all those assholes running around, grabbing things left and right. It was surreal."

"I bet." Reed got up and walked around his desk, put an arm around Christine, and led her to a chair. "Some coffee might help."

Christine nodded.

Reed continued to talk as he calmly poured a cup from the carafe on his credenza. "Any ideas as to what brought this on?"

"All I know is Forman took Dad's deposition yesterday, and it didn't go well. What should I do, Reed? I know I'm not thinking clearly now. I feel like I'm in a state of shock."

Reed took the chair next to his client, slowly read through the warrant, and then said, "This covers everything but the kitchen sink."

"And believe me, that's what they took. You name it—client files, financial records, my laptop, my friggin' cellphone, everything."

"What do you think they'll find when they go through all of that?"

"I don't know. I'm sure they're looking for a financial tie between our firm and Stein, records that show we paid him a kickback for agreeing to that settlement." Christine put her head in her hands, "I don't know, Reed. I'm so confused, and literally scared to death. I don't want to go to jail. This is a nightmare."

"You're not going to jail. I promise you that," Reed said confidently, masking his concern.

Christine glared at him, her eyes red, tears tracking her cheeks. "How can you say that? Look what they just did!"

"Let's step back and go over their proof, okay? First, their expert—this face recognition guru—I've had one of my associates do some research, and we are ninety percent sure we can exclude his testimony. Of course, there are no guarantees in this business, as you well know, but I like our odds. As far as the plane manifests are concerned, I've looked at all the receipts you sent over from your trip. They paint a pretty damn convincing picture of someone going on a European shopping spree, and none of those records put you anywhere near Èze. That's a big problem for the prosecution, not to mention the fact that the French coroner classified Stein's death as accidental."

Christine was feeling better already. Reed could have been a damn good shrink.

"I haven't seen any evidence of kickbacks to Stein. Maybe they'll come up with something and maybe they won't, but until they do, I think we have a pretty good chance of beating all the charges they may throw at you."

Christine knew the kickback payments were made to Security Plus, not Stein, who had promised repeatedly he would create such a financial maze that not a penny could be traced to him. Maybe Reed was right; maybe they couldn't make a case against her.

"All that being said, I think you should explore the possibility of making a deal. Better now than later. No sense in giving them time to wade through all the stuff they confiscated today and taking a chance they might turn up something."

"What do you mean?"

"Just what I said. Look, I am as good a criminal lawyer as there is. If we decide to fight, you couldn't have anyone better in your corner. But," he emphasized the word, pausing for effect, and then continued, "I also have great instincts and know when to cut a deal. And my senses tell me that time is now."

"I'm sorry, Reed, but I don't get it. You just told me how you were going to kick Cowan's ass and now you're advising me to plead?"

"Look, let's be realistic. They'll try you and your dad together, and whatever they prove against him will stick to you as well. And as we both know, there are some facts that don't look good for you. Sure, we have answers for all of them, but like a judge once wisely told me, if you're having to explain away one bad fact after another, it's like having a glob of Jell-O in your hand—sooner or later, it finds a crack and seeps through."

"So what kind of deal do you think I could make?"

"For some reason Cowan is out to get your old man. I don't know why and really don't care, but we need to use that leverage to make the best deal we can for you."

"Which would involve me testifying against him."

Reed nodded.

"I just can't do that." Christine shook her head emphatically. "No way."

"Just think about it. Talk to your dad. See what he has to say. I made some calls to lawyer friends of mine down in Austin who had cases against Cowan while he was a prosecutor there. They tell me he will offer sweet deals to bit players to get a shot at the big game. That fits with the two meetings we had with him in this case. I think he's anxious to do a deal and might—I say just might—give you immunity."

"What should we do about what happened today?"

"I'll file a motion with the court to get all of your property back. We'll get a look at what kind of evidence they filed in support of their application for the warrant. There'll be a hearing, but we probably won't get a ruling for a week or so."

"I hate that fucking Cowan."

"Talk to your dad—the sooner the better."

CHAPTER 38

He had been tailing her on and off since he got to Austin. He knew her routine, her habits, when she got up in the morning, when she went to bed at night, what she wore when she went out, what she slept in, what type of liquor she drank.

He was always amazed at how often people left their blinds and curtains open once darkness set in, exposing themselves to prying eyes from the outside, eyes that could enhance what they were watching with a pair of $200 binoculars, video cam included, zooming in on their subjects when and where they so desired: slouching down in that comfy leather chair in the den, cell glued to one ear, eyes on the iPad; drinking a glass of wine on the sofa while casually thumbing through a magazine; heating up leftovers in the microwave in revealing cutoffs and a T-shirt; coming out of the bathroom wrapped in a towel and dropping it to the floor before wiggling into some skimpy panties and pulling on a loose-fitting nightshirt—all the scenes perfectly framed by windows of different sizes and shapes, the curtains yet to be drawn.

He found it strange how people thought they led private lives, impenetrably shielded from view, by simply stepping inside familiar surroundings and locking the door to the world outside. What better place to get to know someone intimately than to watch them in their own home, carefully observing their every move.

The night sky was moonless, the forecast calling for clouds to roll in after midnight, with severe thunderstorms starting after 2:00 and lasting until early morning—perfect conditions for what he had planned. He checked his watch—7:15. Her car should be pulling into the driveway any moment now.

The stone home was old and didn't have a garage. She always parked in the rear of the house and entered through the back door, which opened to a short hallway, and then to the kitchen. Wooden stairs led up to the door, with plenty of sheltered space underneath for an unwelcome guest to hide. And that's where he was.

The distinct sound of car tires crunching gravel pierced the silence. She was home. He could feel his muscles tense as the car pulled up and the engine died. He watched from the shadows as one of her shoes made its way to the gravel and then the other.

She slid out of the car and closed the door, locking it with the fob. As she walked past, he lunged out and put the chloroform-drenched handkerchief over her mouth and nose. She struggled to reach the gun on her hip, but he was stronger, his arm encircling her waist and penning her arms against her body, his other hand pressing the handkerchief tightly against her face. In seconds it was over, her body limp and seemingly lifeless. He held her in his arms longer than necessary, her head resting on his shoulder, a curious hand cupping one of her breasts, his breath heavy and hot on her neck. He gently placed her down and removed the Glock from her holster, stuffing it in the waistline of his jeans before pulling the cell from the sheath on her belt and throwing it under a bush next to the house.

He retrieved the backpack from under the stoop where he had stashed it and took out a blindfold, gag, and roll of duct tape. After tightly winding the tape around her wrists and ankles, he pulled the blindfold over her eyes, stuffed the gag in her mouth, and placed her in his hiding spot under the steps.

He looked around. Lights were on in some of the neighboring houses, but no one was outside. He jogged to the black van he had parked a block over and drove it slowly down the street and into the gravel driveway. After surveying the surrounding area once more, he exited the van, opened the rear doors, and lifted the body inside.

As the van made its way down the street and out of her neighborhood, Randazzo leered at his prey in the rearview mirror. He had her now, she was all his, he could do anything he wanted to her, anything. He could take as long as he wanted. No one would miss her until morning, at the earliest. And even when they did, they wouldn't know where in the hell she was or what had happened to her. He had planned everything to perfection. He had looked forward to this night, and what a night it was going to be!

Moments later, he was making his way down the stairs inside of his rental house, her body draped over his shoulder. As he laid her on the adjustable bed, he heard something drop to the concrete floor. He immediately looked down. It was one of her shoes—and there was something next to it, he couldn't tell what. He picked up the shoe and what appeared to be an insole that had fallen out when it hit the floor. On closer inspection, he determined it wasn't an insole at all but some type of tracking device.

Shit! No need to panic—just think. Randazzo stuffed the insole into his pocket and examined the shoe to make sure there wasn't anything else inside. He reached over and pulled off the other shoe, carefully inspecting it, turning it upside down and shaking it—nothing. His hands frisked the body, starting at the feet and working their way up. As he did so, he sensed a pang of excitement, which he quickly suppressed—there would be plenty of time for that later, after he had taken care of this inconvenient snag in his plans. There was nothing hidden on the body. She was clean.

Randazzo lifted up the blindfold and, with a finger, cracked open an eyelid. He leaned closer and stared into an expressionless stare—she was still out cold. He checked the duct tape on her ankles and wrists. Was he forgetting something? He furrowed his brow as he considered the possibilities. She probably wouldn't wake up until after he got back, and even if she did, she would be groggy and weak.

No way she could get free—her wrists bound behind her back and her ankles so tightly wrapped there would be no way to twist them free. So what if, worst case, she came to and somehow, someway got free? She couldn't go anywhere. She couldn't escape from her new home. He had made sure of that by installing a lock on the cellar door, the ten-digit combination known only to him. Once he closed the door behind him, there was no way out of that windowless prison.

He bounded up the stairs and closed the door. When he heard the lock click into place, he grinned and mouthed, "Don't worry, I won't be gone long."

He rushed out to the van and drove fifteen minutes to a nearby industrial area. Spotting a vacant, dilapidated house on a street nearby, he parked in front, jumped out of the van, and walked quickly to the front door. He nudged it open with his knee and threw the tracking device on the rotting wood floor before rushing back to the van, the corners of his mouth upturned in a fiendish smirk.

* * *

One eyelid fluttered open, and then the other. Staring up into darkness she closed her eyes for a second and then opened them again—nothing but blackness. What had happened? Where in the hell was she?

She could feel her hands behind her. There was something tying them together, but she couldn't tell what it was. It felt like tape, but she didn't know for sure. And her ankles—she couldn't move them either. The only thing she could do was wiggle her toes.

She stopped trying to move. Was someone there with her? Holding her breath, she listened—nothing but an eerie silence. She couldn't be sure but sensed she was alone.

Slowly she began to sit up, sighing in relief as she met no resistance. She needed light. She needed to see. Leaning to one side of the platform, she nearly fell over—she was on a bed or table of some type. She thought for a moment, searching for a way to snag her blindfold on something, hoping to slide it off. Then it occurred to her. She could use the bed's corner. If she could get off the bed and onto the floor, she might be able to catch the edge of the blindfold on the corner and nudge it out of place. She had to try.

Carefully she swung her feet off the side and slowly began to inch forward, her toes dangling, searching for the floor. Pay dirt! She felt the cold concrete and eased her body off the bed.

Still blindfolded and gagged, her hands and feet bound tightly, she stood up.

Leaning against the frame, she assessed her physical condition—she was dizzy, thirsty, and nauseated. She desperately wanted to rest but knew there was no way she could risk it. She didn't know how much time she had. Willing herself on, her fingers found the top corner of the bed. Turning, she squatted down and pressed her forehead against the corner, moving her forehead slowly upward until the top lip of the blindfold became snagged on the angle and slid down ever so slightly before pulling free. She repeated the exercise until light began to filter through the top of the blindfold. It took a moment for her focus to sharpen. As it did, she gasped in horror at the sexual torture chamber her captor had created. She had to get out of there. She had to think. She couldn't give up. She couldn't let him win. She couldn't let him do the things to her she knew were coming if she froze in fear.

As she looked around her concrete prison, a plan began to take shape. Her eyes fell on an empty beer bottle in the corner of the room. She turned her bare feet from side to side, slowly making her way toward the bottle. And for the first time in years, she prayed.

CHAPTER 39

"Could we have a table with some privacy? We're working on a big case together and . . ."

"Of course, Mr. Connors. Please follow me."

After they were seated, Cal smiled at his daughter and commented, "You look wonderful, my dear. You could have had a career in Hollywood."

Christine blushed. "Oh, come on, Dad. You know flattery—"

Cal finished the saying. "Will get you everywhere. Mae West—gotta love her."

The waiter brought water and took their drink orders: a double Jack over ice for Cal and a vodka martini for Christine.

While they waited, Christine leaned forward and whispered, "What are we going to do, Dad? It seems like everyone wants a piece of us."

"There's always a way out—always. Sometimes you just have to look a little harder to find it."

"I don't see one here. You and I both know the judge is going to throw out that lawsuit you filed against Rosen and *Texas Matters*. I told you not to go after them!"

"I know, I should have listened to you, but that's water under the proverbial bridge. Besides . . ." Cal paused as the waiter served their drinks. Sensing some tension, and realizing they were in no hurry, the waiter moved quickly to another table.

"As I was saying, I don't think it mattered anyway. They already had plans to come after me."

"Maybe so, but that lawsuit didn't help matters any."

"How did your meeting with your lawyer go?"

"As good as it could have under the circumstances. He knows what he's doing. Bottom line, Reed doesn't think they have that strong a case against me."

"I agree with him. They don't. They're just trying to scare you, hoping they'll flip you. Otherwise they wouldn't have called you in twice."

"They should know better. I'd never testify against you. No way."

Cal picked up the menu, pretending to scour the contents. After several minutes, he asked, "You know what you want? Everything on the menu is good."

"I want to finish our discussion before we order anything—unless it's another drink. How are we going to fight this? What's going to happen to the firm? Hell, they took everything! How are we going to represent our clients? Reed says it will take a week or two to get all our stuff back, even if the judge rules in our favor. I don't know how things could get much worse."

Noticing both of their drinks were dry, Cal signaled for the waiter to bring two more.

"I always believe in calling it like I see it. You know that. There's no sense in pretending or wishing for something that ain't going to happen, praying that the Red Sea will part when you know damn good and well it won't. Cowan has got me by the short hairs and he knows it. So does Forman. They hate my guts, think I'm the devil incarnate, and want to bring me down in the worst kind of way. You know I'm right."

"Yes, but—"

Cal cut her off. "Hear me out first and then you can get in your two cents. Okay?" He shot her a look that telegraphed he meant business, and then continued. "They could care less about nailing you. You know why? Stein was a lying scumbag who would do anything to make a quick buck. Remember, he called you about making a deal, not the other way around. He cheated his employer out of millions. And then after the feds were on his ass, he flew the coop and went to France. Once he was safe from the tentacles of American justice, he underscored what a lowlife he was by hanging out with hookers and getting high. And that's what killed him. That will be Travers' opening statement at trial and the jury will *likely* buy into it. But there's always that chance they won't, and that's why you should think about making a deal."

Christine stared at her father, trying to keep her mouth from falling open. "Dad, are you serious?"

"I couldn't be more serious. Look, Christine, I am so proud of you and all you've accomplished. You've always been a wonderful daughter, and I love you more . . ." Cal's voice quivered, causing him to clear his throat and then pause for a second. "You have your whole life ahead of you. Hell, I'm the one who convinced you to meet with Stein. If you'll remember, I was worried about the firm's finances at the time. I would give anything to have that one back."

Christine reached over and put her hand on top of his. "Dad, I'm a grown—"

"Don't argue with me on this. Make a deal. Hold out for full immunity. That son of a bitch will give it to you."

"What are you going to do?"

"What I always do—fight like hell. I've got the best lawyer money can buy. She's a street fighter if I ever saw one—tough as nails. If there is a way to beat this, she'll find it. She'll come at you like a banshee when you get on that stand to testify. You know that, don't you?"

"I haven't made my decision yet."

"Well, let's say you make the smart call, cut a deal, and have to testify against your old man. If you do, my lawyer gets to cross-examine you. And if she does, she'll bear down hard. And you might, just might, get tripped up or forget a few things under her vigorous assault." Cal smiled tellingly at his daughter and raised an eyebrow.

"Ah, I see. I do get flustered under pressure at times."

Cal winked at his daughter. "That's my girl."

As the waiter brushed past their table, Cal grabbed his arm and said, "We're ready to order now."

CHAPTER 40

Randazzo parked the van behind his ramshackle rental house. Rain, mixed with pellets of sleet, peppered him as he ran to the front door. By the time he got inside, his clothes were drenched. He hastily removed his sweatshirt and threw it to the floor, then kicked off his sloshing tennis shoes. Wearing only his sweatpants, he hustled to the door leading to the basement and punched in the combination on the keypad. A familiar click sounded, and he pulled the door toward him.

He hesitated for a second and listened—all quiet—before placing his bare foot on the first step and then the second. He bounded down the last three steps and turned to his left, toward the bed where he had left her. As his eyes widened in disbelief, he heard a grunt and turned as a metal object smashed into his face. His knees buckled and he fell to the concrete floor, bleeding profusely from a deep gash in his forehead, writhing from side to side, sputtering profanities, blood oozing from his lips. He feebly lunged at his attacker's ankles, which sidestepped his grasp, answering with a hard kick to the ribs. Randazzo rolled over and got one last glimpse of Jackie McLaughlin before the tripod in her hands came crashing down again, and again, and one last time.

Jackie glared down at the bloody mess that was Randazzo. His nose was obviously broken, and the head wound was bleeding freely. His eyes were closed, but was he really out? Or was he just playing possum, trying to suck her in, get her to let her guard down? It was hard to tell for sure. Her years with the Austin PD had taught her caution. She couldn't afford to take any chances. She kicked him in the ribs—hard, hard enough to cause an involuntary reflex if he were still conscious. There was no reaction. Randazzo was out cold. There was no doubt in her mind. Running up the steps, Jackie tried the metal door—locked. She stared at the combination keypad and shook her head. How in the hell was she going to get out of here? There were no windows, and the walls, ceiling, and floor were all made of concrete. She could scream all she wanted, but no one would hear her. Glancing at her bare feet she raced down the stairs and retrieved her shoes from the floor next to that bed. Her heart sank: the tracking device was gone.

Now she understood. Randazzo had found the tracking device when he'd brought her here, so he took it and planted it someplace else. That's why he left. That's what saved her—or maybe doomed her. She might die right here in this hellhole.

She glanced over at the motionless body when a thought seized her. Walking over to Randazzo's crumpled body, she thrust a hand into one of his front pockets. Her expression soured—nothing there. Wedging her fingers into the other, she could feel his cell and pulled it out. Staring at the screen in disbelief, her mood darkened. She couldn't use the damn thing; she didn't know the password. As she glared down at the pathetic excuse for a human being lying at her feet, she knelt down, picked up his oversized hand, and pressed the index finger to the home button. On the third try, the software inside read his print and familiar icons lit up the screen. Hands trembling with adrenaline and fear, she dialed a number from memory.

"Gomez here, how can I help you?"

"Jorge, it's Jackie. I'm in trouble. I'm not hurt, but I'm locked in a basement somewhere with no way to get out. I'm looking at that piece of shit Randazzo, and I'm not sure how long I've got before he regains consciousness."

Jorge tried to mask his panic. "We'll find you, Jackie. Give me the number of the cell phone."

Jackie pressed the "settings" icon and then "phone," and a number showed up at the top, which she slowly read to him.

"It shouldn't take my people long to figure out where you're calling from. I'll be headed your way as soon as they do. In the meantime, do what you have to do. Don't take any chances with that guy."

"Don't worry, Jorge. But hurry."

Reluctantly Jackie disconnected, leaned over, and picked the metal tripod up off the floor. There was blood on the mount from the blows she had inflicted to Randazzo's head. And she wouldn't hesitate to use it again if that sack of shit gave her an excuse—any excuse at all.

CHAPTER 41

"Reed, have a seat." Cowan motioned to the chair in front of his massive desk. "It's good to see you again. Coffee?"

"No, I'm good."

"How are things over in Fort Worth? I should make it a point to get over there more often. Great town—so different from Dallas."

"Can't argue with you there." Reed decided to dispense with the small talk and cut to the chase. "You mentioned during our meetings that you would like to do a deal with my client."

Cowan nodded without saying anything.

"That's why I'm here today. I'd like to explore that with you."

"I need her to testify against her old man, you know that. Otherwise I'm not interested. Is she prepared to do that?"

"Depends."

"I might—I said might—be able to drop the murder charge if she pled guilty to commercial bribery. Of course, she would have to do some jail time and pay a substantial fine."

"Come on, Reginald. You're not giving me anything to work with here. You know you don't have enough to charge my client with murder. That's a throwaway."

"We've got the manifests, we've got expert testimony putting your client in Stein's suite right before his death, we've got motive. What else do we need? We've got a solid murder case if I've ever seen one."

"Putting my client in Europe at the time of Stein's death doesn't cut it, and you know it. Europe's a big place, and you have nothing establishing my client was anywhere near Stein's suite in Èze."

"I've got an expert report—"

"That you and I both know is going to get excluded. I can't wait to get my hands on the unredacted report. If we don't make a deal, I'm going to tear your expert a new one."

"I've heard bluster before. We'll let the judge—"

Again, Reed interrupted. "Hey, if you don't want to talk seriously, then I'll head on back to Fort Worth."

As Reed started to stand, Cowan said, "Let's cut the theatrics. What's your counter?"

"Full immunity."

Cowan shook his head. "You know I can't do that, Reed. I've got to have a plea, some jail time, and a fine. I can negotiate the type of plea, the length of the sentence, and the amount of the fine, but I can't give your client a walk."

"Then we can't make a deal, pure and simple. Before I go, let's talk about your proof on commercial bribery. What have you got?"

"As I'm sure your client has told you, we searched her home, her father's home, and their law offices earlier this week. I feel confident that once our forensic accountants finish their review of those docs, they will turn up something."

"So right now you don't have a damn thing—not one shred of evidence showing there was any kind of bribe, is that right?"

"Like I said, we are—"

"Well, my client tells me you're not going to find anything. She didn't bribe Stein, or anyone else for that matter, but you can bet that if she had, she would have covered her tracks. She's too smart to leave a paper trail behind."

Cowan rocked back in his chair and replied, "I've seen some pretty smart people make some pretty stupid mistakes." Leaning forward, he said, "Let's assume for a minute I gave her immunity—purely a hypothetical at this point—what would she testify to?"

Reed sensed he was making progress and replied, "As you pointed out, we are talking in theory only. You agree that nothing we say here—"

"Of course. These are privileged discussions. I would never attempt to use any of what's said today against your client."

"Okay, she might testify that she overheard discussions between her dad and Dr. Crimm about the testimony Crimm would give in some of those civil cases where Cal got millions in jury awards."

"I need more detail than that."

"Testimony that Crimm was distorting the research, that there was nothing in the research data suggesting the drugs were unsafe."

"Does she have any recordings of these discussions?"

"No. Why would she? She didn't bug her dad's office. But she does recall an email she saw that implicated him. She asked him about it, and he politely told her to stay out of his business and he would stay out of hers. Unless it was deleted from the hard drive, your folks should be able to find that email when they go through the computers they confiscated. There may be others, but that was the one that stuck out in Christine's mind."

"Does she have a copy?"

"As far as she knows, it is still on the office computers, which you now have."

"What did the email say specifically?"

"She can't recall what it said verbatim, but the gist of it was that the ends justify the means."

"Does she know anything about her dad putting out a hit on Crimm?"

"I asked her about that. She hadn't seen or heard anything that would suggest he had anything to do with Crimm's death. To tell you the truth, she even acted a little offended when I asked her."

Cowan nodded. "What else?"

"That her dad convinced her to meet with Stein."

"I thought you said there wasn't any kickback scheme."

"Not one you can prove," Reed paused for effect and then added, "without my client's testimony."

"So there *were* kickbacks paid to Stein! I knew it." Cowan grinned, obviously proud of his acumen.

"Knowing it and proving it are two different things."

"So what's she going to say about that?"

"If we do a deal, she might testify that Stein called her about settling those cases, that she met with him, that he wanted to be paid for his services, and that she was repulsed by the suggestion."

"And?"

"When she told her dad, he leaned on her to do it, told her they needed the money to keep the firm afloat. Against her better judgment, she gave in."

"A jury would likely go for that."

"Hmm, makes for a good theme: a devoted daughter trying to please a domineering dad."

"What else?"

"She just might be able to help your forensic team connect the dots on how the payments made their way to Stein," Reed exaggerated, and then added, "which would help Stein's former employer with its claim against the insurance company for millions in damages caused by his dishonest conduct. A result like that would make you look damn good to the general counsel, and you never know when a hefty out-of-state political contribution might come in pretty handy."

"You know I don't consider stuff like that," Cowan huffed, paused for a second, and then said, "I am tempted by your offer, but I'm still having trouble letting your client off completely. She killed someone, Reed. You and I both know that."

"She swears to me she had nothing to do with Stein's death. You and I both know he was nothing but a scumbag who, truth be told, got exactly what he deserved. He ran with a fast crowd over there and ultimately paid the price."

Cowan rose from behind his desk and extended his hand. "I'll have to think about it."

"I figured you would. I need to know within the next day or so. I've got a motion or two I will be filing if we can't make a deal."

"Understood."

The two men shook hands, and Reed left. Cowan buzzed his secretary and asked her to get Agent Tipps on the line. He wanted to do the deal but needed some cover.

CHAPTER 42

"Cal, I have some bad news. I talked with Cowan."

Moving from behind her desk, Sharlene took the seat next to her client. "The grand jury has returned an indictment against you. Cowan called me as a matter of professional courtesy to let me know and to ask if you would turn yourself in. I'm sorry, Cal." She reached over and squeezed his hand.

"Well, that's no big surprise. I think we both saw this coming. What's he charging me with?"

"Pretty much everything—first-degree murder, subornation of perjury, judicial corruption, you name it."

"So what's next?"

"There will be an arraignment hearing where the charges will be read, you will plead not guilty, and then the magistrate will consider your bond."

"I won't have to stay in jail, will I?"

"I talked briefly with Cowan about that. I think we can work something out. If you put up your house as collateral and turn over your passport, he said he'll agree to your release."

Cal nodded. "That's doable. I don't plan on going anywhere." He forced a grin.

"Cal, have you talked with Christine lately?"

"I have. Why are you asking me?"

"I think she may have cut a deal with Cowan. I got that feeling from a couple of things he said when I was questioning him about the evidence he presented to the grand jury. He didn't come out and say it, but I sensed it."

"Hmm. I guess Cowan wouldn't make a deal with her unless she agreed to testify against her old man, now would he?"

"Nope, he wouldn't."

"Okay, here's what I wanna do. I want you to pull out all the stops. I don't give a shit what it costs. We're going to beat this thing. I didn't do anything wrong, and I am confident a Fort Worth jury will see it that way."

"I'm with you a hundred percent. Now, if my instincts are right and your daughter has made a deal, I'll have to go after her."

"I know that. If she has turned on her dad, I want you to do everything you can, use every trick in your little black book to take her down, make her look like the little liar she is." Cal's acting job would have won an Oscar.

"I'll do whatever it takes to get you off, but I need you to understand that it won't be pretty."

Cal stood up. "Got it. When will I need to report and where?"

"I'll talk with Cowan this afternoon and let you know." Sharlene rose and looked up at Cal, her eyes locking on his. "We're going to win this."

"There's no doubt in my mind."

* * *

The door to the interrogation room swung open, and a hunched-over Michael Randazzo, clad in an orange jumpsuit, his wrists and ankles cuffed, shuffled in and took a seat at the flimsy table pushed against the wall. He stared blankly at his feet, his mind somewhere else or perhaps nowhere at all. His right eye was swollen shut, and angry red stitches held together the skin just above his eye. He coughed and grabbed his left side as his three broken ribs cried out in agony.

He looked around the windowless room. He knew the drill. He had been through this before. But this time was different. He had been caught in the act. The evidence was overwhelming. There was no way out. Charged with kidnapping and attempted murder, he was looking at serious jail time, maybe even life. His flamboyant lawyer, Marty McCracken, had been candid about his chances to walk—"zero to none," to quote him, the only consoling words for his client: "At least they can't stick a needle in your arm."

The door swung open once again, and a familiar figure walked through and took the seat across from Randazzo. Their eyes met, and Gomez said, "Well, well, well. We meet again."

Weak but still defiant, Randazzo sneered and hissed back at him, "Nothing worse than a pompous wetback."

Unruffled by the slur, Gomez replied, "That the best you can do?" He then smiled condescendingly at his prisoner, and added, "You don't look so good. Of course, you didn't look worth a shit before, but now you look like some kind of monster, Frankenstein or something."

Randazzo scowled but said nothing.

"Let's get down to business. Why don't you just give me a confession and get this over with? That would make it a helluva lot easier for everyone. What do you say?"

Randazzo hesitated a minute before saying, "You shouldn't even be talking to me. I want my lawyer."

"You're right, Mikey. I tried to call him, but he was too busy to come. Told me he was only taking paying cases and that you were broke as a fucking church mouse."

"You're lying. You haven't talked to him."

"Suit yourself, but I swear on my mother's grave, the only lawyer you're going to get is one the court appoints. And you know how good they are. No more Marty McCrackens for you, I can promise you that."

"I want to go back to my cell."

Gomez's face turned to stone, his eyes on fire. "You'll leave when I say so. You got that, you no-good son of a bitch? Now, tell me what happened. Why did you do it?"

Randazzo stared down at the table and then looked back up at Gomez. "I didn't do it, but I wanted to. You know why. She would have been one good piece of—"

Before he could finish, Gomez was up, his hands in a stranglehold around Randazzo's throat. As Gomez's grip tightened, Randazzo's eyes began to bulge, his cuffed hands tugging desperately to break the hold. As Randazzo's resistance lessened, Gomez came to his senses and drew his hands away. He leaned close and whispered, "No need to fuck up my career by killing you here and now. Besides, you're going to rot in a jail cell the rest of your fucking life, you miserable piece of shit. But if for some reason you get out, you better be looking over your shoulder, because I'll be right behind you, and I'll finish what I just started. You can count on it." Gomez bolted out of the room, slamming the door behind him.

Randazzo yelled for the guard, but only an unintelligible raspy sound came out of his mouth. He tried again—nothing. He began to panic. Would he ever be able to speak again, or had that asshole Gomez done permanent damage to his vocal cords? He waddled over to the metal door and beat on it as hard as he could with his shackled hands. He listened for the sound of footsteps, but there was only silence. He made his way back to the table, slouched down in the chair, and covered his face with his hands. He fought the tears, but they came—slowly at first and then uncontrollably. Gomez smiled as he watched from inside the dimly lit room on the other side of the one-way mirror.

* * *

Abe burst into Leah's office with a bottle of champagne. "Have you heard? It's over. We just got a copy of the dismissal order!The judge threw out Connors' lawsuit!"

"He what?"

"He dismissed the entire case! Time for a celebration!"

Leah's phone was ringing. She was going to send it to voice mail when she noticed it was Jace calling. "Hold on a second, Abe, it's my lawyer." Leah answered the call without waiting for Jace to speak. "Is it true? Has the case been dismissed?"

"Congratulations, Leah!It's all over."

"I can't thank you enough! What happened?"

"Cowan got an indictment against Connors. I think the only reason he brought suit against you and *Texas Matters* in the first place was to go on the offensive and keep Cowan off his back. Obviously it didn't work. Of course, you will still have to be a witness in the criminal case, but you are home free."

"That is great news! Abe is in my office right now with a bottle of champagne."

"Go celebrate. I'll catch up with you later."

Leah clicked off the call and gave Abe a big smile. "We did it! We got the story out, and Cal Connors has been indicted! Pop the cork, Abe, it's party time!"

PART THREE

CHAPTER 43

There were no negotiations, no talk of a plea deal, no discussions of any kind. Both sides welcomed the fight, a bare-knuckle brawl in the arena, a battle to be fought until one side could no longer stand, until the vanquished had to face the consequences of a decision turned bad.

This was Reginald Cowan's big chance—the chance to put away a high-profile trial lawyer with longstanding ties to the Democratic establishment, which Cowan demeaned as a sordid hodgepodge of intellectual elites, card-carrying union members, minorities, sexual deviants, and abortion advocates. And Cowan always took advantage when opportunity came knocking, constantly on the lookout for a leg up, continually searching for any advantage. When one came along, he mercilessly trampled upon anyone and anything that stood in the way of reaching the next rung in his quest for the top. It had always been that way, and his insatiable appetite for success, no matter the cost, had only grown with time.

At UT Law, Cowan had been an outsider, a carpetbagger who had migrated south from New York. His Brooklyn accent, thick and unapologetic, drew puzzled stares from his fellow classmates and the occasional mimicry behind his back, neither of which was lost on him. He sensed the condescension and mockery and put it away for another day, a day when he would pass them all with a sneer of derision, so to hell with them and their parochial views and sheltered perspectives. The vast majority of them had only sparingly ventured outside of the great state of Texas—maybe to Colorado to escape the summer heat, or to Maine, where daddy's family had an ocean retreat. But they couldn't wait to get back, to a place without equal, to Texas, to God's country.

More than once he had asked himself what the hell he was doing in Texas. Why hadn't he stayed up east, where the people liked the things he liked, talked the way he talked, cheered for the Mets and the Giants, and knew how to make a bagel? The answer was pretty damn simple: money. After graduating at the top of his class at Fordham, UT had offered him a more generous scholarship than any other school, by a lot. He guessed they wanted a token Yankee or two, and he fit the bill perfectly. So why not take their money?

With his minimal social life, there had been plenty of time to study, and his grades soared. He became an editor on the law review and graduated in the top one percent of his class. On the road to success, he was way ahead of schedule, already passing those who had treated him with contempt, savoring the intoxicating sense of revenge, an irresistible addiction setting in, the cravings becoming more frequent and severe. And, strangely, he had begun to enjoy living in the Lone Star State—the taste of money, the talk of bigness, that omnipresent attitude that you could get anything and everything you wanted right there, all you had to do was reach out and grab it. And he had done just that.

Politics had always held an interest for him, even back in Brooklyn. He ran for class president his senior year at Fordham, and although he lost, he got a taste of celebrity, of people taking notice, volunteering for him and making him feel important. It was a good feeling, a damn good feeling—one that burrowed deep into his psyche.

His law school record led to countless job opportunities in and out of Texas. But the allure of politics was strong, causing him to opt for a position with the Travis County DA's office. At that time he leaned left, and Austin was a bastion for liberal thinking and politics, the Democratic Party holding sway in all the local elections. He figured that after he got some trials under his belt and formed alliances with the local power brokers, he just might run for DA or city council or even mayor. He would stay active in local campaigns, make some allies, and watch closely for the right opening.

He had met Cal Connors for the first time at a Texas Trial Lawyers Association convention. Cal was a featured speaker, his topic "Rock Stars and Trial Lawyers: What's the Difference?" To the delight of the audience, Cal compared his appeal to Mick Jagger's: "You gotta get 'em right out of the starting block. Mick gets 'em when he struts out on stage. I get 'em in front of that jury box. It's all about charisma—you either got it or you don't, folks."

At the reception afterward, Cowan made a point to snake through the crowd, stopping along the way to shake hands and smile at the rich and famous, until he was standing next to Cal. "Mr. Connors, I sure enjoyed your presentation."

"Hell, call me Cal. I'm sorry, but I didn't catch your name?"

After exchanging small talk, their conversation turned to business.

"So you're interested in politics, Reggie?"

Cowan hated the nickname but let it go. "Very interested."

"I'll keep that in mind."

And he did. Cowan became the assistant DA of Travis County months later, courtesy of a couple of phone calls from Cal Connors, trial lawyer emeritus and defender of the common man. Years later, he received a call out of the blue. It was his old benefactor looking for payback.

"I don't know, Cal. I mean, we don't have anything on the kid, other than he was out with the deceased before she died. He doesn't have a criminal record—nothing, not even a speeding ticket."

Cal was undeterred. "Boy, some folks sure have short memories. Do you know why you're sitting where you are right now? Come on, talk to me." Cal's tone softened a bit. "Look, I don't want you to arrest the son of a bitch—just call him in for questioning, scare the crap out of him, get his dad's mind on something else other than this case I've got against his client. Now, that's not too much to ask, is it?"

Cowan sighed and then desperately sputtered, "Not much to ask, huh? His dad is Jace Forman."

A guffaw on the other end. "So what?" snapped Cal. "He'll never mean jack shit to you and all your high-flying political ambitions, I can promise you that."

Sensing Cal wouldn't take no for an answer, Cowan had reluctantly agreed and hung up the phone; he would be Cal's bitch at least for a while, until the gate swung a different way. And now it had. How sweet it was going to be, sending that cocky bastard to jail for the rest of his godforsaken life.

Shaking himself out of his reverie, Cowan glanced across the courtroom. His sparring partner was wearing a bright red dress, her carefully tousled blond hair short, barely grazing her shoulders. Cowan hated the bitch. Her attitude—and boy, did she have one—took him back to his first days in law school, an unpleasant flashback to a time when he was mocked, ridiculed, and laughed at behind his back.

She caught him looking and mouthed derisively, "Hi, Reggie," causing him to turn away and stare down at the legal pad in front of him. He had called Sharlene Knox right before jury selection to dismiss the murder charge because he didn't have enough solid proof for a conviction.He hated making the call but didn't want to take the chance of giving Cal a double jeopardy defense if he swung and missed and later got the proof to nail him. The call had been painful, and Knox made it a point to smear it in his face for bringing the charge in the first place. People like Knox still got to him, and he knew why. But he always made them pay, always—and this time would be no different.

The case had been all over the news—in the local papers and on the evening newscasts—and the courtroom was packed. The lawsuit junkies were there in force. Not an empty seat in the house. And they wouldn't be disappointed. This would be a multi-act tragedy, with Reginald Cowan III playing a lead role. He would be on center stage with their full attention, as he orchestrated the meteoric fall of their homegrown Icarus.

"All rise. The United States District Court for the Northern District of Texas is now in session, the Honorable Garth Grissom presiding."

A thin man with bushy red hair, cloaked in the robe of justice, bounded up the steps to his perch and slid into the chair behind. He motioned all present to take their seats and then asked the bailiff to bring in the jury.

Cal and Knox were seated closest to the jury and smiled at each of the twelve members as they stepped into the box, sidled along the aisles, and took their seats behind the wooden rail. There were seven women (two African Americans, two Hispanics, and three Anglos) and five men (one African American, one Hispanic, and three Anglos). During the weeklong ordeal of jury selection, Cal had taken notes, passing them to Knox during breaks. They were a team and didn't need a consultant. Between the two of them, they had picked numerous juries. They understood body language, read subtle signs, picked up clues when a potential juror stammered nervously through an answer. They were good at the game, and both liked the jury seated in the box.

Judge Grissom leaned forward, casting his eyes on Cowan, and asked, "Mr. Cowan, are you ready to give your opening statement?"

Clearing his throat, Cowan rose and nodded at the judge. "I am, Your Honor."

In his navy blue suit, starched white shirt, and polka-dot bow tie, he looked more like an Ivy League dandy recently shipped to Texas—out of place and a bit strange. But he had learned long ago to dress like you're used to dressing, be yourself, and don't fake an accent, ever; otherwise jurors would label you as a fraud and not believe a word that came out of your mouth. So no cowboy boots for him, no bolo ties, no Stetsons, no stitched suits, no Texas drawl. He was born and raised in New York and would dress and act the part. He would be himself, at least in appearance.

Cowan walked slowly toward the jury without saying a word. The courtroom was graveyard silent, all waiting to hear what the U.S. attorney for the Northern District of Texas had to say about the man with the swept-back silver hair, the man with the winning smile and piercing blue eyes, the man who had become a legend in Fort Worth for his prowess in the courtroom and his generosity to the city, the man now seated next to the lady in red, the man who was on trial fighting for his freedom and his livelihood.

Pausing at one corner of the jury box, Cowan rested his hand on top of the rail. His eyes slowly swept those of the people seated in front of him, occasionally stopping and then moving again before they came to rest on a middle-aged woman in the front row. "Ladies and gentlemen, I would rather be any place—any place other than standing here before you, asking you to do what I have to ask you to do," said Cowan softly.

The room remained eerily silent. On the legal pad in front of her, Knox wrote "WHAT A LOAD OF MANURE!!!" which Cal caught out of the corner of his eye, causing a subtle smile to form on his lips.

"The defendant is a man I've admired over the years—yes, you heard me—a man I've admired, even envied, a man I wanted to be like." Another pause, and then Cowan turned up the volume, pacing back and forth in front of the jury, stopping at predetermined points to underscore a statement. "That is, until—until I learned that man didn't exist, until I learned that man was living a lie, until I learned that man had cheated companies out of millions, until I learned that man had mocked the judicial system and judges and juries throughout this great state and country of ours, until I learned that man forced his daughter—his own flesh and blood—to make a deal with the devil, a lucrative deal that would line his own pockets with millions."

After this crescendo, Cowan returned to his initial pose at the end of the jury box, his hand once again resting on the rail. "So why did this man, a man who had so much going for him, a man who had been blessed with so much by our Creator, go so, so wrong?" Cowan shrugged his shoulders and answered, "Greed, pure and simple. He just couldn't get enough. He couldn't live like you and me, no sir, that wasn't good enough for him. He needed the island vacation home, the plane, the big house, and the list goes on. And he was determined to have it all, so to hell with the rules and those who might get hurt along the way."

Cowan walked to counsel table, casually poured a glass of water from the pitcher, took a sip, and then returned to the front of the jury box. He had practiced his opening at least twenty times in front of the full-length mirror he had installed on the back of his office door. Every move was carefully choreographed, every start and stop, every pause. He wasn't thirsty but needed to give the jurors plenty of time to soak up what he'd just told them.

"You are going to hear the words 'reasonable doubt' a lot from opposing counsel. So what do those words mean? Let's focus on the first one: reasonable. Let me give you an example. If dark clouds cover the sky, wind is whipping the trees, lightning crashes and thunder rolls, it wouldn't be reasonable to doubt that it was going to rain, now would it? The evidence—the clouds, the thunder, and the wind—all point to rain. And believe me, we don't just have a few clouds, some rumbles, and the occasional gust of wind in this case. We've got a full-blown hurricane."

Knox sighed and rested a cheek on a palm. Cal picked up her pen and wrote "YOU'RE GOING TO KICK ASS" on her pad. She rolled her eyes in a "we'll see" manner.

"You will hear from witness after witness about his judicial scheme, how the defendant and Dr. Howell Crimm conspired to mislead one jury after another, resulting in millions and millions in fraudulent jury awards. You'll hear from the young reporter who uncovered this scheme and had the guts to write about it, and you'll hear how a desperate Cal Connors tried to scare her off the story. And last, you'll hear about a dad who convinced his own daughter to bribe someone so he could continue to live the life of luxury he had grown so dangerously addicted to."

Cowan glanced down at the black shoes he had obsessively shined at 5:00 that morning, and then looked each juror in the eyes, one by one. "Ladies and gentlemen, as I said earlier, I would rather be somewhere else. And I would rather leave Mr. Connors untarnished, a local hero, an example for others to follow, a favorite son of Texas and this great city, a trial lawyer without equal. But the call of justice is strong and demands that I take you down a different path, one that will lead you to the real Cal Connors, a man of lies, deception, and greed, a man who is a menace to society and who must face the dire consequences of his own actions." Cowan's eyes made one last trip around the box before he thanked the jurors, marched back to counsel table, and took a seat.

Knox was on her feet the moment Judge Grissom turned his eyes in her direction, her body language telegraphing she was on a mission.

"Well, ladies and gentlemen, opposing counsel and I agree on one thing: that we'd rather not be here. However, I'll take that a step further. None of us should be here. You shouldn't, I shouldn't, and my client shouldn't. This case shouldn't have even been filed. It's nothing but smoke and mirrors, a fantastical mirage that exists only in the mind of an overly ambitious prosecutor—"

Cowan was on his feet. "Your Honor, I hate to object—"

Judge Grissom cut him off. "Ms. Knox, you're stepping over the line. Stick to what you think the evidence will show."

Knox nodded obediently, her point made, and continued. "You heard opposing counsel talk about this multimillion-dollar fraud he contends my client committed, how my client rigged the system to obtain unjustified jury verdicts, that he accomplished his goal through perjured testimony. You recall my adversary saying that?"

She turned in Cowan's direction, and every juror looked his way and then zoomed back in on Knox. "Let me ask you this: Do you believe two people can have an honest difference of opinion? Have any of you ever asked someone for his or her opinion on an issue and then decided you didn't agree with that opinion?" Knox paused as she noticed several of the jurors nodding in agreement. "Why, just last week I asked one of my lawyers to research a legal point for me. He came back to me with his answer. I read the cases he cited in his memorandum, and guess what? I didn't agree with his conclusion. That doesn't mean I'm right and he's wrong. We just had an honest difference of opinion. Please keep that in mind as you listen to the evidence opposing counsel puts on about Dr. Crimm and his research assistants." She had planted a seed she would water throughout the trial. She opted not to overplay her hand and moved on.

Knox stopped at the corner rail and shook her head as she mockingly said, "Now let me tell you about my client's poor, little helpless daughter—you know, the one he took advantage of and forced to pay this bribe my adversary talked about. You'll see her, hear her testimony, and can decide for yourself: is she really the helpless, naive pawn my adversary described, or is she a conniving, selfish, spoiled, ungrateful brat who turned on a father who gave her everything just to save her own skin? Once she gets off that witness stand over there," Knox nodded to the left of Judge Grissom, "I don't think you'll have much trouble separating fact from fiction. Thank you for listening. I appreciate your time and service." Knox nodded at the jury and returned to counsel table.

Dr. Sanjay Patel was the prosecution's leadoff witness. He didn't come off nearly as well as Cowan had hoped. Visibly nervous and fidgety on the stand, he stumbled and stammered throughout the questioning Cowan had rehearsed with him over and over the afternoon before. Yes, he made the critical points: he was Dr. Crimm's research assistant; he was asked to analyze the data submitted to the FDA on Fosorax; he analyzed that data and reported to Crimm that there were no red flags, that the drug appeared safe except for some minor side effects, which had been warned about in the package insert; and that he was unable to find any evidence of fraud or malfeasance in the approval process.

Then it was Knox's turn, and the wheels came off: Crimm was his superior; he had many more years of experience, clinically and in conducting research, than Patel did; Crimm was well regarded in the professional and academic worlds; experts could differ in their opinions and routinely did. She ended by handing Patel Crimm's résumé and having him read the noted accomplishments, honors, and educational degrees to the jury until Cowan objected and the judge sustained. Sensing the wounds she had inflicted were mortal, and fearing she might alienate the jury if she continued the onslaught, she mercifully ended her cross and handed the battered witness back to Cowan, who in a hushed voice murmured, "No further questions." Patel was excused, sliding out of the hot seat and slinking out of the courtroom.

It was approaching 5:00, and the judge called a recess until the next morning at 9:00. The jury filed out, and after they were gone, Knox caught Cowan's eyes and mouthed, "Nice job." Cowan ignored the insult as he methodically placed each of his files in his briefcase and made his way nonchalantly toward the courtroom exit.

Cal leaned over and whispered to his lawyer, "You killed that poor bastard. I actually began to feel sorry for Patel."

"That's why I let up. I had another hour of cross but thought he was bleeding bad enough as it was. You can overdo a killer cross."

"Good call. Who do you think they'll put on tomorrow? Dr. Coleman, Crimm's other research assistant?"

"I wouldn't. He'll be more of the same—never testified before, doesn't want to be here. I'd go with Rosen."

"You think?"

"Who knows what that asshole Cowan will do? I'm just saying how I'd play it."

"We got time for dinner at Del Frisco's?" Cal asked, a glint in his eye.

"Nope. We've got work to do. I'm glad your office is finally back in one piece. What a mess that was! Let's hunker down in the Boneyard, have something brought in."

Cal didn't like it but knew she was right. Dinner at Del Frisco's would have to wait. Knox was hell on wheels in the courtroom, just like he thought she'd be. And she looked like a million dollars strutting her stuff in that red dress and heels. If he got through this, he'd like to see more of her—literally.

CHAPTER 44

It was late. Leah had been at Cowan's office for hours, with Jace at her side, getting ready for her testimony the next morning. She grilled them on what she should expect from Sharlene Knox.

Leah had wanted to be present during the entire trial, but Knox had wisely moved the judge to enter a sequestration order, arguing that witnesses shouldn't be allowed to hear the testimony of others because doing so might cause them consciously or subconsciously to tailor their own testimony to what they heard. The rationale was sound, and Judge Grissom granted the motion. As a result, Leah had no idea what Patel had testified to that afternoon, and Cowan was prohibited from telling her. She would have to fly blind tomorrow.

Leah knew Knox would come at her with all she had. Her client's freedom depended on it. Knox would pull no punches, give no quarter: it would be scorched-earth warfare in the true sense of the term.

"All you have to do is tell the truth," Jace told her.

It sounded so easy, just get up on that witness stand and tell the truth, nothing to it. Right! With the spectator gallery overflowing, a judge peering down at her, and a hostile lawyer trying to trip her up at every turn, it would be no cakewalk.

They went over Leah's article line by line. She just needed to stay calm and loose, think about the questions before answering and not let Knox interrupt her, take control of the exchange and show Knox she wasn't intimidated by her bullying tactics.

Cowan spent hours grilling her, making sure she wouldn't misspeak on the stand.

As the trial prep came to a close, Cowan asked, "I don't mean to pry, but is there anything in your past that could be a problem?"

Leah almost crumbled but took a deep breath before saying, "If you're asking about my sex life, I've dated around plenty and certainly haven't saved myself for my wedding night."

Cowan grinned. "Nothing there. Rest easy."

"But, there is one other thing." Leah hesitated. She looked at Jace for support.

"It's okay, Leah. We are here to help, not judge." Jace smiled at her reassuringly.

"I got busted for marijuana possession years ago, back when I was a sophomore at UT."

Jace chuckled, draining the tension from the room. "Hell, Leah, you had us worried. We've all smoked a joint on occasion. Haven't you, Reginald?"

Like a true politician, Cowan pivoted, answering the question with a question. "So what happened to the charges?"

"My lawyer worked out a deal where I had to complete several hours of community service and pay a fine, and the charge was wiped off my record."

"'Expunged' is the legal term. If the system works as designed, Knox won't even be able to find that charge. That's the whole point of having it expunged. It's like it never happened. Evidence like that shouldn't come in anyway; it has nothing to do with your credibility." Jace reached over and patted Leah's clenched fist. "You have nothing to worry about, I promise. You're going to do great tomorrow." He turned to face Cowan. "Unless you have something else to cover, I think we need to call it a day and let my client get some rest." Cowan nodded and the meeting adjourned.

On the way to the parking garage, Leah said nothing to Jace, her game face on. She knew tomorrow would be a bitch. But that was the nature of life—a series of rapids testing your mettle and then, if you made it to the other side, a calming pool to leisurely glide down until the ominous sound of turbulent water signaled once again that peace was a temporary state and soon gone. She needed to suck it up and be a money player on that stand tomorrow. Her future depended on it.

* * *

On the way home, Jace called Jackie. He had talked with her every day since her brutal kidnapping. She had seen a lot and been through a lot while with the Austin PD but nothing like what she had just experienced, where death slithered up close enough for her to smell it. She was getting better by the day but hadn't recovered enough to go back to her house, much less sleep there: the memory was just too fresh. She was staying with Gomez, his wife cooking up a storm, their kids sporadically taking Jackie's mind off what had just happened to her. Jace had offered to visit several times, but she had politely demurred. She just wasn't ready to see him. She was not yet her old self, and wondered aloud every time they talked whether she ever would be.

"Jace, so glad you called. How's the trial going?"

"Cowan was not happy with the way Dr. Patel testified today, but you know how that goes. You can never predict how a witness is going to hold up on cross. And, evidently, Knox got him pretty rattled."

"Weren't you in the courtroom?"

"In and out. I had some emergencies come up that I had to handle. Plus, the judge granted the defense's objection to Leah sitting in during the trial. Leah camped out in my conference room, so I came back to the office several times during the day to check on how she was doing. After the court recessed for the day, Cowan and I spent the last several hours prepping her."

"When's he going to put her on?"

"First thing tomorrow morning."

"Ouch. I bet she's nervous."

"She is, just like anyone in their right mind would be, but I've got the feeling she's gonna do just fine."

"I wouldn't worry about her at all. As much as she's been through without buckling speaks volume."

"I agree. So how are you doing?"

"Each day the memory fades a little. I say that—I still have nightmares. I can't get that room out of my mind."

"Are you still seeing the doc?"

"Yeah, she diagnosed me with PTSD and put me on some meds, which I hate taking. They make me feel so out of it. We meet a couple of times a week and talk about all kinds of stuff. I guess it's helping, but who knows. That's my life right now—pretty much sucks."

"After Leah testifies tomorrow, I could come down."

"Jace, I'm still not ready for that. I'll let you know when I am. That doesn't mean I don't want to see you. I do—I really, really do. I'm just not back to where I want to be yet and don't want you to see me until I am."

Jace wondered to himself if she ever would be. People are a product of their experiences, good and bad, and never the same once buoyed by good fortune or pulled under by tragedy. "I understand," he said.

"Let me know how Leah does tomorrow."

"You know I will."

As he stuffed the cell in his pocket, he thought about Randazzo. "You no-good son of a bitch," Jace murmured. "I'll make sure you never, ever get out of that jail cell."

CHAPTER 45

The lunch crowd at Jake's was beginning to thin, and they had to wait only five minutes for a table. After they were seated, the waitress took their orders and rushed away.

Leaning toward Jace, Leah asked, "So what'd you think?"

"You were terrific up there—very believable. I watched the panel, and every single juror was on pins and needles, waiting to hear you tell your story. And as much as I don't like the guy, I gotta give ol' Cowan credit. He did a damn good job this morning. Yesterday was a tough day for the prosecution, but I think he made up some ground today."

"So what should I be prepared for this afternoon when I get cross-examined?"

"Honestly, everything."

"At least give me some idea as to how you think she'll come at me."

"Okay, here's the deal. She likes to get the witness to agree with her on certain things that seem almost impossible to disagree with, which she then uses as building blocks to slowly and methodically cage you in."

"Give me some examples."

"Let's see. She might start by asking you to agree that doctors can, without being dishonest, disagree on a diagnosis or a course of treatment."

"And I would have no choice but to agree."

"Right. She then might follow up with a few more questions like that, until she felt she had painted you into a corner, and then hit you with something like 'So it would be possible for Dr. Crimm, who had more education and years of experience than his research assistants, to honestly disagree with their findings, now wouldn't it?'"

"My answer would be 'Anything's possible, but that's not what happened here.'"

"You would have to support your answer, because you can bet she's going to test it up one side and down the other."

"I would explain that, when you consider the FDA's conclusion that the drugs were safe, the research assistants' opinions that the drugs were safe, the similarity between the reports and affidavits Crimm gave in all of the cases—blah, blah, blah—her assertion's simply not plausible."

"And that would be consistent with what you told the jurors this morning."

"You think she'll try and trip me up on my testimony that Connors hired someone to scare me off the story?"

"I think she has to. She has to create some doubt in the jurors' minds."

"How is she going to do that?"

"Well, we have no direct evidence linking Connors to anything that happened to you. The judge has ruled no one can mention

Randazzo's name in this trial, since he denied knowing Connors after he was arrested the first time and continues to deny it as he sits in the Travis County jail."

"Who, other than Connors, would have had a motive to do that sicko stuff to try to scare me off the story?"

"I bet Ms. Knox will throw out a myriad of possibilities. Or she might just stick with emphasizing that there is no proof whatsoever that her client had anything to do with those despicable acts and leave it at that. And she's right—the trail is clean."

The waitress slid their burgers in front of them and scooted off. Leah was too nervous to eat. She had taken only a few bites before it was time to head back to the courthouse. Jace slid a twenty-dollar bill and a five under the lunch ticket, and the two hurried toward the door.

* * *

The afternoon had been a tug of war between two smart, hard-nosed women. As one appeared to gain an edge, that advantage quickly disappeared, the score returning to deuce. When the mid-afternoon break arrived, the struggle had turned into a dead heat. Sharlene Knox, accustomed to watching witnesses crumble on cross, became frustrated and uncharacteristically desperate to make something happen. Knox knew that desperation rarely led to success in the law business but stepped out of bounds anyway.

"Did you and your lawyer have lunch together?"

Leah replied coolly, "Yes, we did."

"And where did you eat?"

"Jake's."

"And what did you and Mr. Cowan discuss?"

"Nothing."

"You're expecting this jury to believe you and your lawyer had a conversation-less lunch?"

"My lawyer is not Mr. Cowan. Mr. Cowan is the U.S. attorney. My lawyer is Jace Forman, who is sitting right over there." Leah nodded in the direction of the spectators' gallery. "You recall he represented me in that groundless lawsuit you and your client filed against me and *Texas Matters*—you know, the one the judge dismissed last week."

There was laughter in the gallery, and several of the jurors cupped their hands over their mouths, masking their grins. The judge brought order back with his gavel.

Knox was uncharacteristically speechless but quickly regained her composure and continued as if nothing had happened.

"On direct, you mentioned there were several attempts to scare you off the story, correct?"

"That's right."

"The first was a dead fish on your pillow, correct?"

"Correct."

"And you have no evidence that my client had anything to do with that college prank, do you?"

"That's not true. First of all, it wasn't a college prank. I'm sure you've never had anything like that happen to you or you wouldn't be characterizing it that way. It was horrible, something that unfortunately sticks with you forever. Second, Mr. Connors would be the only person to have had a motive to do something like that."

"What about one of those many young men you slept with at UT and then dumped? They might—"

Cowan was on his feet. "Objection, Your Honor."

Judge Grissom, wearing a scowl, barked, "Counsel, please approach." After they'd reached the bench, Grissom leaned forward and asked in a low voice, "Ms. Knox, where are you going with this?"

Knox whispered, "I intend to offer other possibilities as to who might have planted that fish on Ms. Rosen's pillow. Ms. Rosen had an active social life at UT, and it certainly could have been one of the many jilted lovers she left in her wake."

Judge Grissom cut her off and replied, "I'll allow it on one condition: all of the evidence about Mr. Randazzo's possible involvement and arrest, which on your motion I've kept out up until this point, I'll also allow. What do you say, Ms. Knox?"

"Withdrawn, Your Honor."

Knox dispensed with the high-risk rolls and returned to her bread and butter. "You're not a doctor, correct?"

"No, I'm not."

"You've never done medical research of any kind or character?"

"That's correct."

"So you're not telling this jury that you, as an expert, have determined all of these drugs were safe?"

"As I said, I'm not an expert."

"So the answer to my question would be no, you are not telling this jury those drugs were safe, correct?"

"Correct."

"And you're not telling this jury that Dr. Howell Crimm was not qualified to render the opinions that he did, are you?"

"No, I'm not saying that, but—"

Knox cut her off. "And you didn't even know Dr. Patel before you started working on your story, correct?"

"That's correct."

"You have done no investigation whatsoever as to whether or not he is a competent medical doctor, have you?"

"No, but I assume—"

"Ms. Rosen, assumptions aren't evidence. Shall we continue?"

Leah boiled inside but said nothing.

"This was your first big story, wasn't it?"

"You could say that."

"I did say that. Would you agree?"

Leah nodded.

"You'll need to answer out loud."

"Yes."

"Would you say you're an ambitious reporter?"

"I want to be as good a reporter as I can. If that fits your definition of 'ambitious,' then the answer is yes."

"And this story, unjustifiably maligning my client, put you on the map in the world of journalism, didn't it?"

"I don't know what you're talking about."

"Oh, yes, you do. You have a Twitter account, don't you?"

"Yes."

"I've taken the liberty of determining how many followers you had before the story ran, how many you had a week afterwards, and how many you have today. May I approach, Your Honor?"

Judge Grissom nodded.

Knox walked up to the bench and handed the witness a single sheet of paper. "Please read what's on there to the jury."

Leah turned her eyes from her adversary to the paper. "You want me to read this?"

"Yes—out loud to the jury."

Leah took a deep breath. "Two hundred thirty-eight followers before the publication date of 'Texas Justice Gone Wrong,' 12,482 followers a week after the publication date, and 29,000 followers as of yesterday."

"Do you have any reason to dispute those numbers?"

"No, but I can't verify them either."

"You follow your Twitter account, don't you, Ms. Rosen?"

"I do."

"And you're not surprised by those numbers, are you?" Before Leah could respond, Knox passed the witness.

* * *

On their way to the airport, Leah bombarded Jace with questions about her testimony that afternoon. How did I do? I was so nervous up there—was it obvious? How did the jurors react to me? Do you think they believed me? That Knox woman was such a bitch—the jurors didn't like her, did they? The questions came in rapid-fire succession, leaving Jace little time to respond. After Leah settled down, Jace said, "Look, you did great. I would be lying if I didn't tell you Knox made some points, but overall you came out ahead. I'm sure Cowan was pleased with the way things went today."

Somewhat satisfied, Leah asked, "So when do you think the case will go to the jury?"

"Hard to say. I don't know what other witnesses Cowan plans to call."

"Are you going to attend the rest of the trial?"

"I hadn't planned on it. I just wanted to make sure nothing came out during your testimony that could breathe life back into the defamation case the judge dismissed last week, and nothing did."

"Do you think Connors will appeal the judge's ruling?"

"Not a chance. He's got too many other things on his plate right now. Besides, he probably just filed that case as a diversionary tactic, as some kind of show of strength to dissuade Cowan from coming after him. Obviously his strategy didn't work." Jace glanced over and flashed Leah a grin.

"Have you talked with Jackie lately?" Leah asked, concern masking her face.

"I called her last night after we got through meeting at Cowan's."

"How's she doing?"

"She sounded a little better than she did the last time we spoke, but she's still pretty shook up."

"I feel so bad about what happened. If I hadn't written that story, none of this—"

Jace interrupted. "And Connors would still be conducting business as usual instead of fighting for his life in a Fort Worth courtroom. Don't second-guess your decision, Leah. You did the right thing."

"You think Jackie will ever get over this?" Leah asked.

"With time, I'm sure she will," Jace answered as convincingly as he could. In truth, he had no idea.

"It's such a relief to know that monster is behind bars."

"And this time I swear to you he'll stay there."

The Range Rover turned into the entrance to Love Field and, minutes later, sat idling in front of the terminal.

Leah's eyes clouded as she leaned over and pecked Jace on the cheek. "Thanks for everything."

"Glad things turned out the way they did. Have a safe trip back to Austin. I'll keep tabs on the trial and will let you know as soon as there's a verdict."

Leah hurried toward the airport entrance, stopping one last time to wave back at Jace before disappearing inside.

CHAPTER 46

Cowan's jacket was off, his bow tie undone and shirtsleeves rolled up. He glanced at his Rolex; the prep session with Christine Connors was scheduled to begin in a half hour or so. Tipps would sit in and should be getting there any minute. As he waited, he wondered whether the jury had believed Leah Rosen? He thought so, but you could never be sure. And had her testimony made up for the disaster the day before? Hard to say; first impressions were lasting ones, and Patel had been his leadoff witness. Cowan shook his head—he had miscalled that one. But Patel had been one person when Cowan met with him before the trial and a different person on the stand. You could never tell how a witness would turn out. The ones you were most concerned about sometimes kicked butt, and those you thought would knock the lights out often fell to pieces. Trials were unpredictable, akin to high school football games where you don't know what's going to happen from one play to the next and don't know who's going to win until the final whistle blows.

There was a knock on the door. Without waiting for a response, Tipps stepped in, closing the door behind him.

Taking a seat, he asked, "So how do you think it went today?"

"Knox came after her like a barracuda, but Leah held her ground. She did good, better than I thought she would. I think the jury liked her and, at times, was turned off by some of Knox's tactics. She's such a snake."

"So you've definitely decided not to put Coleman on?"

"I don't think he adds anything. And why take the chance that he'll crater like Patel did? No, I think we got what we needed from Leah. We need to try and close the deal with the old man's daughter. It'd be a nice touch of irony if her testimony put him behind bars, now wouldn't it?"

"Yes, it would."

"Have your folks come up with anything else linking him to Crimm's murder?"

"No, but they're still working it hard. We're using our sources in Mexico to try and locate Donato's client. And, who knows, we may get lucky. Maybe he'll return to Santa Fe once he thinks things have cooled down. If he does, we'll be waiting for him."

"How about Donato? You think we ought to bring him in?"

"My instincts tell me there is no way we're going to get him to crack. I could tell that after talking with him for five minutes. He is smooth, really smooth, and can lie to you looking you straight in the eye. He's not going to give us anything, not unless we nab his client first."

Cowan's secretary buzzed in. Christine Connors and her attorney had arrived.

"Stan, you think the written statement buttons her up pretty good, don't you? I read it just a few minutes ago, and there's not a lot of wiggle room."

"Tight as Dick's hatband. I've not seen one any tighter."

"All right then. Let's get started."

CHAPTER 47

Darrin picked up her phone for the third time and then put it back down again. She got up from the table and walked into the kitchen of her Fort Worth condo and poured a glass of chardonnay. After sitting back down at the table, she took a long sip, hoping the alcohol would deaden her senses a bit and help get her nerve up. Thirty minutes later, the bottle was half empty and Darrin had the phone to her ear, praying for voice mail. She didn't get it.

"Darrin? My caller id tells me it's you, but I just can't believe it."

There was a brief pause before Darrin said, "Yes, it's me, Jace." Before he could say anything, she blurted out, "I've moved back."

"You're back in Fort Worth? You've got to be kidding me. That's great news! I haven't hired anyone to fill your position. Hell, I haven't even interviewed anyone. I was hoping—"

"That's nice, Jace, but I already have a job."

"What? With what firm?"

"I accepted a job with Hutton Currie."

"That son of a—"

"Hold on a minute. That's why I'm calling. He wanted to check with you first, but I told him I would take care of it. I know y'all were law school classmates."

"Yeah, well, he should have given me a courtesy call or something." Jace paused, and then asked, "So when do you start?"

"On Monday. I spent last week moving back into my old condo."

"I thought you put it on the market?"

"I did, but fortunately it didn't sell. I had some nibbles but no firm offers. I took the sign out of the yard a little over a week ago."

"I just didn't see this coming. I mean, you didn't return any of my calls. I didn't think I'd ever hear from you again."

Darrin cleared her throat before saying, "I don't want you to take this the wrong way, but I didn't move back for you. I moved back for me."

"Look, it's too hard to talk about this over the phone. Have you had dinner? If not, I could pick you up in fifteen minutes and we could—"

Darrin cut him off. "That's not a good idea, Jace."

Sensing there might be an opening, Jace persisted. "Come on, Darrin. We'd have a—"

Darrin held her ground. "No way, Jace. Sorry."

"So why did you leave Houston?"

"A number of reasons but none worth discussing."

"I bet your sister hated to see you leave."

"Actually, I think she was kind of relieved. She's got a lot on her plate right now. Mark has moved back in, and they're trying hard to make things work. And, of course, the girls are wonderful, but they're a handful."

Jace circled back. "So where does this leave us, your moving back and all?"

"Jace, there is no *us*. It's over."

"Come on, Darrin. I just—"

"It's over, Jace. You're good at arguing—the ol' trial lawyer in you coming out—but you're not going to win this one."

"Well, we can be friends, can't we? Maybe have lunch from time to time?" Jace continued to probe, searching for any opening.

"I need to settle into my job. And I want to fix up my condo. I'm actually excited about that. I'm going to give it a complete makeover."

"After you finish doing all of that?"

"We'll see, Jace."

Jace sensed progress but decided not to push. He needed to end on a good note, come up with a plan, and try his luck at a later date. "I'm really glad you're back, Darrin. Really glad."

"Me too, Jace. Goodnight." Darrin laid the phone back on the table and poured the rest of the wine in her glass. His feelings for her were still there, and they were strong. She was sure of it.

CHAPTER 48

Christine woke up a little after 4:00 a.m. After tossing and turning for what seemed like forever, she finally gave up, threw on a robe, and made a cup of coffee. Sipping the coffee, she noticed a slight tremor in her fingers. Nerves—a condition she'd rarely had to deal with before that asshole Cowan started his holy war against her and her dad. The fall from grace had been swift and harsh, with little time to adjust. Critical decisions had been thrust at her in rapid succession, fires raging everywhere. She couldn't afford a misstep. She wondered whether she had made one, striking a deal with the devil, agreeing to testify against her dad. But like her dad said, it was the smart play, the only play, their only chance to find an escape hatch.

Carrying her coffee to the den, she rummaged through her briefcase, pulled out a manila file, and then slouched down in her favorite lounge chair, propping her bare feet on the ottoman. She opened the file in her lap and stared at the front page of the document inside: "Sworn Statement of Christine Connors." Cowan wasn't content with her telling him what she was going to testify to—he wanted it in writing. She remembered his words almost verbatim: "You either sign the damn thing or you're going to trial alongside your old man for murder, commercial bribery, and fraud. It doesn't really matter to me one way or the other."

She knew at the time he was lying. It really did matter to him: he wanted her signature on that damn document. He was determined to nail her dad's hide to the wall, and her testimony was his insurance policy. But the odds were against her and the stakes high if she rolled the dice—years in prison or worse. She decided to take the get-out-of-jail-free card, with a twist. As she skimmed through the four-page document, which laid out her testimony, she reminded herself that she could do it, that every word was true. Dropping the file to the floor, she stretched, wondering how she'd do on cross.

Walking back to the bedroom and into her walk-in closet she surveyed her options. Cowan wanted her to wear something demure, understated, schoolmarmish even. If the jury were to believe her dad had forced her to do things she didn't want to do, she needed to look the part. To hell with that! Her sworn statement didn't mention anything about the outfit she would wear. That was one base Cowan had failed to cover, and she intended to take full advantage. She pulled out a black dress with a plunging neckline and a hemline that, when she sat, rose well above the knee. Perfect! With those black high heels and bare legs, she would send a strong message, and not the one Cowan wanted. As she stepped into the shower, she felt that familiar adrenaline surge and smiled. It was almost showtime, and she was eager to walk on stage.

* * *

Cowan adjusted his bow tie in front of the mirror. Satisfied, he took the suit jacket off the hanger, carefully weaved one arm and then the other through the sleeves, and then hunched his shoulders forward for all to fall into place. Another look in the mirror and a smile back: he was ready.

He strutted out of the bedroom and into the dining area next to the kitchen where his wife was reading a print copy of the *Dallas Morning News*. Dressed in a frumpy bathrobe and slippers, her troll-like hair in disarray, she failed to look up when Cowan made his grand entrance. Clearing his throat he asked, "How do I look, dear?"

With bored eyes, she looked up from her newspaper and replied, "Like you always do," and then looked back down.

"Oh, come on, give me a little better than that. This is an important day for us. It could pave the way for bigger things, like a move to the Governor's Mansion—"

His wife didn't let him finish. "I hate Austin. You know that. Dallas is much more cosmopolitan."

"It would be a stepping stone, Washington next."

"That's better, but I like Dallas just fine."

Realizing he was fighting a losing battle, Cowan grabbed his briefcase and marched out the door. He hated his wife of 23 years. Their kids would be off to college soon, and he would leave the old bag behind. He liked Austin and couldn't wait to get back there.

* * *

Sharlene Knox had been up and dressed since 5:00, reworking her cross of Christine Connors. Judge Grissom had pinned Cowan down the afternoon before about how much longer his case was going to take, forcing him to admit to having one more witness—and Knox knew who that was.

She had never met Christine but had seen photos of her in Cal's office—photos of her alone and photos of the two of them on trips and at dinners, both wearing smiles that said it all. She just couldn't understand how a daughter could turn on her dad like Christine had. They seemed so close, almost too close. Maybe Knox was just envious. She had been married twice but remained childless. She had no desire to marry again—two times was more than enough for her—but often wondered what it would be like to have kids. She had a few years left to decide and to find the right man with the right genes. If she was going to have children, they had to be winners, just like their mother.

She scratched through some lines on her legal pad and then scribbled notes above. She loved cross-examination. It was her favorite thing about being a lawyer: ripping a witness up on that stand and watching their eyes beg for mercy as she offered none. She had been disappointed in her questioning of Rosen. She had made a few points, but overall the witness had escaped with little more than a scratch or two. But that wouldn't happen today, no way!

* * *

Christine adjusted the microphone in front of her and then cast her eyes in Cowan's direction.

"Would you please state your name for the record?"

"Christine Connors."

Cowan adeptly asked her some background questions and then homed in. "After you graduated from law school, you went into practice with your father, is that correct?"

"It is."

"And your father is sitting right over there?" Cowan turned and nodded toward Cal.

"He is."

"And how would you describe your years practicing with your father?"

"Exciting, rewarding, lucrative—those are the words that come to mind. We made a lot of money and had fun doing it."

"Sounds like the perfect job."

"It was."

"You used the word 'was.' That implies past tense. What happened?"

Christine sighed and leaned forward, her lips grazing the microphone. "I learned some things I didn't like."

"Could you be more specific?" Cowan cocked his head as if he didn't know what was coming.

"About what was going on with my dad's practice."

Cowan wrinkled his brow. "I'm not sure I follow you."

"It might help if I explain how our law firm works."

"Please do."

"You know my dad's nickname is the Lone Wolf. There's good reason for that. He likes to try cases by himself. That's what he did before I hired on and what he continued to do afterwards."

"Okay."

"Well, I had talked with him briefly about these big verdicts he had gotten against various companies—pharmaceutical companies, mainly—before I went to work for him. Nothing very specific but just that he had knocked some home runs. I was impressed, as any young lawyer would be, but didn't really ask any detailed questions." Christine briefly paused and took a sip of water. "After I came on board, I asked if I could work with him on some of those cases. He discouraged it, told me he worked better solo, felt juries sided with him if they sensed the other side was ganging up, with three or four lawyers swarming around, while he sat at counsel table with a grieving spouse next to him. I couldn't argue with his success rate or the logic behind it, so I didn't push things."

Cowan played ignorant. "Sounds like a good trial strategy to me."

"It was, but it turns out that wasn't the only reason he was doing it."

"What do you mean?"

"Those multimillion-dollar verdicts weren't on the level."

There were murmurs and whispering throughout the courtroom, all quickly silenced by the judge's gavel, accompanied by a cautionary stare.

"I'm sorry, Ms. Connors. Please tell us what you mean by that."

"They were based upon fabricated evidence—more specifically, expert testimony that was false, made up, contrived, whatever you want to call it."

"Now you will agree that expert opinions can differ about the same issue and yet not be—"

"I know where you're going, but no, these reports, affidavits, testimony were nothing but lies, straight and simple."

More chatter and whispering from the gallery, which was quickly quelled once again by the judge's gavel.

"You're not a medical expert?"

"No, I'm not."

"You haven't analyzed these reports and opinions, have you?"

"No, I haven't."

"So how can you come into this courtroom and say that?"

"I got curious and did some snooping. My dad and I share a database called Concordance. I knew Dad had routinely used the same expert—Dr. Howell Crimm—in all of his big cases. I searched the database for any documents with Crimm's name on it."

"And what did you find?"

"Reports, affidavits, some court testimony that had been entered into the database."

"I assume you read through some of what you found?"

"I did—all of it. Dr. Crimm's opinions were practically identical in every case. The drugs in question had been approved by the FDA based upon faulty data."

"Is that all you found?"

"No. I knew my dad's login information, so I searched his emails. I thought that maybe I was jumping to conclusions and wanted to see if there was any paper trail between Crimm and my dad."

"Was there?"

"I can't remember the number of emails there were between the two of them, but the first one I read—the most recent—jumped off the page at me."

Cowan picked up a single sheet of paper from counsel table, approached the witness, and handed her the document. "Do you recognize that?"

"I do."

After having the reporter mark the document as the next exhibit, Cowan handed it back to her and asked her to read it out loud.

"Howell, we kicked ass again. Hell, the jurors loved it when I blew up your affidavit and held it in front of them—all your statements about a big ol' Yankee company committing fraud. They couldn't wait to get back to the jury room and spank them boys. In any event, thanks! And don't worry about what we had to do. Just remember, the ends justify the means. Ciao, Cal."

Facing the jury, Cowan asked, "Ms. Connors, would you please read the last two sentences of that document one more time?" As she did, Cowan's eyes locked on those of every juror, one by one. He didn't need to ask the witness for her interpretation. Judging from the jurors' body language, they had already drawn their own conclusions, and he liked what he saw.

"Do you recall which case your dad was referring to in that email?"

"I do. It was the Fosorax case. The one covered in that *Texas Matters* article."

"Did you ask your dad about what you'd found?"

"I was scared to bring it up at first. I didn't know how he'd react. And then, when I did, he just laughed and said he was kidding around with ol' Howell, and that was that, end of story."

"So why didn't you go to the police, or the State Bar?"

"I wanted to believe him. I really, really did. So I did what any dutiful, loving daughter would do. I brushed it under the rug and went on with my practice."

She was sticking to the script to a tee. She hoped the jurors sensed the rehearsed nature of it. Dutiful, loving daughter? What in the hell was that? But there was no way Cowan could ever say she hadn't lived up to her end of the bargain. And she was damn sure going to hold him to his.

"Ms. Connors, I'd like to turn your attention to another topic. Did you ever know a Jamie Stein?"

"I did."

"And how was it you came to know Mr. Stein?"

"He called me."

"About what?"

"He was a claims adjuster for a big insurance company and wanted to settle some cases I had filed against a couple of his insureds."

"What do you mean by that last term?"

"Insureds? The companies that Mr. Stein's insurance firm had issued policies to."

"Okay. And what type of cases were those?"

"Silica cases. Our clients were alleging they had contracted respiratory diseases from exposure to silica, a sandlike substance. It was our position his insureds were responsible."

"And why did Mr. Stein tell you he was contacting you directly? Didn't his insureds, as you call them, have attorneys?"

"They did. He told me they were charging him an arm and a leg in defense costs and that he wanted to get the cases settled."

"Did you find that unusual?"

"Not really. I had had that happen before. Defense lawyers get paid by the hour and have no incentive to settle cases—the longer they drag on, the more the lawyers get paid. That's what Stein was complaining about."

"So did you discuss settlement with him?"

"I did."

"Why don't you tell us what happened?"

"We first met in New York at a restaurant in Union Square that he liked. I threw out a number, he countered, and then he freaked me out."

"In what way?"

"He wanted a kickback if we did the deal."

"Had you ever had that happen before?"

"No, never. I was shocked, and I walked out of the restaurant."

"Was that the end of it?"

"Unfortunately, no. I told Dad what happened when I got back to Fort Worth and he told me I had been too hasty. I was surprised and disappointed by his response, and that's an understatement."

"So how did your discussion with your dad end?"

"He told me to think it over. At that time, tort reform was taking a toll on our practice. To tell you the truth, we were hurting. We were trying to retool our practice to handle more business cases—patent infringement, primarily—but that was taking time. And we were highly leveraged and needed the money."

"And?"

"Dad came into my office one morning and told me I had no choice but to call Stein, get the settlement discussions back on track. Otherwise our firm might fold, and we'd lose everything."

"So?"

"I did what my dad told me to do. I called up Stein, we met at the Ritz in Dallas, and made a deal."

"Do you recall how much Stein paid to settle those cases?"

"Not exactly, but it was millions, with several million going back to him."

"Let's assume your dad hadn't leaned on you for a moment. Would you have done that deal?"

Knox was on her feet. "Objection, leading." Before Judge Grissom could rule, Cowan withdrew the question and then passed the witness. It was a little after noon. The judge recessed until 1:30. Knox would have an hour and a half to fine-tune her cross. There was going to be blood on the tracks that afternoon—she could feel it.

* * *

"Let's pick up where Mr. Cowan left off, shall we, with the settlement you negotiated with Mr. Stein?" Scooting her chair back from counsel table, Knox walked confidently to the witness stand. She forgot to ask for permission, but Judge Grissom let it go. He was as curious as anyone in the courtroom to find out where this was going.

"You were the one in the firm who talked with Mr. Stein, correct?"

"That's correct."

"The only one in the firm to talk with Mr. Stein, isn't that right?" Knox strolled away from the witness stand and toward the jury box, stopping just shy of the rail.

Christine nodded.

"I need a verbal response. You know that, being the seasoned attorney that you are."

"That's correct."

"In fact, your father never had one conversation with this Stein fellow, isn't that right?"

"Not that I know of."

Knox pivoted toward the witness. "And you'd know if they'd talked, don't you think?"

"You would think so."

"I do think so. And you, Ms. Connors, were the only one to meet with Mr. Stein, isn't that correct?"

"To the best of my knowledge."

"So that we are crystal clear on this, your father never met or talked with Mr. Stein, isn't that a fact?"

"Yes."

"You did all of the meeting and all of the talking, didn't you?"

"Yes, but—"

Knox cut her off. "Your lawyer had his turn—now it's mine." She looked up at the judge. "May I approach, Your Honor?"

"You may."

Knox walked closer to the witness stand and handed her several documents. "Would you please review those, Ms. Connors?"

Christine scanned through the documents and then looked up.

"Can you identify them?"

"They are the settlement documents in the silica cases."

"And who signed each and every one of those documents on behalf of the plaintiffs, your clients?"

"I did."

"Take your time and go back through each of them. I want you to make sure your dad's signature doesn't appear anywhere."

"I don't need to. It doesn't."

Knox asked the court reporter to mark the documents as the next defense exhibit and then offered them into evidence.

"So this deal, this multimillion-dollar settlement, was, to quote Stevie Wonder, signed, sealed, and delivered by you and only you?"

"And Mr. Stein."

"Of course. But your dad had nothing to do with it, correct?"

"He knew about it and told me to do it."

"Oh, it's the old 'devil made me do it' defense."

"Objection, Your Honor."

Judge Grissom leaned over and eyed Cowan. "Grounds, Counselor?"

"Argumentative," Cowan bellowed.

"Overruled. This is cross-examination. You may continue, Ms. Knox."

"Ms. Connors, I assume you were concerned about your firm's finances around this time?"

"That would be a fair statement."

"So it wasn't just your father who was sweating bullets over keeping the firm afloat, correct?"

"That's correct."

"You had a lot at stake as well?"

"I did." On the inside, Christine was ecstatic at the way cross was going but struggled to tamp down her feelings, making sure they didn't show on the outside. Knox was all her dad had built her up to be, and more.

"So this money train came along just in the nick of time. It was like manna from heaven. Without it, your world would have come crashing down, isn't that true?"

"I don't know about that, but things were getting tough financially."

"And they'd never been tough like this before?"

"That's right."

"You've never wanted for anything, have you, Ms. Connors?"

"I don't know what you mean by that."

"I mean you've led what many would call a charmed life—attended the best schools, worn the nicest clothes, never thought for a moment about where your next meal was coming from. Am I right about that?"

"I've worked hard to get where I am."

Knox nodded sarcastically. "And getting a head start from ol' dad didn't hurt one bit, now did it? You don't have to answer that. Let's go back to where Mr. Cowan started, with Dr. Crimm's reports."

Christine rolled her neck from side to side and leaned back in the chair, bracing mentally and physically for the upcoming onslaught.

"Have you ever heard the term 'battle of the experts,' Ms. Connors?"

"I have."

"Tell the jury what you understand that to mean."

"In most cases, the attorneys retain experts to render opinions that pertain to pivotal issues in the case."

"Thank you, Ms. Connors. I couldn't have said it better myself. And would it be fair to say that the expert, or experts, on one side of a case might opine differently than the expert, or experts, on the other?"

"That would be a fair statement."

"And this would be true in all types of cases—business cases, personal injury cases, patent cases, you name it."

"That's true."

"Now, you've testified that Dr. Crimm gave untruthful testimony in the cases he worked on for your dad?"

"That's my belief."

"That's what you testified to under oath, correct?"

"Yes."

"But you're not a doctor or a medical researcher, correct?"

"That's what I testified to previously."

"Right. And you haven't analyzed, and wouldn't be qualified to analyze, Dr. Crimm's reports or testimony to determine whether or not any of the opinions he gave or conclusions he reached were, in fact, false, correct?

"I'm not qualified to make that judgment."

"No, you're not. And to cut to the chase, your testimony was really based on two things—the similarity of the opinions given by Dr. Crimm and one email, isn't that true?"

"That's true."

"Have you used experts on your cases?"

"I have."

Knox returned to counsel table, shuffled through some papers until she found what she was looking for, and then asked, "May I approach, Your Honor?"

Judge Grissom nodded, and Knox marched toward the witness, documents in hand.

"Do you recall ever using Dr. Lucius Brock as one of your experts?"

"I can't say for sure, but the name sounds familiar."

Knox had the documents marked as separate exhibits and handed both to the witness. "Please take your time and look these over."

Christine complied and looked up after she had finished. "Yes, I used Dr. Brock in several asbestos cases I had."

"And those exhibits you have were reports he submitted in two separate cases?"

"That's what they appear to be."

"Now, I don't want to waste the jury's time by having you read those entire reports out loud, so I'm going to shortcut this. Would it be fair, Ms. Connors, for me to say that the language in those two reports is almost identical?"

"That would appear to be the case."

"So your own expert did exactly what Dr. Crimm did?"

"Yes, but—"

Her point made, Knox interrupted. "I want to show you some more documents, Ms. Connors." She hurried back to counsel table, shuffled through some more folders, and bustled back up to the witness. "Your Honor, I apologize for not asking—"

"You're fine, Ms. Knox. I'll assume you've asked for permission every time you approach."

"Thank you, Your Honor." Knox handed Christine a stack of documents. "Please look through these and, after you've finished, tell us what they are."

Several minutes later, Christine said, "I've finished. They appear to be emails between my father and Dr. Howell Crimm." She handed them back to Knox, who had them marked as one big exhibit, which she then handed back to the witness.

"Now, in your testimony to Mr. Cowan you zeroed in on one email from your father to Dr. Crimm, would that be correct?"

"I remember that."

"I want to call your attention to the first page of the exhibit you have in front of you."

Christine looked down at the document and back up again.

"Would you read that to the jury?"

Christine complied and read, "I know this one's a close call. Look, if you feel like you're going out on a limb, just tell me. I don't want you to do anything you feel uncomfortable with. Think about it, and let me know."

"Does that sound like your father is pushing Dr. Crimm to lie?"

"That one doesn't, but—"

Knox had her read three more similar emails and got Christine to admit her father hadn't stepped over the line in those either but rather had cautioned Crimm about swearing to something that, as Cal stated in one of the emails, "might cause him heartburn." She finished with the exhibit by getting Christine to agree that all the other emails were friendly exchanges about personal matters that had nothing to do with the cases Crimm had worked on for her father.

"I have one other matter I'd like to discuss with you today." Knox paused and then added, "And that is, why you're here." Knox made a beeline to the jury and kept her eyes on them as she asked, "You made a deal, didn't you?"

"I agreed to tell the truth."

"You made a deal to save your own skin while throwing your dad to the sharks."

"I did no such thing. Like I said, I agreed to tell the truth. Look, I know I'm no angel. I did some things I'm not proud of, but I'm trying to make things right."

"By making up things, horrible things, about a father who doted on you, who worshipped the ground you walked on, who would have done anything for you."

Christine could feel the tears start to well up but managed to hold them back. She glanced over at her dad, who worked hard to fake a scowl. With renewed confidence, she dug deep and hung in.

"How could you do this to a man who loved, and still loves, you with all his heart?" Knox shook her head in disgust and said, "I have nothing more for this witness."

After Knox had returned to her post, Judge Grissom turned to Cowan and asked, "Redirect?"

Cowan thought for a moment and then asked the witness, "Was it hard for you to come here today and testify against your dad?"

"It was the hardest thing I've ever done in my life."

"No more questions, Your Honor."

The judge excused the witness, and all eyes in the courtroom watched as Christine Connors gracefully stepped down from the witness stand and made her way out of the courtroom, tears faintly visible trailing down both cheeks. After stepping outside, she allowed a small grin to take shape. Finally, the cloud of criminal prosecution had lifted. Her end of the bargain was a done deal.

* * *

Closing arguments began at 9:00 the next morning, with Cowan leading off. In his view, the case was simple and straightforward, its blueprint clearly etched in the article written by a young reporter at *Texas Matters* who had dared to reveal to the world the misdeeds of one of the most famous trial lawyers to ever practice law in the state of Texas. A reporter who had documented her sources, dotted all her i's and crossed all her t's, a reporter whose story had been subjected to severe scrutiny by editors and bosses alike, a reporter who had been threatened, harassed, and humiliated, a reporter who had risked it all to expose Cal Connors for the crook he was.

"Ladies and gentlemen, she dared to do what's right, and that's all I ask of each of you—just use your common sense as you interpret the evidence, and do what's right. For not only do we have the testimony of Ms. Rosen, we have Cal Connors' own daughter corroborating every single thing Ms. Rosen and her source, Dr. Patel, told you. There is no doubt, reasonable or otherwise, that the defendant successfully engaged in a scheme to defraud corporations throughout this state and country of millions and millions of dollars. But the story doesn't end there. For the greedy, there is never enough." He crescendoed by recounting Christine's testimony about the sordid Stein affair, painting the defendant as a loving father turned bad, a father willing to corrupt his own daughter to avoid financial ruin.

Then it was Knox's turn at the facts. She began by telling the jury that the honorable U.S. attorney had it all wrong. Her client wasn't guilty of anything but being one of the finest trial lawyers around. Lawyers routinely hire experts, and experts disagree, they argue, they even call one another quacks and charlatans at times. Like it or not, that's the way our judicial system works, and to represent your client zealously, as every lawyer has sworn to do, you have to learn how the system works and play it for all you're worth. And that is exactly what her client had done, and all he'd done. And, not surprisingly, his daughter, accomplished trial lawyer that she was, had done the exact same thing.

"Remember those affidavits she got her expert to sign? You will recall they were almost identical, just like Crimm's were. Was there anything wrong with that? Not a thing in the world. Father and daughter just doing what good lawyers do—representing their clients to the best of their ability. Now, turning to the commercial bribery count, or as I call it, 'the Stein fine,' do any of you really believe what my esteemed colleague was trying to sell you? Do you believe for an instant that Christine Connors could be pressured into doing anything she didn't want to do, by anyone, including her dad? A smart and independent woman like she is? And recall my client did not have one conversation with that Stein character, didn't have one meeting, didn't sign one document. Reasonable doubt? You bet! Ladies and gentlemen, what my adversary told you makes for a good fairy tale, a good story, but that's not what we're after today. We're after the truth."

Knox returned to her seat, and Judge Grissom read a detailed set of instructions to the jury, laying out in difficult-to-decipher legalese the crimes Connors had been charged with, the elements of each crime, the definition of reasonable doubt, and various dos and don'ts that the jurors should abide by during deliberations. After receiving the court's charge, the jurors filed out of the courtroom and into the adjacent refuge where they would decide the fate of Calvin Connors.

CHAPTER 49

The jury had been out for almost four days. There had been a series of notes, requests for testimony and exhibits, but no real clues as to what was going on inside that room. On the second day, the lawyers gave up on a speedy verdict and returned to their daily routines, their minds not far from Judge Grissom's courtroom. And then a call from the court clerk came. The judge wanted the lawyers and the defendant back in the courtroom by 3:00 that afternoon.

Word spread like wildfire among the courtroom addicts who had religiously attended every day of trial, as well as the press, who trolled the courthouse for leads. There were blogs and posts on Facebook, Twitter, and LinkedIn. Would Cal Connors be found guilty or innocent? Was the judicial system corrupt? What kind of daughter would testify against her dad? Should the prosecutor with that stupid bow tie be impeached? Christine Connors was hot—was she married? The topics were all over the board: some serious, some satirical, a few outrageous. And now the time of reckoning was here, come one, come all.

Judge Grissom rose to his perch, a solemn look on his face. "Mr. Bailiff, would you bring in the jury?" A soft murmur filled the courtroom as the seven women and five men found their seats.

"Has the jury reached a verdict?"

A thin, attractive African-American woman at the end of the first row rose and said, "We are deadlocked, Your Honor. God knows we've tried, but we just can't agree."

The courtroom erupted. Judge Grissom banged his gavel again and again until some semblance of order was restored.

"Madam Foreperson, I would ask you and the rest of the jury to continue your deliberations. I'm sure—"

"With all due respect, Your Honor, we have voted and argued and then voted again, asked for testimony, exhibits, done everything we know how to do, but we just can't get there."

"Are you absolutely sure there is no way to reach a verdict on any of the charges submitted?"

"I am, Your Honor."

"Thank you, Madam Foreperson. I would ask that you and the other members of the jury return to the jury room. I want to meet with the lawyers and will notify you shortly on how we are going to proceed in this matter."

The jury filed out quickly, and the judge asked the lawyers to follow him into chambers.

Cowan was the first to speak. "How bad is it, Judge—the split, I mean?"

"I have no idea. As you both know, they asked questions during their deliberations and requested evidence, but I couldn't tell from what they were asking, or asking for, how they were leaning. To tell you the truth, I thought they had reached a verdict when I had the court clerk call you. What I just witnessed caught me as much by surprise as I'm sure it did you. You want me to have them keep trying?"

Knox responded first. "Sounds like that would be an exercise in futility to me."

The judge turned to Cowan. "What do you think, Reggie?"

"Could you find out how far apart they are? That might tell us whether Ms. Knox's instincts are right or not."

"Sharlene?"

"I don't see any harm in that. Let's see what they're thinking."

Ten minutes later, the judge was back in chambers. "Okay, we've got a number of different counts here, but I'm going to focus on the two main ones—fraud and commercial bribery. On the fraud count, the jury is split eight to four in favor of acquittal, and on commercial bribery nine to three."

His face flushed, Cowan asked, "In favor of?"

"Acquittal. Sorry, I wasn't clear on that. So what do you think I should do?"

Cowan answered, "Unfortunately, I don't think we're going to get a verdict—too big a split."

Knox considered her odds for a moment and then agreed.

"Well, it's decided then. I'll thank the jurors for their service and then dismiss them."

The judge left Cowan and Knox sitting on the couch in chambers. Knox turned to Cowan. "You're not going to retry this piece-of-crap case, are you?"

"That's how I'm leaning. I learned a lot during the trial about the weaknesses in the case, and I thank you for that, Sharlene. We've obviously got some more work to do before the retrial, but I just can't find it in me to let a crook and a murderer, and you and I know your client's both of those, go free. It's just not in my DNA."

"Well, good luck with that. It'll just be the same song, different verse."

Cowan stood, picked up his briefcase, and walked toward the door. Before stepping out, he turned toward Knox and said, "I'll be in touch, Sharlene. You can count on it."

CHAPTER 50

Jace was in his office when the court clerk called with the news. After getting her to repeat what she had just said, he hung up the phone and sat there at his desk staring at the clutter that had built up over the past few days. A hung jury! How could that happen? There was no doubt in his mind that Connors was guilty as charged. Sure, he had rigged those verdicts. No doubt he had prodded his daughter to do the deal with Stein. He had probably arranged the hit on his old friend Crimm, but Cowan had played it safe and held back on that charge, hoping for more proof. The Lone Wolf had worked his magic somehow and had prevailed against the odds.

What a good call Cal had made hiring Sharlene Knox! Jace was a hard grader when it came to other trial lawyers, and she was the best he had ever seen—an actress extraordinaire. There was a reason behind everything she did. Every question, every gesture, every glare, every smile, every pause—all were meticulously planned and flawlessly executed. And at the end, the pieces of the puzzle had come together to create reasonable doubt in the minds of a majority of those twelve people behind the rail. A hung jury was all she and her client could have hoped for.

How would he break the news to Leah? He had to tell her personally, and it couldn't wait. He asked Siri to make the call.

"Jace! What's the news? Is there a verdict?"

Jace cleared his throat and answered, "No, there's not. Unfortunately, we have a hung jury."

Leah gasped. "What? You've got to be kidding! With all the evidence, how could that happen? I just don't believe it."

"I couldn't believe it either. But it's easy to get so caught up in a case that it's hard to see the other side. Connors' lawyer presented a strong defense, and some of the jurors bought it. Remember, all she had to do was create reasonable doubt in their minds, and she was evidently able to do that."

"I wasn't as good on the stand as you told me I was. The jurors didn't believe me. Otherwise they would have convicted that bastard."

"That's not true."

"How can you say that? Otherwise we would be celebrating right now."

"The jury had more evidence to consider than just your testimony. I was in the courtroom when Knox crossed Cal's daughter, and that was quite a show. Knox did a number on her, made her seem like an ungrateful bitch trying to save her own skin. Unfortunately for the prosecution, that was the last witness the jurors heard before they started their deliberations."

"So what happens now?" Leah asked.

"Cowan has to decide whether he will retry the case."

"What do you think he'll do?"

"My bet is he won't let it go. He'll have Tipps dig around some more, see if he can pin Crimm's death on Connors. I don't think this is over by any stretch. Cowan's ego and ambition are both too big for that."

"I hope you're right."

"And don't forget that we got Connors' defamation suit dismissed. That was our goal when you hired me."

"I'm sorry, Jace. I just wanted Connors to go down. I know he paid Randazzo to do all those horrible things to me. Speaking of, has Randazzo confessed to anything?"

"Not a damn thing, but there's no way out for him this time. He'll spend the rest of his life in jail."

"Have you told Jackie about the verdict?"

"Not yet. Boy, do I dread that conversation. I don't know how she'll handle it, considering all she's just been through."

"Let me know how she takes it. I plan on going by to see her in the next day or so. It would be good to get a heads-up before."

"You got it."

"And, Jace, thanks for everything. You were all Jackie made you out to be and more. I hope I won't need a trial lawyer anytime in the near future, but now I know who to call if I do."

"Any more thoughts about going to law school?"

"It's still in the back of my mind. I may need you to write me a recommendation some day."

"It would be my pleasure. Take care, Leah."

"Bye, Jace."

Jace closed his eyes and ran his fingers through his hair. He had had more than enough for one day and needed a scotch in the worst kind of way. He opened the cabinet door of his credenza and scrounged around for the Glenlivet. Coming up empty, he cursed himself. "Shit, I must have finished off the bottle after Darrin left." He closed the credenza, threw on his sport jacket, and headed out the door. Ten minutes later, he was perched on a bar stool at Del Frisco's, sipping on a double scotch on the rocks and browsing the menu, his mind starting to unwind. Then he heard that voice—distinctive and unmistakable—and sneaked a peek over one shoulder. Cal and Christine Connors, and their lawyers, were being escorted by the maître d' to one of the tables. He didn't think they had spotted him but couldn't be sure. He considered leaving a twenty on the bar and trying to sneak out the door. But he was out of luck. He had caught Cal's eye.

As they took their seats, Cal whispered something to the maître d'. Minutes later, the bartender placed a drink on the bar in front of Jace and said, "Compliments of the gentleman over there." He nodded in the direction of Cal's table.

Jace stared at the dirty martini in front of him and pushed it to the side. He threw back his scotch, placed a twenty under the empty glass, and made his way toward the exit. He could hear laughter over his shoulder but ignored it. Early celebrations many times soured down the road. The fat lady hadn't sung yet, not by a long shot.

Jace stepped outside into a light rain and began to walk back toward the office, thoughts of the past several months playing out in his head. He needed time to think, time to sort things out, time away from Fort Worth and the daily distractions of his law practice. He had an old college buddy who was living in Nashville, managing a few country music stars. It just might be a good time to pay him a visit and let off a little steam. It was hard to find answers in a cluttered mind, and listening to some live music at the honky-tonks on Broadway and throwing down some Jack might just help him piece together the puzzle. After that, he might even rent a place up in the mountains for a week or two and let his thoughts run free. No need to decide now. Better for once to let the current take him around the bend and not worry where it might lead.

THE END

Thank you for reading The Weight. I hope you enjoyed it. I am an independently published author so I rely on you, the reader, to spread the word about my books. In that regard, if you enjoyed the book, please tell your friends and family, and, if you have time, post a brief review on Amazon. I'd really appreciate it. Also, I have a website at www.hubertcrouch.com with an email link. I read and respond to every email I receive so, if you are so inclined, send me one through that link. Thanks for your support!

Sincerely,
Hubert

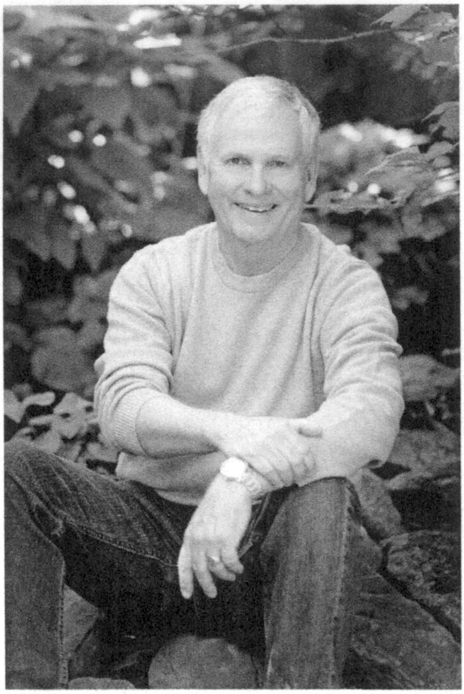

About The Author

Hubert Crouch is a graduate of Phillips Andover Academy, Vanderbilt University, and Southern Methodist University School of Law. He practiced trial law for over forty years. In addition to practicing law, he taught Free Speech and the First Amendment and Legal Advocacy to undergraduates at Southern Methodist University and, during that time, was awarded the Rotunda Outstanding Professor Award. An avid rock and roll fan, he played guitar in a Sixties "cover" band for over thirty years. He and his wife split their time between their home in Nashville, Tennessee and their mountain retreat in Monteagle, Tennessee. He welcomes visitors at his website: www.hubertcrouch.com.

Made in the USA
Coppell, TX
20 March 2022

75293274R00215